Praise for

"*The Devil Wears Prada* meets *Bridget Jones's Diary* with a sinister Hollywood twist, *Enemies Closer* is a hilarious and crazy-making journey inside the entertainment capital, shining a shocking spotlight on entitlement and foul play. Josh Sabarra is a natural-born storyteller." **—Gigi Levangie Grazer, bestselling author of *Maneater* and *The Starter Wife***

"Josh Sabarra's fiction debut is a fizzy cocktail of insider Hollywood gossip, biting, laugh-out-loud humor, and a supremely likable, relatable heroine. *Enemies Closer* is a twisty and delightful page-turner of a novel." **—Lauren Fox, bestselling author of *Days of Awe, Friends Like Us* and *Still Life with Husband***

"*Enemies Closer* is at once laugh-out-loud funny and heartbreakingly poignant. Josh Sabarra understands the heart and soul of an everyday woman who's navigating the glamour and grit of insider Hollywood." **—Jessica Anya Blau, bestselling author of *The Summer of Naked Swim Parties* and *The Trouble with Lexie***

"With the pitch-perfect eye of a true insider, Josh Sabarra skewers the Hollywood machine in this deliciously fast-paced, fun — and occasionally heartbreaking — novel." **—Sarah Pekkanen, bestselling author of *The Perfect Neighbors, Things You Won't Say* and *These Girls***

"I cannot remember the last time I was so riveted by slice-of-life storytelling that doesn't revolve around crimes scenes and investigations. Josh Sabarra captures, with striking authenticity, his modern everywoman protagonist, a hilarious and sympathetic Hollywood-set *Bridget Jones's Diary.*" **—Thelma Adams, bestselling author of *The Last Woman Standing* and *Playdate***

"Honest, deliciously irreverent and laugh-out-loud funny, Josh Sabarra serves up a captivating new American heroine in the fabulously ordinary Marcee Brookes. A new voice in fiction is born." **—Amy Hatvany, bestselling author of *It Happens All the Time* and *Best Kept Secret***

"Sabarra effectively uses his background as a former marketing executive…to provide a witty, insider perspective on Hollywood types, the gossip mill and the life of a publicist." **—*Kirkus Reviews***

ENEMIES CLOSER

ALSO BY JOSH SABARRA

Porn Again: A Memoir

For Michelle –
Thanks for keeping
me looking stylish!
Much love.

ENEMIES CLOSER

xo
[signature]

JOSH SABARRA

10/2017

J|B|S

The following is a work of fiction. Apart from the public people, events and locations that figure into the narrative, all of the names, characters, places, organizations, businesses, dialogue and situations are a product of the author's imagination or are used fictitiously. Any other resemblance to actual events, locales or persons, living or dead, is entirely coincidental.

For further information about the author, please visit http://www.joshsabarra.com. Inquiries about this book and author appearances can be addressed to information@breakingnewspr.com. While the author has made every effort to provide accurate contact information at the time of publication, he assumes no responsibility for errors or for changes that occur after publication.

ISBN: 978-0-9907546-2-6 (Trade Paperback)
ISBN: 978-0-9907546-3-3 (Ebook)
LCCN: 2017903668

For the people I'll always keep close: my parents, Howard and Deborah, my sister, Nancy, and Benée Knauer.

ENEMIES CLOSER

1

ONE THING WAS certain: it was going to take at least two Skinny Cow chocolate ganache cones — maybe three — to soothe the pains of the day. On an average afternoon, Marcee could make it until 4PM before hitting the ninth-floor break room and indulging in 160 calories of frozen goodness. Not today. By noon, she knew that nothing short of 500 calories would do, and, thankfully, she had just replenished her stash in the communal freezer at work. Two boxes had her name on them; yellow Post-Its were affixed with packing tape to both, making clear that each belonged to "Marcee Brookes."

Marcee's clothes were beginning to feel snug. She had made a mental note that morning when slipping into her size-14-going-on-16 grey, below-the-knee skirt and black silk top that it was indeed time to limit her snacking; the cotton-elastic blend that hugged her waistline was finished forgiving — a fact that her mother, Rhonda, had been pointing out just the night before.

"You're going to have to live in navy if you don't curb the eating, Marcee," Rhonda harped. "Thank God for dark colors! They hide almost everything."

Five feet one and 110 pounds, Rhonda was a Valley sprite, a blond-bubble helmet-head who lived in loungewear and backless, two-inch heels. The clicking — not to mention the frosted pink lipstick and daisy earrings — drove Marcee up a wall.

"It's just a few pounds, Mom, and it's all from stress. I'll lose it as soon as my schedule loosens up after Oscar season."

"Honey, the stress isn't going anywhere; your whole business is crazy-making nonsense, and that beast you work for isn't going to lighten up anytime soon. Your father and I wish you would think about another line of work."

"I love movies, and I love doing publicity — I just don't love doing it for Phyllis at Luminary Pictures," Marcee lamented. "So, I'll have to stick it out until something opens up nearby at Disney or Warner Bros."

"I'm glad you can hold out; I am not sure the seams in your clothes will."

"Enough, Mom." Marcee didn't need her mother to belabor the issue; she was depressed enough that it was Sunday night and that her alarm clock would be pushing her out of bed and into her office only 10 hours later.

"You know, Daddy and I just want you to be happy; to find a husband and have a family."

"A husband and kids don't equal happiness, Mom," Marcee said, rolling her eyes as she lounged on a chaise in the backyard of her parents' Woodland Hills townhome. "Plus, at 42, I don't think there's a great likelihood of the fairy tale coming true."

"You're wrong. Remember Myra Bernstein from the Temple? Her oldest — you know, the one with the bad hair and *farbissina* face — just married a guy from West Hollywood. She's 44, and Myra had given up. Now, she's living the dream."

"Who? Myra or her daughter, Hillary?"

"You know what I mean, Marcee. Save that sharp wit for your friends."

"That makes perfect sense, actually." Marcee gave a wry smile.

"Why is that?" Rhonda asked.

"If he's from West Hollywood and married to Hillary Bernstein, he's definitely gay."

"Whatever he is — he's cute and hitched. He makes Myra *and* Hillary very happy."

"Mom, I gotta go." Marcee stood up from her chair and walked over to her mother, who was seated in a hanging swing across the patio. "I have to get home so I can go through all of my navy skirts and blouses. Looks like I'll be living in them for awhile." She chuckled and kissed Rhonda on the top of her head.

"Make fun of me all you want, but anyone will tell you that dark blue covers a multitude of sins. So, go take stock of how much of it you actually own, and I'll tell your father you said goodnight; he's already passed out upstairs."

Marcee got into her silver Audi A3 — a car with brand cache but also sensible on a studio publicist's budget — and drove the 12 miles to her one-bedroom rental in Sherman Oaks. Spending time with her mother always required some form of decompression, which that night included a handful of frozen Thin Mint Girl Scout cookies and a glass of 2 percent milk. Soon enough, she'd have to wake up and face a new week at Luminary, and nothing armed her for battle like a cellophane sleeve of crunchy chocolate.

◇◇◇

MARCEE'S RECENT PROMOTION to senior publicist came with its own parking space on the Burbank studio lot, her name spray-painted red in standard stencil font across a concrete bumper. She had worked more hours and more efficiently than any of her counterparts for as long as she could remember, and the solid stone, she believed, was a well-earned monument to her efforts. Perhaps coworkers and executives would regard her differently now that she was important enough to have her own parking bay. After all, even the smallest perks connoted status in the movie business — secretaries with higher felt walls surrounding their cubicles were seen as senior to their open-desk colleagues.

She stopped and took a minute to stare at her car parked in front of her last name. It would be only minutes before Phyllis Van Buren would undoubtedly ruin the start of her day, and Marcee wanted to soak in the warmth of approval that came with her assigned parking.

"Marcee?" *Fuck*. She heard Phyllis calling for her from the elevator bank at the center of the industrial garage. She quickly pressed the lock button on her car key control and began to walk quickly.

"Marcee? Is that you?"

"Coming, Phyllis," Marcee yelled, her voice reverberating across the entire span of Parking Level 4. The diagonal strap of her Kate Spade messenger bag was cutting into her 36D breasts, and she could feel a bead of sweat soaking into her silk blouse as she headed to the open elevator door.

"I thought I saw you standing next to your car as I pulled in," Phyllis said, looking Marcee up and down while pressing the ninth-floor button eight times in succession.

Phyllis, at five feet eleven, was an imposing figure. With rust-colored hair extensions flowing down her back and sharp, angular facial features, she could easily be mistaken for a drag queen. Her size-10 feet were always stuffed into pointed-toe heels, and her pantsuits were, as she was quick to tell everyone, custom made in Milan. Her shape was awkward, with small, saggy breasts that didn't protrude as far as her distended stomach; they rested on top of her belly like lifeless water balloons that had lost their perk. She was a 56-year-old tree trunk on two skinny legs, and her tailored clothing was more likely a function of her odd shape than her fashion sense. Never mind that she carried herself as though she were the genetically engineered love child of Christy Turlington and Linda Evangelista.

"You sure did, Phyllis. How was your weekend?"

"It's over, and I have a splitting headache," Phyllis answered, her lips, covered in a striking matte red, barely moving. "Listen, I got an e-mail from Rox Madison's office last night. His wife, Claire, is coming in this afternoon to go over our PR plan for *Night Crimes*; I'm counting on you to impress her."

"His wife? What does she know about PR? Isn't she an author?" Marcee would've bet money on the fact that someone had ghostwritten Claire's two books. "Plus, I thought you wanted to be in every meeting relating to Rox and that movie."

"Apparently, she dabbled in marketing before they were married, and he's giving her something to do," Phyllis said. "If the meeting is not important enough for him to show up to, it's certainly not important enough for me to attend either." Phyllis saw herself as the executive equivalent of one of the world's biggest movie stars.

"Do you really think Claire is going to want to hear the plan from *me*?" Marcee asked. "My guess is that she expects to be speaking with *you*."

"She should lower her expectations so you can meet them for her, shouldn't she?" Phyllis used her wine-colored press-on nails to sweep imaginary bangs off of her forehead, a tic that Marcee focused on whenever her boss was spitting vitriol. "I have no interest in doing a dog-and-pony show for a privileged housewife who wants a hobby. When Rox decides to visit, I'll take the meeting; until then, you'll have to do."

"Phyllis, I don't have a PR plan done. You said you were handling everything related to Rox, so I—"

"So, you have until lunchtime to show me how quickly you can whip something serviceable together. I'll look it over before you meet with Claire at 3PM."

By the time Marcee reached her small interior office — with no natural light, even succulents didn't last more than a week there — she was ready for a Chipwich. It was only 8:30AM, though, and hitting the sweets so early in the day would throw her Jewish stomach into a lactose free fall. Not to mention, she had an entire PR plan to write in the next four hours — a nearly impossible task even without taking time to enjoy some ice cream. She did, however, always have time to call her mother.

"She's such a fucking bitch, Mom," Marcee said as she fumbled to close her office door and transfer the call from her receiver to her headset at the same time. "She basically does nothing; she dumps every ounce of work on me unless there's a studio executive or celebrity involved."

"Honey, maybe she does it because she knows you're reliable. Did you ever think about that?" Rhonda was doing her best to soft-shoe around a subject that she and her daughter discussed at least twice a day.

"The fact that I'm reliable is a given, Mom," Marcee replied, feeling unsatisfied with the suggestion that Phyllis might bc operating under any motivation other than laziness and spite. "Please don't imply that Bitchy Bitch McBitch is actually complimenting me with assignments."

"I implied nothing of the sort; you *inferred* it."

"You're driving me fucking nuts, Mom." Marcee was fuming.

"Then why do you call here four times a day? Maybe you want to reach out to someone else's mother. She probably won't annoy you so much."

"Um, OK. Meanwhile, you birth a fucking bovine if I don't call to tell you that I've arrived at the bathroom safely." Marcee's thick, shoulder-length black hair — which was parted at the center of her scalp and curled slightly upward at the ends — was becoming frizzy with the wild gestures that accompanied her rant.

"You know what? Quit. Quit the fucking job. Daddy and I will support you, and you can tell all of your friends that you're moving back in with your parents. You like that idea?" Rhonda had whipped herself into Marcee's frenzy. "Do me a favor, will you? Go in, and give your two weeks' notice right now."

"I can't," Marcee yelled into her hands-free mic, using the loudest whisper she could manage. "I have to write a goddamn PR plan."

"Not if you go in and quit, you don't." Naturally, Rhonda knew that Marcee had no intention of resigning. The conversation might as well have been scripted and printed on a laminated cue card.

"Goodbye, Rhonda." Marcee slammed her headset down, leaving her mother to stew in the upset that she — no, Phyllis — had caused.

With her door still closed — a sure indicator to everyone of personal drama — Marcee logged in to her Apple desktop computer and pulled up a PR plan that she had drafted for *Fear of Day*, another tentpole film she had worked on the year before. *Night Crimes* was the same kind of action-thriller, and it would be easy for Marcee to lift elements from one public relations blueprint and repurpose them for Claire Madison — especially if it had to be done in a few hours. Marcee had always maintained that preparing PR plans was a ridiculous, masturbatory activity; they represented nothing but a time-consuming way of showing clueless actors, filmmakers and producers that the publicity team wasn't just sitting around and waiting for *The Late Show* to call and book a guest. In truth, the "plan" was simply to call as many media outlets as possible to generate as much coverage as possible. Making it look pretty and thought-out didn't make it any more strategic in practice, but that's one of the reasons they called it "movie magic."

By the time 12:30PM rolled around, Marcee opened her office door, feeling confident that she had created a pretty enough PowerPoint deck to please both Phyllis and Claire. Phyllis wouldn't bother to read it, let alone notice that so many pieces had been borrowed from another document, and Claire wasn't likely to be interested in anything more than how the plan would ultimately affect her Bottega Veneta pocketbook. Marcee walked down the long hallway to Phyllis's corner office, an 1,100-square-foot museum that was larger than Marcee's entire apartment — not to mention with a bigger en-suite bathroom — and knocked on the door.

"What is it?" Phyllis said, sitting cross-legged on a raised, ergonomic swivel chair trimmed in real leather. Her back was always to the door.

"I have the PR plan done." Marcee walked into Phyllis's office tentatively; she could never tell if "What is it?" was an invitation to enter or a warning to stay back. Phyllis's computer screen faced visitors, which, Marcee reasoned, served two purposes: 1) Phyllis could use her large, reflective monitor as a means of keeping an eye on who was floating through the corridors behind her; a covert rearview mirror of sorts. And, 2) she could make conversations brief, without ever having to look her staff in their eyes. Should someone important be in the building — such as studio chairman Ken Andrews, superstar Rox Madison, or, say, Tom Cruise — she'd be able to turn and stand quickly for a hug, an air kiss or a lick of his asshole.

"I was wondering when it would be ready," Phyllis snapped. "Just leave it on a guest chair." The overstuffed cream lounge chairs were startlingly deep and close to the floor; Phyllis sat a good foot above absolutely anyone who dared to make himself or herself comfortable.

"Just let me know if it's OK to present to Claire at 3PM." Marcee placed the 25-page document on the seat closest to Phyllis's desk and walked toward the door.

"By the way," Phyllis said, turning her head sideways in an almost-acknowledgement of Marcee's actual being, "Claire's assistant called about two hours ago; Claire can't make it in today after all." Marcee stopped, her back still to Phyllis's. "But at least the PR plan is done, right? You're ahead of the game."

It took every bit of energy Marcee had to continue her stride out of Phyllis's office and into the coffee room on the other side of the hallway. A rage so hot stirred in her already irritated intestines, the likes of which would make Stephen King's Carrie seem like Little Red Riding Hood. She stormed over to the mini-freezer, flinging its tiny door open with both hands, nearly detaching it from its base. Marcee pulled out a Tupperware container of frozen-solid stuffed cabbage that Phyllis's assistant had marked with a pleasant "Do Not Touch" and a Ziploc bag full of weeks-old vegetable soup that someone had forgotten to reheat for lunch. She reached as far back as she could, hitting the depths of the appliance with her right hand. As her arm moved from side to side, the horror of the situation settled into her chest: the Skinny Cows were gone. The thief didn't even leave the boxes behind; it was as though the limited-edition flavor of the month had never existed in Burbank.

Marcee put everyone's leftovers back into the freezer and slammed the door shut. Who would take all eight cones? Not one. Not two. *All eight cones?* They were marked so clearly. It was probably the Ninth-Floor Shitter, Marcee thought; the secretary who worked on the lobby level but took the elevator up multiple stories to bless the bathroom on nine. Apparently, someone was a "Smelly Shelly" and didn't want to be identified — exactly the kind of person who would sneak back to her desk with a handful of sinless ice cream treats.

◇◇◇

THE PR PLAN for Claire had set Marcee back nearly four hours, and with no Skinny Cows to keep her going, she was exhausted by 10:30PM. She turned off the blue butterfly lamp at the corner of an otherwise sterile-looking desk. The light — a gift from her father — was a reliable constant in the daily chaos of her job. The bulb switched on and off with a flip of the butterfly's right wing, a feature that Neal Brookes knew would charm his daughter as much as it did him. When things got out of control — endless phone calls from personal publicists; multiple meeting requests from Phyllis; a piece of casting gossip leaked to the press — Marcee would focus on the glorious glow of the calming insect she named Flo.

"Night, Flo," Marcee said as she tapped the lamp and hustled as quickly as she could down to her car. She had been so busy after discovering the ice-cream-cone crime scene that she'd forgotten to eat, and, if she made haste, she could be at the Chicken Little drive-thru window before they closed at 11PM. It would need to be a secret, of course, or Jordan would kill her. One of the many perks of having a gay best friend was knowing which corporations donated a portion of their profits to anti-gay organizations; Chicken Little's parent company was at the top of the in-the-know Hollywood boycott list, so Marcee would have to make sure that no sandwich wrappers or crinkle-cut French fry boxes were left in her car. She knew she would feel guilty once the fried bird bites sated her ravenous hunger, as though each savory piece of the all-white meat morsels were keeping a lovely same-sex couple from legally getting married or adopting a child. Yet, the madness of the day not only gave her permission to persecute the disenfranchised with her restaurant choice, it laid out a big red carpet for her arrival. That would have been, of course, if there were no traffic on the 101 or Ventura Boulevard.

By the time Marcee rolled up to the remote ordering station in the Chicken Little parking lot, the light on the outdoor menu appeared to short out with a fast flicker. It was fine. Marcee didn't need to read about all of the various combination options; she had decided on a Number 3 with a Number 4 Milkshake before she'd even left the studio.

"Good evening." A muffled voice came through the speaker. Marcee was surprised that it wasn't more animated and that it didn't welcome her to Chicken Little, but, based on their politics, she realized she should have expected the cut-and-dry greeting.

"Can I have a Number 3 with a Number 4 Milkshake, and please throw in two honey mustards and two BBQs." There was nothing worse in her estimation than being on her last nugget with not a drop of dipping sauce left. "Oh, and ketchup for the fries."

"Ma'am, we're closed; we look forward to serving you another time." *That* came through loud and clear.

"C'mon, please? It's 10:59PM," she said into the speaker, not sure if the disengaged teenager who was likely behind the microphone was listening to her. "My cell phone says it's 10:59PM. That means it's actually before 11PM. I raced all the way across town after the longest day just for this chicken." She was hopeful that her passionate plea would encourage the pubescent staff of the local Chicken Little to reconsider their decision to close 60 seconds early. It didn't.

Marcee sped through the parking lot like she was driving an R8 as opposed to an A3 and drove to the most reliable place in the San Fernando Valley: Jerry's Deli. They were open until 2AM, and ordering matzo ball soup and a Reuben sandwich from the to-go counter would at least save some gays; she wouldn't have to confess anything to Jordan when the guilt became too much for her to shoulder.

At 11:15PM, the restaurant's manager looked to be juggling the five jobs that were likely covered earlier by dinner-shift employees. Marcee's order was the least of his concerns, especially considering that Denise Monroe, the nubile star of the country's hottest new sitcom, *Up My Alley*, was enjoying a late-night snack with her rapper boyfriend. It was clear that the soup and sandwich order couldn't distract any straight man or lesbian from staring, starstruck, at the pulchritudinous actress, but Marcee's empty stomach was ready to spew fire.

"Sir, would it be possible to get some water while I wait for my food?" She was trying to keep her cool by imagining the silk pajamas and fuzzy slippers she'd be wearing in less than a half hour.

"Excuse me?" he asked, without turning his head away from Denise Monroe.

"Water," she said. "You know…clear liquid?"

"Oh, yes. Water. I'll get you a glass."

Instead, though, a short-order cook finally emerged from the kitchen with Marcee's order, handing her a paper bag that would provide, at last, the day's only light point. She paid the manager without telling him that he never brought her the water, instead keeping her energy focused on driving home so she could eat, freshen up and crawl into bed with the new issue of *Vanity Fair* — in that order.

During the 10-minute car ride home, Marcee could smell the soup that was now resting on the passenger floorboard. The accompanying corned beef on rye, topped with sauerkraut and Russian dressing, would never see a plate; in fact, it took all of Marcee's resolve to not pull over and eat it right there, on the corner of Ventura and Coldwater.

She swerved onto Dickens Street, dodging two neighborhood dogs and their owners in her hurry to get home and get some solid food into her stomach. She pushed the garage door button on the roof of her car so the gate to her complex would be fully open just as she was ready to pull in, but its red indicator light wasn't activating. She rolled up to the metal bars and pressed the button twice more, but nothing moved.

"Jesus Christ," Marcee screamed, banging her right fist on the center of her steering wheel. She was just about to call a neighbor, which she dreaded at nearly midnight, just as Sherry, the tenant in Unit 4, tapped on the driver's-side window. Marcee almost jumped out of her skin, rattled by the sudden noise at her left ear.

"Honey," Sherry began as Marcee lowered her window, "Gibby is having a little problem."

Marcee leaned her head out and looked down. Attached to a hot-pink leash with a rhinestone collar was a discolored, off-white poodle with an underbite and jagged teeth. While Gibby barked at the sound of the car's engine, she spun around, revealing brown splatter marks across her small tail and the fur on her back.

"What kind of puddle did Gibby fall into?" Marcee asked, politely feigning interest but trying desperately not to encourage a long conversation. Sherry and Gibby were the only things, in addition to the motorized gate, standing between Marcee and her dinner.

"Oh, there was no puddle. Gibby has a sensitive stomach, and, well…"

"Oh, got it," Marcee said, sounding as sympathetic as she could under the circumstances.

"Thankfully, it happened just as I was walking her to the back gate; it would have ruined the carpeting had the 'train' come a minute sooner."

"Well, all's well that ends well," Marcee said with a semi-smile. "I hope Gibby feels better soon. Oh, and Sherry, would you mind opening the gate for me? My car control doesn't seem to be working."

"Sure thing. Also, remind me — I owe you a new copy of *Vanity Fair*," Sherry said, holding up a shit-soaked picture of Sandra Bullock. "I grabbed a magazine from your mail pile so that there'd be no mess on the concrete of the garage area."

Marcee pressed the window button, for the first time wishing that she had selected a car with a manual roll-up option. The automatic, darkly tinted window just wasn't moving fast enough to shield Sherry and Gibby from Marcee's exasperation. She pressed her foot on the gas and drove forward, making a sharp left into her parking space. The smell of burned rubber on the pavement eclipsed what little was left of the food's aroma, and the thought of Gibby letting loose on Sandra Bullock's face almost swallowed Marcee's appetite whole.

The minute she walked into her apartment, she kicked off her shiny black heels — Marcee didn't feel at all shameful for shopping the Jessica Simpson Collection at Macy's; the line was just the right combination of stylish, practical and affordable — and threw her bag and keys onto the convertible queen sleeper sofa in her living room. As she walked to the no-frills galley kitchen with her bag of food, she dialed Jordan from her cell phone.

"Hey, Boo," he said, "you're catching me right under the wire. I'm just about to fall asleep."

"Can you please stay up and talk to me while I eat?" Marcee wanted to have a pleasant conversation with her best friend, the only personal interaction that wouldn't include combat that day.

"As long as you say something interesting enough to keep my lids open," Jordan said. "I have to be up at the crack of dawn tomorrow."

"For what?" Marcee asked as she began to unpack her meal. The soup was now somewhere between lukewarm and cool; she'd make a final determination after the first spoonful.

"I have to turn in my column to *Variety* by 2PM and then I have an audition, so I can't sleep in. I'll have to be up by, like, 11AM at the latest." Jordan's acting career had never developed beyond a handful of under-fives on *The Young and the Restless,* but Marcee gave him points for his stick-to-itiveness. He wrote a column and small news items for the leading entertainment industry trade magazine as a day job while he waited for his big break.

"You've got to be fucking kidding me," Marcee yelled.

"What? I'm entitled to sleep in here and there. Don't judge."

"No, not you, Jordan. I ordered soup and a Reuben from Jerry's. They got the chicken noodle right, but they must have confused my sandwich with someone else's. Everyone was distracted because Denise Monroe was there, and, because of her, I now have chopped liver on rye."

"Marcee, my heart bleeds; it truly, truly does. But I have to get my rollers in and hit the hay; OK, girl?" Jordan's forced ethnic dialect always made Marcee laugh.

"Shut it," Marcee said, trying not to let him hear that she was amused despite his disinterest in her food fiasco. "I'll want to know how the audition went, so call me tomorrow. Don't forget."

"You know I'll call," he answered. "Big kiss, Boo Boo."

Marcee threw the sandwich into the trash; she'd had no interest in chopped liver ever since her grandmother forced her to eat it on Ritz Crackers when she was seven. Instead, she nibbled on the bagel chips that came with her order and ate the room-temperature soup directly from the Styrofoam container with a plastic spoon.

She finished eating quickly and put everything into the sink; she would deal with straightening up in the morning. It was well past midnight, and all Marcee wanted was to be in her lavender PJs and tucked into her luxurious California king.

After undressing and putting her clothes neatly on Slimline hangers — Marcee believed in getting a couple of wearings out of her skirts and tops before subjecting them to the harsh chemicals of dry cleaning — she went into her small bathroom to get ready for bed. She debated jumping into the shower but decided that it would only take away precious sleep time.

Marcee pulled her hair back with a cotton headband, keeping it out of her face while she completed her nightly regimen. She flossed and then brushed her teeth with an electric toothbrush before rinsing her face with a mild bar of soap. Finally, she blotted her cheeks and neck with alcohol-free cleansing pads and applied Cetaphil lotion to her face and décolletage. She was plain and simple when it came to beauty products. Naturally, as a Hollywood publicist, she was familiar with all of the in brands — La Mer, La Prairie, La Whatever — but she stood by the idea that clear skin came from actually making the time to care for it; the products and their ingredients themselves weren't really the secret.

Before turning off the bathroom light, Marcee put her clear night guard into her mouth — severe TMJ would definitely render three years of braces useless if she didn't wear the dental apparatus for at least six hours per day — and slipped into her pajamas. She stopped for a moment to look into the chrome-framed mirror, surrounded by bright, round light bulbs.

She stared at herself for a good three minutes. The glass saw flawless skin and green eyes that looked particularly pretty with her dark hair. It noted her straight white teeth, which complemented a bee-stung mouth as well as an oval shaped face with near-perfect symmetry. Marcee, though, saw an overweight spinster covered in blotches of white cream and with a lisp-inducing dental device that would almost certainly keep her single for the rest of her days. What man in LA would give her a second look, especially with all of the Hollywood babes who were practically handed out, one per customer, upon entering the city?

She pulled the 10 decorative pillows off of her bed — she loved the warm nest they created — and set them on the love seat at the foot of her bed frame. She took a deep breath and exhaled audibly as she crawled beneath her Laura Ashley covers. It was just as well, she thought, that Gibby got to the *Vanity Fair* before she did; she wouldn't have made it past the first five pages before fading into the flower patch design of her warm linens.

With the blackout shades completely down, Marcee's bedroom was pitch dark and surprisingly still considering its proximity to both the 101 and 405 freeways. The double-paned windows kept the traffic's symphony on mute, giving the room a meditative tranquility. Each night, she imagined the bed to be a silent ocean and her five-foot body pillow, only three inches shorter than she was, to be a secure and steady boat that allowed her to float along in her head until sleep took control of its sails.

Hugging the long, light pink pillow with her arms and legs, Marcee considered the craziness of the day and how it fit into the bigger picture of her life. From the moment she arrived at work until the second her head hit the sheets, it had been one slight after the next. She had to figure out how to transition into a job that made her feel respected, something that let her feel useful, productive and appreciated. Everyone around her — other than her parents, who were frustrating themselves at times — treated her with a seeming disregard that she usually assumed she was bringing upon herself. Even Jordan hadn't asked how *her* day had been and didn't want to stay on the phone long enough for it to come up organically. There was an overwhelming pervasiveness to her brand of lonely, like she was wading through life in open water, treading until another vessel would pass by and throw out a lifebuoy — or, at the very least, some blow-up water wings. No matter how many people were physically around her at any given moment, she felt as if she were by herself.

Marcee's mind then leapt to the romantic loneliness that had hung over her since she was old enough to realize she'd never be a size 4. She knew she was bright — her magna cum laude degree in English literature from Princeton confirmed it — but her lack of social confidence and the shame attached to her body shape kept her from putting herself in the pathway of single men. She wanted so much to meet a funny, evolved man to wake up next to, someone to hold who wanted to face the world with her as an unconditional ally.

There had to be men out there whose interest in women went deeper than the superficial. Perhaps those guys lived in other cities, where substance was a commodity and personality counted for just about everything. Maybe it was Hollywood and its alluring web that kept her trapped in a debilitating cycle of self-loathing.

Marcee's eyes began to close, and before she could ponder answers to everything that was spinning in her mind, she felt herself drifting off toward a sleep that would carry her to another Tuesday morning.

2

MARCEE WAS SURPRISED that it took Claire two weeks to reschedule the publicity meeting for her husband's new film. There seemed to be a sense of urgency when Phyllis initially unloaded the responsibility onto Marcee, and, until fourteen days later, interest had gone cold.

"Are you prepared for today?" Phyllis asked as she poked her head into Marcee's office.

"Yep; I've had the PR plan sitting on my desk since the day I wrote it, and I'll study it again before I walk Claire through it." Marcee would simply perform the same song and dance she did for every filmmaker; there was nothing out of the ordinary about this particular project. Same shit, different movie.

"Make sure she knows that Luminary is really behind this film," Phyllis said. "I want her to report back to Rox that we think it's a crowd-pleaser *and* a slam dunk for critics. We're expecting two thumbs up."

"Two thumbs up? You mean from Siskel and Ebert?" Marcee's face froze as the words came out of her mouth.

"Or whomever they are, yes."

"Well, their thumbs are likely to be way down. I mean down down. As in six feet down." Marcee knew that Phyllis's media relationships were tenuous at best and that she was less savvy than someone at her level should be, but not knowing that Gene Siskel and Roger Ebert had both passed away? Someone needed to put this heifer out to pasture.

"Whatever. Just do your best with Claire, and I'll iron it all out with Rox when he and I have an opportunity to chat." Phyllis turned and walked out of Marcee's doorframe, the smell of her Tom Ford Jasmin Rouge trailing her like a billow of kicked-up dust. Phyllis wasn't the "little dab'll do ya" type, and Marcee's sensitive nose always paid the price.

No sooner had Phyllis rolled away on her perfume cloud than the first-floor receptionist buzzed Marcee's phone; Claire was waiting in the lobby. She declined to take a seat because she was "certain that Miss Brookes will be right down." Marcee closed the door to her office and gave herself a once-over in the floor-length mirror she'd had installed on the back panel for these occasions. She'd been deliberate in choosing a brown, pin-striped suit with a light-blue blouse; she thought that she might be taken more seriously in slacks. After all, even with so many women climbing up the food chain, Hollywood was still a boys' club. Fortunately for the men, they didn't need to reapply a powder foundation, blush and lipstick prior to important meetings.

Marcee took the elevator to the first-floor lobby, making her way over to a waiting area that was overflowing with food delivery men, various studio vendors and industry players ready for meetings that might change their fortunes for the better. Claire didn't look comfortable being tanked with the hoi polloi and stood with her back to the guest chairs. She was reading the credits on the various movie posters that were arranged in light boxes across the walls when Marcee approached her with a perky "Hello, Ms. Madison!"

"Marcee Brookes?" Claire asked, lowering her Loree Rodkin sunglasses to the bridge of her nose.

"Yes, lovely to meet you." Marcee stretched out her hand.

"You, as well, but I noticed that there are no posters for *Night Crimes* in the lobby. You've got Julia's new movie, Sandler's next flop and some horror franchise crap that I'm sure you'll market to my kids — but no *Night Crimes*?"

"Oh, those'll go up soon," Marcee assured her. "It's still a little early for the teaser poster reveal; we've promised *Entertainment Weekly* that they can unveil it exclusively in the magazine before we release the image publicly."

"Well, at least you're thinking ahead," Claire answered, following Marcee into the elevator. In a long, flowing black skirt and a grey baby-doll tee, Claire seemed to float on her Tory Burch ballet slippers. The large gold buckle emblems worked in tandem with gravity to keep her roughly five feet two, 115-pound frame tethered to the earth, and she was topped with a thick mane of shoulder-length, wavy hair that was colored a deep chestnut brown. Her well-cared-for 49 looked like a fantastic 35.

"I think you'll find that we've put together a really solid PR plan." Marcee was trying to sound coherent while studying the woman she'd seen on Rox Madison's arm at every awards show and in every tabloid for the last 20 years. In person, Claire's features looked as though they had been smushed into the center of her face, and her nose was deviated enough to be noticeable. She looked like a Cabbage Patch Kid from Xavier Roberts's original collection, minus the yarn hair and the birth certificate taped to her back.

"You say 'that we've put together,'" Claire remarked. "Is there actually another person involved, or are you referring to the proverbial 'we?'"

"My boss, Phyllis Van Buren, and I worked very hard on this." Marcee was gnashing her teeth as the words clogged her throat like a bad case of acid reflux.

"So, she'll be in this meeting, yes?"

"Actually, it's just you and me today, but she and I have reviewed everything together, and she has signed off on the plan." Marcee was tap dancing quickly to cover for Phyllis, who would, if the shoe were on the other foot, throw Marcee under the bus and then drive in reverse to make sure she was flattened.

The ninth-floor conference room was a wood-paneled dream for anyone with an interest in the latest technology. Owned by one of the foremost manufacturers of electronics, the studio boasted stunningly appointed facilities that were equipped with the newest smart TVs and video playback devices, and this meeting space was no exception. Floor-to-ceiling windows offered an unobstructed view of the city, and the iconic Luminary water tower was clearly visible.

As Marcee guided Claire through the oversized double-doors, she offered beverages and snacks from the selection that had been delivered by the studio's food services department.

"None of that is on my diet," Claire said, "I'll have a water, please."

Marcee filled a glass with ice and began to pour from a bottle of Evian.

"Are the ice cubes made from Evian as well? If not, I don't see the point. It becomes just a glass of half tap water and half bottled water." Claire looked serious.

"Would you prefer a glass without ice then?" Marcee was used to the quirks and demands of celebrities and their families. It wasn't out of the ordinary for one star to drink only Poland Springs while another insisted that Acqua Panna be stocked on every set. This, though, was the first ice cube issue Marcee had encountered.

"Let's leave the ice out, and I'll take a straw, please. I

don't like putting my mouth on glasses; you never know how well they've been cleaned."

When Marcee turned around to deliver Claire's room-temperature glass of mountain spring water, she saw that Claire had taken a seat at the head of the table — just where Marcee had spent an hour setting up a computer and projection equipment for the presentation.

"Sorry to make you move the computer," Claire said as she rifled through her black canvas shoulder bag. "I prefer the view from this chair." She found her lipstick, a brand new tube of Chanel Rouge Allure Velvet. Without a hand mirror, Claire colored her thin lips perfectly.

"Oh, no problem at all; it'll just take me a few minutes to rearrange things." Marcee used all of her reserve to remain calm and appear unflappable to the wife of the highest-earning movie star in history. Inside, though, her stomach was eating her heart out.

"Can we get this show on the road?" Claire asked after five minutes, looking up from her iPhone. "I have to pick up my kids from fencing class at 3:30PM."

Now against the clock, Marcee gave Claire the most thorough overview she could, trying to squeeze 90 minutes of information into 30. She would glance from the screen over to Claire every couple of minutes for some kind of acknowledgement — a nod, a smile, an ounce of attention. Instead, Claire was texting furiously, messaging someone Marcee assumed to be a yoga buddy, the housekeeper or Rox himself.

"I have to stop you," Claire interrupted. "Honestly, I'm *so* bored." She stood up, throwing her bag over her right shoulder.

Marcee was gobsmacked. She had worked with all kinds of rude people throughout her entertainment career, but not one time in her experience had someone been quite this impolitic. Maintaining her professionalism — and her game face — Marcee offered a faint smile and shuffled the papers in front of her into one pile.

"No problem," Marcee said, handing Claire a collated packet. "You can read through the rest of this at your leisure."

"You can hang onto it," Claire said, making her way back to the elevator. "I'm sure someone in your office could use an extra copy. Perhaps that girl — what's her name? Phyllis? The one who clearly had more important things to do than come to this meeting? She may need to brush up."

Marcee accompanied Claire to her car on Parking Level 1, a silent march disturbed only by the light sounds of Claire's texting keystrokes.

"How about, maybe this Friday, you come to the Malibu house for lunch? I'll have Mercedes make something healthy, and we can go over all of this more casually," Claire said as she settled into her midnight-blue Porsche Cayenne Turbo. She lowered her window. "Plus, Rox will be home — maybe he'll join us for a little bit." Claire handed Marcee a Crane's stationery card with all of her personal contact information.

"Sure, I can do that." Marcee smiled and waved, neither of which Claire could have seen given the speed at which she tore out of the garage. And it amused Marcee to think that Claire had a Mercedes *and* a Porsche.

The dark clouds that had stationed themselves above Marcee's head during the meeting began to disband, turning her inner upset into giddy excitement. Claire had invited her to have lunch — at Rox Madison's house. What would she wear? Should she bring a small hostess gift? Would the house look like it did in the aerial photos that had been published in *People* magazine? She couldn't wait to call her mother.

"You aren't going to believe this," Marcee squealed into her cell phone. "Are you sitting?" She made the call from the courtyard outside of her office building; Marcee didn't want anyone to overhear her exhilaration, and she wasn't quite sure how she was going to approach the discussion with Phyllis.

"What is it, honey? Your father and I are at the grocery store." This was the first time that Rhonda had received a weekday call from Marcee that didn't begin with shouting or tears.

"Well, I did the presentation for Claire, and she invited me to her house for lunch on Friday. Can you even?" Marcee was speaking quickly while pacing between perfectly trimmed bushes, some cut to look like animated characters from Luminary's most beloved cartoons.

"You must have really impressed her. Mazel tov."

"I don't know about that; she actually said she was bored with the meeting," Marcee said. The words out of her own mouth made her pause. Claire didn't seem the least bit interested in knowing anything about the *Night Crimes* publicity plan, and Marcee didn't feel like she had been with Claire long enough to make an impression. She decided, though, to enjoy the moment instead of letting her rational brain crush this rare burst of positive energy.

"Well, whatever the reason, she invited you. I can't wait to hear what that house is like," Rhonda said.

"How should I handle Phyllis? The minute she hears that I'm going to Rox Madison's house, she's going to either sabotage it or invite herself."

"I don't know that there's a way around it, honey. If you don't tell her, she'll go ballistic. There isn't really a choice." Rhonda was right; Phyllis would likely consider a lie of omission to be grounds for termination.

"Friday is four days away," Marcee said. "I'm going to

sleep on it tonight, and I'll deal with Phyllis in the morning." She and Rhonda said their goodbyes, and Marcee returned to her office with a confident bounce. She was careful not to mention Claire's invitation to the handful of work friends she had — as much as she wanted to broadcast it to even the building's custodian — because Phyllis would almost certainly put the kibosh on the whole thing if the news leaked to her.

◇◇◇

FOR THE FIRST time in her 10 years at Luminary Pictures, Marcee left the office at a reasonable 6PM. She wanted a new outfit to wear on Friday, and it would take her 45 minutes to get to the Ann Taylor Factory Store — leaving her just enough time to choose the perfect skirt and twinset. Typically, her first stop after work — no matter the time — was a local restaurant; on this Monday, however, her appetite was squelched by her excitement.

It took Marcee an hour to scan the racks of clothes. The Factory was never as organized as the Ann Taylor stores, but she avoided paying those prices unless she had a gift card. Plus, this wasn't exactly Alexander McQueen; not many people in LA could identify that one particular skirt was from last season or that a shirt wasn't from the current collection — except maybe Ann herself.

The thing Marcee disliked most about the store was its row of fitting rooms. The swinging doors, when closed and latched, didn't extend to the floor, and she didn't like that her naked calves were visible to other shoppers. Often, she would stand on the bench at the back of the stall so that only the top of her head was visible above the door. She would rather people believe she was relatively tall as opposed to a portly woman with turkey legs. Sure, it was sometimes hard to balance while changing from one outfit into the next, but the risk of a fall outweighed the embarrassment of putting her lower limbs on display.

Marcee found five possible outfits, three of which were marked at clearance prices. She tried on the first — a heather blue-grey skirt with a light-blue sleeveless top. A matching cardigan could cover her upper arms, the second in line of her least-favorite body features. The top half fit beautifully, but Marcee couldn't get the skirt over her thighs. For a moment, her heart sank. Had she gained more weight? She pulled the skirt off and looked at the tag; no wonder it was too small. It was a 10 that some careless person — or evil prankster — had placed in the 14 section.

The second selection was a solid beige skirt with a creamy yellow lace front top and a flowing, striped cotton poncho. All of the pieces fit as though they were tailored to Marcee's curvy figure, and, on sale, the entire ensemble would come in at $89. Not only was the price right, but the colors were appropriately seasonal.

"These are great pieces," the salesgirl said as she removed the aggressively large security sensors and began scanning the bar-coded tags. "At these prices, I'd buy this outfit in every color." She was slender and about 20 years old; it was unlikely that she owned anything from Ann Taylor — be it from the main store, the Loft or the Factory — in *any* color. Marcee laughed to herself as she waited: *security sensors?* Each wired tag probably cost more than the clearance item it was attached to.

"I really like it," Marcee said, "and it's perfect for the special lunch meeting I have on Friday." She was practically begging the waif of a blonde to ask questions.

"Awesome; what kind of meeting is it?" The cashier was making simple small talk as she punched various codes into the register and began to bag the clothes.

Marcee leaned over the counter, her breasts pressed

against the glass top, and lowered her voice to a whisper. "I have a meeting at Rox Madison's house in Malibu."

"Shut the front door! I'm in love with Rox Madison. I'm so jelly." Bryanna — whose name was neatly engraved on a tag that was pinned to her size-0 shirt — looked as though she wanted to throw herself into Marcee's bag so she could tag along to Friday's lunch like a stowaway. "What kind of job do you have?"

"I do publicity for Luminary Pictures," Marcee said proudly, temporarily forgetting the scars she had from Phyllis. People's reactions to hearing what Marcee did for a living — especially those outside of Los Angeles — were part of what kept her soldiering on, regardless of the fact that it stole a little more of her soul every day.

"Oh my God, that sounds like a rad job. I moved out here from Minnesota to work in entertainment; hopefully I can find an entry-level spot soon. I don't care if it's in the mailroom; I just want to get in." Bryanna was one of a zillion kids working retail in Los Angeles, waiting for a chance to be beaten down by someone like Phyllis Van Buren.

"Careful what you wish for," Marcee said pleasantly. "It's not all glitz and glamour." Unless, of course, you've been invited to a movie star's house for lunch.

As Marcee began to walk to her car, her stomach rumbled, reminding her that she had neglected to eat dinner. She scanned the strip mall, hoping there'd be a Chipotle or a Tender Greens. Unfortunately, the Ann Taylor Factory wasn't exactly in a destination shopping plaza — so a Mrs. Fields would have to suffice. That evening's extra-large white chocolate macadamia cookie was an earned treat. Marcee rationalized the 9PM baked good as a celebration of sorts; she had been invited to a celebrity's home, and she wanted to taste the accompanying good feelings.

She ate the last bite of the cookie while sitting in her car, the kind of nighttime lingering that her mother had advised against since Marcee was old enough to get behind a wheel. Rhonda frequently warned her daughter about muggings, attacks and abductions, which Marcee wrote off to Rhonda's bizarre obsession with Nancy Grace's TV specials. So, when she dialed her mother from the car, she didn't mention that she was pulling out of a desolate parking lot in Glendale that was also home to a pawnshop and a check-cashing business. It was as though it had been designed to be the scene of a crime.

"Hi, Mom. I'm just leaving Glendale," Marcee said as she found her way onto the 101. "Can I swing by and show you the clothes I bought for Friday?"

"Of course, honey, I'm up."

"I want to make sure that, if we decide it's not the right outfit, I have a day or two to find something else." Marcee wasn't going to roll the dice on anything related to The Big Day.

"Where'd you buy an outfit?" Rhonda asked.

"I stopped at the Ann Taylor Factory Store."

"You're going to show up at Rox Madison's house in something from an outlet? Is that how I raised you?"

"Mom, I've gotten some nice things there in the past. I think you'll like what I picked out." Marcee's tone bordered on a whine.

"Listen, honey, after the Monica Lewinsky/Bill Clinton Oval Office scandal, everyone was shocked that she had saved the outfit with the semen on it. Remember that? The 'love dress'?"

"What on earth does that have to do with what I'm wearing Friday, Mom?" Marcee wasn't following the logic.

"You know what *I* was shocked about? Not that she saved a stained dress. I was appalled that she wore an outfit from the GAP to the White House. Do you see what I'm saying?"

"OK, OK, I get it. But, just look at these clothes with an open mind. I don't think anyone's expecting me to show up in Gucci." By now, Marcee was only 15 minutes away from Woodland Hills, and her mother could pass judgment in person soon enough.

She pulled into the first cluster of guest parking spots at Briarcrest Estates, grabbing the flimsy plastic shopping bag from her back seat. Unfortunately, outlet stores rarely provided the kinds of sturdy bags with rope or ribbon handles that could be reused, but, as her father would remind her, "You can't get old and retire into a nice shopping bag anyway, can you?"

Marcee used her key to open the front door, rushing into the foyer and setting her purse on the slim glass table that sat beneath Rhonda and Neal's framed ketubah. The cathedral ceilings — which Rhonda insisted on calling "vaulted" so as not to recall anything related to Christianity — made the entryway look considerably larger than it actually was; Marcee liked feeling tiny every time she entered the townhouse.

"Lemme see, lemme see," Rhonda said as she ran barefoot to the front door, grabbing the shopping bag out of Marcee's hand and kissing her on the cheek at the same time. She examined the skirt, the top and the poncho, holding each piece up to the light as though she were inspecting the work of the sweatshop minors who had, no doubt, sewn the fabric together in a rush to get to their lunch breaks. "You know, this isn't so bad. I mean, the stitching on the top could be better, but this is the shape of things with manufacturers these days. It's not like when Grandpa was in the garment business. People cared about quality then."

"So, you think I can get away with this?" Marcee cut

to the chase, having heard too many times how Grandpa Jacob was a giant in ladies' sportswear.

"Actually, I think it might be perfect. Throw it on; let me see how it looks." Rhonda always taught Marcee that what works on a hanger doesn't always work on a human. Without moving into the living room, Marcee removed her work clothes and changed into the new outfit.

"Oh, honey, you look lovely. You chose nicely!" Rhonda sounded impressed that Marcee was able to pick event-appropriate clothes that fit well without her assistance. They usually shopped together.

"You really think so, Mom? It looked nice in the dressing room, but those mirrors and fluorescent lights have tricked me before."

"Cross my heart; I swear. Do you think I would lie to you about something so important?" Rhonda walked around Marcee as she stood in place, looking carefully at every fold in the fabrics.

"Alright, so we can cross wardrobe off the list," Marcee said. "Now, what should I do about Phyllis? Obviously, I'll tell her, but what mode of communication has the least potential for damage?"

"You know, I was thinking about it when I was getting my pedicure today." Rhonda put her right foot forward, displaying her hot pink toenails with white flowers that had obviously been hand painted on each one. "What if you send Claire an e-mail to confirm the date and time, and copy Phyllis? This way, if she tries to pull anything, it'll be in front of Claire, so to speak. Does that make sense?"

"That's a good idea; but what if Phyllis confronts me in person or by phone? Claire wouldn't even know." Marcee always thought it sound to consider every possible outcome; in her anxious mind, upsets and disappointments were easier to manage if she had already formulated a plan to handle the worst.

"We'll burn that bridge when we get to it. Let's not worry ahead of time — or try to even guess what Phyllis might do."

"OK, but I'm going to be at Claire's house on Friday, come hell or waters high. I don't care what Phyllis says." Marcee could feel a backbone forming inside her, one small bit at a time.

"That's the right attitude, honey. Now, go home, and get some sleep. Hang that skirt in the bathroom when you shower tomorrow so the few creases get steamed out."

"Yes, Mom," Marcee said, kissing Rhonda goodnight. "Whatever you say." She walked to her car as Rhonda watched from the front door.

"Text me when you get to Sherman Oaks and not until you've parked. You know how I feel about these kids who are texting and driving. It's like a death wish," Rhonda said. Marcee knew her mother would wait to close the door until she saw the taillights of her daughter's car fade into the Southern California fog.

◇◇◇

MARCEE ARRIVED AT her office, Starbucks in hand, at 7:30AM the following morning — nearly an hour earlier than usual. It would be easier to draft the perfect e-mail to Claire without the noise of phones ringing and the water-cooler chatter of employees who had watched *The Bachelor* the night before. She'd wait to hit "send" until 9:30AM, when the city was up and running, but at least she'd have had enough time to thoughtfully craft a note that would endear her to Claire and keep Phyllis's mouth from foaming onto the Berber carpet.

She wasn't quite awake enough to deal with the harsh

overhead bulbs, so she tapped Flo's magic wing. She could always count on the blue butterfly to give her just the right amount of light. Marcee fired up her computer and went right to the "drafts" folder in her e-mail interface. She wasn't distracted by new messages from the studio's New York office, having already answered all of the pressing questions from her iPhone before she'd even gotten out of bed. Marcee took a deep breath and began to type.

To: Madison, Claire <starlover2000@gmail.com>
From: Brookes, Marcee <marcee.brookes@luminarypictures.com>
CC: Van Buren, Phyllis <phyllis.vanburen@luminarypictures.com>
Subject: Friday

Dear Claire,

Thank you so much for taking the time to visit Luminary Pictures yesterday. It was my pleasure to review the *Night Crimes* publicity plan with you, and both Phyllis and I appreciate your interest in the PR campaign. We are hopeful that you conveyed our enthusiasm to Mr. Madison.

Per our conversation, I look forward to seeing you at your home this Friday afternoon. We can continue to discuss details of the press strategy, and I can answer any outstanding questions that you or Mr. Madison may have.

Please let me know what time you'd like me to arrive, and I'll be there.

Again, many thanks.

Warmest regards,

Marcee

After reading the note no fewer than 50 times, Marcee called her mother.

"Hello? Who is this? What?" Rhonda hadn't been awake and was audibly jarred from her sleep.

"Who's calling so early, Rhonda? We need to put the phones on silent until we get up. Don't people know we've retired?" Marcee's father was grumbling in the background.

"Mom, it's me. Sorry to wake you guys, but I wanted to read you the e-mail I wrote to Claire." Marcee didn't do anything without seeking her mother's approval except, of course, when it came to food choices. Even without being asked, Rhonda weighed in with advice on everything from when her daughter needed a haircut or lip wax to the best options for low-calorie, late night dinners.

"Hold on; let me walk into the other room so your dad can go back to sleep."

"Hurry, Mom. People are starting to come into the office, and I don't want anyone to overhear this." Marcee was on pins and needles.

"OK, go ahead," Rhonda said.

Marcee read the e-mail in its entirety, including the salutation and signature line.

"That sounds great, honey. And, I like that you didn't mention lunch — it makes the whole thing seem less threatening to Phyllis, like it's all business. Good thinking."

"OK, thanks, Mom. Glad you picked up on that. Gotta run." Marcee's watch read 9:25AM, and she was 300 seconds away from launching her nuanced message. She needed to make sure that she got at least two bags of Hostess Mini Muffins into her system before she detonated the bomb.

She reached into her messenger bag and pulled out one small packet of chocolate chip muffin bites and another of blueberry. Now, with only a minute left on the ticking clock, she washed down the eight pieces with a swig of her iced mocha latte.

"Here goes," she said out loud as she hit the Send icon with her mouse and waited for the "swoosh" sound to signal the successful delivery of her e-mail. For the next five minutes, she sat anxiously in front of the screen, braced for either Claire or Phyllis to reply. She refreshed her in-box every couple of seconds, faster than someone could realistically respond.

To pass the time and settle her nervous energy, Marcee put on a pair of earbuds and listened to her iTunes library, hoping that Adele would distract her. After all, zaftig girls had to be there for each other, right? She knew that the British pop star wouldn't let her down.

It was about 30 minutes later and eight songs into the *21* album when an e-mail reply popped onto Marcee's monitor. She paused for a moment before opening the bold unread message, preparing herself for whatever nastiness Phyllis might have written. Her heart was beating at a frightening speed, but she decided that there was no time like the present. She removed the earphones and clicked on the e-mail before she could scare herself out of it.

To: Brookes, Marcee <marcee.brookes@luminarypictures.com>, Madison, Claire <starlover2000@gmail.com>
From: Van Buren, Phyllis <phyllis.vanburen@luminarypictures.com>
Subject: RE: Friday

Hi, Claire:

So sorry I wasn't able to be at the meeting yesterday. I was pulled onto a conference call with the studio president.

Marcee said that you were happy with the document I put together for her to present. Thrilled to hear.

I'll plan to see you on Friday with Marcee. It'll be nice to get out of the office, and I can give you a better idea of how Luminary sees the campaign unfolding.

My very best,
Phyllis Van Buren

The document that *she* put together? Marcee wasn't sure why she was surprised by anything that Phyllis would say or do, but the outright lie — not to mention taking credit for Marcee's work — made her bleached arm hairs stand on end. And, now she'd probably have to drive Phyllis to Claire's house on Friday as well as sit there and listen to the gaping asshole applaud herself for the success of the whole company.

Before Marcee could steep in her fury, she noticed that an e-mail reply from Claire Madison had just come in.

To: Brookes, Marcee <marcee.brookes@luminarypictures.com>
From: Madison, Claire <starlover2000@gmail.com>
CC: Van Buren, Phyllis <phyllis.vanburen@luminarypictures.com>
Subject: Re: Friday

Marcee —

So great meeting you yesterday, and lunch on Friday will be fun! How does 12:30PM sound?

Bring a light jacket on the off chance that we decide to sit out by the water for part of the afternoon. I know it's summer, but it can get breezy out here.

Hugs,
Claire

P.S., PHYLLIS: I didn't realize you were in a meeting with Ken Andrews. He and his wife, Jill, are good friends of ours. I'll have to mention it to him when they're at our house for dinner tonight. As far as Friday, Marcee should come alone. We prefer to have only people we've previously met in the house. Thanks for understanding, and maybe we'll see you at the premiere!

3

EVEN THE INDUSTRIAL-SIZE umbrella that Marcee received as a cardholder gift from Bloomingdale's wouldn't have been strong enough to protect her from the downpour of work Phyllis funneled onto her desk. Press releases, publicity plans, phone calls and status reports were now all on an impossibly long to-do list. To Marcee, her steno pad of action items seemed as laughable as subprime mortgage paperwork: full of numbers and ideas that existed in theory but didn't indicate actual home ownership. She wasn't likely to get through half of the assignments Phyllis hurled at her, let alone the preexisting tasks that were scheduled for the day.

"I really need you to power through all of this before the end of the week," Phyllis said, hovering in the hallway outside of Marcee's office door. She made no mention of the e-mail exchange with Claire, and Marcee was certain that the mountain of work sitting in front of her was Phyllis's attempt to keep her talons around a small amount of dignity.

"I'll do the best I can to tie everything up by Thursday evening," Marcee replied, just to keep Phyllis's mouth shut.

"If not, you'll have to skip lunch on Friday," Phyllis snapped. "Work comes before playtime." It seemed obvious that she had increased Marcee's workload in an effort to impede Claire's exclusionary plans.

"I would hardly call driving 40 miles in Friday traffic 'playtime.'" Marcee, during the decade she'd been working for Luminary, was rarely confrontational with Phyllis; for the most part, a frozen Dove bar would calm things down before Marcee was pushed to the use of contentious words. All of a sudden, though, Marcee felt strength in her position. "Plus," Marcee continued, "it's not 'Tea Time at the Madison's.' It's a meeting to further discuss the publicity strategy for *Night Crimes.*"

"I suppose if you had done your job right the other day, there'd be no need for a second meeting," Phyllis countered. "Perhaps my department would be better served by someone who gets it on the first take."

Marcee took a deep breath, exhaling and then counting to three in her head. "Well, Phyllis, you'd better leave me to finish all of this," Marcee said, pointing to the stacks of folders on her blotter and breaking eye contact with the fire-breathing bag of rawhide.

Marcee stayed at the office until 11PM, noshing on a bag of caramel-flavored Popcorners and drinking an oversized tumbler of Crystal Light iced tea. The upside to the late hour was the low-calorie meal; had she left at a reasonable time, there was no doubt she would have scarfed down an In-N-Out burger with a Dunkin' Donuts Boston Kreme chaser. In this instance, Phyllis had saved Marcee from herself.

Licking the sweet saltiness from her fingers, Marcee stood from her chair and grabbed her shoulder bag. She shut down her computer; her eyes were too bleary to look at one more document. With a quick tap of Flo's magic wing, Marcee's office went dark, signaling the end of another treacherous workday.

Marcee waited to dial her mother until she had pulled out of the parking structure. *Amazing,* she thought. *They can put a man on the moon, but no one can figure out how to deliver cell signals to garages? In Tinseltown, no less?*

"Hi, honey," Rhonda said. "Daddy and I just got home from dinner at the Frankels; that woman doesn't shut up. Everything OK on your end?"

"I am literally leaving the office now, Mom," Marcee whined, begging for sympathy with her tone. "Phyllis hammered me with work, probably because she was so pissed about the Claire Madison invite. I'm going to have to live at the studio this week if I plan to spend the day in Malibu on Friday, and, even then, I'm not sure I'll finish everything."

"Do the best you can; you have to go to Rox and Claire's house on Friday either way," Rhonda said. "If you continue to make a good impression on Claire, Phyllis can't be so threatening. I don't think anything can make you more indispensable than being in the good graces of Rox Madison's wife." So much of the Hollywood politics were beyond the understanding of Marcee's parents, but Rhonda seemed to have a handle on this situation.

Marcee arrived at her apartment and quickly changed into her pajamas. She was showered and moisturized in record time, hitting her four-poster bed with a loud sigh. She nestled herself inside a faux-fur acrylic blanket from Restoration Hardware that had been gifted to her a couple of years prior by an annoyingly vegan Secret Santa at the Luminary holiday party. She'd been meaning to donate the throw — polyester lining and all — to a local thrift shop, but she hadn't had time to swing by the Jewish Women's Council. The Salvation Army was just around the corner from her home, but they didn't supply the same tax-friendly itemized receipts issued by the Chosen ladies. Not to mention, Jordan had educated her about the Salvation Army's supposed belief in gay reparative therapy and their lack of antidiscrimination policies to protect their homosexual employees. If that weren't enough, the fucking bell ringing outside of her local grocery store drove her nuts. *Can't they solicit funds in a more peaceful way?* Marcee always thought to herself. Even the Girl Scouts were less annoying when accosting her during their annual cookie drives — but maybe that was a personal thing; they offered shortbread for cash as opposed to paper poppies that wound up in the trash after Marcee walked out of view.

The one-sided conversation in Marcee's head was keeping her awake. She went off on her own tangent about her dislike for supermarkets, particularly those that allowed young adults to loiter outside with clipboards. Marcee hated having to pretend that she was on a phone call, motioning to her ear in an effort to keep the do-gooders at a quiet distance. No, she didn't want to sign a petition for world peace or to put a stop to global warming at that moment. Rather, she wanted the Tampax Pearl Plastic Tampons and Mallomars at their advertised sale prices in addition to a checkout lane that didn't require she pay with cash for her 10 items or less. It was that simple.

◇◇◇

BY THURSDAY NIGHT, Marcee was running on empty. She'd completed two weeks' worth of work in only a few days, and Phyllis had acknowledged none of it. It was just as well, really; no word from Phyllis meant no conflict and a lesser likelihood that the subject of lunch at Claire's house would come up again. Phyllis never stayed at the office later than 5:30PM, so Marcee knew there was no risk of running into the bitch when she walked to the elevator at 9:30PM.

Exhaustion turned into excitement after Marcee drove away from the studio, and no one would be able to appreciate her enthusiasm as much as Jordan. She pressed number two on her speed dial.

"Girl, please," he answered, without so much as a hello. He'd taken cultural appropriation to a new level, eschewing his middle-class Jewish upbringing for that of Nicki Minaj.

"Tomorrow's the day," Marcee said. "The big lunch at Rox Madison's house."

"I cannot wait to hear about their crib," Jordan said, "and kindly try to find an item for my gossip column, will you? You know I always cover your premieres, even when the movies suck. You still owe me for that Nicole Kidman film."

"Jordan, I can't give you anything to publish; they'd know who it came from. And, by the way, can we focus on *me* right now? Just for a few minutes?"

"You have exactly 90 seconds. After that, Boo Boo, the conversation turns back to this black woman."

"Jordan, you're not a black woman." Marcee had loved him since the day they met at the Woodland Hills Jewish Community Center Preschool, and she knew for certain that he was as white as sourdough.

"*How. Dare. You.* I'm beyond insulted."

"Well, get over it. We have to discuss my manicure. I think I'm going to get my nails done on my way to Malibu instead of first thing in the morning. Should I go with a dark color or something lighter for the beach?"

"That's such an important decision, Marcee. Are you sure I'm up to this? Maybe we should call a special meeting of the UN."

"Shut it, Jordan! This is important. Claire's probably going to be judging every little thing, and I want to make sure I'm on point. Like it or not, this meeting could mean a lot to my career."

"OK, in all seriousness, go with a dark color. Make a

statement but not with anything as pedestrian as OPI. You need to drive to one of those upscale salons where they have Christian Louboutin's Bianca or Chanel's Vert Obscur. Wear a blue-grey or dark green color that's bold and confident." Jordan knew his high-end nail lacquers because he owned most of them himself. He turned his nose up at anything with an $8.50 name, such as Lincoln Park After Dark or Light My Sapphire, even for his toes.

"OK, done," Marcee said. "I am so nervous."

"Why? You've been around these kinds of celebrities for ages."

"It's not about their level of celebrity," Marcee continued. "I guess I want her to like me, that's all."

"It's impossible to *dislike* you, and I'm not saying that just because you're now a source of information about Rox." Jordan laughed.

"Oh, girl, please," Marcee said, mimicking his phrasing as she smiled and disconnected the call. During the remainder of the drive to Sherman Oaks, she remembered being drawn to Jordan's unique sensibility at age four. He was a reedy underweight with a mop of straight black hair that was deliberately disarranged into a "just woke up" style. His milky skin framed almond-shaped china-blue eyes, an aquiline nose and two pillowy lips that rested on top of each other like fluffy pink marshmallows. He spent most afternoons by himself on the playground, wardrobe styling the various dolls that were in the school's toy chest. He was quiet and timorous, usually ignored or teased by other kids who perceived him to be a "weirdo" or "too girly."

Jordan grew into a similarly wispy young man — a five-feet-seven sylph with the same haircut. Marcee always rallied around her best pal, recognizing how special he was and how much he'd bring to the world someday. "People just don't understand you yet," she'd say, at once reassuring him that his differences would eventually become assets and taking pride herself in the fact that she was so intuitive and forward thinking.

Phoebe and Charlie Levine, Jordan's parents, became close to Rhonda and Neal in the mid-70s; not only did they live around the block from each other, but they shared a value system that lived and breathed through their children. Both families were relieved when Marcee and Jordan were accepted to Yale, as neither of the kids had to navigate the East Coast or the Ivy League alone. They'd never existed away from each other, and there was a great comfort in knowing that Marcee and Jordan would brave the New Haven winters as a team.

The sound of Marcee's Audi scraping against the sloped pavement ramp into her apartment building's garage jolted her into the present. Memories of growing up with Jordan had been flying across her windshield — a three-dimensional timeline of two lives forever linked by shared histories — distracting her from the matters at hand. She needed to rush indoors, brush her teeth, throw on a hydrating mask and get eight hours of sleep before the damning circles of fatigue darkened her undereyes.

◇◇◇

RUTHANNE WOULD NEVER know that Marcee wasn't faithful, which provided some comfort to her cheating hands. It was bad enough that Eun-sao Kim had lost the name-tag lottery when the Studio City Nail Terrace first opened, let alone that she got saddled with *two* names instead of the customary Alice or Wendy. Over the years, RuthAnne had relayed all of the injustices she'd suffered to Marcee; the shitty name and sole waxing duties were among the most harrowing. According to RuthAnne, depilating the pubic mounds of the San Fernando Valley — the porn capital of the country — was a follicular nightmare. Her clients wanted elaborate shapes and configurations, a difficult art when applied to especially coarse short and curlies. "Beverly Hills bush much better," she'd say. "Water over there make hair softer."

Marcee didn't want to further slight the oft put-upon aesthetician, but Jordan was right: Marcee would have to travel to the other side of the hill if she wanted to escape the Essie and Color Club selections that cornered the nail color market in the Valley. Only a designer coat would do for Claire, and PrettyCures was the crème de la cuticle.

Always sensible when it came to putting mileage on her leased car, Marcee decided that it did, in fact, make sense to get dressed and blow out her hair early Friday morning. This way, she could hit Beverly Hills on her way to Malibu via the PCH. Los Angeles traffic was always an unreliable nightmare, so Marcee made sure she was at PrettyCures by 10AM. Her nails would be done in an hour, and she'd have 90 minutes to get to Claire's for lunch at 12:30PM.

As she entered the salon, her eyes began to water. Was a basic manicure really $45?

"Mani/pedi?" A voice from a back room of the rectangular shop grabbed Marcee's attention. Sharon, a tall, shapely blonde, was fastening her personalized, embroidered apron as she walked toward the front to formally greet her new client. Her desert chest — an overtanned stretch of scaly skin above some surgically enhanced cleavage — was on full display. "Sorry, I'm the first one here this morning. There's usually someone at reception." Sharon's chatter gave Marcee a moment to think about how she would politely decline the $95 combo treatment that likely didn't make a Beverly Hills housewife bat a false eyelash.

"I wish I could do both today," Marcee said, "but a basic manicure should have me out of here right on time."

Sharon lowered her chin slightly so that her reading glasses, which were tethered to her neck by an iridescent pink cord, slid to the tip of her manufactured nose. She peered over the rim of her purple frames, giving Marcee a thorough stare-down. "Are you sure?" she asked. "We're known for our pedicures." Marcee could hear judgment in Sharon's attempt to up-sell the salon's services.

"I'll have to come back and get one." Marcee smiled, knowing full well that this would be her first and last appointment at PrettyCures. She grabbed a bottle of Christian Louboutin Lady Twist — a shiny blue-green shade from the Noir collection — and sat in the first motorized recliner while Sharon filled a bowl with warm sudsy water and pearlized marbles. The bottle of polish was made of heavy glass and topped by a pointed brush handle that was about six inches in height. Marcee had a flash daydream about impaling Sharon's snotty ass the minute she offered a paraffin wax treatment for $30 but was woken by the sound of Beyonce's newest single filtering through wall-mounted speakers. She reached for the latest issue of *Us Weekly* with her left hand while Sharon began to file the nail tips on her right. Usually, looking through the gossip and entertainment rags on her own time felt too much like a day at the office, but reading "What's in Snooki's Purse?!" was, in that instance, more relaxing than making small talk with a skinny white woman who had a stick up her ass. Plus, it wasn't really personal time, so the magazine "research" made Marcee feel like she wasn't playing hooky during the hours leading up to her lunch meeting.

As fate would have it, stars…"are just like us!" After pages and pages of comparative, side-by-side images of celebrities in the same outfits, Marcee reached her favorite section: paparazzi snaps of celebrities doing everyday chores. Jay-Z pumps gas? Really? Madonna takes her kids to the park? How is that possible? As it turns out, it was just as possible as Rox and Claire taking their 10-year-old, adopted biracial twins on a trolley ride around the Grove. There it was, in full-page, four-color glory.

Sharon moved around to the other side of the chair as Marcee shifted the magazine to her right hand. In the shuffle, Sharon caught a glimpse of the photo.

"He's too good looking for her," Sharon said with the authority of a Hollywood insider and the discretion of a two-year-old. After all, she had no idea that she was doing the nails of Claire Madison's lunch date. "He reminds me of an even more famous Hugh Jackman, slumming it with an ordinary girl who got her hooks into him before fame did. If he'd just waited, Rox could've had any woman. Perhaps even me."

Marcee couldn't help but feel offended. Why couldn't a hot guy be attracted to an average-looking girl with an above-average brain and sense of humor? If Marcee had met a man like Rox and married him in her 20s, would some starlet-turned-manicurist be saying the same things about her to a client who was thumbing through the pages of soon-to-be birdcage lining? It took all of the willpower Marcee had to not tell Sharon that she was heading to Rox's house the minute her nails were dry.

"Maybe they're actually in love," Marcee said. "Is that impossible to believe?"

"In this town? Yeah, not a likely story." Sharon was obviously as jaded as she was weathered. She directed a tiny white fan onto Marcee's nails and left a small manila envelope in which Marcee could leave a cash tip. Marcee had forgotten to pay before the nail color was applied, and Sharon was obviously too busy having an opinion on Claire's marriage to suggest precolor payment.

"Can I put your tip on my card?" Marcee asked.

Sharon tossed an icy glare. "Nope. Cash only. Have a

great rest of your day." And, just like that, she disappeared into the back on a wave of fumes from acrylic and acetone.

By 11AM, the salon was bustling; it was time for Marcee to get on the road. She paid at the front counter while looking through her purse carefully for cash; she would be damned if she'd smudge a nail because of the tipping requirements. She scraped together the $9 that represented a 20 percent gratuity, but, as she signed her name on the credit card slip, something came over her. "Do you have a small piece of paper?" she asked the receptionist.

Marcee scribbled a note on the four-by-four blue square: "*Additional tip — you may consider treating new customers a little better.*" She folded the note in half and placed it neatly in the mustard-colored envelope along with the money. She wrote "Sharon" across the front, accented by an "xo." Shoulders high, Marcee marched out of PrettyCures to the parking lot.

Using the underside of her right hand, Marcee delicately opened the door to her car, settling into the driver's seat and fastening her seatbelt before dialing her mother.

"Are you on your way to Claire's?" Rhonda asked. "How was the manicure?"

"Yes, and expensive," Marcee answered. "And the manicurist could not have been any more of a bitch. I taught her a little lesson, though." She let go a few bars of maniacal laughter.

"A lesson? What happened?"

"The woman seemed to be judging me the whole time, and she wanted me to spend more than the $45 for a basic manicure," Marcee said.

"$45 for a manicure? For that money, she'd have to live in the house and clean, too. I hope she irons!"

"Can you believe the nerve? You know what I did, though?"

"Tipped less than the customary 20 percent, I hope," Rhonda replied.

"No, I gave her the $9, but I put a note in the envelope, too. It said that she should be nicer to new clients." Marcee's voice had a tone of indignation. "I'm sure that was a first for her."

"Good for you, honey. She'll definitely think twice before making other customers feel so insignificant." Rhonda sounded proud of her only child. "So, are you ready for the lunch meeting? How does the outfit look?"

"I think it looks OK but a little tight," Marcee said, "I just want this to go well. If I can get Rox in my corner, it could be a huge asset."

"You'll be great, and Claire obviously likes and trusts you enough to have you to their home. Will you call me as soon as you're on your way back to the Valley?"

"Of course," Marcee replied, as if there were a chance she'd call someone else first.

On a scale of Wilson to Phillips, Marcee was feeling like 1990s Carnie. The skirt screamed Chynna in the fitting room but was uncomfortably restraining in the confines of her driver's seat. Claire would undoubtedly notice the imperfect fit. Perhaps the loose-fitting poncho would do its job, working in tandem with the dazzling nail polish to distract from Marcee's pooched midsection. She was hopeful.

◇◇◇

MARCEE'S 16GB IPHONE didn't store as much music as she would've liked, but her go-to women of rock-and-roll were always only a touch away. If a power ballad was in order, no band could outdo Heart; likewise, if an anthem of strength was necessary, Pat Benatar was on standby. During her drive to Malibu, Marcee needed to feel "Invincible," in that *Legend of Billie Jean* kind of way. Belting at a volume that was quite possibly startling to other motorists, she sang about the "power of conviction" as she channeled the short-haired songstress whom Marcee was certain was the top-billed act on a county fair main stage that very evening. Pat meant more than that to Marcee, though; the entire Benatar catalog was a musical memoir of sorts. "Le Bel Age" could easily flash Marcee right back to high school, when her mom would play the *Seven the Hard Way* cassette over and over.

Marcee saw a reflection of her perfectly made-up face as she repositioned the rearview mirror, quickly looking behind her own eyes to a 15-year-old version of herself in the back seat. The braces that had transformed her teeth into perfectly straight rows gave her mouth an unnatural pout, and her oversized neon pink shirt from Wet Seal covered a morbidly overweight teenager whose chubby thighs were sweat-stuck to the pleather seats of Rhonda's Nissan Maxima. Marcee recalled being pushed against the right door, sardined into the coupe by the neighborhood carpool kids whom her mother schlepped to and from school every third week. Somehow, Jordan always charmed his way into the front passenger seat, claiming "shotgun" because of motion sickness or needing extra space to complete an overdue homework assignment.

"There isn't enough room back here, Mrs. Brookes," Jonathan Parker yelled into the front of the car one morning.

"There'll be plenty of room next year, when you have your own car and can drive yourself," Marcee's mom retorted, stirring a laugh from Jordan.

"Shut up, Jor-DANA," Jonathan hissed, emphasizing how he'd made Jordan into a girl with the addition of only one syllable. He then elbowed Lauren Gardner, who was perched on the dreaded hump between the two back seats.

"Maybe Marcee should sit in the front from now on," Lauren chimed in. "Then there'd actually be room for three people back here."

"Maybe each of your moms should drive you to school from now on," Rhonda said, raising her voice to an uncharacteristic growl. The car got quiet, except for the gravel and smoke of Pat Benatar's voice coming from the speakers. Marcee stared out of the window in an effort to avoid eye contact with anyone, even her mom. She looked at the blur of shrubbery, orange cones, traffic lights and street signs that blended into a high-speed oil painting of confusion. Jonathan and Lauren weren't blinded by the flashy shirt or its extra fabric. They saw the unlovable fat girl beneath the rayon.

In those moments — which came a few times per week, at various points during the school day — Marcee tried to remind herself that her "gifts," as her father liked to call them, would ultimately get her farther in life than the cheerleader looks and bumptious attitudes of her peers.

"This one is smart and has drive," Neal Brookes would tell family friends while hugging Marcee at holiday dinners and gatherings. "Watch out for her!" Marcee desperately wanted to escape his embrace on those occasions, hopeful that she could fade into the background before any more attention was channeled in her direction. She knew that her intellect was well above average — gifted classes and AP courses, not to mention unprecedented standardized test scores, left no doubt about her brainpower. It was her pyknic physique that made her want to vaporize and seep beneath a closet or pantry door as quickly as a blowy draft could sweep her away.

"OK, so my mom is Smurfette, and my dad wears size small. How did I lose the genetics competition?" Marcee complained to Jordan time and time again.

"The same way that my mom is a tennis pro, and my dad coaches football," he answered. "Meanwhile, the only balls I want to play with are attached to the jocks on the varsity team."

"Ugh. It's totally unfair," she'd continue. "It's not like I eat *that* much."

"Marcee, when you're having a rough day, you add a Happy Meal to your Big Mac combo."

"I get stressed on test days," she shot back, "and I make sure that the soda is diet!" Marcee knew she didn't have a Quarter Pounder to stand on; Jordan was being truthful. She ate her feelings, and, overall, her emotional attachment to food felt stronger than her want for a smaller body. Sure, barbs from the pretty Lauren Gardner would now and again make her rethink that position, but something coated in chocolate would inevitably come along to keep her on course.

Marcee was fast approaching Point Dume — known in town as the "Malibu Riviera" — and had to shift her focus back to the Waze navigation app. Claire's assistant, Sarah, had given her directions by phone, but she was so fast-talkingly officious that Marcee was barely able to scribble legible notes on a buck slip. She said something about a right at Bob Dylan and a left at Barbra Streisand — or was it a left at Cindy Crawford? — but Marcee wasn't as familiar with the maps of the stars' homes as Sarah obviously thought she should be. Marcee knew the storied Hollywood lore behind the stretch of oceanfront land that entertainment legends had called home since the 1920s, but she wasn't as knowledgeable about Malibu's more current dwellers.

"I'll e-mail you my cell phone number; please call when you arrive," Sarah had instructed her the previous afternoon. "I'll have a valet take your car and bring you to the house in a golf cart." So, as told, Marcee dialed Sarah's mobile phone as soon as she was among the neighborhood's winding streets.

"Thank you, Ms. Brookes; Javier will meet you out front to take your car."

Sarah's tone added a layer of fire to Marcee's nerves. The pressure was already on in terms of presenting Claire with polished PR materials and strategy, but she'd likely be meeting the world's biggest action star as well. On top of that, she was going to be in his home — the inner sanctum of a Hollywood god, which, after a Google search, she learned that he'd bought for $45 million. Sarah's style, initially, did nothing to put Marcee at ease or warm the proverbial pathway. It was no surprise to Marcee that Claire would employ an executive assistant who could mirror her own off-putting veneer.

Marcee slowly rolled her car to the property's humble-looking entryway, noticing someone who looked like a Latin telenovela star approaching her door. As much as she would have loved to consider the scenario in a daydream or while enjoying her Jimmy Jane Form 6 in the bathtub, she wasn't quite ready to be greeted. She was hoping to reapply her lipstick and smooth her outfit before actually meeting any staff, but their efficiency worked against her.

Javier was strikingly handsome; he had green eyes and jet-black hair that complemented the body of a gym fiend. His pants were perfectly tailored to his round ass and ample-looking crotch, and his red T-shirt stretched across his broad chest like it was sprayed-on latex.

"Hello, Ms. Brookes," Javier said. His accent was surprisingly American — not the Spanish soap-opera dialect she'd expected — and he had a voice so rich and deep that she was certain he'd broken no fewer than a dozen hearts in his 26 or 27 years. "Please give me your keys, and I'll take you up to the house in a cart."

“I’ll let you take me anywhere,” Marcee wanted to say, but, instead, she swallowed the saliva that was pooling in her mouth and quickly averted her eyes from Javier’s perfectly round bubble butt; “a cute tucchus,” her mother would call it. Five years had passed since Marcee’s last sexual encounter, and his look got all of her juices flowing. Her latent libido had to wake up now? Right before such an important meeting?

Fortunately, before she could get a word — or a dribble — out of her mouth, Javier helped her out of the car, taking her shoulder bag and work binder. “Let me show you inside,” he said politely, opening the deliberately distressed wooden pedestrian gate that looked as though it might fall from its antique hinges if moved too quickly.

4

THE GRASS WAS, in fact, greener in Point Dume.

As Marcee stepped through the wooden door to the left of the motorized vehicle gate, she was taken with the emerald color of the grounds surrounding the stone driveway. The cut lawn smelled like newly minted cash, and the lush trees were draped in a fragrant moss that a storybook would describe as "enchanted."

"Hop in the golf cart, Ms. Brookes," Javier said. "I'll run you up to the house."

"I can see the front door from here," Marcee replied, looking ahead to the stocky figure standing at a near distance. "I don't want to waste your time." The yard was much wider than it was long; Marcee reasoned that she could have been at the front door already if not for the strict arrival protocol.

"That's Sarah, Ms. Brookes, and she'll be extremely unhappy if I don't give you a ride. Mr. and Mrs. Madison don't like their guests to walk." He gave Marcee a pleading stare that she interpreted as a silent command: *Just hop in the cart so I can avoid trouble and get on with my day, OK?*

Marcee gathered the excess material at the bottom of her throw-over and sat on the white foam passenger seat in the first of four electric golf carts. Before Javier sat down, she adjusted the left leg of her Spanx; she didn't want a hint of the black compression undergear to reveal that the objects in her skirt were larger than they appeared.

"Ms. Brookes, can I kindly ask you to have a seat in the back? The view of the grounds is much better when you're facing out, and we want you to enjoy the scenery."

Had she entered a Stepford community? The cadence of Javier's rhetoric seemed overly rehearsed, and his pleasantries were as inorganic as her favorite to-go foods from Taquita Chiquita in Encino.

"Um, sure," Marcee mumbled, moving swiftly in an effort to chase the awkwardness out of the situation.

Shirtless twentysomething men were working in every corner of the yard, each cuter than the last. One handsome all-American waved as Javier rode past, adjusting the bandana around his head to stop beads of sweat from dripping down his chiseled face onto his million-pack abs. Marcee gave him a faint smile and returned his wink with a hesitant wave, redirecting her attention to a light-skinned black gentleman who was similarly in shape. He was feeding fish in a bridge-covered pond to her right. Was this some kind of charity calendar in the making? The LA Fire Department had one; so did the UCLA men's rowing team. They'd all stripped to raise money for a variety of causes, and there was no question that Rox and Claire's landscaping staff could show some flesh for the homeless, a school building fund or the proposed playground next to the Malibu Country Mart.

In the 18 seconds it took Javier to drive Marcee to the front entrance, she'd seen enough eye candy to describe to Jordan later that night. She was dying to get a look inside the main attraction, though: a 16,000-square-foot bluff-side estate that was designed by one of the world's most sought-after architects. Or, at least that's what Marcee's online research had turned up.

"Hi, Ms. Brookes," Sarah said as Marcee stepped out of the golf cart and took her bags from Javier. "Nice to meet you in person." She put out her right hand to shake Marcee's, smiling broadly as though she was thrilled to see another human being.

"Thank you for arranging all of this," Marcee answered, surprised by Sarah's appearance. Usually, when Marcee imagined the face of the person attached to a voice or an e-mail, she was on-target — not to mention that the vast majority of Hollywood assistants had a stock look; therefore, she'd expected Sarah to be a leggy fawn. She'd pictured a dark-haired Taylor Swift, cat-eye makeup and all. The woman she met, however, was a warmly round size 18 in an Ashley Stewart knit dress and a strand of opalescent pearls.

"Oh, not a problem," Sarah said, adjusting her headband to keep her waist-length mane out of her face. The after-her-time Crystal Gayle could go from country songbird to Cousin Itt in a hot second without the right hair accessories.

"Claire is just finishing coffee with a couple of girlfriends; can I grab you a cup?" Sarah guided Marcee through the stained-glass doors and into a cavernous foyer. A stunning found-wood table sat in the center of the room, over which hung a cluster of cords that lit various shaped light bulbs, all with different filament patterns. A chill wafted through in a circular flurry, and Marcee wasn't sure if it was coming from the ocean or the décor itself. She clung to her woven poncho.

Sarah opened the door to the room directly at Marcee's left, which housed a modern-looking library. The tall shelves featured a rolling ladder that was tracked to move around the perimeter, and the books were organized by the color of their spines: the rainbow began with red in the near top corner and hit the far bottom of the last shelf with violet. Two cream-colored couches faced each other in the middle of the study, sandwiching a small glass coffee table.

Claire was perched on one sofa facing two slightly older women on the other.

"Wow!" Marcee said as she entered, struggling to find her words while overwhelmed by the grandeur and competing colors of the space. "Have you read *all* of these books?" Her eyes looked the shelves up and down as though she were assessing every title in the collection.

"Some of them twice," Claire answered as she jumped up and threw her arms forward for a disarmingly warm hug.

"Frankly, I don't know how she'd even find what she wants to read," one of the other women said, standing to introduce herself. "I'm Gabbi Green." The moment she said her name, Marcee made the connection. Gabbi was a former salon makeup artist who had developed her own line of luxury cosmetics. Now a premium and revered brand, Gabbi Green was a beauty-industry icon. Or rather, she was a woman lucky enough to have married a rich man who could provide capital for the launch of her business.

"What the fuck are you talking about, Gabs?" Claire asked jokingly.

"Do you walk into the room and say, 'Gee, I think I'd like to read a book with a blue cover today?'" Gabbi had a point. The organizational style was visually appealing but completely nonfunctional to someone who actually *read* books.

"Why don't you stick to powder and lip liner, and I'll worry about my library," Claire said with a forced laugh. She shifted her eyes to Nina Walker, who stayed seated but reached up to shake Marcee's hand across the table.

"Nina and Gabbi, this is Marcee Brookes. She's the studio flack who's doing the publicity for Rox's new movie." The two women nodded and smiled but showed little interest beyond that. Claire returned to her seat on the couch.

There was no mistaking Nina Walker; Marcee had

studied all of the ever-present media coverage of her tragic career crash. As an informed publicist, Marcee stayed abreast of just about every story in every rag mag, from *People* to the *National Enquirer.* She'd learned that Nina, who had been the standout of the *Wacky Weekend Live* ensemble cast in the mid-90s, bought into her own hype. Like many had done before her, she left the sketch comedy show at the height of her run, assuming that Hollywood would embrace her the same way it welcomed *Saturday Night Live*'s Eddie Murphy and Will Ferrell, among others. Unfortunately, her cold real-life persona — not to mention her fondness for fermented beverages and her limited mental capacity — left her jobless and living in a prefurnished unit at the Park LaBrea housing development.

"I guess we should let you get down to business," Gabbi said, nudging Nina and pushing her toward the door. "I'll call you Monday, and we'll plan a weekend at the Santa Barbara house." Marcee got the impression that Nina was socially tone-deaf and needed Gabbi as a guide dog of sorts.

"Oh, I'd love that," Nina interjected as Gabbi led her by the arm out of the library. It was obvious from the look on Gabbi's face — and the theatrical arch of her aggressively plucked right eyebrow — that the suggestion of a getaway wasn't inclusive of Nina.

"I could use a minivacation," Claire answered as she blew kisses from her pillowed roost on the sofa. "I'm exhausted by everything lately."

Sarah walked by and closed the door to the study the moment Gabbi and Nina exited. Claire's lack of patience for the two women was evident in her dramatic sigh. "So glad *that's* over," she said. "I mean, I can take those ladies only in small doses." Claire motioned for Marcee to take a seat across from her.

"It's clear that they really admire you," Marcee replied.

"It's kind of a nuisance. I don't mean to sound like a total bitch, but I just can't stand Gabbi anymore." Claire took a sip of her coffee. "And that Nina Walker. I never enjoy spending time with her, but Gabbi trots her around like a special-needs kid she's trying to mainstream. They're like a two-for-one fire sale."

"What *is* Nina Walker up to these days?" Marcee asked.

"Nothing but whining about losing her house, which she'll be the first to tell you was owned at some point by Charlie Chaplin. I don't think she understands entirely that her career is over. The Kristen Wiigs and Tina Feys have leapfrogged her bad nose job and grabbed the career she wanted. Plus, I hear she's a cunt on set. No one wants to put up with that shit from such a marginal talent."

"Having a reputation for being 'difficult' is definitely a drawback if you're not A-list." Marcee chose her words carefully, not wanting to sound too interested in gossip but hoping that Claire would go on.

"Plus, did you see how skinny she is? She's been anorexic for the 10 years I've known her," Claire continued. "Anyone who has an eating disorder for that long and doesn't die is doing something wrong. Just another way in which she's a failure."

Marcee was taken aback at first by Claire's pointedly forceful comments, but it felt good to think that she trusted Marcee to be discreet with such insider information.

"By the way, do you want that?" Claire asked, motioning toward a small, black laminated shopping bag that was foil stamped with the Gabbi Green Cosmetics logo. "She always brings a supply of makeup, but her products fuck with my skin. I think she uses cheap ingredients."

Marcee took the bag from the table and looked inside. It was jam-packed with the entire line. "Thank you so much, Claire. I'll definitely get use out of this." To Claire, it might have been second-rate product compared to Chanel, but it was a brand that Marcee aspired to. The only time she treated herself to Gabbi Green was when Nordstrom ran a 20 percent-off special on top of a "free gift" promotional bonus. Did she ever use the Lilliputian lipsticks or pea-sized pods of sparkling bronzer? Not even once. But the Gabbi Green makeup brush carrier, filled with useless samples, justified the $25 for a long-wear eye pencil.

"Listen, I'd rather you enjoy it than tax Sarah with the chore of deciding which of my kids' teachers to regift it to," Claire said, laughing. "Of course, Gabbi thinks I swear by her brand, but, to me, it's just Revlon in prettier packaging — like a turd in a shiny box. God bless her, though, for bilking scores of women out of zillions of dollars. If only they knew that her only qualification to manufacture and distribute makeup is a half-completed trade degree from some community beauty school and an affair with a stupidly suggestible, rich fat guy."

"Well, it's going to a good home." Marcee smiled. "Now, should we start taking a look at the proposed *Night Crimes* publicity campaign?"

"You must be hungry, and Mercedes should have our salads ready. Plus, I'm sure you want a tour of the estate," Claire said. "Just leave your bags here. Don't worry, no one is going to steal *that* makeup."

◇◇◇

THE HOUSE? STUNNING. Claire's career as a docent? Going nowhere.

Marcee figured that a tour of the 12-bedroom ocean-view house — replete with conversation-piece furniture and stunning artwork — would, even on fast-forward, take an hour. Claire had concluded the entire walk-through in 30 minutes.

"It's great, isn't it? Don't you want to just move in?" Claire asked rhetorically as she walked Marcee toward the kitchen.

"It's like heaven *is* a place on earth," Marcee replied, smiling to herself at the 1980s Belinda Carlisle reference. Sometimes, Marcee liked to pepper her conversations with song titles and lyrics, just to see if anyone caught on. It was a game she played with herself.

"I know; it's nothing like our other homes," Claire continued. "They're all only about 10,000 square feet. This place is divine."

"That Moreau," Marcee said, pointing to a wall opposite a small breakfast nook, "is breathtaking."

"The what?" Claire looked confused.

"The Moreau. It's so pretty."

"Oh, you mean that picture? Rox says it's worth a fortune, but it's really not my thing."

The kitchen was large enough to cater a meal for 100 people, and Mercedes moved around it as fluidly as the Pacific Ocean soaked the sand at the property line. A mid-50s Latina who looked as though she had tasted a healthy portion of every dish she'd ever prepared, she wore her coarse hair in a shoulder-length ponytail. Her deep saucer eyes were set back in a rounded face, her shiny, flushed skin making clear that she had been laboring over the stove the entire morning.

"Mercedes, are the salads ready? Marcee and I are starving."

"Jes, Mrs. Madison," Mercedes answered with a hearty accent. "They're sitting right over there." She pointed to the two place settings that had been prepared on the island in the middle of the room. "Hope you en-yoy."

"Gracias, Mercedes," Marcee said, "la comida se ve delicioso."

"¡Tu español es muy bueno!"

"Si, aprendi español en la escuela," Marcee said. "No soy perfecto, pero trato."

Claire stood silently by a side counter, moving her head back and forth as she listened.

"Lo estas haciendo muy bien," Mercedes complimented her, seemingly excited to speak with someone in her native language.

"This is adorbs," Claire finally interrupted, "but the refried Spanish is mind-numbing, and the salads aren't getting any fresher. Can we vamanos, por favor?"

"Sorry, Claire, I was just checking to see if I remembered anything from high school." Marcee couldn't discern whether or not Claire was trying to be funny or if she really *was* that ravenous.

"OK, well, now that the 'que pasas' are out of the way, let's eat. I haven't had so much as an almond since my meditation class this morning, and my stomach is starting to eat itself."

Marcee perched herself on one of the counter stools, both of her legs hanging straight down. Claire sat cross-legged in an uncomfortable-looking yoga configuration, at a right angle to Marcee. The arrangement was intimate for a business meeting, the way a man and woman might position themselves on a date, and Claire's "Hollywood-casual" loose-fitting leisure wear — an aqua velour track-suit and a pair of orange Nike Air Max sneakers — made her look like a puff of day-old circus cotton candy. It wasn't a wardrobe choice Marcee would even attempt to pull off, but it sat sweetly on Claire.

"Those are great running shoes," Marcee said. The outfit begged to be acknowledged, and she thought the footwear represented the safest accessory to compliment. Claire's seated pose had inched her pants toward camel-toe territory, and Marcee didn't want to call attention to the issue.

"They are, aren't they?" Claire answered, looking at the two feet tucked halfway under her tiny ass. "Nike sent them to me; they're prototypes. I love that no one else has them."

"So, should we look at the rollout plan for *Night Crimes*?" Marcee asked as she grabbed a folder from her bag.

"Rollout plan?" Claire asked. "What do you mean?"

"The timeline we want to use for Mr. Madison's publicity appearances." Marcee was confused. "Sorry, I didn't mean to throw jargon out there. I know you have a marketing background, so I was being careful not to overexplain."

"Marketing background?" Claire laughed. "I took one communications class in college. That's the extent of my 'background.' Rox told a teensy white lie to the studio so it would seem natural for him to send me in his place. He hates this movie and wants as little to do with it as possible." Marcee smiled conspiratorially.

"Should I explain it all more thoroughly then?"

"Honey, I just want this movie to go away; I'd be happy if it premiered on WebFlicks instead of at the Bruin in Westwood. I mean, have you *actually* seen it? It's a mess because of that dumbass director."

"I was entertained by it," Marcee said, trying to hold onto the company line at least a little bit.

"Only Andrea Bocelli could possibly be entertained by it, and that would be if his hearing went out, too. I call bullshit, Ms. Brookes," Claire interrupted. "It sucks, and you know it. How do we bury it?"

Marcee couldn't disagree with Claire's sentiment; *Night Crimes*, was, indeed, a cinematic shit-storm. Somehow, though, she would need to figure out a way to balance Claire and Rox's disdain for the film with the studio's mandate to make it a tentpole blockbuster.

"Anyway," Claire said, as though she were making a natural segue into a related conversation, "what's dating like for a good-looking girl in LA? Those days are so far behind me." Marcee couldn't process the words in her head; half of her brain was still figuring out how to sound diplomatic about *Night Crimes* and the other couldn't believe that Claire had just described her as "good looking."

"I don't really know," Marcee stumbled. "I haven't had a date in years. I'm always so busy with work." She felt she needed to explain the absence of a romantic life.

"Is that because you *want* to be busy with work or because you just haven't met a guy? You won't find him if you don't put yourself out there." *Fuck. Claire just morphed into my mother,* Marcee thought.

"Well, the job is pretty much 24/7, but, if I'm being honest, I don't look for social opportunities that involve single men," Marcee admitted. She was being more truthful than she'd been with even her mom.

"You need to lighten up on this work shit and go hunting," Claire said as she speared a piece of lettuce and shrimp from her salad bowl. "How old are you? 32? 33?" Marcee smiled.

"I'm 42," she replied. Marcee took pleasure in revealing her true age to those who assumed her to be younger.

"You're in your 40s? I never would have thought," Claire continued. "We need to find you a man. It's ridiculous that you're single."

"My friend Jordan set up accounts for me on Match.com and JDate; he goes as far as writing messages to guys on my behalf."

"He must be your best gay," Claire said, which was a fair assumption. Marcee knew she was a zaftig, single woman in her 40s, a textbook fag hag if ever there were one.

"You're onto me, aren't you?" Girl-chatting with someone

who seemed to understand her situation was a welcomed change; Marcee didn't have a group of close female friends. "Am I that easy to figure out?"

"Let's just say I've heard similar stories," Claire replied. "So, no interesting online daters *at all*?"

"Not even one," Marcee said. "All of these guys want to text and exchange a ton of pictures before meeting in person. I hate it." Claire stopped eating and stared at Marcee, who was relaying a humiliating online dating misadventure.

"You know," Claire said, cutting Marcee off midsentence. "I have an idea. How would you feel about a setup?"

"Why, do you know a smart, handsome professional who's in the market for a middle-aged chubby Jew from the Valley?" Marcee's self-deprecating humor didn't appear to resonate with Claire.

"I'd hardly call you middle-aged," Claire quickly pointed out. "*I'm* middle-aged." *No,* Marcee thought. *If the average age at death is 84, 42 is, in fact, middle-aged. By Claire's logic, old would be over a hundred, which most people never see.* "But, to answer your question, yes, I think I know *the* perfect man — if you trust me to play matchmaker."

"Of course," Marcee answered. "You've obviously been successful at landing a great guy — and writing about it."

As if on cue, Rox walked into the kitchen. He was wearing small white tennis shorts and a sweat-soaked, striped Polo shirt; his thick head of jet-black hair was matted to his forehead. He went right over to Claire and dipped his chin to kiss her lightly on the top of her head from behind.

"Hi, honey," Claire said, "did you have a good game?"

"It was fine; who's this?" He leaned his head toward Marcee.

"Marcee Brookes," Claire answered. "Remember? I told you I was meeting with the PR girl from Luminary about *Night Crimes*."

"Oh, yeah, right," he said as he continued through the kitchen toward a hallway. "Hope she has fun trying to sell *that* movie."

Marcee was taken with Rox's striking features. A towering six feet five, he had muscular legs and exploding, superhero pecs. His imperfectly rugged nose gave a rough edge to an oval face, a steely strength that was accented by the dreamy sparkle in his light-brown eyes. He was a walking GQ cover.

"Well, now you've met The Man," Claire said proudly, as though that had been Marcee's reason for driving all the way out to Malibu in the first place. "Anyway, back to Brent Wetherley."

"Brent Wetherley?" Marcee asked. She didn't recall Claire mentioning the handsome up-and-comer.

"Yeah, remember? Before Rox got home, I was saying that I know a great guy for you." Claire got up from the counter, leaving two-thirds of her salad in its bowl.

"You mean the *actor* Brent Wetherley? The cute guy on *People* magazine's latest 'Ones to Watch' list?" Marcee was stunned.

"Yep, that one," Claire said, using her iPhone to Google pictures of the heartthrob. "Look at that face! And, he's so kind." She held up her screen so Marcee could see a virtual catalog of photos of Brent on various red carpets and in magazine spreads.

"Claire, there is no way that Brent Wetherley would be interested in me."

"How do you know who would interest Brent? My guess is that I know him a lot better than you do." Claire had a point. Marcee knew him only from magazine interviews and talk show appearances, and Claire obviously knew him personally.

"I've seen online photos of him with stunning women,"

Marcee said. "You really think he'll want some plain Jane from Sherman Oaks?"

"I'm sure you're very photogenic," Claire answered. "Plus, there aren't that many pictures of Brent's girlfriends floating around. He tries to keep his private life out of the press. Can you even name a woman he's supposedly dated?" Marcee could picture a few photos with one blonde or another, but she'd have been hard-pressed to actually ID one of them. "Listen, he needs a new publicist anyway, and you can advise on which of those nasty bitches to hire, right? Those sycophantic screamers dressed in all black are the worst."

"I can certainly point him in the direction of the least offensive," Marcee agreed. "They're all kind of a waste at $5K per month, but if he wants a new one, I'm happy to chat with him about it." Marcee surprised herself; she wasn't usually so candid about her publicity agency colleagues.

"Great. I'm going to put the two of you in touch. I'll tell him I have a nice girl for him to meet who just happens to know the PR world."

"You're not going to send him a picture of me, are you?" Marcee was having a hard time wrapping her head around Claire's thinking. Brent Wetherley could presumably have his pick of Hollywood starlets; what was he going to do with some dowdy publicist from the studio troughs?

"First of all, you're more than your looks," Claire said. "I've known you only a short time but long enough to recognize that there's a smart girl under that beautiful hair." Marcee blushed as a stroke of comforting heat moved from her ears down the back of her neck. Self-consciously, she rubbed her right hand along the back of her head. The whole situation was surreal: the wife of one of Hollywood's biggest movie stars was trying to connect her — romantically and professionally — with another of the industry's celluloid elite. "Second, Brent's not the kind of guy who would ask for a picture." Claire continued to talk as her phone started to ring with a FaceTime call. "He trusts my judgment, and he's a gentleman." She paused for a moment and looked down at her screen. "Oh, fuck."

"What's wrong?" Marcee asked, only partially focused on Claire's obvious upset. Her mind was still on Brent Wetherley.

"Fucking Claudia Erickson. She wants to FaceTime." Claire grunted. "She'll chew my ear off for an hour about her divorce from Nick." It took Marcee only about two seconds to figure out that Claudia Erickson was *the* Claudia Erickson, wife of the eponymous bass player for Erickson Wells. The band had some of the bestselling albums of all time.

"You know what, I'm just going to answer. Maybe if she sees there's someone here, she won't keep me long." Before Marcee could say anything, Claire pressed the green indicator on her touch screen, and there, in full motion, was an image of the woman who had inspired some of rock music's most enduring hit songs. "Hi, baby," Claire said, holding the phone out in front of her so that Claudia could see both her and Marcee in the kitchen.

"I'm falling apart, Claire," Claudia said, with perfectly flat affect. "This divorce is going to kill me." Her makeup was masterfully applied; she had clearly paid very close attention to the makeup artists working on her face throughout the years.

"Claudia, this is Marcee Brookes." Claire leaned toward Marcee to make sure Claudia knew the conversation wasn't private. "She's doing PR for Rox's new movie. Remember? I told you I met her at Luminary last week."

"Oh, right," Claudia said, "she looks lovely." Marcee's eyes widened as she sat up a little straighter on her stool.

They had discussed her previously? She had been a topic of conversation between Claire and Claudia Erickson? No one would ever believe it.

"Do you want to talk a little later?" Claire asked. "I assume you need my undivided attention."

"It's OK," Claudia answered. "I just wanted to tell you one quick thing."

"Is it alright for Marcee to hear? I know you like to keep everything within the family, so to speak." Claire glanced at Marcee and then immediately back to the iPhone.

"It's fine," Claudia said. "It's nothing I wouldn't say publicly."

"Just looking out for my best friend," Claire responded, smiling and twisting her hair between her right thumb and index finger.

"Anyway," Claudia began, "I ran into Risa earlier. Do you remember if we had discussed that my divorce was finally going through at our last TTT?"

"I don't think Nick had served you with papers until a couple of days after," Claire replied.

"Regardless, she was at the next table at Hinoki and the Bird today, and she seemed surprised when I told her. She's not a good enough actress to appear legitimately shocked."

"She'd argue that her awards say otherwise, but we all know that a couple of Emmys for that stupid *Head in the Clouds* show don't amount to a pile of shit. They give those trophies out like free condoms at a gay men's health clinic." Marcee had always loved Risa Turner, the star of that 80s sitcom, but the actress sounded like a sore subject for Claire and Claudia.

"Please. Emmys are like Grammys. They'll hand you one if you made a good mix tape 30 years ago," Claudia said. "That aside, she made some comment like, 'I'm so sorry for you, Claudia,' as though I'm the same kind of pathetic has-been she is."

"She's a piece of work." Claire shook her head in disbelief. "What did you say?"

"I said, 'Were you sorry when Elizabeth Smart was returned to her family? Because that's how *relieved* I am.'"

"She probably doesn't know who Elizabeth Smart is," Claire said as the two began to laugh.

"Whatevs. I'm just not in a good place right now, but I had to tell you that story." Claudia's rolling laughter wasn't exactly that of a woman on the edge. "Anyhow, call me back when you're alone. I'll cry into all of my expensive jewelry until then."

"By the way, can you have your girl let Sarah know the date for our next TTT night? I want to make sure she puts it on the schedule before my calendar fills up." Claire obviously didn't realize that Claudia had already disconnected the FaceTime chat before she got her question out. She began to text furiously. "I don't feel like getting on the phone with her again; I'll have Sarah call back to get the TTT details." Claire tossed the alliterative acronym out as though it were something anyone should know. Marcee nodded but worried that she appeared as confused as she felt when Claire looked at her sideways.

"To The Tomb," Claire explained. "It's what we call our small, core group of friends. Everything that's said during our dinners and weekends together goes to the grave; like a 'cone of silence' sort of thing."

"It's nice that you have such a tight-knit group," Marcee said. "And that there's so much trust."

"Yeah, it's great." Claire stood up from her stool. "On that note, I have to get going. My yoga instructor is out of town for a month, so I have to actually *go* somewhere for classes. Can you even imagine? She just picked up and went off for five weeks with one of her celebrity clients who's shooting a movie."

"That's a real inconvenience," Marcee said, trying her best to sound understanding.

"In some respects, I could use a break from her; she has a face that not even a mother could love, and she's not interesting enough to talk to for three hours a week," Claire continued. "But I owe her for this body." She did a quick spin around on the toes of her flashy sneakers, allowing Marcee to catch a full view of her lean figure, front-to-back.

Claire gave Marcee a hug and kiss on the cheek. "I'll talk to you next week — I want to hear all about what happens with Brent." She twirled out of the kitchen just as Sarah showed up to walk Marcee to the front door.

"Perfect timing," Marcee said. "We literally *just* finished."

"I know," Sarah responded. "I saw Claire do her 'goodbye dance' on the monitors in my office."

"Ah," Marcee said. "Cameras?"

"Claire has them *everywhere.*" Sarah stared into Marcee's eyes with the intensity of someone trying to send an SOS with her expression. Marcee had seen the look before — in movies, when a victim is being held captive and tries unsuccessfully to pass a secret cry for help to the outside.

"Well, on the upside, if you ever forget where you put something, you can just run the video back instead of physically retracing your steps." Marcee had to think fast to come up with a silver lining,

"There's always that." Sarah smiled. "Javier has your car just beyond the gate. He'll drive you down there."

"Thanks so much for arranging everything, Sarah." Marcee gave her a hug. "Hope you'll be starting your weekend shortly!"

"I'll probably be here for a few hours still," she lamented. "But drive carefully. Call me if you need anything, but I'm sure Claire will be in touch." Marcee desperately wanted to ask Sarah what she knew about Brent Wetherley and what her opinion was based on her own interactions with him. But she didn't know how much Claire shared with her assistant, and she didn't want to risk breaching a confidence. After all, Claire's true friends were planning to take everything to their graves.

◇◇◇

"SO? TELL ME all of it." Rhonda's voice was difficult to hear clearly over the sounds of the PCH traffic and the ocean waves. Marcee had all of the windows down so she could enjoy the heady, salted air that circulated through her car.

"Oh my God, Mom, it was awesome," Marcee said. "It was like sitting in the middle of a real-life magazine photo shoot for a whole afternoon. I couldn't even eat my salad." She realized that she hadn't taken more than a few bites of her shrimp Cobb during all of the excitement.

"You'll eat tomorrow," Rhonda said. "In the meantime, I don't want you to leave out one detail, from the house to the husband."

As Marcee started to recount everything, she thought about her stomach that, although empty, felt sated. Somehow, Claire's personal interest filled her up in the same way food usually did; there'd be no need to stop at a drive-thru.

5

MARCEE CONDITIONED HER hair with Moroccanoil's Intense Hydrating Mask one time per week; $35 for eight ounces wasn't exactly bupkis, according to her mother, regardless of the shiny veil it draped over her scalp. Friday at Claire's had been so uplifting, though, that Marcee wanted to begin her Monday lathered in luxury — never mind that she'd treated her hair only four days prior. She doubled her time in the shower, taking 30 minutes to exfoliate with a dollop of St. Ives scrub, and then cleaned her face with alcohol-free toner before drying off completely and applying her new Gabbi Green cosmetics.

The eye shadow was a daring choice; to Marcee, "Citrus Creamsicle" sounded like a shade that Kate Moss or Gigi Hadid might wear for a designer runway show. When mixed with a small amount of "Earth Smoke," however, the orange coloring blended into a more sensible shade that politely whispered "confident" instead of screaming it. Marcee went heavier on the eyeliner, which produced a more dramatic look than she'd been bold enough to wear previously. Over the weekend, she had watched a few makeup tutorials — all from semifamous preteens and adolescents on YouTube who had clearly mastered the art of beating a face before getting a handle on algebra — and learned the virtues of contouring with bronzer. The shimmery Gabbi

Green powder gave Marcee's rounded cheeks slightly more definition, and the coral lipstick matched the palette that her face had become.

With a diffuser at the end of her standard-issue blow-dryer, Marcee worked her hair into something that resembled a popular Jennifer Aniston style during the *Friends* years, adding a little bit of hairspray to achieve body and hold. When she looked at the finished product in her counter-to-ceiling bathroom mirror, she tilted her head from side to side, examining from every angle the woman she'd created. She had put extra time into herself and wanted to assess the payoff. *Not half bad,* she thought. *Why haven't I made this kind of effort before?*

She threw on the outfit she'd worn to Malibu — no one at the office would know — and the summer tones of her patterned poncho looked as though they were made to accompany her eye makeup. Without the stress of having to impress Claire, the skirt didn't feel quite as figure-hugging as it had on Friday, but, for added security and comfort, she used a heavy-duty safety pin to allow some give to the waist. Perhaps the outfit was on clearance because the metal clasp was attached to fit a size 12 instead of the average American woman. The notion of the possibility made Marcee smile.

Since she was a teenager, tunes from the Go-Go's and the Bangles made her feel upbeat, like she could take over the world for about three minutes. Whether it was "Head over Heels" and "We Got the Beat" or "Hazy Shade of Winter," a bouncy girl group hit of the 80s was a slam-dunk mood elevator. Likewise, Marcee cued her favorite playlist and drove the 10 miles to work like she was an Egyptian. She didn't worry that she pulled into her parking spot at 9AM, the official start of the day, even though she was used to being at her desk a good hour and a half before any of her colleagues. Something about her time with Claire on

Friday — not to mention her brushes with Gabbi Green, Nina Walker, Claudia Erickson and Rox himself — was fueling a sense of worthiness. For a few hours, she was a member of their club, and it straightened her shoulders.

"Morning, Mar," Lila, one of the department assistants, said as Marcee walked past a pen of open cubicles. "How was your weekend?" It was a typical post-Sunday inquiry, delivered with a tone that implied that the answer didn't really matter. The just-out-of-college newbie probably didn't want to hear more than the word "fine," if anything at all.

"It was great," Marcee said, stopping for a moment. "I got a lot accomplished work-wise at Rox Madison's house on Friday and then had a productive weekend organizing things in my apartment."

"That's great," Lila said. "You have a hot date tonight? You look really good."

"Sadly, no," Marcee replied, "but thank you. I ran into Gabbi Green at Rox's house, and she wanted me to try some of her new colors." It was a little bit of a stretch, but it sounded better than admitting she was playing "makeup" with a bunch of Claire's toss-aways.

"You mean Gabbi Green herself?" Lila's eyes widened; she now seemed genuinely interested. "She's my hero; she went from being, like, some makeup artist to running this ginormous company. I love her stuff. Just wish I could afford more of it."

"She's lovely." Marcee smiled, leaving Lila's cubicle and gliding down the hallway to her own office.

She unlocked the door and threw her shoulder bag onto one of the two guest chairs behind the computer screen. It wasn't until she walked around her desk and turned on her electronics that she saw a stack of paperwork accompanied by a note from Phyllis:

Marcee —

These press releases are disastrous. Please rewrite them before submitting to the legal department for final sign-off. I'd like to think that you can write better than this.

— PVB

On an ordinary day, Marcee would have needed four deep breaths and six calls to her mother before melting down like a Weight Watchers Fudgesicle. Now, however, she felt like she was standing on firmer ground: First, because she hadn't even written the media announcements that were paper-clipped to Phyllis's notecard; they'd been drafted by a subpar colleague who was Phyllis's pet employee. Second, because those connected to people like Claire shouldn't take shit from anyone. And, third, because her lunch in Malibu had given her a contact high that was still going strong; nothing could break her stride. Likewise, throughout the week, Marcee reminded herself about her new friend in Point Dume whenever Phyllis jabbed her with a nasty remark or added busywork to her plate. It was almost as if Claire had given her strength by osmosis.

By Thursday evening, Marcee had powered through the editing of 12 press releases, attended 15 standing meetings with various related departments at the studio, answered 400 e-mails, returned 98 phone calls and watched one nighttime screening of Luminary's summer space action film. She was more productive than ever with no signs of fatigue, and the siren song of her pajamas and comfy bed had softened. Everything seemed so effortless that she didn't even realize how much she'd accomplished in only four days.

Marcee peeled out of the parking garage about five miles per hour faster than usual and full of energy; her "Ladies of the 80s" playlist was still in rotation. She waited to call her mother until Taylor Dayne had finished singing "Tell It to My Heart" because, as much as she wanted to gab with Rhonda, she had to show respect to Leslie Wunderman, the nice Jewish girl from Nassau County, New York, who'd transformed herself into a pop singer with a porn name. *Good for her,* Marcee thought. *Even if this song* is 30 *years old.*

"Hi, Ma," Marcee said the moment her mother answered. "All well since this morning?"

"Everything's fine," Rhonda replied, "other than your father, who keeps complaining about Aunt Lenore and Cousin Amanda coming for the weekend. Don't forget that I'm making dinner for everyone on Saturday night."

"I kind of understand how Daddy feels about Aunt Lenore," Marcee said. "She's so fucking annoying."

"Well, she's my sister, and she's coming, and that's it." Rhonda sounded frustrated. "They're here for only two nights so Amanda can look at UCLA as a possible graduate school, and Lenore hardly gets out to California."

"Is Uncle Arnie still having an affair with that Asian woman Aunt Lenore pretends she doesn't know about?"

"Shhhhh," Rhonda whispered into the receiver, as though a government organization might have tapped the phones. "I wasn't supposed to tell you that. Lenore confided in me."

"Mom, you tell me everything." It was true; Rhonda didn't spare Marcee one detail about anything happening with anyone in the family.

"Well, Lenore would be very upset if she knew I'd said anything; *her* daughter doesn't even know."

"As much of a dingbat as Aunt Lenore is, Mom, Amanda is a pretty bright girl," Marcee said. "This whole thing has been going on for seven years, and she's not a baby. I'm sure she's figured out that Daddy likes to eat Chinese."

"Did I raise you to talk like this?" Rhonda asked. "I think we should change the subject; how awful was work today? I haven't heard you mention Phyllis in a few days."

"Work is fine," Marcee said.

"What do you mean, 'work is fine?'" Rhonda pushed. "It hasn't been 'fine' the entire time you've slaved away there." Before Marcee could respond, she heard the beep of another call coming in. She looked at her dashboard console to see that "Madison, Claire" was on the other line.

"Mom, there's an important work call beeping through; I'll give you a buzz in the morning." As the words came out of her mouth, she pushed her hair back behind her ears on both sides, as though she had to look more presentable to take a call from Claire. She hit the "swap" button on her iPhone. "This is Marcee," she said, trying to sound professional.

"Yeah, I know who I dialed," Claire said. "You won't believe the horrible day I've had."

"Hi, Claire! How are you?" *Dumb question,* Marcee realized. *The woman already said her day had been rough. Think before you open your mouth.*

"Like I was saying," Claire continued, "Rox and I had a huge fight this morning, and I can't shake it."

"Do you want to talk about it?" Marcee was already just around the corner from her apartment, but she pulled over so she could talk to Claire uninterrupted.

"Um, yeah," Claire said, "why do you think I called?" Marcee smiled to herself. She was fairly certain that she and Claire had bonded on Friday, and this was a solid confirmation. "Anyway, I want the kids to transfer to Harvard Westlake, and Rox wants them in public school. What the fuck?"

"I know a lot of people believe in—" Marcee tried to get a thought out.

"Rox went to public schools growing up, and he says it's good for them to taste the real world a little. I just can't have that."

"Why not?" Marcee asked. "Think of the money you'll save. Isn't Harvard Westlake like $40K a year per kid?"

"You don't honestly think I'm worried about the money, do you? You saw *one of my houses*, right? Anyway, I just think adopted biracial twins are up against enough to begin with. Why throw them into a public cesspool when all of their friends are at places like Campbell Hall and Harvard Westlake?" Claire was ranting nonstop, throwing out rhetorical questions like darts; Marcee was unsure of when to assert her point of view.

"I understand," Marcee said. "But maybe—"

"Plus, what are the other parents going to think? That Claire Madison's kids can't cut it in private school? I have enough money to *buy* my kids a fucking school. Rox just doesn't understand the position he's putting me in. Could this day be any worse?" Claire went on for another 40 minutes; Marcee listened to every word. She realized, after the last time she tried to interject, that Claire simply needed someone to agree with her.

"I can totally see what you're saying," Marcee replied. "Sounds like a pretty heinous day. Is there anything I can do to make you feel better?"

"Not really; I just needed to vent." Claire's voice dipped out for a moment. "You know what, Marcee? Claudia is finally calling me back. I'll talk to you soon." The call disconnected from Marcee's Bluetooth, and "I Think We're Alone Now" from Tiffany appropriately filled the car.

She parked and then walked into her apartment, racing through her nighttime wash ritual so she could curl up in bed with her cordless landline phone. Everyone else she knew had migrated all of his or her telecommunications business to one mobile number, but Rhonda insisted that Marcee keep a traditional line in case of an emergency that knocked out the cellular towers. And, at times, Marcee was grateful to have an extra number, such as when her cell phone was low on battery or she wanted to multitask with various apps while having a conversation at the same time.

"Girl, what are you doing?" Jordan asked the moment he answered Marcee's call. "I am just on my way to cover an 8:30PM panel discussion about the lack of work for actresses over 40 in Hollywood. Because *Variety* — not to mention every other magazine — hasn't covered *that* subject to death already." She could practically see his eyes rolling.

"I just spent nearly an hour on the phone with Claire," Marcee said, as though she were tossing a piece of rye bread to a flock of pigeons, "and now I'm falling into bed. It's been a crazy week at work."

"Child, you need to roll this movie back." Jordan sounded excited. "Did you just say that you were on the phone with Rox Madison's wife for an hour? Did I hear that right? Didn't you two get all of your work talk finished on Friday?"

"She wanted to chat about private things," Marcee said, knowing that she would pique Jordan's curiosity with such a tease. Claire's personal interest in her would undoubtedly be seducitve to Jordan. Rox and Claire were Hollywood royalty, and Marcee's association with them would give her the patina of someone special.

"So, is she your new best friend? I don't remember the last time you talked with *me* for an hour in one stretch." Jordan's tone was playful, but Marcee could sense a thread of jealousy in his comment.

"Of course not," Marcee said, but she and I definitely have some sort of connection. Plus…and you have to swear to keep this between you and me…"

"Would I repeat anything you tell me?" Jordan asked.

"You would and you have," Marcee replied. "So, do I have your word that this goes no further than us?"

"Yes, yes, yes. What is it?"

"She wants to fix me up with Brent Wetherley." Marcee was grinning as she relayed the news.

"Get the fuck out. He's so hot." Jordan sounded even more blown away than Marcee. "That's what she called to talk to you about?"

"No, she brought up Brent on Friday; today was about some little tiff she was having with Rox."

"Wait," Jordan said, "so she mentioned wanting to fix you up with Brent Wetherley on Friday, and you failed to tell me until almost a week later? Talk about burying the lede."

"I gave you the entire play-by-play of my meeting at Rox and Claire's house," Marcee replied, "but I wanted to wait on the Brent Wetherley thing until I could get it through my own head." In truth, Marcee didn't want to make herself vulnerable by telling anyone other than her mother about the potential romantic setup. What if Claire was just politely blowing smoke? Marcee would look ridiculous.

"This conversation ain't over," Jordan said, "but I am just about to get to my event. We'll be picking this up tomorrow."

"Say hi to all of those old, haggard, washed-up actresses," Marcee said, laughing. She shut her Panasonic handset and placed it in its charging cradle on her nightstand. On her iPhone for two hours, she played games in the Boggle and Word Brain apps to distract her from the thoughts of Brent Wetherley swimming in her head.

◇◇◇

THE DIRTY-BLOND FLECKS in Ben Paull's wavy brown hair

highlighted the tousled thickness that rested on top of his endearing face. It was the messy, bed-head kind of look that many Angeleno men were deliberate in creating with waxes and pastes even though they wanted their surfer locks to look effortless. Marcee could tell that Ben woke up with the adorably chaotic shag because he always dressed similarly: neat enough but without a discernible style. It were as if he wore the adult equivalent of Garanimals, which Marcee thought was refreshing — especially for one of the studio's senior lawyers. The rest of the company's legal counsel had a good 10 years on Ben's boy-wonder 38; they were mostly stuffy suits who frequently told her why she *couldn't* plan a particular event or send out a certain press release instead of helping her actually get the job *done*.

"Ben, why are you the only lawyer at the studio who makes me walk across the entire backlot to his office instead of e-mailing his comments?" Marcee asked playfully.

"How long have we worked together?" Marcee's pet peeves included when adults answered questions with *new* questions, but her rapport with Ben was so established that his quirks had become charming over the decade they'd known each other.

"Ten years," Marcee said as she sat down at a small round conference table in a far corner of his office.

"So, is it so strange that I'd want to see your face? We Jewish kids from the Valley need to stick together."

"I suppose so," Marcee answered with a laugh. "Valley Jews unite!" She punched her right fist into the air like a comic book heroine.

"Are you one of the Powerpuff Girls now?" Ben's crooked smile revealed a perfectly white set of teeth. "Cause, if so, you're at the wrong company. Warner Bros. distributes that cartoon."

"Is our entire meeting going to be like this?" Marcee

looked at her watch and smiled. "I've got four hours to do about 15 hours' worth of work, so, if we could just—"

"The way I see it," Ben interrupted, "is that you can't really move forward with *your* work until I've given *my* feedback on these press releases. You're kind of stuck, Marcee Brookes."

"Fine," she said in mock exasperation. "You have 15 minutes before I shift into business mode."

"What's new in your life? I haven't seen you in more than three weeks." Ben sounded sincere in his interest and was accurate about the passage of time. "I like to hear from you — even when you don't need to know if something you've written will get the studio into legal trouble. Plus, you're looking fantastic." Marcee picked at the skin around her thumbnail and then looked down to make sure her skirt was smooth and not bunching around her waist.

"Well, one interesting thing happened," Marcee said, shifting attention away from her updated look. "I had lunch at Rox and Claire Madison's house last Friday, and she and I have sort of struck up a friendship."

"That's fun," Ben replied. "What's their house like?"

"It's huge and amazing, exactly where you'd think a movie star would live," Marcee said. "And their art collection is crazy. There's a fucking Moreau hanging in the breakfast area at the back of the kitchen."

"Can you imagine living that way? It's like an alternate universe."

"It totally was. I felt like I was walking in a diorama made from pages of *Architectural Digest* and *Dwell* magazine."

"I've heard Rox is really nice. What was he like?" Ben seemed as interested in the gossipy chatter as anyone else, which surprised Marcee considering that she always thought of him as the odd executive who was unimpressed by the Hollywood scene.

"He looked really busy, so he and I didn't talk much," Marcee said, bending the prism of truth ever so slightly so it reflected more flatteringly on her. "But I got a good sense of their life together from Claire, who couldn't have been friendlier."

"That's nice to hear; glad you made a new pal," Ben said. "So, what's on tap for the weekend?" He moved on to another subject quickly, suggesting to Marcee that he may have been more interested in her excitement about Rox and Claire than his own.

"I have to go to my parents' house tomorrow because my aunt and cousin are in town from Florida," Marcee answered. "Or, maybe I'll hang myself tonight to avoid it. Still deciding."

"Well, I'm just having a lazy weekend, so, if you want to escape early, give me a buzz. We could grab a drink or dessert."

"That sounds so much better than a plate of overcooked salmon and small talk with my Aunt Lenore, but my mom would plotz if I tried to leave before 11PM."

"Well, you can't say I didn't try to save you from your relatives." Ben laughed. "Should we plan to have lunch next week? I miss our regular catch-ups." Marcee opened her iPhone calendar and scrolled through the next week's schedule.

"I can do Thursday," she said. "Does that work for you? Maybe just a quick bite on the lot? I have to be back at my office for a meeting at 2PM."

"Sounds good," Ben replied as he handwrote the appointment onto his paper desk calendar. "Now, should we go over those press releases?"

◇◇◇

AUNT LENORE COULD drive the Dalai Lama insane; it

was her gift. By the time Marcee arrived in Woodland Hills — only 20 minutes later than Rhonda's 6PM scheduled call time — her father had already downed two tumblers of scotch on the rocks and an entire serving bowl of peanuts mixed with raisins; the evidence of Neal's frustration lay on a small side table next to his favorite living room recliner.

As Marcee stood in the foyer, placing her keys and small bag onto a silver tray of miscellany, she glanced at her dad, who rolled his eyes and then refocused his attention on the TV. *Terms of Endearment* was on Turner Movie Classics, and it was nearing its dramatic, tear-jerking finale.

"Dad, why are you watching this?" Marcee asked, taking a seat on the couch beside his chair. "You hate this kind of schmaltz. Isn't there a Hitchcock movie or something on another channel?"

"Marcee, I can honestly say, for the first time ever, that I envy Debra Winger in this movie. At least she doesn't have to live through tonight. I'd suffer her fate to avoid having to put up with Lenore." His eyes didn't leave the screen.

"I think Debra Winger dies in just about everything, doesn't she?" Marcee took a stab at a joke to lighten the mood. "Where are the ladies?"

"They're futzing in the kitchen," he said. "Although I am sure your cousin Amanda isn't doing anything but texting or Twittering or whatever it is you all do now on those phones."

"What kind of futzing is involved with baked salmon and vegetables? It's the one and only meal Mom has down to a science."

"Couldn't tell you," Neal said. "But if it keeps Lenore out of *this* room, I'm all for it."

Five feet four with a thick brown, highlighted bob, Lenore's look was obviously rounded out by an off-label, distant cousin of Eileen Fisher's. She had evolved into a

65-year-old Miami Jewess, the kind who spent her spare time raising money for ORT and sitting on the board of the local synagogue. Her career as a couples therapist took a back seat after she'd married her deadbeat, philandering husband, Arnie, and it wasn't until their daughter, Amanda, went to high school that Lenore looked for things to keep her busy. She decided to become a Bat Mitzvah, a rite of passage that she hadn't been through at the traditional age, which sparked an obsessive interest in her faith. She was one bad wig and a floor-length denim skirt away from living on a kibbutz, which, she'd admitted to the family, alienated those friends whose relationships with her preceded this extreme religious awakening.

Marcee remembered how, growing up, she'd be excited about her aunt's visits. Lenore was single until Marcee was in her mid-teens, and she'd fly to California for every holiday to spend time with her only niece. In the mid-70s and throughout the 80s, Aunt Lenore was young and pretty and childlike with long, straight hair and no bangs. She looked like she could be a sister to Cher or Barbie's younger sibling, Skipper. She would play for hours and hours with Marcee, inventing secret languages and spy games that would end only when Marcee could no longer keep her eyes open. Their bond lasted until Lenore married Arnie Braunstein, the same time it became clear that Marcee had outgrown her aunt's unsophisticated and credulous worldview. Essentially, Marcee matured, and Lenore hadn't.

The Brookes' relationship with Lenore didn't become tenuous until Marcee's grandmother Beatrice — Rhonda and Lenore's mother — passed away in 2004. The estate was divided evenly between the two daughters with the exception of one diamond ring valued at $50K. The whole family knew that Beatrice had earmarked the bauble for Marcee, her first grandchild, but she hadn't been specific about it in her will. Lenore and Arnie became embroiled in a feud with Rhonda and Neal over the piece of jewelry, resulting in a years-long rift that remained until Lenore finally decided to separate from her awful husband. She confessed that her still not-quite-ex had been fueling the fight and was more interested in the ring's monetary value than the sentiment that sat beneath the precious stone. Neal never forgave Lenore, though— "She went along with her husband, which makes her just as bad," he'd say — even when Rhonda decided to mend fences. The ring never left Marcee's safety deposit box, and she resolved to stay out of the fray unless she wound up with a legal reason to put some skin in the game.

"Marcee Beth," Lenore squealed as Marcee walked into the kitchen. She reached forward with both arms and stood still in a dramatic, punctuated hold.

"Hi, Lenore," Marcee said, giving in to the obligatory hug and kiss.

"I'm your *Auntie* Lenore," she said with the same giddy laugh she'd had since Marcee could remember. "I haven't seen your punim in way too long." Marcee bit her tongue and smiled faintly, even though she wanted to mimic Lenore's giggle to her face before kicking her in the teeth. Marcee shifted her eyes toward Amanda, a thin-as-a-rail 22-year-old who sat cross-legged at the kitchen table wearing rhinestone-encrusted headphones.

"Hi, Amanda," Marcee said at a low volume. She could tell that her cousin was engrossed in a movie or music video streaming to her phone, and she didn't care enough about greeting Amanda to make any more of an effort. The girl had been an entitled brat since the day Lenore delivered her in a blow-up kiddie pool during a risky home birth, and her attitude clearly hadn't changed.

"Amanda, what have I told you about being on that

phone all the time? Your cousin is trying to talk to you, and you haven't even looked up. Amanda!" Apparently, it hadn't occurred to Lenore at first that her daughter was not being exclusionary; she simply wasn't hearing or paying attention to anyone. Lenore walked over and lifted the earphones from Amanda's head.

"Mom, what the fuck? I'm trying to watch this WebFlicks show." Amanda's face was caked in foundation, and her eye makeup was severe enough to make RuPaul look plain. Her long brown hair was pulled back into a taut ponytail.

"Amanda, Marcee is trying to talk to you; the two of you haven't seen each other in years."

"Hi, Marcee," Amanda said, getting up from her chair and giving her cousin a forced hug. "I didn't hear you walk into the kitchen."

"No worries," Marcee said. "Mom, do you need help with anything before I go back into the living room with Dad?" Amanda had resumed her program already in progress. She clearly didn't feel an urgency to catch up.

"No thanks, honey. Aunt Lenore and I have everything just about ready. In fact, you can tell Daddy that we're going to sit down to eat."

Marcee returned to the living room just as the credits began to roll on *Terms of Endearment*. "It's time," she said with the seriousness of a death-row guard tasked with escorting an inmate to the electric chair. "Dinner is about to be served."

"When I drop dead, I want to be reincarnated as Debra Winger in *Shadowlands* so I can die again before having to see Lenore and that kid one more time."

"Just make sure that God doesn't get things confused and send you back as Debra Winger in Lifetime's *Dawn Anna*. I think she actually survives a brain tumor in that one."

"Let's just get this mishigas over with," Neal whispered to Marcee as he got up from his La-Z-Boy and seated himself at the head of the dining room table. Rhonda, Lenore and Amanda were already sitting.

"Rhonnie, this salmon looks amazing," Lenore said as she poked her fork into the seasoned fish plated in front of her. "Doesn't it, Amanda?"

"Rhonda knows how to turn Costco cuisine into a decent meal," Neal said, already having polished off half of his food.

"Their fish and meats are from hunger," Rhonda replied. "This is fresh, from Whole Foods."

"Well, it's delicious," Lenore continued, "no matter where it comes from." The simple globe light above the table shone directly on a basket of brioche rolls. They were so appealingly lit that Marcee had to have one; she reached across Lenore to grab some extra carbs. "So, Marcee, honey, your mom tells me you're still working in Hollywood."

"Yep, I've been at Luminary Pictures for about 10 years now," Marcee answered.

"It must be a fun job. Don't you think so, Amanda?" Lenore elbowed her daughter in what seemed to be an effort to engage her in the conversation.

"Totally fun," Amanda said, without looking up from her plate.

"What kinds of projects do they have you working on?" Lenore asked.

"Lenore, Marcee is off from work today. I'm sure it's the last thing she wants to talk about." Traditionally, the subject of Marcee's job was off-limits during weekends, and Rhonda tried to shift the conversation so Marcee didn't have to.

"Oh, it's OK, Mom," Marcee said, all of a sudden perkier than she had been earlier. She turned toward her aunt. "I'm working on a movie called *Night Crimes* with

Rox Madison." Rhonda and Neal looked at each other; they seemed surprised that Marcee was so amiable about discussing work.

"You mean you've *met* Rox Madison?" Lenore asked. "I think I would die on the spot."

"You'll have to introduce your aunt to Rox sometime," Neal interjected. No one other than Marcee appeared to pick up on the joke.

"I actually just had lunch at his house in Malibu last Friday," Marcee said. Amanda put her fork down and looked at Marcee.

"You actually *know* him?"

"I sure do," Marcee said, beaming. "He and his family are really great; his wife, Claire, has become a good friend."

"Like, do you have his number in your phone?" Amanda asked. "Does he call you?" This was the first time Marcee had ever seen her cousin give a shit about anything.

"Of course I have his number," Marcee said. "It takes a lot of communication to market a big movie like that."

"I'm so jealous. My friends are never gonna believe this; it's almost like I know him, too," Amanda said. "Mom, can I go call Allie? I totally have to tell her this. She's obsessed with Rox Madison."

"Sure," Neal interrupted. "Go call Allie." He didn't want to take the chance that Lenore would force Amanda to stay at the table any longer.

"Marcee, I'm so proud of you," Lenore said. "It's hard to believe that my little munchkin 'spy' is now schmoozing with the rich and famous."

"Oh, those folks are just part of the job," Marcee said, pushing the remaining food around her plate. She felt a surge of energy that made her too anxious to continue eating.

"Tell me more! My life is so boring compared to your glamorous existence. I want to live vicariously through you for a few minutes." Lenore was frothing at the mouth, as though she were Cujo with a piece of raw steak.

For two hours — and long after Neal had eaten dessert and excused himself from the table — Marcee told stories about her elevator ride with Channing Tatum and her near fender bender with Charlize Theron on the 101 freeway. She gave Lenore a verbal tour of Rox and Claire's house and dished some studio gossip. From the sound of it, Marcee had all but forgotten her daily grunt work and the psycho boss who lorded over her like a poor man's Disney villainess.

"I'm just so impressed," Lenore enthused. "Your life is mind-blowing; the things you get to do are awesome."

Marcee smiled and passed a confident laugh. "All in a day's work," she said.

6

MARCEE COULD ALWAYS tell how hectic her work week would be by 8AM on Monday mornings: if more than 25 e-mails had arrived between the time she went to sleep on Sunday night and when she walked into her office the next day, the outlook was bleak; her yardstick never failed. Having survived Saturday night with Aunt Lenore — which turned out to be slightly less unpleasant than she'd originally thought — she felt she deserved a quiet five days at the studio. Her in-box indicated otherwise.

She sifted through 87 e-mails, a few of which were obligatory invitations to various coworkers' birthday parties and baby showers; the bulk, though, related to important work issues that required immediate replies. Marcee plowed through the messages that could be answered quickly and with little thought and then began looking through those that needed more attention. When the phone rang at 10AM, Marcee had barely scratched the surface of her e-mail backlog.

"This is Marcee," she answered in a hurried tone that basically said, *Why are you using a phone? Everyone iMessages or e-mails these days.*

"Hi, Marcee, it's Sarah Lawrence." She wasn't an alumna of the Bronxville, New York, liberal arts university; there must have been some mistake on their donor list.

"Sorry, you have a wrong number," Marcee said, "and kindly remove me from your call sheet."

Sarah spoke quickly, before Marcee could hang up. "It's Sarah, Claire Madison's assistant."

"Oh my God, Sarah, I am so sorry." Marcee was mortified. "Your e-mails come up as 'C. Madison Assistant,' so I didn't realize that your last name is Lawrence."

"It happens a lot," Sarah said, laughing. "My parents weren't too thoughtful about picking names. My older brother is Martin, which, you can imagine, makes people assume he's a black comedian."

"That's hilarious," Marcee said, "but at least your namesake is a well-regarded institution of higher learning."

"It could've been worse; if they'd named me Sharon, my career would have ended after one network police procedural."

"Oh, stop," Marcee continued. "That's so not true. You would have starred in a dozen TV movies after *NYPD Blue*."

"You're so funny," Sarah said. "It's no wonder Claire likes you." Marcee was smiling in her office, even though no one else could see her. "On that note, Claire wants me to get your personal e-mail address. She has a couple of things to send your way, and she prefers to keep personal business off the Luminary network."

"Sure, it's MarceePR@gmail.com. I have that account on my iPhone, so I'll get the e-mails as soon as she sends them."

"Great," Sarah answered. "I know one of them has to do with helping Brent Wetherley secure a new publicist." Marcee's heart sank; she thought Claire was using that only as a guise under which to set her up on a date. Sarah made it sound formal and professional.

"No problem," Marcee said. "I'm happy to help out however I can." She was gnashing her teeth quietly.

"Brent is such a nice man," Sarah offered without inquiry. "He and Rox hang out a lot; he's always a gentleman whenever he's at the house."

"It's nice to hear that he's one of the good guys." Marcee tried to sound upbeat, but she felt dejected. She'd already told her mother and Jordan about the potential date, and now, after less than two weeks, it seemed that Brent Wetherley actually *was* searching for publicity representation more than he was a matching glass slipper. Or perhaps, Marcee thought, Claire just didn't tell Sarah the true intent behind the introduction.

"OK," Sarah said, "I guess I'd better get back to work. I have a zillion things to do for Claire today."

"Thanks for calling, and I'll look out for those e-mails." Marcee paused for a moment before officially ending the conversation. "You know, Sarah, we should get together for lunch or drinks sometime."

"You and me?" Sarah asked. She sounded surprised. "That would be really nice. I don't think one of Claire's friends has ever asked to spend time with me." Marcee loved being referred to as "one of Claire's friends."

"Well, it seems like we're all going to be in touch a lot, and we definitely have similar senses of humor. So, why not get to know each other better, right?"

"I'm all for it," Sarah said excitedly. "I'll e-mail your personal account with my contact info, and we can make a plan."

Marcee went back to her work messages but couldn't help being distracted. Every two minutes, she glanced at her phone to see if Claire had e-mailed yet. She was hoping that a note from the lady herself would bring some clarity to the "*Is Brent a romantic setup or just business?*" question that had been plaguing her since she'd hung up with Sarah. The answer came four hours later.

To: Brookes, Marcee <MarceePR@gmail.com>, Wetherley, B. <WetherOrNot@wetherleymediagrp.com>
From: Madison, Claire <starlover2000@gmail.com>
Subject: Intro

Hey, Marcee & Brent!

Brent, Marcee is a PR executive at Luminary. I mentioned her to you the other day. She'll be able to steer you in the direction of the least cunty publicist in town. She knows the best of the worst, so to speak.

Oh, and she's smart and cute! I'm sure you'll have more to talk about than snatchy PR agency girls. ☺ Happy chatting!!! She's at (818) 555-1912.

xoxo

cm

Marcee wanted to jump from her chair and high-five someone, but, instead, she kept her excitement contained behind her desk. Obviously, Claire hadn't told her assistant that she wanted to match Marcee and Brent — or Sarah was skilled at staying tight-lipped. Either way, the uneasy feelings that turned her stomach throughout the morning were nothing but wasted energy; Claire was following through on her word and obviously still believed in Marcee as a dating candidate. *Note to self,* Marcee thought, *don't be too forthcoming at your lunch with Sarah. It appears that Claire might not tell her everything.*

Before Marcee could marinate in the warmth of Claire's first e-mail, another popped into her in-box.

To: Brookes, Marcee <MarceePR@gmail.com>
From: Madison, Claire <starlover2000@gmail.com>
Subject: TTT Dinner

On a another note…

I was thinking that you might like to join me and the girls for the next TTT dinner. They'll love you!!!

It's two weeks from today at Craig's on Melrose, near Robertson. 8PM. What say you? Come!!!

xoxo

cm

The whole building could have gone up in flames at that moment, and Marcee would have been able to walk through it unharmed. Or, at least, that's how she felt. She sat at her desk quietly for a few minutes, reviewing both of Claire's e-mails. She studied every word and punctuation mark, even the number of exclamation points at the ends of particular sentences. It was clear that Claire had an enthusiasm for their new friendship, and Marcee was thrilled by it.

She must have pushed her hair behind her ears six times while she stared down at her phone, all of a sudden remembering her freshman year at Yale. Marcee recalled avoiding sorority rush, knowing that her full figure and bookish personality would likely keep her from ever becoming a pledge. So, proactively, she joined Alpha Phi Omega, a coed service fraternity, instead of rolling the dice with Pi Beta Phi and Kappa Alpha Theta. There wasn't one blonde in APO, but do-gooding for the campus and community — and nation! — allowed her to turn her back on the cool kids before they slammed the door in her face. Marcee had learned as early as elementary school to perceive most social situations as slights and personal attacks, whether real or imagined; the chubby girl was rarely the first picked to be on a team or in a club. If only her detractors knew whom she was having dinner with 20 years later, they'd be tripping over themselves to include her.

"Mar, can you sign this memo before I start running off copies?" Lila asked, walking into Marcee's office without so much as a polite knock or pause. The most overzealous of the department assistants, Lila had a knack for dropping in at inopportune moments; this time, though, Marcee welcomed it. The interruption pushed her into the present. Belaboring her early years, even if in her own head, was fruitless, especially considering how far she'd come. She had e-mails from Claire to prove her worth.

"No problem," Marcee said as she read the memo out loud and then put her signature at the top. "How was your weekend, Lila?"

"You know, the usual," she answered. Marcee nodded as though she knew what "the usual" meant, but, in truth, she had no idea if that indicated a movie and pizza or a rave at a Sunset Boulevard club. She had vowed to keep her own personal life — or lack thereof — private, so she rarely solicited that kind of information from anyone other than Addie Willis, a junior publicist who doubled as her work confidant. "How about you? Anything exciting on Saturday or Sunday?" Lila asked. She began rereading the memo she'd drafted as Marcee started to respond, making evident her limited interest.

"I had some family from Florida in town," Marcee said, "and I did some clothes shopping. I have a date coming up; I felt like I needed something new to wear." She hadn't purchased one article of clothing over the weekend, but, all of a sudden, she wanted the people around her to believe she had some semblance of a romantic life. She also wanted to tell Lila about Claire's e-mails and that the date she'd just mentioned would be with Brent Wetherley, but she kept herself measured and under control.

"Good luck with that," Lila said as she exited Marcee's office with the signed memo. *"Good luck with that?" Should I be insulted?* Marcee thought. *As though I need luck to have a successful date?*

The day couldn't end fast enough, for two reasons. First, Marcee was tired of trading messages and phone calls with the director of *Duck and Cover,* a lewd *Porky's*-style comedy that Luminary had acquired at a festival for very little money. The filmmaker thought he'd shot *Gone with the Wind,* but the studio bought the movie only because of its potential in the home video and on-demand markets. Nevertheless, it was part of Marcee's job to make the deluded hack think that the company was supporting his project; treating him with the professional respect he didn't deserve exhausted her.

Second, Marcee couldn't wait to analyze Claire's e-mails with her mother and Jordan on her way home. The Valley side streets were congested with enough traffic to give her 45 minutes on the phone with Rhonda, and the line of cars at In-N-Out Burger provided a good half hour for her to chat with her best friend.

"Wait, girl. You just finished telling me that the Brent Wetherley date will likely happen, and now you're having a double with fries? Child, please. I hope the dress you're planning to wear has some elastic in it."

"Jordan, you know I eat when I'm excited. Can't you enjoy the moment with me?" Marcee was serious. "I already lied to my mom and told her I was stopping at Costco to pick up a roasted chicken and some vegetables — just so I didn't have to hear this lecture from *her.*"

"You eat also when you're depressed, angry, sad and happy," Jordan reminded her.

"I'm an emotional eater," Marcee replied. "I have a preferred food for every mood swing."

"Well, you need to swing your car out of that line and get your ass to the nearest grocery store for protein and some spinach."

"OK, OK," Marcee said. "I give in." She maneuvered her Audi out of the restaurant's parking lot and headed one mile down Ventura Boulevard to Ralph's Fresh Fare.

"You'll thank me later. You're about to be going on a date with a movie star; you don't want to be pouring out of your clothes until *after* dinner. You know I speak the truth." Jordan *did* have a knack for telling it like he saw it.

"What the hell are *you* talking about?" Marcee replied. "I know you've had a number of dates in which you and the guy never even made it *to* dinner. Unless, of course, you count whatever tube steak was served in the bedroom."

"I'm clutching my pearl necklace, as it were." Jordan laughed. "Bitch, please. Go get yourself a chicken titty and some leafy greens, and call me the minute Brent responds to Claire's introduction. Girlfriend is off to a premiere."

As Marcee walked into the enormous supermarket, she thought about Jordan's comments and again about feeling like an outsider her entire life because of her weight. She rolled her cart down one aisle after another, reviewing the kinds of foods and drinks she'd need to stock in her kitchen if she planned to slim down quickly: skim milk, not whole; fruits and vegetables, not Swedish fish; steel-cut oatmeal, not Pop Tarts. *I can do this,* she repeated to herself, thinking that she'd consider the TTT dinner in two weeks to be her first weight-loss milestone. *This way, it'll be easier for Claire's friends to imagine me with someone like Brent Wetherley.*

Marcee filled her shopping cart with low-fat soups, skinless, boneless poultry, broccoli and red potatoes. She threw in some Greek yogurt and presliced fruits for breakfasts, wheat bread and lean turkey breast for lunches, and a bag of raw, unsalted almonds for daytime snacks. She did nothing half-assed, and if she was going to get herself in shape, she would have to diet hardcore. Not to mention exercise. She planned to map out a lunchtime walk that amounted to at least two miles per day; she figured that distance would be effective yet still manageable.

By the time Marcee got to the checkout, her cart was brimming with just about every healthy offering that Ralph's had on their shelves. Even though it was dinner rush hour, she had the lane to herself; she was *that* person, the one no one wanted to be behind because of the size of the cartload in front of him or her.

"No powdered donuts or Cheez Doodles tonight?" the cashier asked pleasantly. Marcee cringed as she realized that the heavyset, youngish senior recognized her face from a few late-night junk-food shopping sprees. "Plus, I gotta be honest with you — those fat-free Fig Newtons are pretty bland."

"I can't imagine that they taste that much different; the regular ones have only a small amount of fat anyway." Marcee strained to look at the checker's name tag, which was slightly obscured by her overstarched collar. "Don't you agree, Morgen?" She loved to address people directly, out loud, whenever possible because she'd read somewhere that adults like the sounds of their own names. And the theory had proven true time and again; she always got friendlier, more favorable responses from people who believed she regarded them on a personal level. *PR 101*, she thought.

"I'm so far gone, baby, that I don't even look at the

Newtons. I go straight for the cream-filled Chips Ahoy and the Mega Stuf Oreos." Morgen chortled. "My husband likes a big woman, and I enjoy giving him what he likes." She was a 300-pound frosted blonde with a poofy mullet and poorly bonded teeth. "I admire your willpower, though. If you eat like this, you'll be skin and bones by next month." Comparatively speaking, Morgen was probably right. Yet, would Marcee's new, self-designed eating plan have her looking good in an Hervé Leger banded sleeveless within weeks? Not likely.

"Hon, did you bring your own bags, or do you want the paper ones for 10 cents each?" Marcee could have sworn she heard judgment in Morgen's voice, and therefore felt shameful about not making more of an effort on behalf of the environment.

"I'll take the paper, please," she answered, shoulders hunched. She often forgot to carry the reusable bags from her trunk into the grocery store. At least she gave back in other ways, she reasoned; like buying a handful of World's Finest Chocolate bars when some grade school 4-H club member was peddling the almond-studded bars *that happened to melt perfectly onto a graham cracker.* Just thinking about it gave her a s'morgasm.

When she got home, it took Marcee nearly an hour to unpack the 12 bags that Morgen had arranged so carefully. When she'd finally placed the last package of peeled carrot sticks into her refrigerator's hydrating drawer, she realized that she hadn't eaten — the whole reason she'd gone to Ralph's in the first place — and that she hadn't checked her phone in more than two hours. If there were things that Marcee Brookes was desperately attached to besides her mother, they included food and her communication devices. Going hours without any of them was unheard of.

Marcee picked up her phone and scrolled through the

home screen. Nothing much was happening on the work front; the storm of e-mails that had touched down at the office that morning seemed to have lightened up, and there were only two messages waiting at her Gmail address: one from Sephora and another from Brent Wetherley.

To: Brookes, Marcee <MarceePR@gmail.com>
From: Wetherley, B. <WetherOrNot@wetherleymediagrp.com>
RE: Intro

Hi, Marcee. Great to e-meet you, and thanks in advance for your help with finding the right publicist. They all seem to be disasters; I've already been through two of them.

Anyhow, I'm shooting in Vancouver for the next three weeks, but I have morning call times. I'm usually done by 4PM. Are you around tomorrow night to chat? Maybe 8PM? If that works for you, I'll call the number Claire gave me.

And then let's do dinner when I'm back in LA! My treat.

Talk soon,
Brent W.

Ordinarily, Marcee would have been overjoyed about the free canvas tote that Sephora was offering with any purchase of $50 or more. The beauty emporium's shopping incentive, however, took a back seat to correspondence from the hottest new face in Hollywood. Too bad her mother was out to dinner and a movie and her best friend was at a work event; there was no one else with whom she was comfortable enough to discuss Brent's note.

Marcee decided to turn in early and get a good night's

rest. The sooner she went to bed, the sooner her call with Brent Wetherley would come, so sleeping through her jitters seemed the best option — even if it would take a .5mg Xanax to keep her from having a restless night. Without eating so much as a crumb, she washed up and tucked herself in, rehearsing in her mind what she would actually say to Brent on the phone. The conversation she imagined eventually swirled into a stream-of-consciousness spiral that relinquished control to the alprazolam until her alarm rang at 7AM the next morning.

That Tuesday was, at some moments, an endless drag and, at others, a fleeting blur. In reality, it was simply an unremarkable workday, cluttered with standing meetings and phone calls from producers and directors who didn't think their films were getting the same amount of attention as their colleagues'. To Marcee, however, every second was a means to an end, one moment closer to her phone call with Brent. She stopped to reread his e-mail a number of times, taking note of the fact that he had removed Claire from the chain and that he'd already planned to take her for dinner in a few weeks. Or, would that just be a thank-you for her help in guiding the publicist situation? Then again, if he had been thinking ahead about showing his gratitude, he could have arranged to send flowers or cookies, neither of which would require any of his personal time. Her brain was on an endless spin cycle of similar considerations, none of which included the fact that she hadn't eaten in almost 24 hours.

She made sure to leave the office promptly at 6PM so she could be home and showered by 7PM. She wanted to be as comfortable as possible during the call, which meant flowing, cotton pajamas and her hair up in a short ponytail. She was lying in bed with the newest issue of *O: The Oprah Magazine* when the phone rang at exactly 8PM.

She'd planned to avoid answering until the third ring, but her eagerness got the better of her; she accepted the call after only the first.

"This is Marcee." She delivered her standard greeting as though she had no idea who might be calling.

"Hey, Marcee, it's Brent, right on schedule," he said in a light tone. Marcee liked the familiarity with which he spoke, not announcing himself by his full name.

"What girl doesn't appreciate a man who's punctual?" Marcee said, afterward kicking herself for what she realized sounded flirtatious.

"I'm really big on being respectful of other people's time," Brent answered. "I don't like anyone to be waiting for me."

"You're a publicist's dream." She tried to push the chat into the subject of work, but Brent didn't follow her lead.

"Where do you live in LA?" he asked.

"I'm in the unfashionable 818; Sherman Oaks." She imagined that he was inaudibly groaning, as would just about everyone who lived in more desirable parts of the city; Angelenos regarded the San Fernando Valley as a distant land.

"My house is in Brentwood," he said, "so, really, I'm just seven or eight miles down the 405. I could always helicopter over to you." He laughed at his own joke, and Marcee chuckled as though she hadn't heard similar lines hundreds of times before. She was more focused on the fact that he was even thinking about getting to her apartment and that *Brent* lived in *Brent*wood.

"I'll make sure the landing pad on the roof of my building is ready for you." Marcee played along.

"That would make things a whole lot easier," Brent said. "Our friend Claire seems to think you're worth the flight."

"Well, I'm no skinny Hollywood girl," Marcee blurted,

"but I'm working on it." Marcee was relieved that Brent couldn't see the shade of red her face had become. She realized that her own discomfort with her weight forced an unrelated reply that was subconsciously designed to manage his expectations.

"I'll admit that I Googled you, so I know exactly how pretty you are. You have a rocking corporate headshot." Was this guy for real? Marcee wanted to melt into his charm even though she couldn't understand how someone so adorable could find *her* remotely appealing.

"So, you're cyberstalking me already, before our first phone call?" It wasn't out of character for Marcee to crack a joke when she felt insecure and nervous; she had mastered the subtle art of subject change over the years.

"Maybe just a little," he answered sheepishly. "I saw you went to Yale."

"I did, indeed." Discussing her education was more in her comfort zone. "But look what happened; I wound up doing PR in Hollywood. I'm surprised that my parents haven't asked for the tuition money back."

"It can't be *that* mindless," Brent said. "There is some strategy involved, I'm sure."

"I think it used to be more that way, back when I started, but, now, there's no 24-hour news cycle. Everything happens in real time," Marcee explained. "Instead of issuing a well-crafted press release, it's acceptable to make a 140-character announcement on Twitter."

"I don't even do my own social media," Brent revealed. "I pay some mom in New Jersey to deal with all of my Facebook, Instagram and Twitter posting."

"Don't ever make that public." Marcee went into business mode. "Fans will stop engaging if they know it's not you. I've seen it happen with celebrities."

"Note taken," he said. "And now you know a secret

about me, so I guess I'll have to be sure to stay on your good side."

"About a personal publicist, by the way; you know they're all a bunch of nasty bitches, right?" Marcee felt comfortable enough to be forthcoming about the hare-brained gatekeepers who plagued her — not to mention the industry — on a daily basis.

"The two I fired were horrible. They would be really nice to me and then awful to the studio staff and journalists. I don't want people thinking that's how I do business."

"Most celebs never catch on; they think their publicists are as friendly toward everyone as they are to their clients." Marcee was relieved to hear that at least one notable actor had learned the game.

"So, now that I've been through the ice queen with the cat-eye reading glasses and the power lesbian who is more interested in getting herself covered in *The Wall Street Journal* than she is her roster of clients, whom do you suggest? I feel like I need to have *someone*, just to field interview requests and event invites."

"I'd go with Linda Slater at Pressed PR," Marcee advised. "She's not perfect, but she's pleasant enough, and she has always been efficient in my experience. Plus, she owns a boutique firm, so you'll be a big fish in a small pond. It won't be like your experiences at those mega-agencies."

"Done deal. She's hired. Should I tell her you referred me?"

"I can call her first, or at least make an e-mail introduction," Marcee said.

"That would be great. Just tell her we're friends and that you're helping me out," Brent answered. *He already considers us friends?* Marcee thought. *It sounds nice, but he can't possibly be that taken with me.*

"Will do," Marcee said. "Will you let me know how the

conversation goes? I'll be curious to know how you respond to her."

"Of course! In fact, I was going to suggest that we FaceTime later this week, just to check in. Sound good? I'd love to chat more."

"Me, too." Marcee was about to jump out of her skin, even though she knew she'd need to have her hair, makeup and clothes on fleek in order to do a video chat. "I'll look forward to it."

"You can also look forward to dinner as soon as I get back to LA. You pick the place; I'll even drive to your village if I must."

"I'm holding you to that, Brent Wetherley. And, because of that comment, I will absolutely be choosing a restaurant in my — what did you call it? — village."

"Goodnight, and sleep well," Brent said. "Talk to you in a couple of days. Feel free to say hello by text in the meantime."

The moment Marcee hung up the phone with Brent, she dialed her mother. For two hours, she repeatedly discussed every detail of the conversation. They analyzed each word and nuance, as described by Marcee, until they both decided that Brent Wetherley, might, in fact, be interested in more than professional counsel. Or, at least, that was the verdict for the evening.

Marcee's heart was beating so fast that she was conscious of its pumping; it felt like it was ready to burst through her chest. She went to the Google app on her phone and searched through every web image of Brent she could find, saving the best pictures to a new photo album she'd just created. This would give her easy access to shots of his gorgeous face whenever she wanted to study them regardless of the fact that she was still having a hard time understanding his interest in her.

She knew that she'd never get to sleep without her reliable light-orange pill, so she swallowed a Xanax with a swig of Arrowhead water. It had been years since a viable relationship seemed within reach, and now the possibility of a storybook romance was right at her door. Marcee drifted off to sleep, thinking about how her first kiss with Brent Wetherley might taste, if things ever went that far.

◇◇◇

WHEN CLAIRE CALLED on Wednesday morning, Marcee had just gotten settled into her office for the day.

"Did Brent get in touch with you? I didn't see that he replied to my e-mail introduction." She began talking the minute Marcee answered the phone; it was clear that Claire liked to get right down to business.

"Hi, Claire," Marcee said. "Are you OK? You sound out of breath."

"I'm fine," Claire answered, "just doing a quick run after yoga. What's the story with Brent?"

"We actually talked last night. I gave him the name of a new publicist and put them in touch by e-mail."

"And? Is that it?"

"I think our call went well; we're going to have dinner in a few weeks, when he's back from Canada." Marcee was tentative and still too doubtful to speak with confidence about her chemistry with Brent.

"Well, I would say it went just fine if he asked you to have dinner," Claire replied.

"Or, maybe he just wants to thank me for my help," Marcee suggested. "But he did seem interested in texting and FaceTiming between now and when he gets back to LA, so…"

"So," Claire, interrupted, "why do you sound unsure,

then? If he didn't like what he heard, why on earth would he want to talk to you more?"

"That's true," Marcee conceded. "I guess I'm just out of practice when it comes to this dating stuff."

"He's so nice and unassuming," Claire said. "And totally charming. Could you tell?"

"Absolutely," Marcee answered. "He seems very genuine."

"OK, well don't fuck it up. It sounds like my instinct was right — so do me proud. Keep things going until he gets back. We'll discuss further when I see you at the TTT dinner."

"I will, and, yes, I'll see you at Craig's," Marcee said, but she wasn't sure if Claire actually heard her. It sounded as if the call had been disconnected before she finished speaking.

7

As Marcee walked from her office building to the studio commissary, a floating mass of uncertainty shaded the concrete below her. For two days, her moods had been subject to quick about-faces. One moment, she'd be feeling high about a man as notable and beautiful as Brent Wetherley wanting to take her for dinner, and the next she'd be certain that he couldn't possibly be into her. It was an exhausting wheel of high exhilaration and debilitating self-doubt.

"Do you want the usual?" a petite Latina woman in a hairnet asked the moment Marcee walked through the double doors. The cafeteria was divided into various stations — the salad bar, the sandwich board, hot foods and snacks — and Blanca managed the Panini press.

"I think I'm going to skip the tuna melt today," Marcee answered. "I might try something on the lighter side." She was trying to stick to her diet, and her nervous stomach was in knots; she couldn't risk the potential gastrointestinal side effects of the mayonnaise. Since Marcee was a little girl, Rhonda had advised her against eating similar dairy products, such as egg salad and coleslaw, outside of their own home; she always questioned the freshness of such items and had instilled in Marcee the same fear. For that reason, Marcee never admitted to her mother that she ate

Blanca's chunk-white tuna between two slices of Muenster cheese and an English muffin at least three times a week.

"Do you want me to throw some turkey on wheat with a little mustard?" Blanca gave Marcee a big smile, partially revealing a gold tooth that was implanted on the upper right side of her mouth. She had worked for Luminary throughout Marcee's entire tenure, and the two had a warm rapport that represented their decadelong work friendship.

"I'm actually meeting a friend for lunch today, so I might just wait until he gets here to decide what to order." Ben was usually very punctual, so Marcee was surprised that he hadn't already been there waiting.

"No problem," Blanca called out. "You just let me know when you're ready, and I'll make you whatever you want." Marcee waved and took a seat at a small table in the dining area. She was anxious to talk to Ben about the whole Brent Wetherley situation and wasn't as focused on food as usual. Her appetite had been squashed by the uneasy feelings in her gut.

Marcee placed her purse on the surface of the two-top table and began staring at her phone. She had answered all of the e-mails that had come in since she'd walked out of her office before realizing that Ben was now 15 minutes late.

"Where are you?" Marcee texted. "Did you get stuck in a meeting?"

"I was just about to text YOU," he replied. "I thought you forgot about me. I've been waiting awhile."

"I'VE been at the commissary, facing the front door, for the last 15 minutes. You can't miss me; I'm at the first table."

"Commissary? I'm at the Apex," Ben answered. "You didn't really think I'd take you to lunch at the commissary, did you?"

"I'm on my way," Marcee typed with one thumb. "I'm so sorry; I just assumed we were going casual." Marcee grabbed her bag and rushed outside. It would take her a good 10 minutes to walk to the Apex, the executive dining room that was on the opposite end of the studio lot. She had eaten in the exclusive plush restaurant — appointed with luxurious booths and bountiful floral arrangements — only a handful of times before. With a limited 20 tables, the restaurant's seats were reserved for the industry elite — directors, producers, actors and studio brass. Employees who were ranked below the vice-president level were barred from making reservations.

Marcee practically galloped through the backlot, racing between soundstages in a mazelike zigzag that she knew would get her to the Apex as quickly as possible. She passed New York Street and Midwest Boulevard, two areas of the studio that had doubled for Manhattan and the Middle America suburbs in thousands of films and television shows, and weaved through a dozen production office bungalows before making her way to the front door of the restaurant. She pulled her Gabbi Green compact from her handbag and gave her face a quick look. Never mind that Ben had now been waiting nearly 25 minutes; Marcee couldn't risk running into any senior staff members looking like a sweaty, disheveled mess.

Ben stood up as soon as he saw Marcee approach with the maître d'.

"I'm so sorry," Marcee said, giving Ben a friendly hug before joining him at the table. "When we talked about eating on campus, I figured it would be at the Commissary." As she slid into the booth, he immediately reached for her bag; there was more space on his side of the table than hers.

"Well, I figured since we planned to meet at 12PM, and you don't have to be back until 2PM, we had time for a nice meal." Ben tilted his head slightly and raised the corners of his mouth into a faint smile. "And we still have an hour together, so it's all good."

"You look pretty casual today, even for you," Marcee commented playfully.

"I have B&G downtown tonight," Ben answered. "Now do you feel bad for shaming my ensemble?"

"B&G? Am I supposed to know what that is?"

"The Boys & Girls Club; I've been coaching basketball at the community center a couple of nights a week. It makes me feel like I'm doing something more than fighting over the amount of Jennifer Lopez's next paycheck." Ben had an earnest look on his face, one that called Marcee's attention to his perfectly smooth olive skin. He pushed a linen-lined basket of artisan flatbreads toward Marcee.

"I want one of those so bad," Marcee said. "But I should be good."

"One piece isn't gonna kill you." He nudged the cheddar-crusted crackers even closer.

"I can't," she said. "I just spent $300 on healthy food at Ralph's, and I have to stick to my plan."

"Who *are* you? I've never known you to turn down good food," Ben said, laughing.

"I know, I know," Marcee said. "It's been only a couple of days, but I'm getting through it, Bonnie Franklin-style — may she rest in peace."

"One day at a time, huh?"

"Yep. My goal is to lose 10 pounds within the next few weeks. I am not sure how realistic that is, but I am going to give it all I've got." Marcee slid the bread back in Ben's direction.

"What prompted this health kick? It seems so extreme for you," Ben said as he rolled up the sleeves of his shirt. The cuffs were stretched to their seams by his prominent bicep muscles.

"Wait, where did those arms come from?" Marcee hadn't noticed them before, perhaps because they were usually covered with fabric.

"I guess the gym is finally starting to pay off," he said. "Plus, I run with Jackson every morning."

"I love that dog," Marcee replied. "How is he?"

Ben grabbed his iPhone and pulled up photos of his beloved Weimaraner. "Can you believe I've had him for five years? It's probably about time for his Aunt Marcee to pay a visit."

"Do you still take him hiking in Runyon Canyon? Maybe I'll go with you sometime. I need to fold a little exercise into my routine."

"We're doing Runyon this weekend, on Saturday morning," Ben answered. "Should we count you in?"

"I think I need to work up to it for a couple of months first. I'll start with some lunchtime walks around the studio before running up a mountain. I'm not sure steep inclines and rocks are for beginners."

"Well, Jackson and I are here for you whenever you're ready. But I still want to know what prompted this whole health thing." Ben brushed his shaggy hair off his forehead, showcasing the intensity of his hazel eyes.

"If I tell you, do you absolutely swear to keep it between us? I've told no one but my mom and my gay bestie, Jordan." Marcee sounded serious, as though she were about to reveal she had an illness that required a swift lifestyle adjustment.

"Have I ever breached a confidence?" Ben asked.

"No, but this is so personal, and I'm still trying to figure out how *I* actually feel about it." Marcee started to reach for a piece of bread almost by reflex but stopped herself before touching it.

"We've been friends for a long time," Ben said. "Whatever it is, I will do anything I can to help you through it."

"Here goes: Claire Madison introduced me to Brent Wetherley." Marcee ran her hands through her hair, pushing the ends behind her shoulders. "And I think there might be a little chemistry."

"Brent Wetherley, huh?" Ben reached for his iced tea and added an extra packet of Splenda.

"Crazy, right? The new It Boy," Marcee said with a proud inflection.

"Was this at a party or something?" Ben asked.

"No, we haven't actually met in person yet, but we talked on the phone and made plans to have dinner when he's back in LA in a few weeks."

"So, how do you know that there's really chemistry? A phone call is a phone call. Sort of like when people are convinced that they're hot for each other after a couple of text messages these days." Ben began breaking off pieces of the nibbles in the bread basket and crunching little bits at a time.

"Claire thought I could help him find a new publicist, and he called me to discuss various possibilities. We just sort of had this natural, effortless banter, and he asked me out." Marcee felt like she was having to explain what would spur Brent Wetherley to invite *her* to dinner, the same kind of rationalizing she'd had running on a loop in her head for two days. "Why, do you think maybe he sees dinner just as a friendly thank-you for my help?"

"I guess it could go either way, but I would be a little guarded until you see how dinner plays out," Ben advised. "I'd hate to watch you get too caught up and then be disappointed."

"Why, have you heard things about him? I know nothing other than the innocuous stuff I've read in the rags, but he was really personable on the phone." Marcee wondered what intel Ben might have gathered through the grapevine.

"I don't know any more than you do; you know I try to stay away from the drama." Ben stared into his drink, poking the ice cubes repeatedly with a skinny straw like he was playing some sort of video game.

"Claire raves about him and thinks he's really genuine. Even her assistant mentioned how nice he is. Apparently, he and Rox are close, so he's around their house a lot."

"If he comes with a seal of approval from someone you trust, I'm sure he's a good guy." Ben stared out the large window to his left as he downed half the glass of tea in one exaggerated sip.

"Are you humoring me? That sounded a little disingenuous."

"No, I just don't understand it entirely," Ben said. He refocused his attention and looked at Marcee head on.

"What, that someone like Brent Wetherley could be interested in *me*?" Marcee felt an uncomfortable prickly sensation that radiated down her back.

"That is not what I meant at all, Marcee," Ben said. "You're projecting."

"Projecting? That's about as original as the $150 check I write to my therapist each week."

"Come on," Ben continued, "that's not fair. You asked me a direct question, and I answered honestly. It wasn't a comment on your appeal." Ben looked as though he'd been caught at a crime scene holding the murder weapon. "Cell phones and texting sometimes create the illusion of something that doesn't really exist in person. It could be an issue between any two people — my comment wasn't about you and Brent specifically."

"So, you're just giving me general dating advice, regardless of the fact that there's a movie star — and *me* — on the other end of it?" Marcee pushed.

"Listen, my mom has been trying to marry me off to

every single Jewish girl in the Valley," Ben said. "She'll give me their numbers and make me call them. They all sound like possibilities, but, inevitably, I meet them for coffee or a drink and there winds up being nothing between us."

"Just because that's been your experience doesn't mean it will be mine." Marcee was trying to be as quiet as possible in her discomfort, speaking at a low volume.

"That's absolutely true," he said, "but there are a couple of things I don't quite get. With Brent's current status in Hollywood, why is he depending on setups? Wouldn't you think women are throwing bras and panties in his direction wherever he goes? Plus, do you really know Claire well enough to trust her judgment in men?"

The fiery doubt that had spread through Marcee's body, in that instant, turned cold.

"Where's the ladies' room?" Marcee asked as she stood up abruptly and looked around. "I'll be back in a minute." Ben pointed her in the direction of the restrooms, and she moved in a hurry. She walked into the last cubicle, which, thankfully, had a door that just about touched the ground; should other women pop in, they wouldn't be able to tell who was occupying that particular stall. Marcee closed and locked the door behind her and then grabbed some toilet paper to lift the lid. She lined the entire surface of the seat with multiple strips of Charmin — exactly the way her mother had taught her as a child — and sat on the makeshift germ barrier. Marcee stared ahead at the slats in the wood, an orderly pattern of stripes, trying to get her feelings under control.

Ben was right; chemistry could not be determined by one conversation, so it was very possible that Brent's dinner invitation *was* simply a nice gesture. That's not what Marcee wanted to hear, though. She always liked that Ben acted as a brother figure, yet she couldn't help but feel stabbed by their conversation. He seemed to be suggesting that she needed to protect her feelings, that she shouldn't be so quick to consider a "happily ever after" with the town's hot new actor.

Earlier in the day, Marcee couldn't wait to tell Ben about her call with Brent and her anticipation of their upcoming dinner, but now she felt stupid for opening her mouth. Being vulnerable with her mother and Jordan was one thing, but putting her heart and hope on display for anyone else was a ridiculous mistake. It now seemed obvious that the whole Brent Wetherley thing was a whimsical fantasy, and Ben sniffed it out at almost the first mention. Only those extremely close to her would help perpetuate the daydream; others would wince at the sadness of it all. She was mortified that Ben had gotten a front-row view of her romantic immaturity.

Marcee went over to the row of sinks and blotted her eyes with a hand towel she'd run under the faucet. The cool water, she thought, would calm her, followed by a dry cloth that would erase the remaining evidence of upset — and, unfortunately, most of her makeup. With a deep breath, she threw the linens into the laundry bin and returned to the table.

"Marcee, I honestly didn't mean to cause trouble; I'm just looking out for you." The crease between Ben's eyebrows was strong and furrowed.

"I understand," she said, "but I really should get back to my office. I realized I have a few things to read over before my 2PM meeting."

"Come on, Marcee," Ben said, "You know that I care about you. Maybe too much."

"What does that mean?" Marcee asked, still too embarrassed to focus on his words.

"I don't know; I just want you to be happy, and this whole thing worries me a little." Ben looked down at the black napkin in his lap. the Apex was classy enough to avoid giving white cloth to those in dark pants.

"I appreciate that," Marcee answered flatly. She was already thinking about the conversation she'd have with Jordan on her way back to her office. She reached her right arm across the table toward Ben. He grabbed her hand in a peaceful gesture. "Um, could I have my purse, please?"

"Oh, right, sorry," Ben said, releasing her hand right away. "I forgot I was sitting next to it."

"I'll talk to you next week," Marcee said as she rose from the table and stepped outside, hoping that the fresh air would chase away her sudden nausea. She put on a pair of Michael Kors sunglasses as well as some white earbuds, holding her phone in the palm of her hand to create the appearance that she was on a business call. This way, if she ran into any colleagues, she had an excuse for not engaging.

Rather than taking the fast route, Marcee strolled across the lot. There was so much film history around her, which she very rarely stopped to appreciate. Judy Garland had run up and down the very alleyway that Marcee was standing in, and Fred Astaire had danced on the cement that was just under her shoes. *It really is extraordinary,* Marcee thought. *So much happened here.* The scenery was a temporary distraction from the feelings of worthlessness that Ben had unwittingly stirred inside her. She dialed Jordan immediately.

"Hey, girl," Jordan answered. "Is everything OK?"

"Why are you assuming that there's something wrong," Marcee asked.

"Um, because you never call in the middle of the day."

"I just had lunch with my friend Ben; you know, one of the lawyers at Luminary," Marcee began. "And he basically told me that Brent Wetherley couldn't possibly be interested in me."

"Wait, what did he say?"

"I told him about the phone call and about Brent asking me out to dinner, and then I asked him if he thought it was an actual date or just a polite consideration." Marcee's eyes started to water. She stepped behind a building to keep out of view.

"What was his exact answer?" Jordan asked.

"He said I shouldn't get carried away until after I meet Brent in person; sometimes people can have phone and text chemistry that doesn't translate to real life." Marcee let out a loud, frustrated sigh.

"First of all, is Ben straight?"

"Yes," Marcee answered.

"OK, so, number one, why are you even asking a male breeder to help you decipher romantic code? He's *a straight man*. What does he know?" Jordan snapped. Marcee pictured his thumb and middle fingers *actually* snapping. "And, number two, he didn't say, 'Brent couldn't possibly be interested in you.' He just pointed out the obvious about modern-day dating."

"Did I just make a total fool of myself? I got so embarrassed that I basically walked out on lunch."

"You had a Britney-level meltdown," Jordan replied. "If there had been tears at the table, you could have been in Lohan territory."

"Fuck," Marcee said. "What do I do? I basically made myself look like an ass because of my own insecurity."

"You'll call him after the weekend, and tell him you were up the crimson creek without a pad, so to speak." Marcee laughed as she grabbed a tissue from her purse and patted her eyes.

"Jordan, what is wrong with me? I feel like I went from a 42-year-old woman to a 14-year-old girl over the last couple of days." Marcee looked up at the bright Los Angeles sky.

"You're kind of underdeveloped when it comes to

men," he said. "You've had almost no dating experience, so you're processing things the way you would've as a teenager. You're acting clumsy about it. You need to calm down and see what happens on your date. You could wind up hating Brent."

"I guess so," Marcee said. "I'm so mortified now about what just happened at lunch."

"If Ben is really your friend, he'll understand when you explain it to him next week. In the meantime, don't ask any other straight men to weigh in on your personal life. You'll put all the gay BFFs out of work."

"I promise," Marcee said.

"Listen, crazy bitch, your time is up. I have two articles to finish before I leave the office. Keep your chin up and your mouth shut for the rest of the day, alright?" Jordan was as reliable as ever when it came to making Marcee smile. "Don't even utter the name 'Brent Wetherley' until further notice."

Marcee hung up and threw her glasses and cell phone into her purse; she walked the rest of the way in the sun's glow, even stopping to chat with a few colleagues who were scurrying back to their desks with takeout containers. The moment she got back to her office, she called her mother from the landline.

"It's been a day, Mom," Marcee said as soon as Rhonda picked up. "Will you and Daddy be home tonight?"

"Yep, we're reorganizing the earthquake preparedness pantry. Are you alright?"

"Everything's fine. I just need to talk." Marcee was relieved that her parents didn't have dinner plans or a bridge game.

"Should I order some pizza and spaghetti from Nicola's? I know that's your favorite. I can even have them add some of that apple crumble that you love." Rhonda could obviously hear in Marcee's voice that she needed some TLC.

Otherwise, she would have undoubtedly suggested something broiled with a baked potato.

"No, thanks. I'll pick up a salad on my way. I'm trying out a new eating plan, which I know will make you happy."

"Your health makes me happy," Rhonda replied. Thankfully, she couldn't see Marcee's eyes roll to the back of her head.

"I'll see you around 7:30PM, Mom."

◇◇◇

GELSON'S HAD THE best salad bar in the valley, and, even though their prices were slightly higher than those of surrounding grocery stores, Marcee had treated herself. She'd piled sliced egg, garbanzo beans, tomatoes, sprouts and a few slices of grilled chicken breast on top of some iceberg greens, all of which were visible through the clear plastic container.

"That looks like a hearty salad," Rhonda said as soon as Marcee sat down at the kitchen table. "Can I get you some water or tea? Or maybe some seltzer?" Since Marcee was a little girl, her mother had peddled Canada Dry seltzer water like she owned stock in the company.

"Water would be great, thanks," Marcee replied, pouring a packet of low-calorie ranch dressing over the top of her greens. "Is this all of the canned food you're replacing in the earthquake cabinet?" Marcee asked. The table was covered with dusty, unopened cans of string beans, mushrooms, chicken noodle soup and water chestnuts.

"Nope, this is what we're *keeping*," Rhonda answered. "I just need to wipe everything down with a damp cloth."

Marcee dug into her salad with one hand and began to examine the emergency food reserves with the other. "Mom, this soup passed its sell-by date in 2008."

"Daddy says it'll be fine in a pinch. Apparently, that

whole 'expiration date' thing is a myth." This from the same woman who, for the 42 years Marcee had known her, led the worldwide boycott on store-made tuna salad.

"Well, if you survive the earthquake, you'll probably kill yourselves with this food supply," Marcee said. "Remind me, if I happen to be here when the Big One hits, to stand under an unstable, heavy fixture. I'd rather just go out quickly than try to survive on those lima beans."

"Bite your tongue, pu pu pu," Rhonda replied. "Don't even think like that."

"Wait, what's in this Ziploc bag?" Marcee put her fork down and reached to her right. She lifted a plastic bag that was perfectly fastened; the "yellow and blue make green" technology made the secure seal obvious.

"I think those are your father's backup toiletries," Rhonda said. "If there's a serious shaker, we probably won't be able to get to any stores for a while."

"Mom, there are four packs of Tucks and 11 tubes of Preparation H. Are hemorrhoids a bigger concern than, say, his blood-pressure meds, toothpaste and, I don't know, maybe water? I see absolutely no extra water supply on this table."

"What do you want from me, Marcee? Dad clearly has his priorities." Rhonda sounded resigned to Neal's logic.

"With the number of canned beans you two have hoarded, I guess I can understand why he'd want to look out for his ass. Plus, all of this cream and witch hazel will be a godsend to every displaced earthquake victim with a burning rectum; there's certainly enough here to slather all of the West Coast population." Marcee went back to her dinner. "Where *is* Daddy, by the way?" Her father hadn't come into the kitchen to say hello.

"He probably fell asleep watching a movie upstairs," Rhonda said. "It was his idea to weed out the cabinets, but, of course, that means I'll be doing the entire project. Anyway, what went on at work today? You sounded like you were in a little bit of a spin when you called earlier." Rhonda stood over the sink and rinsed the outside of each can of food one by one.

"Basically, I made the mistake of telling Ben Paull about the whole Brent Wetherley situation."

"Why is that a mistake?" Rhonda asked. "He's the Jewish lawyer, right? You two have been friendly for years."

"Yes, but he seemed skeptical about all of it, and I kind of freaked out." Marcee took her last bite and met Rhonda at the sink. She threw her empty salad container into the trash and grabbed a blue-checkered towel that was folded neatly over the dishwasher handle. Marcee hand-dried each can as her mother finished bathing it under the tap.

"What do you mean, 'freaked out?' And what exactly did you tell him?"

"I told him that Claire had introduced us by e-mail and that Brent and I talked on the phone," Marcee said. "And also that he asked me to have dinner in a few weeks."

"That's all true, isn't it? I don't see the problem." Rhonda continued to hand Marcee cans.

"Ben suggested that I might be getting too carried away and excited about a guy I haven't spent time with yet in person."

"It's nice of him to look out for you, I guess. Dating is a two-way street; you may find that *you're* not as enamored with Brent by the time you're face-to-face." It hadn't really dawned on Marcee before her chat with Jordan that she had a dog in the fight, too; it wasn't *all* about Brent.

"Ben also thinks it's a little strange that someone who is that gorgeous, famous and of-the-moment needs a setup. He suspects that women are tossing themselves at Brent left and right."

"Well, that's a possibility, too," Rhonda said. "But it might also be hard for him to find someone of substance. A girl who throws herself at him might not be the kind he wants to end up with. You have to consider both scenarios."

"I know, that makes perfect sense," Marcee agreed. "But when I was talking to Ben, I kind of jumped to the conclusion that he couldn't understand how someone like Brent would go for anyone less than a supermodel."

"I'm sure that's not what he was trying to say, Mar. It sounds to me like he was being a watchful friend."

"Jordan had a similar opinion," Marcee said. "I called him after I basically ran out in the middle of lunch. He totally calmed me down and made me realize that I was being oversensitive. Maybe I am just better off staying out of the dating game."

"Don't be ridiculous." Rhonda had finally washed off the last can, years-old corn that would eventually wind up clogging a drainpipe one way or another. "You'll be fine. You just have to remember that love is a bunch of ups and downs, whether you're looking for it, you've found it or you can't find it. There's a reason there are millions of country songs."

"And I have to apologize to Ben; I feel awful. I dumped my insecurities all over him." Marcee helped her mother organize the emergency cabinet with the now sparkling cans.

"Just call him tomorrow; tell him it's a particularly emotional time of the month for you. He'll know what you mean." Rhonda winked.

"Are you and Jordan the same fucking person?" Marcee shook her head in disbelief. "He told me to use that exact excuse."

"The way I see it is, if we have to suffer through it, we are entitled to use it to our advantage when necessary,"

Rhonda said. "It's too bad that, at my age, I can't play that card with your father anymore."

"I'll call Ben either tomorrow or Monday to explain," Marcee said. "In the meantime, I need to manage my own expectations about Brent." Marcee picked up her things and headed to the front door.

"When is that dinner?" Rhonda asked.

"The date with Brent? When he gets back from Canada, in about three weeks."

"No, honey, the one with Claire and her girlfriends." Rhonda walked Marcee to the curb, where her car was parallel parked.

"Oh, that's a week from Monday," Marcee said.

"If Claire is such good friends with Brent Wetherley, I'm sure her pals know him, too," Rhonda suggested. "When you're all chitchatting, you'll probably get a better sense of what he's like."

"We'll see," Marcee said. She threw her bag into the back seat and got into her car. "Tell Daddy I'm sorry I missed him, and I'll see him over the weekend. Love you, Mom."

"I love you, honey. Call me so I know you got home," Rhonda called out as her daughter pulled away. Marcee waved in her rearview mirror.

As Marcee drove home, she tuned her SiriusXM radio to the Coffee House channel. Every now and then, a little singer/songwriter melancholia captured her mood and made her feel understood. If Joni Mitchell could see everything from both sides, dammit, so could Marcee Brookes. Jordan and her mother made sense, as did Ben. And, hopefully, her soon-to-be new friends — the TTTs — would be able to lend some valuable perspective as well.

8

"L84LNCH" WAS TAKING up two spots in front of the valet stand. The gunmetal grey Maserati GranTurismo Convertible certainly looked pretty outside of Craig's, but it was impractically parked when Marcee arrived on the dot of 8PM. No one seemed to be getting in or out of the Italian sports car — it was a stationary fixture, for at least the moment — making it more of an oversized ornament at the entrance to the restaurant than someone's actual means of transportation.

Through her windshield, Marcee caught the eye of one of the parking attendants, who motioned to her from the curb. She stopped her car and waited until he arrived at the driver's-side door to exchange a ticket stub for her keys; before she could thank him, he'd whisked her comparably modest Audi out of view.

Just outside the front doors — elegantly constructed from dark wood and frosted glass — was the usual huddle of paparazzi and two well-dressed, young couples who looked like they were on their way to a post-dinner event. As Marcee stepped to the side to freshen her lipstick and blot excess oil from her T-zone with a small piece of rice paper, she saw one of the valets give each of the two women a small, white paper bag that was folded at the top and sealed with a round "Craig's" sticker. The taller and prettier of the two blond glamazons opened her packet, lifting out chocolate chip cookies and immediately handing them to her date. She had the figure of a 13-year-old boy, and it looked unlikely that she'd even tasted a cookie in the two-plus decades she'd probably been intimidating every average-sized woman who crossed her path.

Marcee had been on the phone with her mother during the drive from Sherman Oaks to West Hollywood, trying to keep her nerves under control. This would be the first time she was actually seeing Claire since her visit to Chez Madison in Point Dume, not to mention her initial introduction to Claire's closest group of friends. She so much wanted the other women to take to her the same way Claire had and with a similar immediacy, and, if that seemed to be the case, she would allow herself to eat the complimentary cookies on the way out. They would be her "cheat treat" for navigating the dinner successfully.

Marcee was wearing a red cotton dress with an empire waist and a black bolero sweater. She had lost seven pounds in the previous two weeks, which gave her clothes some breathing room, but she counted on the dark sleeves to cover her thick upper arms and the high-waisted detail to disguise her still-rounded midsection. A pair of black wedge heels accented a look that was modern enough to be fashionable and comfortable enough to keep Marcee from feeling self-conscious.

The grey, black and white tiles directly in front of the restaurant's entrance created a houndstooth-type pattern on the sidewalk, which continued inside just past the double doors. Marcee's outfit worked in harmony with the ground beneath her feet but was not at all a match for the labels on the clothing of the women standing at the bar to her left. That waiting area was crammed with casual designer threads and a sea of faces that looked like they *might* belong to notable people; it was hard to be sure in the low lighting.

Marcee approached the host, a silver fox in a form-fitting suit, who was stationed behind a computer screen and a reservation book. He was chatting with a well-preserved actress whom Marcee recognized from *Knot's Landing* or one of the other primetime soaps of days gone by. Whether it was Joan van Ark, Michele Lee or Donna Mills — and Marcee didn't know the difference — the woman didn't pause for even a second to acknowledge that there was someone waiting to be seated; neither did the maître d'. Marcee moved a step closer to the desk, placing her arm on the ledge in hopes of being noticed. They still didn't glance her way.

"I'm sorry to interrupt," Marcee spoke up, "but I am meeting a group of people—"

"Just a moment," the host replied without breaking eye contact with the has-been soap queen. Marcee had been to Craig's for business dinners a number of times before and always felt like a second-class citizen in their dining room. There was a conspicuous design to the flow of the restaurant that yielded a perceptible seating hierarchy based on one's STARmeter status. As a studio marketer, Marcee was typically parked at a freestanding table behind a waitstaff service station. This time, though, she would surely be sitting in a prominent location with the A-list end of the spectrum, which made her bolder about making herself known.

"I am already a few minutes late to meet Claire Madison," Marcee interjected, "so if you could just point me in her direction..."

"You're here to meet Mrs. Madison?" The host sounded surprised. "Let me show you to her table right now," he said, cutting off his conversation with the faded television star like a piece of string hanging from a worn-out sweatshirt. "Madison" was clearly the magic word.

Marcee was shown to a rounded, light-blue booth at the far back corner of the restaurant, just under a piece of art created from an old Frank Sinatra police mug shot. Already seated were Claire and Claudia Erickson, both of whom had empty cocktail glasses in front of them. They'd obviously arrived early.

"Marcee," Claire said, blowing an air kiss from behind the table, "I'm putting you in that chair opposite me." She pointed to the seat that had been added to accommodate their party of six. Typically, Marcee didn't like sitting with her back to a room — it made her feel exposed — but it seemed as though the "To The Tomb" members had a standing seating arrangement.

Before Marcee sat down, she reached across the table to shake Claudia's hand. "I know we met briefly on Claire's phone, but it's nice to see you in real life," Marcee said.

"Yes," Claudia replied. "I've heard lovely things about you. Glad you could join." She didn't offer a smile or move one muscle in her puffy, round face. Her jet-black hair had the stick-straight, telltale ends of a Brazilian blowout, and her smokey eye makeup — highlighted with a hint of white-pencil "dew" in the interior corners — was flawless. Claudia's strikingly blue eyes looked as though they were glowing through the ashy, charcoal shadow.

"Meanwhile," Claire piped up, "Claudia was just telling me about her cheating shit-bag of a husband." Marcee took a seat on the lone chair and placed her handbag underneath. She smiled warmly in a quiet expression of sympathy. She wanted to engage like an insider but also tread lightly at her TTT debut.

"It's always something," Claudia answered. "I found out that Nick has been having an affair with some homely

Canadian girl. If I'd known that, I would have served *him* with divorce papers instead of the other way around. Or, maybe I wouldn't have. I don't know. Being Mrs. Erickson has tons of perks, and he'll be dead soon enough anyway."

"That's horrible, Claudia," Claire said, laughing. "Just because he's 75 doesn't mean you can close the casket already."

"Are you kidding? He'll probably have another heart attack the minute that loonie-toonie mounts his shriveled little cock. I should probably call the Recording Academy now so they can get a jump start on his 'In Memoriam' package for the Grammys. I'm sure they'll want to book someone like Mick Fleetwood to do a tribute." Claudia lifted a glass of water to her mouth and sipped through the cocktail straw that was floating around with a piece of lemon. "Oh, look; Risa just walked in. I saw a pile of extensions make its way past the entrance like a shark fin." Marcee turned in her chair.

"Did she tell you that they've asked her to compete on the next season of *Celebrity Ballroom*?" Claire asked. "She already mentioned to me that she expects us to come to as many shows as possible to cheer her on."

"*Celebrity Ballroom* is basically a viewing at this point," Claudia said. "You know, one last look at a dwindling career before it's buried and marked with a tombstone. The network should just call the show *Forest Lawn Memorial Gardens.*"

"I'm sure she'll want me to bring Rox; she probably promised the producers that she would have celebrity supporters in order to book a spot on the show in the first place," Claire interjected. "I can tell you right now that he's not going. He would never be seen in *that* audience; plus, he can't fucking stand Risa."

Just as Claire finished her sentence, Risa Turner showed

up at the table. Five feet tall and about 170 pounds, she was a chubby ball of energy topped off by a stack of obviously fake brown curls. Her yellow, sleeveless sundress called attention to the stretched skin of a 47-year-old woman who'd experienced extreme weight fluctuations throughout the years. All of her major gains and losses since the early 1990s had been documented in *OK!* magazine.

"Can you believe the paps didn't even take my picture on the way in? I mean, I saw Joan van Ark getting snapped when I pulled up to the valet. Do they really think pictures of 'Plastic Surgery Barbie' are going to sell to the tabs before shots of me?" Risa slid into the far end of the booth next to Claire, leaning in to kiss both women sitting to her right.

"Maybe they didn't recognize you under all of that imported hair," Claire joked. "I'm sure they'll get you on the way out, unless, of course, George Clooney leaves at the same time we do."

"Is he here?" Risa asked, craning her short neck to scan the restaurant.

"Yeah," Claudia answered, "I saw him when I walked in earlier."

"Risa, this is Marcee Brookes," Claire interrupted, directing her attention to the opposite side of the table. "She's my new friend from Luminary, the 'featured guest' I mentioned in my e-mail, remember?"

"Hi," Risa said, distracted by her search for George Clooney. She waved her fingers by way of introduction.

"I've always been a big fan of *Head in the Clouds*," Marcee said. "That show defined my entire adolescence."

"Adolescence?" Risa gave up on her effort to spot her superstar crush and looked at Marcee with a piercing glare. "How old are you?"

"Um...42," Marcee said. *Shit; I totally fucked up*, she thought. Marcee knew better than to tell a celebrity that she was "raised" on her work or that "my mother loves you." Her skin absorbed the rose-colored makeup she had generously brushed onto her cheeks, and every bit of natural color drained from her face.

"I'm only five years older than you are," Risa snapped. "It's probably a stretch to suggest that you 'grew up' on my show. We're practically the same age." Marcee's hands became clammy as she started looking around the room nervously to find another point of focus. Her heart began to palpitate; she could feel her wrists pulsating at a rapid speed and put both hands on her lap, hidden beneath the table skirt. Marcee was more accustomed to working with celebrities for brief periods, not socializing with them on such a personal level. *Stay on your game, Marcee, or you won't be included again.*

"Whatever, calm down," Claire said, diffusing the situation. "Marcee's comment was more of a compliment than the photographers outside paid you. Anyway, tell us about *Celebrity Ballroom*; it's such a great opportunity."

"I know, right?" Risa squealed. She'd gone from annoyed to excited in one second flat. "I just wish I knew who the other cast members are going to be. They don't tell you when you sign the contract, so, for all I know, I could be fox-trotting next to a *Playboy* playmate or someone from a Bravo reality series."

"You wouldn't want those pseudo-celebs dragging you down, would you?" Claudia asked rhetorically. "But, at the very least, maybe you'll get to fuck one of the hot professional dancers. Word all over town is that they really lay out the welcome mats for the stars they're paired with."

"Oh my God, I would totally take those two dancing Hungarian brothers at the same time. Jeffrey is already worried about losing me to a *Celebrity Ballroom* carney." Risa looked down at her square-tipped, French-manicured acrylic nails.

"Don't you think it's time to end things with Jeffrey at this point anyway?" Claire asked. "It's kind of gross to be boffing the guy who played your little brother on TV. Plus, the fact that he's married and has two kids...but who am I *not* to judge?" Claudia and Claire giggled in harmony as Marcee's lower lip dropped.

"You're dating Jeffrey Cameron?" Marcee blurted out before she could stop the thought from leaving her head. *Way to go, Marcee.* Her mind was racing. *You did it again.*

"You don't have to announce it to the whole restaurant," Risa said in a terse whisper. "Plus, it didn't start until we saw each other a few years ago at an *Entertainment Weekly* 'Where Are They Now?' photo shoot. It's not like I was having sex with him when we were on the show together."

"But he has a wife and young kids," Claire reminded her, coming to the rescue once again. "You must have some sort of conscience about that, no?"

"Jeffrey says his wife is a total bitch and hasn't had sex with him since she was pregnant with the second baby; I kind of feel bad for him."

"Risa, every cheating asshole has some sob story as to why he needs the comfort of another woman. Don't kid yourself." Claudia's tone deepened. "I'm sure Nick gave his horse-faced Canuck mistress a similarly sad tale."

"Ladies, you know I literally wrote *the* books on finding men and keeping them satisfied, right?" Claire's back-to-back bestsellers, *Meeting the Man* and *Keeping the Man*, had become relationship bibles after her appearances on *Oprah*. "Always give your guy sex, even when you're not in the mood. Right or wrong, if he's not getting it from you, he's gonna get it somewhere."

"So, do you put out for Rox every night?" Risa questioned.

"With *his* sex drive? I have no choice. And, a few times

a month, I actually get on all fours and take it in the back door," Claire said. "Frankly, I'd do it in the ass every day of the week for my shoe collection alone."

Marcee's head moved back and forth like she was watching a ping-pong match at Chuck E. Cheese. The conversation bounced in every direction, revealing pieces of information about everyone that seemed extremely personal. As hard as it was for Marcee to keep up with — let alone keep track of — what was being said, she felt a tingly sense of acceptance. These three women, all of whom were public figures, must have trusted her enough to be so forthcoming with details of their private lives. No one in Marcee's life had ever discussed his or her sex life so openly and proudly, not even Jordan, who should have been stereotypically required to give blow-by-blows after every single date. She used two fingers to sweep some flyaway strands off her face and cocked her head slightly with a sense of belonging.

"I love anal sex," Claudia chimed in, "but Nick never really wanted to do it. I think we tried twice."

"It's not my favorite thing, especially because Rox has such a huge dick, but I don't mind walking funny sometimes to keep him happy," Claire said. "I consider it like getting my period; just part of life."

"I remember the first time I messed around with a guy, back in high school." Claudia looked up and then off into the distance, as though she were reminiscing about a favorite childhood moment. "I would let him fuck me only in the ass. I was convinced that I'd remain a virgin until the day I actually got it in the cooch."

"That's hilarious," Claire said, giggling, "but someone should have taught you early on that your poophole ain't a loophole, Claudia."

"I let Jeffrey stick it anywhere he wants," Risa replied.

"And, right now, I'd let the waiter do the same for one drink." Claire waived the server over to the table.

"Marshall, baby, can we get a round of Grey Goose and sodas for the gang? We're still waiting on the other two, but my friends here are a little thirsty." Claire took the liberty of ordering for everyone, which meant that Marcee's Sprite would have to wait. She hated the taste of vodka but didn't want to upset what she assumed to be the typical flow of a TTT dinner. "Actually, make that five drinks. I see Jill Andrews walking over now."

Jill Andrews? Marcee didn't realize that Ken Andrews's wife was part of the powwow. She'd seen Jill on Ken's arm at various company events, but she'd never been formally introduced. Marcee wasn't high enough up in the organizational food chain at Luminary to be on the studio chairman's radar, but a connection to his wife could land her in his line of vision. She'd have to be mindful of every word that came out of her mouth.

"How's the famous vegan?" Claudia asked, getting up to kiss Jill on the cheek. Claire and Risa also rose from the table, prompting Marcee to stand as well.

"Sit, sit, sit," Jill said, throwing her coat into the banquette. "I'm going to run to the ladies' room."

Marcee had always admired Jill. She'd created a vegan cooking and fitness empire from scratch — before she even became Ken's second wife — and had cultivated a brand that crossed just about every medium: TV programs on the Good Eats Network, cookbooks and fitness videos. She appeared to be a smart and savvy businesswoman who also happened to be a dead ringer for Michelle Pfeiffer: milky, translucent skin, steely grey-blue eyes, and thick, blond waves.

"Is there fur on that coat?" Risa asked from across the table as though she were Miss Marple finding a novel's biggest clue. "She's a mega-vegan!"

Claudia lifted the jacket and looked at its label. "It's a cotton/poly blend," she announced. "No animals were harmed in the making of this schmata."

"Let me see that collar," Claire said, reaching to grab the coat. "Uh, that is awful up close."

"It doesn't look so great from far away either," Risa replied. "Who knew she was a closet Etsy shopper?"

"I swear it came from Build-A-Bear Workshop," Claire continued. "It looks like she skinned a fucking brown plush Teddy." She returned it to Claudia, who set the garment back in its place.

"And, by the way, did you see the discolored ridges along the bottom of her front teeth?" Claudia asked. "Throwing up all that stomach acid is going to do her in."

"What do you mean?" Marcee didn't want to pry, but the comment begged for additional conversation. Until that point, there hadn't been much of an opportunity to insert herself into the chatter, and, the few times she had tried to engage, she didn't like the taste of her own foot.

"That crazy vegan either throws up or uses laxatives to immediately shit out every bite she puts in her mouth," Claire continued. "Each time I see her run to a toilet, I call her the Salad Shooter in my head."

Jill returned to the table and sat at the end of the left side of the booth, just next to Claudia. "You must be Marcee," she said. "Claire mentioned in an e-mail that you work for my husband." Marcee shook her hand.

"Well, indirectly, yes," Marcee answered. "I report to his head of corporate communications and publicity."

"You mean that Phyllis creature?" It was obvious that Jill wasn't a fan.

"So the two of you have met." Marcee smiled. "She's definitely a character."

"'Character' is a nice way to put it," Jill said. "You're

polishing a piece of shit with that description. Ken thinks she's vile."

"She must be doing something right." Marcee wanted to tell Jill what a calculating asshole Phyllis actually was, but she decided it was more prudent to breast her cards for the evening.

"Jill, honey, what's the latest?" Claire asked. "Other than what you had for lunch, of course; I already saw a picture of the bean soup on Instagram."

"That Ikarian stew was to die for, and totally vegan," Jill said. "Wait until you see my breakfast post tomorrow — rice cereal in soy milk with fresh berries."

"If God wanted us to drink soy milk, he would have given the beans udders," Claire quipped, "and he wouldn't have made animals so tasty."

"You know which picture really made me think of going vegan?" Claudia jumped in. "The one of that groundbreaking new snack you created the other day; you know, the apple wedges with organic peanut butter. It was really inspiring." Marcee looked at Claire and Claudia, both of whom were noticeably avoiding eye contact with each other.

"Make fun all you want, but it's such a simple thing to throw together and really satisfying," Jill answered. "Plus, no animal products. I'm so glad people are at least paying attention to my social media updates. Speaking of which, I'm going to post this photo tomorrow as well." Jill held up her iPhone and showed the screen to everyone at the table.

"That's tragic," Risa said, averting her eyes while reaching for a piece of focaccia from the basket of bread.

"Jill, come on, I want to enjoy my dinner," Claire said, handing the phone immediately to Marcee.

"I can't; that's so upsetting," Marcee said, turning the device facedown and sliding it back to Jill. The picture of four small, bloody pigs in torture cages made Marcee's stomach turn.

"This is why we all need to do our parts." Jill raised her phone again for last looks.

"Make it stop!" Claire raised her voice and put her hands over her eyes. "You know what's worse than a vegan? A vegan with a Botoxed forehead. You can't spout that bullshit when your frozen face is the product of animal testing. So, can we just enjoy our dinner while you plan your next aggressively militant Facebook status?" Her face loosened into a smile, the kind of half-reaction that made it hard for Marcee to tell if Claire was just lightheartedly ribbing Jill or actually tearing her apart.

"Plus, Jill," Risa said, "I don't understand why you guys get to call your food 'vegan crabcakes' and 'vegan chicken.' If the point is to save the animals, why even evoke them with the names of your menu items?"

"In all fairness, it would be hard to market tempeh parmigiana and seitan stroganoff, but I kind of agree with Risa." Claudia used her fork to jab the piece of lime lingering at the bottom of her vodka soda. "If you're really making a statement, you shouldn't be referring to animals at all when it comes to your meals."

"Listen, bitches, I didn't build a billion-dollar business because people don't share my vision. I'll remind you of all this when you're begging for tickets to the Meatless Ball at the Beverly Hilton in April."

"Speaking of meatless balls, look who's here," Claudia said, staring straight ahead as Jamie Cross approached the table. "Please tell me you're not wearing your Lesbian Jesus sandals."

"You know we love a good pair of Tevas or Birkenstocks," Jamie answered, sliding into the banquette next to Risa. She blew everyone kisses and then turned to face

Marcee for a head-to-toe scan. "But no. I'm wearing my most sensible pair of Doc Martens."

"Hey, there, I'm Marcee Brookes," she said, reaching out for a handshake.

"Um, sure, hi," Jamie replied, shifting her attention to Claire. "Sorry I'm late. What did I miss?"

"In a nutshell, Nick is having an affair with an ugly Canadian, Risa will still be banging her married TV sibling while she hoofs it on *Celebrity Ballroom* this season, Rox and I fuck like bunnies and Jill is still a whack-job vegan," Claire answered. "What do *you* have for us?"

"Wait, *Celebrity Ballroom*?" Jamie looked at Risa, surprised. "You're actually doing that show?"

"I am," Risa said. "They're trying to turn the star power up a notch, so I figured I'd throw my dancing shoes into the ring." It was clear from her delivery of the statement that she'd repeated it to the point of believing it herself. Or, it was the best acting she'd ever done.

Jamie, a lanky five feet ten with close-cropped brown hair, let out a snort as though no one were around. It was easy to see that she wasn't wearing a bra under her white linen tunic, but, other than as a nipple cover, extra support wasn't necessary for her A-cups. She wore a leather necklace with a dangling brass key that was engraved with the word "believe"; the charm rested directly between her breasts, calling attention to the dark color of her large areolae just under the fabric.

"You know what, when your last girlfriend — or was it the one before that? — was on *Star Rehab*, I showed up for the big intervention episode," Risa commented. "So don't be so quick to knock *Celebrity Ballroom*."

Marcee had seen Jamie Cross's face all over the weekly entertainment magazines; after all, she'd been in the Hollywood mix for more than 15 years. First, she dated Fontaine

Corte, a throaty folk singer whose marriage was supposedly on the rocks when Jamie "seduced" her at an LA Gay and Lesbian Center charity gala. When that hit the skids, she became involved with Mimi Chase, the out-and-proud daytime talk-show host, and later landed in the arms of Jessica Stewart. Jessica had been a child performer who blossomed into a respected, award-winning actress and filmmaker; when she came out during an Academy Awards acceptance speech, Jamie — the official Hollywood celesbian — was on her arm. Their wedding photos landed on the cover of *People.*

From what Marcee could glean, Jamie was nothing more than celebrity-adjacent, a woman who generated attention for herself through her romantic attachments to notable women. She had no discernible career or income — she was always referred to as a "producer"; of *what,* though, Marcee was unclear — yet, in every "Star Tracks" photo, she was dressed in the finest Tom Ford men's suits.

"Whatever," Jamie said, dismissing Risa with a flick of her hand. "I think getting someone through rehab has a little more gravity than doing the cha-cha next to a bunch of injured sports has-beens and washed up daytime hosts."

"When there are cameras there to capture all of it for a TV audience, Jamie, one is no more noble than the other." Claudia was on at least her fourth drink and had become even looser with her comments. "And at least on *Celebrity Ballroom,* there are pretty costumes. You always look like you're going to the Renaissance Faire when you're on TV or in pictures."

"Well, this dinner is fun so far," Jamie said sarcastically. "For the first time, I think I might actually want to hear what Jill is eating these days."

"No beavers, clams or pussies, unfortunately," Jill retorted. "I'm all about protecting animals."

"Not to worry, Jill." Jamie glared. "I prefer a nice, moist, vegan muffin myself."

"Oh, a 'twat swat' from the president of the 'Scissor-a-Celebrity Council.'" Jill used her fingers to make air quotes around the slurs.

Marcee sensed a tension at the table that was previously absent and decided, at last, to participate a little more. "Can I interrupt for a second?" she asked, bringing the group to a silence. "I just want to thank you ladies for including me. You're all such amazing, accomplished women, and I'm raising my glass to new friendships." With her right hand, Marcee lifted the one vodka beverage that she'd been nursing throughout the meal.

"To friendships," Claudia reiterated, clinking stemware with those right next to her. Marcee was seated too far away from everyone to physically touch glasses without standing. Throughout the main course, she'd actually considered the seating arrangements; the other ladies were all stationed around a half circle — Claire in the middle — and Marcee was the one guest across from them, alone along the out-facing, straight edge. It was as if she were at an interview, sitting in front of a school admissions board.

Just as the brief toast ended, the waiter delivered two chocolate pizzas to the table. "These are courtesy of Craig," Marshall said as he placed the round plates in front of the women. Craig had been the maître d' at Dan Tana's for more than 20 years and left to open his own hot spot in 2011.

"I'll have to give him a big kiss on the way out," Claire cooed. "He always takes such good care of me." She pulled a slice of the sugared dough, gooey with melted chocolate and cookie crumb topping, and took a bite. "To die for," she said. "And I love that it's a secret, off-menu item that most people don't know to ask for."

Marcee exercised self-control and refrained from

having a small triangle of the dessert pizza. She knew she'd be getting chocolate chip cookies on the way out, and she'd allow herself the sweets when she wasn't in front of the firing squad.

"You're not having any, Marcee?" Claire asked. "You're missing out."

"I'm trying to be better with my food choices," Marcee admitted.

"Could that have anything to do with Brent Wetherley? Isn't your date in about a week or so?" For the few days prior to the TTT dinner, Marcee had refocused her energy and thoughts on how she would impress Claire's friends as opposed to marinating in dating self-doubt. Just the mention of Brent, though, hollowed her stomach to a gaping pit.

"Wait, what?" Jill asked. "Brent Wetherley, the actor?"

"No, Jill, Brent Wetherley the circus clown," Claudia garbled. Jamie and Risa laughed.

"I have a feeling that Marcee and Brent are going to hit it off," Claire said. "I introduced them by e-mail a couple of weeks ago, and he asked her to have dinner when he's back from his shoot in Vancouver."

"He's so hot," Risa said. "I'd climb on top of him and ride that shit. If you want me to end my affair with Jeffrey Cameron so much, why didn't you set *me* up with Brent Wetherley?"

"I think Brent would like to meet someone without a Hollywood past," Claire answered. Before she could continue her thought, a tall, slim bottle-redhead walked up to the table.

"I'm so sorry to interrupt your dinner," the woman said in a faint Russian accent, "but when I saw Jill Andrews sitting near me, I had to come over. You completely changed my life."

"That's so sweet," Jill replied, standing to hug her fan.

"I have every single one of your cookbooks and DVDs, and I haven't missed an episode of *The Valiant Vegan*. I don't usually geek out like this, but you really made me a better person. Would you mind if we took a quick selfie?"

"I'd be honored," Jill replied graciously, smiling while the startlingly skinny ginger snapped a shot on her phone. "I'm on Facebook, Instagram and Twitter — so post that photo everywhere!"

"And, Miss Turner, I owe you a lot, too." The gushing admirer looked directly at Risa.

"Aw, thank you, ma'am. It makes me feel great to know that I bring some smiles and laughs into people's lives," Risa enthused.

"Well, actually, it's more than that," the woman continued. "When I first moved to America, I learned English by watching your show."

"Um, thanks, I guess," Risa said disappointedly, dismissing the fan by looking down at the table and folding her cloth napkin. It wouldn't take a detective to figure out that she was put off by the comment.

"OK, that's funny," Claire said with a riotous laugh. "You didn't make her smile; you taught her the English language. She probably adopted all of your ridiculous sitcom phrases. What was that dumb thing your character used to say all the time?"

"The line was 'What do you meeeeeaaaaaannnn…?'" Claudia answered quickly, as though she were on a game show. "That poor bitch has probably been repeating Risa's dumbass dialogue for years."

"I guess it's sad then that my stupid old sitcom lines have lasted longer than your marriage," Risa spat. Claudia squinted at her with an overly articulated, drunken gaze.

"Well, at least there's one wacky Hollywood housewife

who appreciates the two of you," Claudia grumbled at Risa and Jill. "I don't know about you, but Nick hates it when people approach him at restaurants for pictures and autographs."

"I don't mind," Jill said, "because if they have one good experience with me, they'll buy every fucking thing I put out until the day they die. With each signature and photo, I can hear money being deposited into my accounts."

"That's the truth," Claire added. "I always make sure I'm pleasant when people ask me to sign books. Rox, though, is grumpy sometimes with fans."

"I just act grateful when people approach," Risa said.

"What other choice do you have?" Jamie mumbled under her breath.

"Well, girls, another lovely TTT dinner," Claire announced, looking at her watch and obviously trying to wrap things up. It was 11PM. "I took care of tonight's bill; it's your turn next, Claudia." Typically, the restaurant was so up its own ass that the reservationists mentioned a 90-minute table time limit at the moment of booking — a rule that obviously didn't apply to the famous and powerful.

"Thank you so much for a fantastic meal and for welcoming me," Marcee said as everyone gathered her bag and accessories and began to walk toward the exit. "I hope there will be a next time." She suggested future inclusion in case they weren't already considering it.

"Of course there will be," Claire answered. She held open the front door, greeting the two lingering photographers who quickly snapped photos. In eight or nine flashes, Claire, Jamie, Jill, Claudia and Risa were captured forever, leaving one of LA's most popular restaurants on a Monday night.

They all approached the valet parkers with tickets in hand. "I'll group-text you guys later so that everyone can be in touch. We'll all want to know how the date with Brent Wetherley goes," Claire said. An attendant handed her a set of keys and a bag of cookies as she slid a $50 bill between his fingers; she kissed everyone before speeding away in the Maserati that had been parked near the front door all evening.

Marcee made small talk and hugged the others goodnight as a parade of their Porsches, Teslas and Bentleys passed by. Her Audi A3 was the last to arrive at the curb, and Marcee was just as happy; there was no need for the ladies to see her economy car. The valet waited next to the driver's-side door while she reached into her purse for $10. The eight-dollar fee and two-dollar tip would have to suffice, especially if she had to start saving up to pay for a TTT dinner within the next six months. From what she could gather, each group member paid for the entire meal twice a year — and there was no way that Craig's had cost Claire less than $800.

"Thank you, and have a good evening," Marcee said as she took her keys from the parking attendant and handed him two $5 bills.

"You, too, miss," he replied as he looked down at the money in his right hand. Marcee couldn't help but peek at his extended palm as well. She had no idea where he was hiding her cookies. She started her engine, leaving the door open. "Drive carefully, miss," he continued.

"OK, thank you," Marcee answered, still paused in hopes that he was going to suddenly remember to grab a packet of treats from the umbrellaed stand on the sidewalk. "Have a good evening," she said, realizing that she had just repeated herself. After an awkwardly long period, she closed the door and drove forward without dessert. *Four things could have happened,* Marcee thought. *1) The valet actually did forget the complimentary parting gift. 2) Craig's ran out of cookies by 11:15PM. 3) The valet wasn't satisfied with his tip and kept the cookies for himself to be punitive. 4) He'd decided that her figure wouldn't benefit from baked goods.* Marcee decided to believe in the first two possibilities rather than ruin her evening by thinking about Options Three and Four.

She made a left on Robertson and then another onto Santa Monica Boulevard, heading toward Beverly Glen for her ride back to the Valley. At nearly 11:30PM, she didn't want to bother her mother or Jordan with a call, and yet she wasn't in the mood to listen to one of her usual playlists. The quiet in the car gave her time to catch her breath and replay the evening in her head. She felt special, like she was part of something exclusive — particularly when considering the company; they were being photographed and approached by fans, and she was sitting at *their* table.

Marcee thought of all the things she learned about Claire, Claudia, Jill, Risa and Jamie; details about people who, before that night, existed for her only as two-dimensional screenshots on TMZ and Joaquin Richie's widely read gossip blog. Sure, they'd snapped and nipped at each other's Louboutin heels, the way all types of families do, but they clearly regarded Marcee as a solid addition to their circle. Why would they have shared so much otherwise?

9

A VERIFIED, BLUE check mark on a Facebook, Instagram or Twitter account — an "FIT home run," if you were lucky enough to have all three — meant everything in terms of social media status. Marcee knew how valuable these online acknowledgements were to the celebrities, filmmakers and wannabes who were able to score exclusive online badges, but, for the most part, she avoided jumping onto the ever-spinning wheel of social networking herself. Sure, she had accounts on all of the popular platforms as mandated by Phyllis, but she used them only to showcase the movies she was promoting. Marcee was the last person to post a picture with a movie star or a photo with Jordan for National Best Friends Day, so it was no wonder that her followers and online connections were few. Until that Tuesday morning, she was just as happy to keep it that way.

She woke up at 5AM, an hour before her alarm clock typically beeped on a weekday. Her sleep had been restless, and her brain was still processing all of the conversations that took place during the TTT dinner the previous evening. If that weren't enough, her home screen was lighting up like a marquee with messages from Claire providing contact information for each of the ladies in one group text. Marcee propped three pillows against her pickled-wood headboard and held her phone in front of her.

"Thank you all so much for an amazing evening," she texted, following Claire's lead and ignoring the early hour. "I'm looking forward to staying in touch and hopefully seeing all of you again soon."

"It was fun, right?" Claire shot back immediately. "I think you might be our newest TTT member, and, by the way, I followed you on Twitter last night." Had she read Claire's text correctly? She was now a member of their club? Marcee pushed her head back into the ultrasoft down pillows and closed her eyes before checking her iPhone again.

She quickly flipped to her social media apps and opened her Twitter account. Sure enough, she'd been followed by @TheClaireMadison, bestselling author and wife of *People* magazine's "Sexiest Man Alive." Naturally, Claire had the coveted blue check next to her name, as did four of the others listed in her latest tweet:

> Loved, loved, loved our dinner! @jillandrewsveg
> @risacloudsTV @CrossJamie90
> @ericksonwellsfrevr @MarceePRGirl #TTT
> #friends

Marcee was surprised to see that her number of followers had increased from a static 123 to an admirable 765, simply because of Claire's post the night before. The others had yet to respond or retweet, but surely their eventual participation in the message chain would generate even more traffic later in the day. *Maybe I should be more active online,* she thought. *This is kind of fun.*

Even though she had plenty of time to potshke around her apartment for another hour and still be at work before anyone else, she decided to jump in the shower and get ready so she could make a Starbucks stop in Studio City on her way to the office. Because she never got her complimentary to-go cookies from Craig's, she figured she'd treat herself to four cream cheese-filled bagel bites and a Caramel Crunch Frappucino *with* whipped cream. She deserved them.

Conveniently, Jordan called just as Marcee had securely positioned her frozen drink in the cup holder at the center of her car. "Hey, Jordie," she said as she made a sharp right turn out of the shopping plaza at Ventura and Laurel Canyon.

"How was the dinner? I can't believe you haven't called me already to spill the tea."

"I swear I was going to check in. My text messages and Twitter were blowing up this morning, and then I was trying to tell my mom all about last night while I was doing my makeup," Marcee answered.

"Wait, did you just say 'Twitter?'" Jordan sounded shocked. "I have been trying to get you going on social media for, like, four years, and now you're saying you didn't have time to call *me* because you were on *Twitter*? That is some kind of whatthefuckery if I've ever heard it."

"Change your brake pads, honey," she said, laughing. "Claire sent out a tweet including each of the TTT girls, and all of a sudden, my account came to life. It's amazing."

"Oh, so now that Claire Madison opened the door, you're ready to walk through; when I suggested it, you couldn't be bothered. I see how you play, girl."

"Hate on the game, not the player," Marcee snapped, clicking her tongue against the roof of her mouth in a style she'd observed on *The Real Housewives of Atlanta*.

"You're starting to speak like I do, and I don't like it even a little bit," he teased. "Anyway, how did everything go last night?"

"It was great. They seemed very comfortable with me,"

Marcee said, "and they really opened up about their personal lives. Claire even texted this morning with an invitation to stay in their group."

"She doesn't waste time, does she?" Jordan asked. "I guess she likes your vibe, but you know these Hollywood bitches are full of shit and totally wrapped up in themselves. You better not forget your friends down here on earth."

"I'll be more likely to remember you if you get a blue check mark next to your name on Twitter."

"Oh, bitch, no you didn't," he shouted into the phone.

"Buh-bye, Jordie-Pie," Marcee said as she smiled and disconnected the call, pulling into her parking space in the Luminary garage.

By the time she threw her bag under her desk and turned on the butterfly lamp, she had all but finished her venti beverage — just at the point where sucking the remaining drops through an oversized green straw would cause an embarrassing slurp. She'd seen e-mails coming through to her phone all morning but had decided she would deal with whatever entertainment "emergencies" were brewing when she was actually seated in front of her computer.

Before she began to look through the various correspondence from the East Coast staff and media outlets begging to book celebrities from upcoming Luminary films, she pulled up her Twitter page. She now had retweets from Risa and Claudia and 2,944 followers. She was quickly gaining popularity in the Twitterverse and decided she'd better post something to keep people engaged — just as she would counsel a starlet who was looking to maintain an online fan base. She took a quick shot of Flo and uploaded it with the caption "The #light of my life, Flo. #lamp #love #officelife." Within minutes, the post had been "liked" by eight people.

As if the day couldn't get better, she looked at her

phone to find that she had one personal e-mail — from Brent Wetherley.

> **To:** Brookes, Marcee <MarceePR@gmail.com>
> **From:** Wetherley, B. <WetherOrNot@wetherleymediagrp.com>
> RE: Hey, baby…
>
> So sorry I haven't been in touch as I'd hoped. The schedule has been grueling, and I've been out cold after shooting each night. The good news is that I fly back to LA at the end of the week.
>
> How does dinner this Saturday night sound? I'll pick you up in the Valley, but I can't promise we're going to eat local. ☺
>
> Lemme know if we're on.
>
> Hugs,
>
> Brent W.

Marcee had been plagued by Brent's inattention for nearly two weeks but avoided mentioning her mind-set when Claire brought up the subject the night before. The texts and FaceTime calls he'd suggested during their one chat never materialized, and only constant reassurance from her mother and Jordan — as well as her excitement over the TTT dinner — kept her from falling into a snack-food spiral. This e-mail, though, highlighted by the words "baby" and "hugs," retriggered the exuberance she felt had been attached to their initial exchange. She put on her headset and dialed Rhonda from her desk phone.

"Hi, honey, everything OK?" She sounded out of breath.

"I should be asking *you* that question," Marcee answered. "It seems like you're gasping for air."

"Dad and I are finishing a game of tennis at the country

club," she said, "I was just reaching for some water when I heard the phone ring."

"Well, an e-mail from Brent Wetherley just came through, and he asked me out to dinner this Saturday night. He apologized for falling off the map; apparently his work schedule was crazier than he'd anticipated." Her voice had a matter-of-fact tone, but she was beaming inside and out.

"Isn't that what I told you over and over?" Rhonda replied. "I knew he'd eventually follow through. You need to have a little more faith."

"Should I answer him now or make him sweat it out for a day or two?" Marcee had read *The Steps*, the famous dating guide, and had taken the author's advice seriously.

"I wouldn't operate under guidance from a years-old pop-culture book, Mar," Rhonda suggested. "Brent is not some average guy you met in a bar; the rules are different here."

"You're right, you're right," Marcee said as she turned around in her swivel chair, her back now to the door of her office. "I don't want to seem desperate, though, like I've been sitting at my phone waiting for his message."

"So, wait an hour or two, but don't turn this into some kind of sport." Rhonda went silent for a moment. "Sorry, I had to take a drink." Before Marcee could respond, she heard a light knock on her door; she swung around in her seat.

"Jill!" she exclaimed, surprised to see the vegan goddess herself standing in the doorway.

"Is this a bad time?" Jill mouthed.

"I'll have those photos e-mailed to you right away," Marcee said into her hands-free headset, "and thanks so much for your interest." She motioned to Jill to come in while she pretended to end a business call. Jill put her lemonade-colored Matt & Nat handbag on the edge of the desk.

"I love that purse," Marcee said while she removed her headset and stood up to hug Jill.

"Thank you, I love it, too," she said, stroking the front panel, "and it's made without any animal-based materials."

"It's gorgeous," Marcee continued. "I'll have to check out their website."

"I hope I'm not interrupting anything important; I was having breakfast with Ken at the Apex, so I figured I'd take a walk over to say hello."

"I'm so glad you did," Marcee said, sitting in one of the two guest chairs in front of her desk. Jill sat in the other. "I had such a nice time last night; I'm already looking forward to next month's get-together."

"There are some strong personalities in our little bunch, but you seemed to blend right in." Jill was wearing a black Lululemon jogging suit and a red baseball cap that was embroidered with the Luminary logo; her blond hair hung through the back in a ponytail. "Those girls aren't always so welcoming, but they'll usually follow Claire's lead. She's sort of the de facto ringleader."

"Then I feel honored to have her stamp of approval." Marcee smiled.

"I suppose someone like you would." Jill must have seen Marcee's face lose its expression in a sudden flinch. "What I mean is someone who doesn't usually move in celebrity social circles," she amended. "Anyway," she went on, glossing over her discourteous comment, "it'll be fun to have you in the group." Marcee wasn't sure if Jill was warning her that Claire could be exclusionary when it came to the nonfamous or if she was trying to explain the Hollywood food chain in a not-so-roundabout way.

"What do you have on tap for the rest of the day?" Marcee asked. She wanted to move the conversation along cheerfully rather than letting Jill know that she felt stung by her previous remarks.

"Let's see," she said, pulling out her phone and swiping

to her calendar. "I have a pottery class at 1PM, a phone interview with *Vegan Times* magazine at 2:30PM, and then I'm supposed to meet Claire and her kids for sushi in Beverly Hills."

"It sounds like you're pretty busy," Marcee said while thinking to herself what a luxury it would be to have *that* schedule.

"I just wish I could get out of dinner tonight. Rox is shooting something in Vancouver this week, and, whenever he's away, Claire ropes me into family meals. Between you and me, I can't stomach their kids."

"I haven't met them." Marcee was surprised that Jill was so openly disdainful of two ten-year-olds.

"Savages," Jill continued. "It's not hard to believe really; they've basically been raised by nannies and au pairs."

"I've never understood the difference between a nanny and an au pair." Marcee was trying to walk the line between sounding sympathetic toward Jill and staying positive about Claire's family.

"The nanny takes care of your kids, and the au pair fucks your husband; I think that's how it works," Jill said, still swiping away at her phone. Before Marcee could get a laugh out, Phyllis barged into the office.

"Jill Andrews, how did I not know sooner that you were in the building? A little birdie just mentioned it to me." Phyllis, in a pea-green mock turtleneck and brown pants, held her arms out for a hug.

"I guess your staff forgot to send out the press release," Jill snapped, neither standing nor looking up from her phone.

"What brings you over here?" Phyllis continued to engage despite Jill's frosty greeting.

"Just some girl chat with Marcee," Jill replied curtly.

"It's funny, I was telling Ken last week that I'd love to have the two of you over for dinner sometime soon."

"That's lovely of you, Phyllis, but we're pretty booked this year." She looked up with an impassive glare.

"Well, I'll leave the two of you to finish chatting," Phyllis said, obviously realizing that she was getting nowhere close to Jill's good graces, "and, Marcee, please pop by my office sometime after lunch." She turned and left, her odious scent lingering in the air.

Jill laughed. "Oh shit, you're in trouble now," she said as soon as Phyllis was out of earshot. "But don't worry about whatever she says to you; I'll make sure Ken has your back."

"She's going to hate the fact that I'm hanging out with *her* peers," Marcee said.

"Oh, fuck!" Jill stood up and grabbed her bag from the desk. "I have to run."

"What's wrong?" Marcee was unnerved by Jill's sudden upset over a message that had just come through.

"Madonna and Gaga got into it, and apparently there's blood. I'm so sorry."

Marcee couldn't believe what she was hearing. Two grown-up superstars had gotten into a physical brawl, and one of them was seriously injured. Jill Andrews — the woman sitting in *her* office — was among the first to know about it. *It has to be Madonna who's injured,* Marcee thought, *because Gaga probably packs a stronger punch.*

"Hopefully it'll stay out of the press," Marcee said. "Just know that *my* lips are sealed."

"What are you talking about?" Jill looked confused.

"Surely the tabloids are going to find out about a fight between Madonna and Lady Gaga," she said, shocked that Jill didn't seem concerned by the possible public fallout.

"How cute are you?" Jill said, looking at Marcee pitifully as she would a homeless child begging for coins. "Madonna and Gaga are my miniature pinschers. They sometimes get intro skirmishes that land at least one of them at the vet's office. Anyhow, gotta go. I'll text you later."

Marcee moved back to her desk chair, sitting straight up rather than in her usual hunch. Jill's impromptu visit and Phyllis's subsequent displeasure left her unsettled during a day that had initially promised all good things. Rather than drown in the wake of negative energy — her typical go-to mode when she felt marginalized — she decided to shift her focus to Brent Wetherley. After all, the possibility of a romance with a Hollywood hottie was what she had to hold onto. In the love department, all Jill had was her 70-year-old "daddy" of a husband, and Phyllis was nothing more than Miss Havisham with a day job.

She opened Brent's e-mail and spent the next hour drafting and editing her subtle reply.

To: Wetherley, B. <WetherOrNot@wetherleymediagrp.com>
From: Brookes, Marcee <MarceePR@gmail.com>
Re: Hey, baby…

Dear Brent,

Saturday evening sounds great, and I appreciate your offer to drive *all* the way to the Valley. I'll take you up on it! Just let me know what time to be ready.

Sorry to hear that the shoot has been so tiring. I hope the last few days are a little easier on you.

Travel home safely. I look forward to seeing you this weekend.

Marcee

She worried that jokes about the driving distance to the Valley had been overplayed and wondered whether "looking forward to seeing you" should be changed to something less needy, such as "see you this weekend"; her keyboard was getting a workout. Reviewing the 70-word e-mail more than 20 times, she made copious changes before finally hitting Send. Then, she wasted no time calling Jordan to get his approval.

"It sounds a little formal to me," he answered, "and maybe end with a warmer valediction, something other than just 'Marcee.'"

"It's already gone," she said with a deep exhale. "I just wanted to make sure it wasn't horrible."

"A better time to chart directions is before the ship has sailed," he quipped. "That said, the note is fine. Stop obsessing."

"Are you sure? Now I feel like I didn't read it over enough."

"A better use of time would be finding the right outfit for Saturday. You need to look like a million bucks, obvs," Jordan advised.

"More like 500 bucks," she countered. "I can't afford to burn so much money on one date."

"Child, we can't even leave the Sherman Oaks Fashion Square Mall for $500. Go into your savings, and prepare to call in sick on Friday. We'll be on Wilshire in Beverly Hills by 11AM."

◇◇◇

MARCEE HAD SPENT quite a bit of time on the third floor of Neiman Marcus but never to shop for herself. Studio Services, the department that liaised with film productions and PR departments, was hidden in a far corner, somewhere between Donna Karan and Lela Rose; she knew that particular part of the floor plan well. What she didn't know, however, was which designer would be the most likely to offer dresses in sizes flattering to her curvy figure. Her eyes and sensibility were all about Tom Ford, but her tummy told her to keep looking.

"Actually, I think we should go back down to the second floor," Jordan said. "Most of the couture collections are there." He was no stranger to high-end retail.

"I just feel so guilty for using a sick day," she said as they rode down one flight on the escalator. "Especially after Phyllis ripped me a new one on Tuesday for fraternizing with her boss's wife. What was I supposed to do? Jill came to *my* office on her own volition."

"I actually just had an amazing idea," he answered. "What if Neiman's convinced Escada to chip in for more ornate, detailed escalators, and there were a sign at the bottom of each one that said, '*Escada*lator'?"

"Did you hear what I just said about Phyllis and taking today off?" she whined as they landed on the second floor.

"I would much rather ride on an *Escada*lator," he continued, making clear to Marcee that he wasn't entertaining her neuroses. "Anyhow, let's start with Carolina Herrera, and we'll work backward to Zac Posen." Marcee ran her hands along a row of dresses.

"These all look too formal for a dinner date," she said. "It's not a prom or a fashion show in Paris."

"Baby doll, the pieces that are already hanging in your closet are right off the runways of Paris, Kentucky," he shot back, "so let's at least get you a little closer to France." He added an "OK" with the obligatory, drawn-out pronunciation of a sassy sidekick.

"Everything on these racks was designed for a size 4." *An afternoon in Lane Bryant,* she lamented to herself, *might be more fruitful.* Before she could continue along that line of thinking, a swirl of color came charging at her in the body of an overly sun-touched South Florida yenta.

Five feet tall and sporting a fuchsia Toni Tennille haircut, the mid-70s-looking crone moved with purpose. Her well-worn legs had the agility of someone half her age, which helped her arthritic hands reach Marcee's right shoulder at record speed. "Darling, what can I help you with?" Marcee turned to face her attacker, whose wrist was banded with an elastic spiral gummy bracelet holding keys to the store's various display cases. The ubiquitous department store employee accessory reminded her of the see-through, anti-theft pencil-case purses that cashiers were required to carry when she was a kid.

"She has, shall we say, an *event* tomorrow night and needs a nice cocktail dress," Jordan answered before Marcee could get a word out.

"Let me guess, something orange for that leukemia fundraiser that everyone is going to at the Montage?" The sales associate's bright red lipstick had bled into the deep creases surrounding her mouth.

"No," Marcee replied, "I actually have a date."

"Oh, thank God," she said. "Leukemia is kind of passé. I hear that even Brad and Angie stopped kicking in for that long before they split up. Hold out for something in pale yellow a couple of months from now; the Spina Bifida Soiree is going to be all the rage this season."

"I want something black and understated." Marcee was too focused on the silver, rectangular tag pinned to Millie Bergman's lapel — and the fact that it offered her entire name, first and last — to address the woman's perspective on the in diseases of the moment.

"Of course you want something dark," Millie said, as though she'd heard the same thing from a hundred people already that day. "Black doesn't do as much to hide things as you would think." *What kinds of parents were responsible for this Jewish Boca Raton transplant?* Marcee wanted to scream. *My mother could teach her a thing or two about colors and tact.*

"Well, then, Millie Bergman," Marcee said in almost a growl, "what would *you* recommend for a size 14 woman?"

"The shoe department." Millie darted away, the sound of her jingling keys fading as she disappeared into a sea of Oscar de la Renta gowns.

"Pay no mind to the Crypt Keeper," Jordan said. He grabbed Marcee's hand and walked her toward Mary Katrantzou's newest line the second he saw her face drop into a dejected frown.

"Am I *that* fat?" she asked. "I mean, I know I won't die from the same illness as Karen Carpenter, but I'm not exactly a white version of Precious either."

"Honey, you're not fat," he replied. "That old bitch is just an urn of ashes waiting to be scattered; *you're* the proverbial phoenix. And what would the phoenix be without some ashes? Nothing but a fucking bird trying to get up."

Marcee laughed. "I don't know what I'd do without you, Jordie," she said, rubbing her hands up and down his back.

"I need this touchy-feely nonsense to cease immediately," he barked playfully. "And look at this dress. It's a 14. I knew Mary wouldn't let us down with her size run." She took the hanger from his hands and checked for a price tag.

"At $1,675? I don't think so," she said.

"That's pennies at Neiman Marcus. Just try it on."

"Nothing's fine, I'm torn," she replied.

"About what, Natalie Imbruglia? I love that you just tried to sneak those lyrics into our conversation, by the way." Marcee's face burst into a wide smile; she liked it when Jordan would catch on to her private word games. He was one of the rare few who did.

"On one hand, I want to splurge and buy something I'll feel glamorous in," she said, "and, on the other, I want to be prudent about how I spend my money."

"Mar, nobody outside of Yale uses the word 'prudent' in casual conversations," he chided. "What are you, a walking SAT test? If that's the case, *you* are to this dress…let me think of the right analogy…as *I* am to a muscle-bottom with a ten-inch schlong."

"OK, that makes sense," she said. "I'm heading into the fitting room now."

Within two minutes, she emerged from her stall in the colorful and creped fabric that Jordan had handpicked.

"You know, if I'm being honest, I'm not loving it on you."

"Praise all that is good and holy in the world," she replied, breathing a dramatic sigh of relief. "I thought you were going to try to talk me into it. Can we just go back to my place and put an outfit together from my own wardrobe?"

"I'll agree to that only if — and I mean *only if* — you'll buy yourself a pair of sexy heels on the way out. You owe it to yourself and to Brent."

She agreed to his terms, and they headed downstairs to scope the selection of designer footwear. She had seen every episode of *Sex and the City* years before, so the Manolos she spotted right away seemed dated and too obvious.

"What about these Lanvin Mary Jane pumps," Jordan suggested, holding up a chunky black shoe with a distinct metal buckle. "Are they too lesbian? They're only $800."

"*Only* $800? I'll take them in every color," she joked. "Don't be ridiculous." She walked around the circular grey carpeting, inspecting styles from Gucci, Givenchy and Giuseppe Zanotti. Overwhelmed by the choices, she plopped down on the taupe curved sectional sofa and surveyed the shelves from her seat. "Wait, what about those." Marcee pointed to a pair of sleek, silver Christian Dior stilettos that were staring at her from across the couch.

"You mean these?" he asked, picking up a size-8 floor sample and studying it from all angles. "I definitely approve." Covered in plain, shiny satin, the shoes were accented at the bridge with a small, crystal-studded grey sphere. The sparkly detail was the only flair on an otherwise ordinary choice, but Marcee was taken with them.

"How much?" she asked, prepared for the answer now that she'd studied the entire department.

"They're $1,595, but they're nondescript enough to wear a few times." Jordan looked serious.

"A few times? For that price, I'd sleep in them."

"Listen, girl, how often do you treat yourself to something extravagant?" He didn't wait for an answer. "Never. So go crazy. Buy these shoes, will you? I'll kick in $50, so consider them on sale."

Marcee held the right shoe in her hand, examining the arch, structure and design. "My date *is* with Brent Wetherley, after all," she said in a mutter that was barely audible to Jordan.

"Exactly," he agreed. "And think about it this way: if things go well, he'll be paying for your next pair of expensive shoes."

"I'm getting them!" she exclaimed. "Tell the guy that I want to try them in a size 8. Then hand him my credit card quickly, before I change my mind." Jordan flashed a toothy grin and went about taking care of business.

"Miss Brookes, can I get your signature on the top copy?" the salesman asked as he delivered a receipt with the shopping bag. The final, tax-inclusive figure — $1,754.50 — rattled Marcee from her seat. She steadied a near fall by redirecting her attention from the register slip to his name tag. She still couldn't wrap her head around why Neiman Marcus required employees to identify by their entire names. *It seems so invasive; I could totally google "Henry Davison" if I wanted to know everything about him.*

"Alright, let's head back to my apartment," she directed, shuffling Jordan toward the parking structure. We'll pick out a black dress and a nice pashmina scarf and let the shoes be the star of the show."

"Oh, Miss Brookes," Henry called out after her. "You might want to visit our hosiery salon on level three before you go. They'll have something that'll look fabulous with those Diors."

"Salon?" she asked, tilting her head sideways and looking to Jordan for an explanation.

"Honey, that's just where they keep the 'socks' in Beverly Hills."

10

SHE SHOULD'VE LEFT the white shoebox in the living room. From on top of her dresser, it stared her down, even chasing her in the few parts of the distressingly uneasy dreams she could remember. Most women would have been ecstatic about anything marked with the grey Dior logo, but Marcee felt like she'd woken up, woozy from the night before, next to a man she didn't remember bringing home from a college mixer. *Did I really buy a pair of shoes for nearly $1,800?* At least her lapse in judgment, she reasoned, didn't come with the risk of pregnancy or have morning breath.

Anxiety had woken her in the middle of the night — long before there was any work for the window shades to do — and, as hard as she tried to will herself back to sleep, her body wasn't having it. After tossing and turning for an hour, it was evident by 4AM that a full night's rest wasn't in the stars: she was up at the same time as a Dunkin' Donuts morning shift manager. Fortunately for him, though, he didn't have to look halfway decent for a date with Hollywood's screen idol du jour.

Throughout years of constant worry about everything from her career to romance to finances, Marcee had memorized the entire pattern on her bedroom's popcorn ceiling. She would count the dots and discolored specs in an effort to release the tightness in her chest when the fear of growing old alone clamped down on her like a bear trap. It didn't matter that she knew plenty of women who were just as happy to live an independent lifestyle, free of responsibility to a man. *She* wanted the elusive husband, the guy she'd hoped to meet 15 years earlier, and, more important, she wanted to believe that he could love her despite her full figure and the myriad of insecurities that rendered so many of her nights sleepless.

Marcee got out of bed and, without turning on any lights, walked over to the 5x19 cardboard box that was partly responsible for *A Nightmare on Dickens Street.* She lifted the lid and looked down at the shoes, one wrapped in clear plastic and the other beneath a branded storage bag that probably accounted for 25 cents of the purchase price. The gleaming shine of the luxurious fabric and the sparkling circular ornaments sewn just above the pointed toes were, indeed, stunning and would unquestionably look dazzling on the feet of a Jennifer — Lawrence, Lopez or Aniston. *But on me?* she thought. *They're just useless ornamentation meant to distract from a dowdy 42-year-old with childbearing hips. And they cost two-thirds of a month's rent.* She repacked the shoes neatly and put them under her bed, completely out of sight.

A hot bath could, as her mother always said, cure just about any unease, and she was hopeful that some steam and a dip would chase her nerves down the copper piping. As she started to run the water, she spotted the glass jar with lavender bath salts at the far left corner of the basin's ledge. Something about the early hour coupled with her jitters of insecurity — not to mention a critical case of buyer's remorse — moved her to sprinkle double the suggested amount of the scented balm under the flowing tap. Pulling off her hairband, Marcee stepped gently into the water, letting her feet adjust to the temperature before lowering herself into the warmth.

She folded a towel and placed it behind her head so she could recline comfortably; her heels rested just above the waterline and below the faucet. Neck to ankles, she was submerged, her small arm movements creating the tiniest ripples around her. From above the surface, she could see her midsection, which was magnified through the distorting prism of clear liquid. There was a lot of love on her handles, and her tummy, as she saw it, looked like Pillsbury biscuit dough that had expanded after the initial pressure release from its can. *This*, she said to herself, *is unlovable. Even I can't stand to look at it.*

Marcee tasted the tears before she felt them pooling in her eyes. Her face and shoulders were already covered in bathwater and sweat, so it was the saltiness dripping down to her quivering lips that signaled a sudden convulsive cry. Frequently, she was able to stave off the enveloping sadness that followed her panic attacks with a call to her mom or Jordan, but, at 4:15AM, she had limited resources. The despair worked against what little energy she had in reserve, forcing her feet to fall into the tub. Her doleful heaves created such a disturbance in the water that she was no longer able to see her torso below the small waves. *For the best,* she thought as she turned her head to one side and continued to sob. *What if Brent gets to the front door and is too turned off to go through with the date?*

The five-minute meltdown felt like it had lasted five hours, so she was disappointed to look up at the her stainless-steel wall clock and find that it was still too early to call anyone. She unplugged the drain and stood while the remaining gallons funneled out. Before the last drops disappeared, she pulled the plastic curtain across the metal tension rod and started to run the shower. Marcee wanted to rinse off the residue that the Dr. Teal's soaking solution had left on her skin as well as cloud the mirror with enough condensation to keep it from reflecting her off-putting body.

Back in bed, remote control in hand, she flipped through just about every cable channel hoping to find an on-demand stand-up comedy special or an out-of-the-way documentary about people who live in tiny homes. She landed on a Hallmark movie that featured a female florist-turned-detective who becomes embroiled in a small-town murder case. *So, this is what eventually came between Brooke Shields and her Calvins,* she thought. And thankfully for Marcee, *Flower Shop Mystery: Mum's the Word* was as dull as its title; she fell fast asleep before the comely shopkeeper ever figured out "whodunit."

It was 10AM when the landline rang. Marcee lowered the volume on the television and reached for her cordless phone.

"I've been trying you on your cell for, like, an hour," Jordan said. "Where have you been?"

"Ugh, I was up most of the night," she answered, "having a nervous breakdown."

"Why didn't you call me? You know my phone is always on in case a huge gossip story breaks."

"It was 4:15AM, and I was a mess." Marcee was still feeling somewhat disoriented.

"If you should ever need me, I'll be there in a hurry," he replied. "And, in the meantime, keep smiling; keep shining, knowing you can always count on me. For sure."

"You will not beat me at my own game," Marcee said, sitting up in her bed and feeling some life in her face for the first time in hours. He had worked Diana *and* Dionne into one thought.

"Whatever you say, but that's what friends are for." He

laughed. "I'm picking up a bagel and a plateful of onion rolls along with some coffee at Noah's. I'll be at your place by 11AM; the day of beauty will commence immediately upon my arrival." And now Barbra in *Funny Girl*, too?

"You're the wind beneath my wings, Jordan, and I mean that," she said, doing the best she could to shoehorn Bette Midler into the mix.

"Well, you've got to have friends," he replied, hanging up the phone before Marcee added any lines from Tina Turner.

She threw on a pair of Splendid sweatpants with a promotional T-shirt from a years-old chick flick and then tied her lifeless hair into a knot on the top of her head. She knew she was far from a glamorous "before" picture but hoped that the "after Marcee" would, at the very least, keep Brent from running in the opposite direction. A 45-minute call to her mother calmed her down just before there was a knock on the door.

"How'd you get through the front gate?" she asked, surprised that Jordan had shown up without having to call for a buzz-in.

"Your neighbor Sherry was outside walking her rat-poodle, so she let me in."

"She should be careful," Marcee replied. "I heard a rumor that Candy Spelling once had a doorman at *her* building fired because he let Tori up to the penthouse unannounced."

"Um, Mar, have you taken a look around?" he teased. "You don't even have a secure lock let alone concierge personnel."

"Give me a bagel and some of that coffee," she said, grabbing the carrying tray of breakfast goodies. "We need to sit down and map out today's strategy."

"What's to figure out? We'll go get manicures and finish at Paint Dry for your makeup and hair. You've had all of your flaps and folds waxed, right?" Jordan sounded certain that she'd already attended to her bikini line.

"Waxing? Why?"

"What happens if Brent gets a little frisky after dinner?" he asked. "You don't want him to feel like he's on the Jungle Cruise."

"I highly doubt that he's going to want to see me naked, and I would never go that far on a first date anyway." Marcee was resolute, as though she'd had to fend off many lecherous men in her extremely limited romantic experience.

"Whatever; you still need to tend to your lady garden," he continued. "It'll make you feel better, trust me, and, should your skirt come off, I'm sure he'd rather see a few red bumps than too much grass on the lawn. Is there a decent aesthetician you use around here?"

"I usually go to Cindy at Bright Eyes & Bushy Tails on Van Nuys," she said. "The technique they use is really big in Japan."

"Right, well, so are David Hasselhoff and Alyssa Milano's singing careers, but let's forget about that. Did you just say *Bushy Tails*?" He laughed. "That is the best name ever. I love a man with a nice bushy tail."

"First, ew, and second, my hunch is that the few men you'll see leaving there have fairly smooth asses."

"Do they bleach buttholes, too? I'm asking for a 'friend.'"

"Shut up, Jordan," Marcee said, taking her coffee and keys from the kitchen table. "Let's go so we can be back by 5:30PM. Brent is picking me up at 7PM; I want to make sure my outfit looks perfect before he gets here."

They raced to the Studio City Nail Terrace, where she opted for a neutral pink gel color, and then worked their way back toward Sherman Oaks for some hair removal. By the time Marcee and Jordan arrived at Paint Dry for her 3PM makeup and blowout, everything but her head had been clipped, oiled, stripped and plucked.

"Do you want to put a smock on?" the receptionist asked. "We can get you washed while Ambrosia finishes up with her previous client."

"Ambrosia?" Jordan whispered as he walked with Marcee to a changing room. "Is she a hairstylist or a pole dancer at the Hot Pants Lounge?" He helped her change into a neon pink cape and held her T-shirt and bag as they walked toward the sinks.

Marcee began to feel her nerves flare up when she passed a row of adjustable swivel chairs positioned in front of individual lighted vanities. In one after the other was an Aqua Netted blonde or redhead, each looking like she'd stepped off the set of a cable news show. There was either a competition for Best Network Hair or the Mrs. San Fernando Valley Pageant was happening right in that very strip mall.

"Jordan, is it me, or does it look like they do only over-sprayed helmet styles here?" A technician had just finished rinsing and massaging her scalp.

"Yeah, it seems a tiny bit like a B'nai B'rith meeting. Should we bolt and try Blow & Go on Ventura?" Before they had time to reconsider the beauty plan, Ambrosia introduced herself and showed them to an empty seat.

"Nice to meet you," Marcee said, shaking her hand. Ambrosia was a beautiful midtwenties brunette with a modern, layered haircut and large green eyes.

"Ambrosia, as the official gay BFF, I would be remiss if I didn't mention that my friend would like a more relaxed, contemporary style than some of these local bubbies are going for." She winked in understanding and proceeded to give Marcee a supermodel bob that would have made Heidi Klum proud.

"How'd I do?" Ambrosia asked as she turned Marcee to face the mirror. "Is this what you wanted? You have such gorgeous, thick hair; it would be kind of hard to mess it up."

"Oh my God, it's amazing." Marcee was transfixed. "I've never seen it look this good." Jordan, seated on an ottoman a few feet behind Marcee, nodded and flashed a wide grin of approval.

"Just wait until I get to that face with my brushes," she continued. "I hope this is for a date; some guy is going to feel very lucky."

"Actually, it *is* for a date," Marcee replied, smiling with the small amount of pep that the compliment had generated.

"Tell me about him," Ambrosia said, making light conversation while she worked. "Is this the first time you're going out?"

"Yes, it's the dreaded first date. I'm so out of practice." Marcee sighed with a deep exhale. "It's a setup by a mutual friend."

"I assume you've seen pictures of him," Ambrosia said. "What does he look like?"

"He's the Brent Wetherley type," Marcee answered. She turned and shot Jordan a stern look the moment she glanced in the mirror and saw his lips start to move.

"Wow, so this guy must be pretty hot." Ambrosia mixed powders, pigments and creams on her handheld mirrored palette. "Kind of chiseled and smoldering but with a grungy edge?"

"Yep," she said, following Ambrosia's directions to look up, down and sideways for the application of eye shadow and then lashes. "He's really cute."

"Well, you'll look great on his arm." She sprayed a light mist of finisher over Marcee's face, stood in front of the chair to give her work a final quality check and then looked to Jordan for a sign-off.

"Amazing," he said. "Mar, I've never seen you look better."

Marcee stared straight ahead, trying to become familiar with the face she saw in front of her. The spackle and blush had definitely hidden a few imperfections, but, in her mind, they didn't distract enough from the plain face that Brent would be looking into all evening. *Why am I even going through with this?* She didn't move. *What am I thinking? It's all ridiculous.*

"Mar, we gotta get going," Jordan said, putting a hand on her shoulder and breaking her descent down yet another rabbit hole. "It's 5:15PM, and you need to be dressed and ready in the next 90 minutes."

The moment they walked into her apartment, Marcee removed her shirt carefully while Jordan sat on her unmade bed. For half an hour, they considered two black skirts and two potential companion tops.

"We're basically choosing between the same couple of outfits," Jordan said after circular conversations about how Brent might take to a Peter Pan collar more than a traditional style. "You can't go wrong either way, especially considering what an amazing job that girl did on your hair and makeup."

With her knee-length, flared A-line skirt and dark hose, the silver Dior shoes were particularly striking. A simple men's collared button-down, opened to reveal a little cleavage — along with a thin scarf for coverage — completed a classic presentation that was polished and upscale.

"Boo, you look absolutely gorge," he said as she chose a satin clutch from her closet. She transferred her driver's license, some blotting papers, a small amount of cash and some Listerine breath strips into the tiny bag.

"I wish I felt it," she answered. She walked into the bathroom to give herself a last look. "I still don't understand why Brent Wetherley would go for *this* when he could have any girl out there."

"He's the lucky one," Jordan said, giving Marcee a hug as she walked him to the door. "And it's not like this is some random online date you set up through Match.com. Claire has reasons she thinks you two will hit it off. Keep that in mind."

◇◇◇

WHEN MARCEE TOLD Brent she'd meet him in front of her apartment, she didn't expect to find a Prius in Blue Crush Metallic waiting by the curb. She knew from her online research that he supported a variety of environmental causes such as Global Green, but, when he called to say he'd arrived at her building, she figured she'd be stepping into the newest Tesla — and not the basic Model 3.

Her heels were slightly higher than she was used to, so she walked outside slowly and carefully. She took deliberate steps — one foot in front of the other — to avoid a face-first tumble onto the pavement and so as not to scuff the sides and bottoms of her indulgent purchase.

"Those are some hot shoes," Brent opined, walking over to help her down the six steps that led from the entrance of her complex to the sidewalk level. She smiled as he gave her a warm hug, taking her hand and getting her settled in the passenger seat of his Toyota. He was wearing a pair of red skinny jeans and a vintage David Bowie concert tee that predated his birth. His black leather boots — replete with brushed metal side buckles — matched his waist-length, silver-studded jacket. He had obviously grown out his light brown hair, which was pulled back into a short ponytail. Marcee recognized his fresh scent — Jo Malone's English Pear & Freesia, her favorite — which belied his overall style; he had a Johnny-Depp-in-need-of-a-shower hipness yet the smell of a country orchard.

"It's so good to be home," he said. "I don't have to leave town for another 12 weeks."

"It must be hard to be away for months at a time," she responded as he made a U-turn on Dickens and headed toward Coldwater Canyon. "How long does it take you to settle back into your routine after a long work trip?"

"Having two assistants makes it pretty easy," he answered, his eyes on the road. "I can jump back into my LA life without much effort." *Of course he has people who keep things running. Dumb question, Marcee. Step up your game, or this date will be over before it actually begins.* "What kind of music do you like?"

"Embarrassingly, I love a good 80s song," she admitted, "but if you want to know how much of a geek I really am, you should check out my showtunes library." She decided to crack a self-deprecating joke. *Why not tell him you're a nerd before he has the opportunity to think it on his own?* Brent pushed a few buttons on his steering wheel until "Move On" from *Sunday in the Park with George* flowed through his speakers.

"Oh my God, I love Sondheim, not to mention Bernadette Peters and Mandy Patinkin," she enthused, thrilled that he'd picked a song she knew backward and forward. "Are you a Broadway fan, too?"

"A couple of my buddies started a band, and I'm on the mic," he answered. "We take classic theater ballads and rearrange them to sound like gritty, alternative songs."

"So, you guys are like Soundgarden covering tunes from *Cabaret*?" She was trying to wrap her head around the idea of Chris Cornell stumbling through a rendition of "Maybe This Time."

"Exactly!" he yelled, reaching over and grabbing her left hand with excitement. "No one else I've told understands the concept." *I'm sure people understand*, she thought; *they just don't want to hear it.*

"I love the idea," she replied. "I'll be the first to download the album on iTunes."

"An album is so far down the road, but you'll come hear us at the Troubadour next month. We're playing two weekend shows." Marcee had a surge of confidence; he was already planning on being in touch four weeks later. "And, by the way, you haven't asked where we're eating tonight," he said.

"I'm guessing that it's in Beverly Hills since we're more than halfway there," she replied cheerfully.

"Yep, and I hope you brought your appetite." Just like that, her heart fell back into her stomach. Marcee couldn't tell if he was assuming, from her shape, that she was a good eater or if he was merely referencing the amount of food he planned to order. "We're going to Mastro's, my favorite steakhouse." She was very familiar with the LA hot spot; she had yet to dine there herself, but TMZ always featured footage of celebrities such as Tom Cruise and former One Directioner Zayn Malik entering and leaving. "Sound good to you?"

"I've heard the food is delicious," she answered, "and I'm always up for something new."

"I'm glad you haven't been there," he added. "I love introducing people to my favorite hangouts."

As they pulled up to the valet on Canon Drive, one attendant opened Brent's door and another opened Marcee's. They were clearly accustomed to Brent's visits because neither provided a ticket stub.

"Thanks, Bernardo," he called out after his car. "Take care of Martha."

"Martha?" Marcee asked as she and Brent walked under the black awning to the aqua-tinted glass doors at the entrance.

"My car," he answered. "As in, *Who's Afraid of Virginia Woolf?*"

With his hand resting lightly on the small of her back, Brent guided Marcee past the hostess, who nodded with a familiar smile, and showed her to a half booth large enough for six but set for two. He motioned for her to slide into the chocolate-brown leather banquette while he took the middle of the three armless chairs across from her. A column made from exposed, slate-colored bricks separated their table from the others, all of which were closely sandwiched together with an uncomfortable community feel.

"Are you sure you don't mind sitting with your back to the room?" Marcee wanted to make sure that Brent wasn't bothered by one of her own dining-out quirks, even if it had to be at her expense.

"Nope," he replied, "I'm here only to see you." He smiled and reached across the table. She pushed the shrimp and crab cocktail — which he'd obviously been chivalrous enough to preorder — toward him. "I'm not looking for seafood, babe," he said. "Give me your hand." Tentatively, she moved her arm from her lap and put her palm in his. "I'm so glad this is finally happening; I've really been looking forward to it." Disquieted by his undivided and amorous attention, she stared down at the red cocktail sauce to avoid eye contact. Then, at just the right moment, Dorothy Wang approached the table with a voice like a bullhorn.

"Brent Wetherley," she screamed, practically announcing his presence to the entire roomful of Hollywood "definite-lies" and "maybes." "Where have you been hiding?" Dorothy was a Taiwanese-American comedian and wannabe actress whose dry brand of humor had soured on her dwindling audience.

"I've been in Canada shooting a film," he answered, standing up to hug the chubby funny lady. "I just got back last night. And, by the way, this is Marcee Brookes." Dorothy smiled and gave a quick bow of the head. "What are you working on, Dot?"

"I haven't been on stage *or* camera much lately," she replied. "I did a few red carpet commentaries for *Inside Hollywood Tonight,* but the acting parts are all but gone. Haven't you noticed? Roles for Asian women are going to white actresses; Tilda Swinton just got one, and now I hear they're trying to make Scarlett look Chinese. Crazy, right? They could just hire *me* — closer to the real deal — for a fraction of the money."

"It's definitely an industry-wide problem," he lamented in a tone that sounded disingenuously polite. "But if anyone can find a way around it, it's Dorothy Wang. You're a survivor."

"That's for sure; I'm not letting any grass grow under my feet." She looked at Marcee. "I am actually recording an album."

"I didn't realize that you sing," Marcee said, trying to seem interested in Dorothy's sudden career turn.

"Um, yes, I sing," she scoffed, as though the planet should know. "Who is this girl?" she continued, pointing at Marcee and locking eyes with Brent for an answer.

"She's a fantastic woman," he said, "and she has great taste in music."

"Well, she'll be happy to know that I'm simply waiting for word from a *very* notable record label. It's been a while, but no news is good news."

"Not always; sometimes it's bad news that's taking a long time to arrive," he said brusquely, obviously standing up for

Marcee. "I'll wait for you to e-mail me the MP3 tracks if it ever gets released."

"Always nice to see you, Brent." She turned quickly and waddled her squat frame back to an undesirable table at the center of the room.

"Wow, that was a loaded exchange," Marcee commented. "I was just trying to add to the conversation." *I should never open my mouth,* she thought.

"You were perfectly fine," Brent assured her. "She's an oversensitive, bitter has-been who should be happy she can even get a table here."

"How do you know each other?" Marcee asked.

"We met at an Elizabeth Glaser Pediatric AIDS Foundation event a few years ago," he answered. "Mary Lou Retton dropped out, and I guess Dorothy was the closest semi-celeb in terms of size and haircut." He gazed at Marcee adoringly as her laugh forced her to spit out a small amount of the water she'd just sipped. "You have a beautiful smile."

"That's hilarious," she said, touching the corners of her mouth with a dark napkin and talking right over his compliment.

"Speaking of Mary Lou Retton," he continued, "you know that her picture on the original Wheaties box was actually life-size, right?"

They laughed constantly throughout dinner — he ordered for both of them, the most expensive and delicious meats accompanied by Gorgonzola mac and cheese, creamed spinach and green beans — and traded stories about all of the ill-behaved celebrities they'd encountered.

"How did you and Rox become so close," she asked, just as the waiter delivered Mastro's signature warm butter cake and coffee to the table.

"When I was getting started, after a bunch of guest spots on some vapid CW shows, I landed a tiny part in

Eaten Alive; like two lines," he said. "I guess it's the classic story of the big actor taking the baby actor under his wing."

"That's really sweet and *so* not like a Hollywood superstar," she replied, sipping her decaf and sampling one small bite of cake. *If I eat more than a mouthful of dessert, he'll definitely pay attention to my weight.* "I've met him only once, briefly, but Claire and I have become pretty friendly over the last month."

"Claire's my girl," Brent gushed. "She's always looking out for me. Just take this date, for example..."

"What about it?" She flashed a closed-mouth smile that bordered on coy and shook her head lightly backward as though she were auditioning for a Pantene commercial. Marcee felt good about how easily their conversation had flowed throughout the evening, and she loved his biting sense of humor. His fondness for the same SiriusXM channels didn't hurt either.

"She made a good call, didn't she, or am I misreading things?" Brent took her hand, and she did nothing to interrupt his gesture. *OK, I need to call my mom and Jordan right now. I think he's really into this date; I can't believe it.*

"Not at all." Her stomach was in knots but she outwardly stayed the course. "This has been a fantastic evening."

"So, then, while I run to the restroom, look at your calendar." He stood up and took his iPhone out of his pocket. "We'll lock in our next date on the drive home."

As she waited at the table, she quickly texted both her mother and Jordan with the "thumbs up" emoji and scrolled through her e-mails and Facebook page to keep from jumping out of her skin with exhilaration. She slid her phone into her bag as soon as she saw him walking back from the men's room five minutes later.

"Sorry it took so long," Brent said. "There was a line." Marcee always chuckled to herself when people made it clear that they were cued up for a stall and not delayed by the calls of their bowels. God forbid someone cop to a number two in the land of illusions. "Shall we get the car?"

She took her napkin from her lap and placed it on the table and then grabbed her purse as she slid out of the booth. He took her by the hand and walked her to the exit.

No sooner did Brent push open the doors than Marcee was blinded by a sea of popping flashbulbs. All she could hear were the sounds of pushy paparazzi screaming, "Brent, over here," "Brent, who's the girl?" and "Brent, give me that Wetherley pout." None of it was new to her in theory; in fact, her job sometimes required that she help celebrities through similar barrages. This ambush, however, on a night during which she felt particularly vulnerable, rattled her. She put her chin down and moved forward, not meeting the eyes of anyone surrounding her path to the car.

Brent moved his grip from her hand to her arm, intertwining his right elbow with her left. He slowed his walk, smiled, turned at every command and waved to the few looky-loos who were circling the scene. It was clear that he was used to the hubbub.

"Hey, lady, give us some face." The crowd of men with cameras — all wearing black hoodies and grimy pants — yelled similar directives as they moved in on her. She looked up, startled and off-balance, and hustled to the open passenger door as fast as Brent's steps allowed.

The blitzkrieg continued even after she was seated in the car — which, fortunately, the valets had waiting and running. Some overly aggressive photographers attempted to snap shots through the densely tinted glass.

"It's a fact of my life," Brent explained during the drive to Sherman Oaks. "I'm sure this is all old hat to you, being in the business."

"Of course," she said, "it's part of the job, I know." She

didn't want to let on to Brent how unsettling and violating it felt to be screamed at so forcefully by strangers. He reached over and stroked the back of her neck.

"I'm hoping you've put me on the books for this coming Friday night." He looked over at her for a quick moment. "They're doing a concert version of *The King and I* at the Hollywood Bowl, and I love a good picnic." She glanced at him and giggled.

They pulled up in front of her building just as she finished typing their plans into her calendar. Brent quickly got out of the car and rushed to open the door for Marcee. "I had such a fabulous night," he said as he walked her up the steps to the main entryway. It looked as if he was about to move in for an embrace when the glass doors flew open.

"Gibby!" Sherry reprimanded the small scampering dog, even though *she* was the one who had failed to attach the mongrel's leash. "I'm so sorry; she has a mind of her own." Brent reached down and picked up the squirmy, white bundle of fur.

"This must be the naughty Gibby," he said, handing the poodle to Sherry. Marcee was warmed by how Brent managed the intrusion and the fuzzy pet. *Nothing is hotter than a sexy guy tending to a cute animal.*

"Sherry, meet my friend Brent…" She started to introduce her date.

"Oh, I know just who he is; I'm obsessed with him," Sherry raved. "That movie he did with Ryan Gosling and Cate Blanchett? One of my all-time faves. I was on the edge of my seat the whole time, wondering who she'd end up with."

"*Love Comes Third* is some of the best work I've done, so thanks for that, Sherry," Brent answered with a present and charming affect.

"That scene where Cate moves in to kiss Ryan, and you

push him out of the way," she babbled. "I was screaming in the theater."

"It looks like Gibby's legs are crossed," Marcee interjected. "You probably want to get her out to the grass." She was trying to disengage her annoying neighbor as delicately as possible.

"She'll be fine if I hold her." Sherry brushed Marcee off. "What was Ryan Gosling like?"

"He's a great actor," Brent replied politely. "I loved working with him."

"Do you think you'll do a sequel?" Sherry wasn't giving up and neither was Gibby's bladder. The dog began to let out crying squeaks.

"Brent has to be up early for a family event tomorrow, so we should probably let him go," Marcee said. She walked him back to the sidewalk and mouthed, "I'M. SO. SORRY," as Sherry's incessant chatter continued.

"Goodnight, ladies," he said as he got into his car. "I'll speak to you tomorrow, Marcee." And, like that, he was off into the night as quickly as his fuel-efficient car could glide down Dickens.

◇◇◇

"JORDAN, MY FAVORITE golden gay, the date went really well, I think." Marcee called him as soon as she'd placed her shoes into their protective sack.

"I'm your *platinum* gay," he snapped back. "My mother had a C-section. Gold is for the second-tier queens who actually passed through a vagina. And what do you mean, 'I think?' Did he kiss you?"

"We didn't get that far because of fucking Sherry Montesano," she said. "That dumbass busybody decided to walk Gibby just as Brent was saying goodnight — and who knew she'd morph into a sycophantic maniac."

"Ugh, that sucks," he answered. "Did it seem like he *wanted* to kiss you, though?"

"I'm pretty sure he was leaning in for at least a hug, but I don't know for sure. He asked me to go to the Hollywood Bowl with him this coming Friday, so isn't that a good sign?"

"You mean for *The King and I*?" Jordan sounded surprised.

"Yeah, how'd you know?"

"Girl, I've been waiting for that to open in LA since they announced it last season. I bought tickets for the Saturday night performance when they first went on sale; Patrick Stewart is going to rock as the King of Siam."

"Anyway, can we please, please, please focus on me," she begged.

"Mar, if he asked you on a second date, you don't even need my opinion. He clearly likes you enough to spend more time getting to know you."

"Likes me *enough*, or really *likes* me?" She knew it was impossible for anyone to have an actual answer, but she wanted to fall asleep with the security that came from her best friend's unfiltered opinion.

"Of course he really likes you, Mar," Jordan said in a comforting tone. "He'd have no other reason to ask you out again."

11

"BEA TISCHLER JUST saw you on the Google; you better go on your computer right now!" Rhonda sounded joyfully frantic at 6AM.

"Mom, slow down," Marcee groaned, rubbing her eyes and adjusting her pillows before pulling her MacBook Air from a drawer under the bed. She'd had her first full night of sound sleep in months so the discordant ring of the home phone was an unwelcome introduction to Sunday morning.

"You're apparently all over the Worldwide InterWeb," her mother continued. "Bea's daughter Ruby called her from New York about 10 minutes ago to spread the word." Marcee propped herself up and opened the laptop, her pulse racing from zero to one hundred without so much as a warm-up.

"Oh fuck," she gasped. "Did you see Joaquin Richie's site?"

"Honey, you know I can barely send an e-mail without calling an Apple genius for help," Rhonda reminded her. "Who's this Joaquin Richie character?"

"He's, like, the biggest Hollywood blogger on earth." Marcee couldn't believe that she was explaining Joaquin's cultural relevance to anyone living in 2017 — or that she was seeing herself splashed across his home page. "He has pictures of me, arm in arm with Brent, leaving Mastro's last night, and the headline says, 'A NEW ROMANCE FOR HOLLYWOOD HOTTIE BRENT WETHERLEY.'"

"I take it that the date ended well," her mom replied. "I'll have to tell the Frankels and the Weisbergs to look online. It's so exciting."

Marcee quickly navigated among all of the big gossip outlets — *TMZ, Radar Online*, the *Daily Mail*; her date with Brent was the top story on each of them. "Mom, I'll call you a little later with details about last night, but I have to talk to Jordan immediately." She dialed his cell, never mind that it was only 6:20AM. Hadn't he told her just the day before that this type of breaking news was exactly why he left his phone on at all hours?

"Bae, this better be fucking good," he answered. His voice had the raspy timbre of dawn.

"Girl, what do you do with all of the time you save?"

"What are you talking about?" He sounded groggy.

"Dropping the second 'b' from 'babe' is really efficient. Cumulatively, it probably adds a good hour back into your day."

"Listen, struggle bitch, if you're calling just to throw shade on my style, do it after lunch," he said. "I need to sleep for another six hours — at the very least."

"OK, OK, kidding aside, you need to go on *Joaquin Richie* right now."

"If he scooped me on a story again, I'm going to need shock therapy to calm down." She heard the 'ding' of his computer firing up. "*Variety* will kill me if I don't start beating these other sites to the punch with exclusive articles."

"Well," she answered, "you missed one that was right under your nose."

"Fuck me!" he screamed, clearly having discovered

exactly what she was talking about. "You're the lead piece. I need to post about this right away."

"No!" she shouted. "I don't want it in the trade magazines."

"Um, Mar, the photos have already been sold to tons of outlets," he shot back. "It's not like I'm posting something that the rest of cyberspace hasn't already seen."

"But none of them has my name."

"That's just a matter of time," he pointed out. She knew he played the gossip game better than anyone else. "And it's the very least you can do for me. Help a sister out, will you?"

"Ugh, fine." She gave in. "But remember this crumb I tossed your way when I need you to run something about Luminary next week."

"'Crumb' is an overstatement," Jordan said. "More like a speck. Someone is going to ID you in the comment sections of these articles anyway, if he or she hasn't already. I gotta go so I can get this posted right away. Bye, Felicia."

"You better dial me right back," she groused. "I called to discuss the pictures with you, not give you a hot tip so you can generate web traffic." He had hung up before she'd finished talking.

She sifted through the media coverage of her date, enlarging every photo and studying her expressions and angles. *I look like a sad-sack moose.* She always told celebrities to keep their chins out and pointed slightly downward, and here *she* was doubling for Kim Jong-un. She worried that Brent might want to cancel their second date if he paid even the smallest amount of attention to the images. For the next three hours, she sat in the sanctuary of her bedroom and clicked through all of the trashy, muckraking pages that turned up in a search for Brent's name. She stopped only to answer Claire's call at 10AM.

"I see somebody's date with Brent went well, or at least it says so on *Entertainment Tonight*'s website," she began without so much as a "Good morning."

"Hi, Claire," Marcee chirped. "I had a really great time, but, for some reason, I didn't think about the paparazzi ahead of time. I should have realized that he'd wind up in the press the minute he mentioned Mastro's."

"It could have happened wherever you two went together." Marcee knew Claire was right; the cockroaches of entertainment journalism were known to crawl out from beneath any surface — sometimes even at dive spots in areas like Reseda. "It goes with the territory. Plus, all of the pictures are cute."

"You really think so?" Marcee asked. "I was afraid that I looked like a pudge pop."

"Don't be ridiculous," Claire went on. "You guys look adorbs together."

"I hope he had as much fun as I did," she said, dying — but not daring — to ask if he'd reported anything to Claire. Brent had yet to reach out to Marcee since dropping her off the night before, sending bursts of doubt and insecurity from her stomach to her chest.

"I haven't heard a peep from him, but I'll text in a little bit," Claire said. "He's a late sleeper, so he's probably still passed out. In the meantime, though, I wanted to know if you're free this afternoon. Claudia and a couple of Rox's friends are coming to hang out by the water, and I thought maybe you'd want to join. We need to hear all about your evening."

Marcee was relieved to know that Brent's sleeping pattern was likely responsible for his silence and flattered that Claire and Claudia were so interested. "Actually, my day is completely free. What time were you thinking?"

"Just throw on a bathing suit and head over when you

can," she said. "No need to bring anything else; we have food, cocktails, towels and sunscreen. Sarah's working this weekend, so just message her when you're at the front gate."

Shit. Me in a swimsuit in front of those women? Oy.

Marcee put on a clear shower cap that she'd lifted from a Las Vegas hotel and raced into the shower with the confidence of an Olympic runner ready to cross the finish line. *I'm getting a second day out of this blow-dry,* she thought as she considered how her outlook had brightened in only 24 hours. The morning before, she was drowning in a mineral bath of despair, and one day later, she had both the start of a flashy romance *and* an invitation to a private beach party at Claire's house.

She dried herself and applied a light dusting of makeup before stepping into a black, vintage one-piece bathing suit that was generous enough to hide her hips. To a sarong skirt tied around her waist, she added a dark, crocheted cover-up to the outfit — along with a pair of grey Havaianas flip-flops — and topped it all with a wide-brim, floppy hat. Marcee was Four Seasons-ready on a Marriott budget because, even at a size that made her self-conscious, she learned early from her mother that one couldn't live in sunny Los Angeles without affordable, figure-appropriate cabana-wear.

She drove to Nothing Bundt Cakes, a bakery with a delicious, albeit limited, menu, and picked up one of her favorite treats — a dark chocolate round with fudge frosting — in a size large enough to serve a party of 10. She didn't want to arrive at Claire's house empty-handed and figured also that the ladies might want to indulge in something sweet on a lazy Sunday. For a few extra dollars, she had fake flowers and colored ornaments added to the icing and then asked that the dessert be boxed for travel. She placed it on the passenger-side floorboard, securing it next to her canvas tote in order to prevent a double-fudge disaster if she was forced to stop short.

It was 11:45AM by the time she was on her way to Point Dume, and the volume of her car stereo was cranked. She loved the Motels — Martha Davis's raw vocals recalled the other musical artists she admired — but "Only the Lonely" didn't seem as appropriate for the ride to Malibu as it had on her way home from work that previous Thursday. "Suddenly Last Summer," though, was a beat she could get behind. She skipped ahead on the *No Vacancy* album and increased her speed by 12 miles per hour. *So what that Topanga Canyon is whip-winding enough to make even a golf cart difficult to control?* Feeling invincible and a little bit reckless, she made it to the PCH within a half hour and then to Claire's house only 15 minutes later. Sarah, her hair up in a tight bun, was waiting outside for Marcee when she pulled up.

"How are you?" Sarah asked, hugging her as soon as she stepped out of the car and taking the cake from her hands. "Sorry, there's no staff other than me today, so I'll show you in."

"I didn't realize that you work on weekends," Marcee said. "I was surprised when Claire mentioned that you'd be here."

"I'm taking a couple of days off this coming week to get some of my own errands done." Sarah looked exhausted. "Today is all about organizing Claire and Rox in preparation for my mini-staycation."

"Do you want to come by the studio for lunch while you're off from work?" Marcee realized they hadn't scheduled the get-together that they'd talked about weeks before.

"I can do Thursday, if that works for you," she said, suddenly livelier following the suggestion of a meal together.

"Yep, that should be good," Marcee replied, knowing

that her week was fairly open. "Consider it booked." As she went to put the appointment in her phone, she noticed that she had 20 text messages, 12 voicemails, 87 unread e-mails, 10,000 newly hatched Twitter followers and more Facebook friend requests than she had actual friends — all since Jordan's column item had gone live an hour earlier. "Holy shit."

"What's wrong?" Sarah looked concerned. "Don't worry if Thursday isn't the best day for you; we can plan something another time."

"No, Thursday is fine, but my phone is blowing up with messages." Marcee, overwhelmed by the unusual amount of cellular activity, closed the protective, faux-leather case and put it at the bottom of her bag.

"That's not surprising," Sarah said nonchalantly as she walked Marcee through the house to the shoreline in the back. "Especially after all of the play you got on the Internet this morning." Sarah said nothing more about the date or Brent.

The moment they stepped onto the sand, Marcee heard Claire call to her from an outdoor lounge area that was staged with plush resort furniture. "Brookes, get your ass out here." She didn't look up from her chaise; neither did Claudia or the two buff, shirtless men lying next to her.

Sarah handed the cake back to Marcee so she could present it to the hostess herself. "You have fun," she said in a whisper. "I'll be in the back office. Text me if you need anything."

Marcee started to walk toward the group just as a toddler dashed between her legs, seemingly out of nowhere. Already a bit wobbly on the uneven, damp sand, she lost her hold on the box, the cake hurtling downward like a lead weight.

"Sriracha! What did you do?" A perfectly fit Ken doll

got up from his chair, running toward Marcee and the now-crying child. He scooped up the blubbering, diaper-clad tot from the ground. "You tell the nice lady that you're very, very sorry," he instructed in a singsong lilt, as though the whole incident had been a game.

"Not to worry," Marcee replied, secretly upset that Donna Summer's prophecy had materialized: it, indeed, looked as though someone had left the cake out in the rain. "It's probably better on the floor than it is on my thighs anyway," she said, laughing, as she tried to brush off the embarrassing incident and move on.

"Sriracha is going through the terrible twos; I'm Mark Benitez-Mason, by the way." She recognized him from TV the moment he leaned in to give her a friendly hug.

"I love the name Sriracha," she said, trying to distract Mark's attention from the blob of chocolate splattered all over her calves and feet.

"Thank you; my better half and I love it, too," he said proudly. "It's unique and spicy, just like our little girl." He clutched the child to his chest, his armband tattoo — obviously designed to look like barbwire — resting next to her reddened eyes and tear-stained cheeks.

Mark and Tommy Benitez-Mason were the Style Network's biggest stars. Their home makeover shows, including *Decorator Wars* and *The Great Clutter Cleanse*, were long-running cable hits, and their line of cleaning supplies was at the center of a multibillion dollar business. In fact, Marcee knew that her mother lived by their MotorMop, a revolutionary gadget that was available exclusively at Target and on QVC. Both men were tanned, expertly groomed and so handsome that their average female viewer overlooked the fact that they were banging each other in hopes that they'd sweep her off her spotless linoleum. Sriracha Louise was their miracle embryo, as featured in *OK!* magazine; Mark provided the sperm, and Tommy's sister offered the egg and the oven. Marcee remembered reading about the ridiculously gorgeous duo and their modern-day family a couple of years prior.

"Enough about Baby Hot Sauce," Claire yelled, "it's time to relax in the sun." Marcee walked over and kissed the ladies hello, introducing herself to Mark's husband.

"Nice to meet you," Tommy smiled. "I apologize for our daughter; I'm sure the cake would have been delicious."

"Don't give it a second thought," she said, even though she couldn't stop thinking about the $40 she would have saved if she'd just regifted a bottle of wine from her stash at home. "I'm just going to rinse my feet off at the edge of the water. I'll be back in a minute." She walked onto the beach and cleaned the remnants of chocolate off her skin before settling into the one empty seat beside Claire.

"You're so covered up." Claudia looked Marcee over. "Do you always wear so much when you're sitting outside?" She took a sip of vodka straight out of one of eight mini-bottles that were sitting on the glass table next to her chair.

"I know it gets cold at the water sometimes, so I prepared," she answered. Marcee had checked the projected temperatures and knew that it would be a comfortable 70 degrees all day. But even if it were 110, she would have wrapped herself like a mummy to conceal her bulges.

"Forget the outfit," Claire interrupted. "It's not worth discussing. What I *do* want to hear about is your night with Brent."

"Who's Brent?" Although Tommy seemed to be lying peacefully in a *Baywatch*-red speedo and Gucci sunglasses, he clearly wanted in on the chat.

"Brent Wetherley," Claire replied. "I set him up with Marcee; their first date was last night."

"He's so sexy; I'd love to get my hands on him." Tommy stayed in position, not even moving his head to look at the women.

"You and Mark would love to get your hands on any man with a nice package in his pants," Claudia said. "Do you two still bring other guys into your bedroom?"

"Not always; sometimes we just fuck them right on the kitchen counter." Tommy smiled. "The more the merrier." It was obvious that he enjoyed baiting the ladies.

"Would you consider your relationship to be open?" Claire asked.

"Yeah, we give each other free passes here and there, but since Sriracha came along, things have slowed down."

"Children *will* ruin your life," Claire commented.

"Speaking of which, where are your beautiful twins?" Marcee inquired.

"They're having a weekend sleepover at Marcia Gay Harden's house. Out of my hair, hallelujah."

"And when does Rox get back from Vancouver?" Marcee continued.

"Oh, he's back. His shoot wrapped early; he wound up coming home on Friday night," Claire said. "He was supposed to hang out with all of us today, but, at the last minute, he was talked into attending some fundraising brunch in Brentwood."

Mark returned to the gathering with Sriracha, who was now wearing a *Dora the Explorer* two-piece. "Someone is changed and fresh," he announced as he made googly eyes, holding up his daughter like she was Simba from *The Lion King*. "Did I miss anything?"

"We were just talking about how much you and Tommy like to have extramarital sex," Claudia answered. She poured the last of her miniature liquors into the tumbler of iced tea she was holding.

"Don't say that stuff in front of the baby," Mark snapped. "Who knows what she might pick up."

"She's two, for the love of Jesus," Claudia slurred. "Measles and chickenpox are about the only things you have to worry about. Maybe lice, but she has an alarmingly small amount of hair anyway."

"How did this conversation degenerate so quickly?" Claire sat cross-legged in a blue string bikini. "Can we please get back to the date with Brent?"

"It was fantastic," Marcee said. "We have so much in common — from our senses of humor to music to the kinds of food we like."

"I knew you two would click." Claire picked up her phone. "I'm texting him now for a report."

"He asked me to go to the Hollywood Bowl with him this Friday; I hope that means he had a good time." Marcee didn't want to assume anything.

"For *The King and I* concert?" Tommy asked. "Mark and I are going, too. We can't wait."

"Yes!" Marcee exclaimed. "How did everyone but me know about that event?"

"When Miley Cyrus and Patrick Stewart are starring in a Rodgers and Hammerstein musical, how could anyone *not* know about it?" Mark shook his head in seeming disbelief.

"Marcee, Brent just wrote back," Claire blurted excitedly. "I quote: 'You done good, Claire Madison. She's awesome. Can't wait to see her on Friday. Big smooch.'"

"I could fucking barf." Claudia stared blankly at the water.

"Don't pay any attention to that sagging snatch; she's bitter because she's no longer Mrs. Erickson," Claire said. "Nick's new young girlfriend gets the backstage passes now." She turned her head to Claudia and narrowed her eyes. "It doesn't feel good to be on the outside of the red ropes, does it?"

Marcee took no offense to Claudia's comment; she was fairly certain that it was the alcohol talking. And if she paid any attention to the drunk ramblings of a jilted Hollywood wife, she wouldn't be able to focus on the text that Brent had sent to Claire. "He used the word 'awesome,' huh?"

"You *are* awesome," Claire maintained. She held up her water and clinked Marcee's bottle of Snapple lemonade. Marcee breathed easier knowing that he and Claire had connected and that he was as enthusiastic about the date as she was. Sure, it would have been nice to hear it from the horse's mouth, but she felt good knowing that they shared a similar sentiment, no matter how the news arrived.

As the sun moved throughout the afternoon, Mark and Tommy adjusted the four pole umbrellas to keep everyone cool and protected from the damaging ultraviolet rays. The gang gabbed, laughed and picked from the elaborate cheese board that Claire had set out. It was a quintessential Sunday at the Malibu shore — except with better food and more interesting people. *I could get used to this,* Marcee thought.

"Well, I'm sorry we missed Rox, but we have to head back to West Hollywood," Mark said. He and Tommy gathered the water toys that were strewn around and said their goodbyes. They exchanged phone numbers and e-mail addresses with Marcee, as if there would ever be future contact.

"And, as much as I would like to stay longer, I need to get home, too." Marcee didn't want to close down the party or wear out her welcome. "I have work in the morning." She bent down to hug Claire and then Claudia.

"OK, party poopers," Claire said. "Sarah will let you out, and we'll do this again in a few weeks. Marcee, make sure you let me know how everything goes on Friday."

"Of course," Marcee said before following Sarah through the living room and out the front door. She shook as much sand off of herself as possible before stepping inside her immaculate car and then blew a goodbye kiss in Sarah's direction. With her window lowered, she slowly pulled away from the curb. "I'll see you Thursday," she called out. She speed-dialed Jordan as soon as she was out of view.

"OK, so you're never going to believe my afternoon," she said.

"Slow your roll, child," he replied, stopping her mid-thought. "Did you see the story I posted for *Variety*?"

"Not yet, but I know everyone else did," she answered. "My phone has been en fuego all day."

"What are people saying?" he asked.

"I haven't looked at any of my messages because I've been at Claire's house having a beach day with Claudia Erickson and those gay husbands from HGTV."

"Wait, what? Mark and Tommy? I'm obsessed with them." Jordan screeched as though he were a 12-year-old girl. "I would kill to be in the middle of that *man*wich."

"Well, there's hope for you." Marcee giggled. "They like to have men over for threesomes, and they're in an open relationship."

"They told you all of this over lunch?" He sounded shocked. "How does something like that even come up?"

"Just by chatting during the day," she replied, feeling in the know. "They had their little daughter with them, too. Can you believe her name is Sriracha?"

"Oh my God, yes," he said, laughing. "I remember hearing that on their *Fathers Know Best* special. I bet that little one could beat up Blue Ivy, Apple, Pax *and* Willow with one leg tied behind her back."

"I feel kind of bad to make fun of the kid's name," she said. "They seem like really nice people."

"Whatever, they named their baby after a condiment. That's hilarious, whether they're nice or not."

"On another subject, I'm worried about work tomorrow," Marcee said. After a weekend of mostly emotional highs, she was concerned about how her colleagues — and Phyllis — might react to her moment in the spotlight.

"Why? You'll be the talk of the office. Do you know how many women would kill to be in your Diors?"

◇◇◇

MARCEE HADN'T BEEN at her desk for more than one minute before two of the department assistants, including Lila and her favorite junior publicist, Addie, were standing in the doorway.

"How come you never mentioned that you were going out with Brent Wetherley?" Lila asked. "That's totally major, major, major."

"You know I don't usually talk about personal stuff," Marcee answered.

"I can't believe you kept it a secret for this long." Addie was full of energy for a Monday. "We literally had lunch about a week ago. How were you able to sit on this? I would have been telling anyone who'd listen."

"I guess I was still trying to process it," Marcee explained. "At the time, it seemed like some bizarre dream. You know, one of those fantasies where a basic girl gets swept off her feet by a rock star or a billionaire businessman."

"Brent Wetherley is definitely a fantasy guy, but don't underestimate yourself." Addie had been Marcee's biggest cheerleader at the office since she'd started working for Luminary five years earlier. "He's lucky to have met such a great girl."

"Was Saturday your first date?" Lila inserted herself again; she was known for being the town crier and asked questions accordingly.

"It was," Marcee answered, trying to decide whether to reveal that another one had already been set.

Lila beat her to the punch. "Will there be a second? I mean, *Variety* made it sound like you two are an item." *Fucking Jordan.*

"We'll see," Marcee replied playfully, "but all signs point to yes."

"Do you all need a water cooler to stand around?" Phyllis broke through the crowd that was now assembled inside and around Marcee's office. "It's hard to imagine that, by 9:30AM on a Monday, there isn't enough work for all of you to be doing. But, if that's the case, I could probably make do with a smaller staff." The mob disbanded immediately, scattering to far corners of the ninth floor before the Wicked Witch of Burbank could set her beady eyes on them.

"Good morning, Phyllis," Marcee said, the entire corridor now cleared of every other breathing human. "How was your weekend?" She tried her best to sound business as usual.

"About the weekend," she answered, "I think we're due for another little chat in my office. Why don't you finish whatever bit of work I interrupted and be at my desk in five minutes." Phyllis turned sharply and left the room.

Marcee started to panic; confrontations with her terror of a boss were so nerve-wracking and uncomfortable. She could feel her neck and shoulders tense up, a reflex that had become innate after toiling under such a bitch for so long. She took a few deep breaths and then, in a moment of clarity, remembered what Jill Andrews had said in reference to Phyllis during their impromptu chat that past week: "Don't worry about whatever she says to you; I'll make sure Ken has your back." *Well, I've got Jill and Ken on my side; that's a winning ticket right there. I might as well get this over with.* She swallowed a gulp of iced coffee and walked into Phyllis's den.

"Close the door please," Phyllis instructed, turning in her chair, "and have a seat." Marcee braced herself for attack. "I'd like to know what *you* think makes you a valuable asset to my department."

"Well, all of my work is done correctly and on time," Marcee began tentatively. "Also, I get along with the internal staff, and I'm well liked by filmmakers." Her professional prowess was the one attribute that gave her confidence, but Phyllis's predatory glare was eating away at it.

"And do you honestly believe that those are what represent a path to success in *this* business? *I'm* sitting in the corner office, and none of the items on your list was ever important to *me*." Phyllis looked down at her nails and then back at Marcee. "The key is playing the game properly, and, sadly, befriending Jill Andrews was a grave misstep."

"Yes, Phyllis, we talked about that last Thursday," Marcee answered. "I wasn't proactive in seeking her out, as I explained. It just sort of happened."

"Aligning yourself with the wife of the studio chairman could be your downfall, especially if their marriage is as tenuous as I hear." Marcee wasn't sure if Phyllis already knew something or was fishing for information.

"I don't know much about their relationship," Marcee replied. "We're not as close as you think."

"Let it suffice to say that vegans don't eat meat, and Ken is known to spend his extracurricular time with young women who do. Do you understand what I'm saying?" Phyllis's not-so-delicate euphemism made Marcee feel like throwing up; the thought of an aspiring female executive or starlet on her knees, sucking an old man's penis, was nauseating. "If they wind up on the outs and things get nasty, it would be nearly impossible for me to employ one of Jill's confidants."

"I appreciate that you're looking out for me," Marcee replied, trying to sound sincere. "I'll make sure, in the future, that I think things through more carefully." She bit her tongue so hard that she was surprised blood didn't drip from her mouth.

"Along those lines, do you care to explain your romance with Brent Wetherley?" Between her right thumb and index finger, Phyllis held up a printout of Jordan's *Variety* article as though it were a piece of rotting trash.

"I wouldn't call it a romance," Marcee said in an attempt to downplay the situation. "Claire Madison wanted to set us up on a date; I thought I was doing the right thing by going along with it."

"You're obviously aware that Brent is starring in one of our upcoming holiday films," Phyllis replied. "Do you think that you might be bending a little too far backward to please our actors?" Marcee's face turned red at the sexual implication, especially since she hadn't even kissed Brent. "Not to mention, you called in sick on Friday but were clearly well enough to be photographed in Beverly Hills 24 hours later."

"Um, well, I..." Marcee stammered. Phyllis was indeed a raging pit bull, but she had, in fact, caught Marcee skipping school.

"You *what*? Go on, I'm listening." Phyllis raised her voice. "You needed the day off to choose some clothes from Goodwill?" She picked up the copy of the *New York Post* that was siting on her desk and opened it to "Page Six." "It seems like Friday was all about bad judgment," she said, pointing to a large black-and-white photo of Marcee holding hands with Brent.

"Phyllis, I apologize. I don't know what else to say."

Marcee realized that she had to cop to the crime. "I made a mistake."

"*A* mistake? As in *one*," she continued, brushing her extensions off her jacket. "Why would you ever show so much of your legs? That skirt alone is a felony. You make Diane Keaton look like a sharp dresser."

Marcee did everything she could to hold back the tears that were beginning to well in her eyes. "Again, I'm so sorry I wasn't honest about Friday. It'll never happen again."

"I'll certainly never *trust* you again, that's for sure," Phyllis growled. "And I will absolutely not be counting on you for fashion or beauty advice." She handed Marcee yet another tabloid page that featured a paparazzi photo. "Did you even glance in a mirror before you left your house looking like *this*?"

Marcee fidgeted in her seat, searching for a piece of art or something just outside the window to focus on. If her body had to be in the room, she could at least try to let her mind go elsewhere.

"I can't imagine that Brent actually wanted to take you outside once he saw you." Phyllis appeared to be studying the pictures on her desk like they were courtroom evidence. "Or maybe he sees you as charity work."

"If that's everything, Phyllis, I'm going to get back to my office," Marcee said in almost a stutter; she was about to break down.

"You might as well go ahead and pour yourself into your job," Phyllis said loudly enough for anyone in the immediate vicinity to hear. "Brent Wetherley is not interested in some past-her-prime oinker with the personality of peeling wallpaper."

Marcee stood quickly and hurried out. She held her hands in front of her face so no one would see the tears as she raced to the emergency exit stairwell. The sound of her crying echoed against the concrete steps while she practically flew down nine flights. She'd tried so hard to stay calm, but the Hollywood animal had ultimately crushed her spirit to pieces.

As soon as she made it outside, the daylight caught her in its net, slowing her speed. She inhaled the fresh air and then exhaled with long, exaggerated breaths. She walked to a landscaped area between her building and the adjacent production offices, taking a seat on a wooden bench. She used her left sleeve to dry her eyes and stared ahead for a few minutes at the tranquil greenery.

Marcee reached for the cell phone in her side pocket and started to dial. "Hey, are you sitting down? You won't believe what just happened."

12

MARCEE FELL AGAINST the door and dropped her purse to the ground the second she saw that her office had been packed up. Everything but her desk phone and computer was securely wrapped in protective paper or bubble-wrap and boxed neatly in organized stacks. *I can't believe this is happening,* she thought. She sat on the floor, legs straight forward like a battered rag doll, while the shock crashed on her shoulders as though it were molten lava. The heat moved past her chest and into her stomach; she closed her eyes and threw her head backward. *My life is ruined; I'll never work again.*

Marcee had never been fired from a job. In fact, other than by Phyllis Van Buren — who was notorious for reprimanding even the office goldfish — she hadn't gotten so much as a sideways glance from a previous supervisor.

Marcee was in early, as usual, so there was no one around to deliver the seemingly obvious news. After 10 years as a revered publicist at Luminary, had Phyllis actually pulled the rug out from under her? Before she could make heads or tails of anything, a burly man from the studio facilities department appeared.

"I'm really sorry," he said. "We were told to have this finished before business hours, so I figured I had until 9AM."

"Yeah, well, being the early bird doesn't always get you

the worm," she muttered, closing her eyes again as though it would somehow transport her right out of the building. "Do you need my address? I assume you'll deliver the boxes to my apartment." Marcee looked up at Dominic, whose name she could now see embroidered on his filling-station shirt.

"I was given specific instructions," he replied, "so I'll have to call my boss about transporting property off the lot."

"It's *my* property," she said, "and I'm certainly not going to be able to carry it all to my car in less than 25 trips."

"I'll move everything as I was told and then we can figure the rest out later, OK?" He looked confused.

"Where are you storing my things for the time being?" Marcee, even in her disbelief about the whole situation, wanted to know where her possessions were headed for the day.

"I was asked to take everything from room #9-1010 to room #9-104."

Room #9-104? Marcee used her hands to push herself up from the industrial-grade carpet. *Why are my personal things going to Phyllis's corner suite?* Bewildered and growing furious, she began to walk through the halls, poking around in her bag for her phone.

As she stepped inside Phyllis's office, her jaw dropped. The space had been emptied entirely and vacuumed, the smell of Lysol and carpet cleaner permeating the room. She had no time to make sense of the situation before Dominic walked in, carrying two of her boxes.

"My instructions were to leave these packed cartons in this office," he said. "If you decide you want specific items delivered to your apartment, I'll need to get permission."

"I think there's some misunderstanding," she answered, still perplexed. She sat down on one of the guest chairs and looked out the window. *What is happening?* She nearly jumped out of her seat when her phone rang, startled as though she were in a horror movie waiting for the killer to be in touch again. *When a Stranger Gets Fired.*

"Honey, I tried to reach you earlier." Jill's voice was perky; she'd probably already done two runs and whipped up a vegan breakfast, all by dawn.

"My phone was on silent until I walked into work," Marcee said. "So sorry."

"About work," Jill continued. "There have been a couple of changes."

"Um, yeah," Marcee stumbled, "I walked in 20 minutes ago, and, well…"

"I was so shaken by your phone call yesterday morning," Jill interrupted, "and I couldn't help but talk to Ken about it."

"Oh God, no. Am I being let go? I didn't mean to cause problems between the two of you." *Did I make the wrong decision? Fuck, I shot myself in the head.*

"Let go? What are you talking about?" Jill answered. "You've been promoted to executive vice president of corporate communications and publicity, effective immediately. Phyllis, on the other hand, has been relocated to an itty-bitty office on the other side of the lot while she job hunts. She can also write the press release about her own departure."

"Wait, what?" Marcee's ears started to ring; if she'd been standing, she would have lost her balance.

"She can draft something about how she's moving to Northern California to take care of a sick relative or that she has plans to start a consulting firm. You know, one of those transparent excuses that communications executives spin when they get shit-canned."

"I understood what you meant about the press release, but I'm still trying to wrap my head around what all of this means." Marcee moved from the guest chair to one of the four couches.

"It means that I convinced Ken to give you a gigantic promotion, and you'd better live up to the hype," Jill said, laughing. "In all seriousness, though, Ken has always hated Phyllis; I'm not a fan either, as you know. Once you told me that she was questioning my marriage, she was as good as Cobblestone Mill toast."

"And this happened all in one day?" Marcee was dumbfounded.

"Nothing takes more than a call when you're married to the man who runs the studio," Jill answered. "Anyhow, I have a million things to do, so you settle in and then get your ass in gear. Ken will want to meet with you in the next week to go over his expectations."

"Jill, I don't know what to say. I'm so overwhelmed right now."

"Don't thank me," Jill replied. "I presented a problem and suggested a solution. That simple. Oh, and I want to hear about the whole Brent Wetherley thing, so let's try to grab coffee when I'm at the studio next." She hung up before Marcee could say another word.

Within a couple of hours, Marcee set up her new office, and the IT department had her computer and phone line transferred and functioning. When staff members started to trickle in, she was seated behind her new desk talking to her mother.

"Are you telling me that Phyllis got the boot and you have her job now?" Rhonda was as shocked as her daughter.

"It sounds too good to be true," Marcee said, "but I'm pretty sure that's what just happened."

"See, I knew how invaluable a relationship with Claire would be," Rhonda gloated in her best "I told you so" voice. "Those TTT women have done a lot for you."

Marcee heard a knock. "Mom, I have to run," she said, turning around in her chair to find Addie standing in the doorway. "I'll call you on my way home."

"What the hell happened? Is this for real?" Addie threw her arms around Marcee. "I'm thrilled that a house finally fell on Phyllis, but I'm more excited about who lives in it."

"I'm still stunned, to be honest," Marcee admitted. "I keep waiting for some reality show producer to walk in and tell me I'm on an episode of *Joke's on You.*"

"You had no idea this was in the works?" Addie asked. "Since your dating life exploded in the media, nothing would surprise me. You're good at keeping things close to the vest, clearly."

"I had absolutely no clue," Marcee replied. "I found out about two hours ago. Can you even?"

"Well, no one deserves it more," Addie said, hugging Marcee again. "As a single mom trying to build a career, you give me some hope."

"You certainly work hard for the money," Marcee said, smiling to herself. "And, hey, maybe *my* new opportunity will create one for *you.* You never know, right?"

"I'm going to leave you to get adjusted; let me know if you need anything." Addie walked out just as Ben Paull appeared at the entrance to Marcee's new office.

"Does the executive vice president have time for a lowly schlepper from the legal department?" He flashed a broad grin and closed the door behind him.

"Well, well, well," Marcee said, walking over to give Ben a friendly peck on the cheek. "I think this is the first time that *you've* come to *me.*"

"You outrank me now," he answered. "So, it's protocol."

"How'd you find out about this so quickly?" Marcee questioned.

"Are you kidding? Everyone hates Phyllis Van Buren so

much that news of her demise ripped through the studio like a blaze."

"I should have figured," Marcee said, laughing. "So, you're here to congratulate me?" She smirked, fluttered her eyes and sat behind her desk.

"Sure," he answered, "and to find out about this new boyfriend of yours. I read all about your date in the papers."

"I wouldn't exactly call him my boyfriend yet," she said, glancing at her computer monitor to find one congratulatory e-mail after another popping onto her screen.

"When are you seeing him next?" he asked.

"He's taking me to the Bowl this Friday night." Marcee watched Ben's face go blank.

"That's great," he said, sounding less than enthusiastic. "I'm sure it'll be a nice time. And maybe you'll make weekend headlines again."

"Your sincere good wishes are appreciated," she teased, staring him right in the eyes.

"You know I want you to be happy," he said. "I get nervous with these Hollywood people, though. They're always up to something."

"First of all, let's not go down that road again," she said, cutting him off quickly. "And you *are* one of those Hollywood people."

"I'm an attorney who *happened* to get a job at a studio," he insisted. "I could be just as satisfied at a law firm or a bank."

"I see," Marcee said. "That's good to know. I'll keep my eye on the job boards at Wells Fargo."

"Make fun all you want," he shot back, "but you know I'm a solid, stand-up guy. You're just intimidated by my charm."

"Oh my God, that's it!" she exclaimed with mock enthusiasm. "I couldn't put my finger on it all these years, but the light just shined down. Your spellbinding allure has been at the root of all my troubles."

"I can only imagine," he continued. "Your life must have been hard to get through."

"Listen, nobody knows the trouble I've seen," she said. "Don't you have someone else to terrorize? Can't you be a menace to a colleague in your own building?"

"Eh, I've already frightened two people today, so I reached my quota early." He dismissed her veiled suggestion to move along. "Plus, I have more fun agitating *you*." Ben looked like a handsome schoolboy in an open-collared blue dress shirt and khakis; he reminded Marcee of a cute Blockbuster Video employee circa 1999.

"How's everything with you?" Marcee asked. "Have you and the puppy dog been stomping the canyon trails?"

"Twice a week," he said proudly. "You've yet to join us for a hike, by the way."

"My weight has been coming off," she said. "Maybe you didn't notice, but I'm down a good 14 pounds — just from watching my diet."

"You always look good to me." His dimples became pronounced as his face opened into a delightful beam of fraternal concern. "But, remember, exercise is just as important as your food choices."

"Thanks for casting me on *The Biggest Loser*, Bob Harper," she joked. "I'll consider your counsel. Now, why don't we table this conversation for the time being, and you can annoy me over lunch next week; my treat." Marcee was getting anxious as she saw her e-mail count doubling by the second.

"Fine, you're off the hook for today," he relented, "and I'll take you up on that offer."

"Don't threaten me," she called after him as he turned to leave. She noticed how nicely his pants cradled his backside. "And close the door behind you, please."

Marcee took a few minutes to survey her surroundings. The high-end furniture was an enormous upgrade from the standard-issue fixtures in her previous cave. *I'll have to get some art,* she thought. The Brazilian rosewood credenza alone begged for a worthy wall accompaniment.

She checked her computer again, now jammed with more bold, unread e-mails than she could possibly answer in two weeks. Gabbi Green's note might have gotten lost in the sea of messages had it not come at the split second Marcee looked up.

To: Brookes, Marcee <marcee.brookes@luminarypictures.com>
From: Green, Gabbi <gg@gabbigreencosmetics.com>
Subject: Tomorrow/Exclusive Invite

Marcee! I hope this finds you well.

I'd been meaning to get in touch after we first met but seeing you in all the papers this past weekend reminded me to reach out. I hope you don't mind that I got your info from Claire.

I'm launching a new, limited-edition highlighting powder at Nordstrom in Santa Monica tomorrow night. Cocktails start at 6PM; the big demo will be at 7:30PM.

Can you come with Brent Wetherley? It'll be a fun night out, and I would love to see you again.

Hope I can count the two of you in. Claire and her whole gang will be there — Jill, Claudia, Risa and Jamie — so it will be a good time. Promise!

xoxo,
Gabbi

Have I been invited to one of Gabbi Green's signature events? Marcee read the words a second time, just to make sure she wasn't delirious. After all, the entire morning seemed like a hallucination, and it was still only 10:30AM. She called Jordan to fill him in on the day's adventures and to discuss Gabbi's note.

"That's kind of weird," he said, dribbling the first drops of rain on her parade. "I mean, you met her only one time, weeks ago, right?"

"Claire has obviously mentioned me," Marcee reasoned. "The whole TTT group is going."

"Gabbi's e-mail specifically asked you to bring Brent, though," he pointed out, "which makes me think that she wants star power for the red carpet. You and I both know that no media outlets will cover a new product event without a few A-listers in front of the step-and-repeat."

"You're so jaded." Marcee read the e-mail again to herself while she was talking. "Maybe she just thinks it'll be a fun group."

"You're a big-girl executive now," Jordan replied. "You better learn to think like one. I'm fairly sure she's using you to get Brent to her flagship makeup counter for a photo op. Why else do you think she's sending you an invite the day before? She probably looked at the press tip sheet and realized there weren't enough big names."

"Whatever," Marcee huffed. "I'm going to see if Brent will agree to go. I don't want to miss a chance to be with the ladies, and he'll look good on my arm."

"That goes without saying," Jordan acknowledged. "He'd look even better on mine."

◇◇◇

BRENT AND MARCEE agreed to meet on the second level of the Santa Monica Place garage. He was coming straight from a voiceover session in Culver City, and she had left Burbank at 6PM to be at Nordstrom for a fashionable 7PM arrival.

"The traffic was a bitch," he said as he hugged Marcee hello. "I can't believe I actually made it on time."

"I wish you didn't have to run out by 7:30PM, though." Marcee was thrilled that he was interested enough in seeing her to make the drive west but disappointed that he couldn't stay for more than a half hour.

"Me, too," he groaned, "but I have to rehearse with the band tonight and then do a radio phoner with 104.1 2DayFM in Australia. They love me there."

"I understand; you're busy," she said. "Plus, you need to make sure you're in top form for next month's shows. I'll be in the audience, and I'm prepared to be impressed." He took her hand as they walked into the store through the cosmetics department. No sooner had they made it to the Gabbi Green display than they were greeted by a young woman who looked like a high schooler with a walkie-talkie and a clipboard. She showed them to the press line immediately.

"They're trafficking these PR girls younger and younger, aren't they?" Brent whispered into Marcee's ear, smiling as he pulled her with him in front of the 14 paparazzi penned between stanchions.

"Brent, look over here!" The men behind the cameras directed the action, yelling out various poses they wanted to capture. "Can we get you and your girlfriend holding hands and then maybe a kiss?" Like a pro, Brent put his arms around Marcee's waist from behind and then squeezed her against his chest before leaning in to kiss her cheek. "Stay just like that," one of the shutterbugs shouted. Even though Marcee remembered to keep her chin out and down this time around, she was no more comfortable in front of the flashes than she'd been at Mastro's over the weekend. This was the most demonstratively affectionate Brent had been, and Marcee was unsure of what to make of his advances with, essentially, the whole world watching. She smiled like she was enjoying the commotion; she knew it was expected. "Now, can we get *her* out of the way? We need some single shots." And, just like that — on command from the photographers — Marcee was shuffled to the side by the young publicist who'd welcomed her minutes before. She felt like one of the lifeless mannequins positioned at Nordstrom's entrance, there to make things look appealing but easily moved with the change of seasons.

Access Hollywood was the only broadcast show to send a video crew. It had been discovered earlier in the day that Sherilyn Lane — the legendary singer/actress who held a record for releasing multiple number one hits in every decade since 1960 — was on life support at Cedars-Sinai; most TV news outlets were on hospital watch. And since there was only one top-tier star scheduled to appear at Gabbi's soiree — Brent Wetherley — *Entertainment Tonight, Extra* and *E!* didn't bust their asses to attend.

"What brings you to a Gabbi Green event?" the producer asked, holding a microphone in front of Brent's face. He grabbed Marcee, who was now standing behind him, into the frame.

"My lady here loves Gabbi's products, and I support whatever makes her happy," he answered.

Time stood still. Did Marcee hear him correctly? Had *he* just referred to *her* as his lady? She wanted to ask the cameraman to run the footage back so she could hear the soundbite again, but she'd just have to wait for the episode to air the following evening for confirmation. *Note to self: remember to set the DVR as soon as you get home tonight.*

As they finished with the media, Brent headed toward the front door. "Don't you want to say hello to the girls?"

Marcee asked, hoping she could get him to stay at least a few extra minutes.

"Baby, if I get caught up in a conversation with Claire and Claudia, it'll be even harder to sneak away," he replied. "Better that I duck out now. Have fun for both of us, and get as much free product as you can squeeze out of Gabbi. I'll text you tomorrow or Friday." *And now he's referring to me as "baby"?* Brent spun around so he was facing Marcee and then began moving steadily away from her. Without breaking his backward stride, he blew her a few kisses. "I have to be at rehearsal in 15 minutes; the guys are waiting on me."

"Oh, oh…" she said softly. "OK." Her voice trailed off into such a faint murmur that she was unsure if the words actually left her lips. She waved self-consciously as she watched him turn to jog out of the store. She knew all too well the feeling of being at a school prom alone, and that same isolating loneliness dripped into her gut. She looked around until she found Claire huddled with the TTT gang around a circular high-top table.

"How's the new executive?" Jill inquired as Marcee pulled up a stool to join the group.

"I'm doing well, thanks," she answered. "I just feel bad that Brent had to dash out so early."

"Is he gone already?" Claire stretched her neck and looked around as though she might catch him on his way out.

"Unfortunately, yes," Marcee continued. "He has to practice with his band tonight and then record a radio interview with some pop station in Australia. Apparently, he's really big Down Under."

"That's the word on the street," Claudia said, sipping one of the green cocktails that were being passed around on trays. She looked as though the caterers had slipped her a few already.

"Gross," Jamie said. "I don't want to think about a veiny dick while I'm eating." Marcee was surprised that Jamie even stood up to kiss her, considering how dismissive she'd been at Craig's. More surprising to Marcee, however, was the long underarm hair that she noticed poking from beneath Jamie's cap sleeve.

"I, for one, can't wait to hear about his cock," Risa interjected. "Maybe by our next dinner, you'll have some dimensions to report." Marcee's life suddenly seemed of interest to the fading sitcom queen.

"Have you always been such a pud-hungry troll, Risa?" Claudia blabbed. "How hung is that TV brother you're having an affair with? I've never heard you mention his bundle."

"It works; that's the best I can say for it." Risa tittered. "It's nothing close to what Marcee will be getting, from what I understand."

Marcee couldn't have been happier that Gabbi stopped by to suck all of the attention away from the discussion of Brent's assets. "This launch is a bust," Gabbi said softly, leaning in so only the small circle could hear. "Sherilyn Lane couldn't have waited one more fucking day to have a medical crisis? She's stealing all of my thunder, even on social media. Usually, my name is trending during these events."

"I think Sherilyn is a little more iconic than your bronzers," Claire commented. "All anyone in town is doing right now is posting old photos of themselves with her — or drag queen look-alikes."

"And they're micro-blogging about that one time they drove past her gothic mansion in Malibu," Claudia added. "It's like when Mr. Purple Paisley died, and, boom, my entire online feed became Prince-tagram. Everyone loves a good celebrity death; even better when the star is hanging on for a few days. It's just too bad it's not my almost ex-husband."

"Don't you worry, Claudia," Claire said. "I'm sure Nick is one of the next on God's list. Famous people are dying left and right this year."

"Anyway," Gabbi said, looking at Marcee, "I'm so glad Brent could make it. This whole thing would have been a complete disaster without him."

Although Jordan had already warned her that Gabbi's invitation likely came attached to an ulterior motive, Marcee felt completely insignificant. Now there was no doubt in her mind that the cordial e-mail was simply a ploy to nab an actual movie star, someone other than a roster of B-listers and Hollywood wives turned self-help authors.

"Marcee?" Jill tapped her shoulder. "You look like you're off in a dream world somewhere."

"It's been a crazy week," she said, snapping back into the moment. "I guess I'm just a little tired, sorry. Did you say something?"

"Nothing important," she answered. "I'm going to run to the restroom; I'll be right back."

"Do you want me to go with you?" Marcee asked. "I could use the ladies' room myself."

"No, no," Jill insisted, "I'm fine. You all keep talking." Marcee got the sense that Jill did, in fact, want a companion. She excused herself after a minute and began to look for the lounge.

Nordstrom had closed early to accommodate Gabbi's party, so there were no customers milling about while Marcee walked past Clinique, MAC and NARS and then through the costume jewelry department. As she turned the corner toward the bathrooms, she noticed Jill standing in an alcove between fine fragrances and timepieces. Marcee stayed out of view as she watched Jill furiously stuff bite-size pieces of food into her mouth as though she were a feral dog that hadn't eaten in months.

Marcee waited until Jill left her plate on a glass display case and walked away before she moved in to get a closer look. There, on rented, gold-rimmed china, sat prosciutto-wrapped figs, chicken bites fried in waffle batter and a half-eaten mini-slider with bacon and cheese. None of it, from what Marcee could tell, had been made with plant-based substitutes. She was shocked that she'd just seen the country's most prominent vegan scarf down the equivalent of a baby animal.

Jill was just walking out of a stall when Marcee entered the restroom.

"Oh my God, you scared me." Jill jumped. "I didn't hear anyone come in."

"It's just me." Marcee smiled. "I had way too much water. If I don't go now, I'll never make it back to the Valley without having to stop." Their conversation bounced off the commercial tile, creating an awful din.

"Did you follow me from the table?" Jill, looking nervous and jittery, washed her hands three times.

"No, why?" Marcee asked. She tried to sound casual and composed.

"Oh, nothing." Jill relaxed her shoulders slightly and dried off with the Gabbi Green paper towels that had been placed at each of the sinks. "I'll see you back at the table."

"Sounds good," Marcee said, walking into one of the cubicles and locking the door.

"And Marcee?" Jill continued to talk. "I hope you'll always remember who gave you the professional opportunity of a lifetime, OK?"

As the sound of Jill's Lulus suede lace-up heels faded and Marcee heard the main door to the bathroom swing closed, she let out a sigh a relief. For a moment, she thought there might be some kind of soy-brain showdown, and she had no interest in losing her new gig the day after she landed it.

While she layered the toilet seat with almost an entire roll of tissue — over which she placed two paper covers — she resolved to keep Jill's secret. The woman's entire platform was built on a lie but one that Marcee didn't want to risk getting tangled in.

When Marcee returned to the table, Jill was arranging a crudité plate using what few pieces of celery and red pepper garnish she was able to pick from platters stationed around the party.

"Throw this in," Risa said, tossing a baby carrot onto the display. "It'll add some extra color. Your posts have been too beige lately. I like to see a pop of orange when I visit your Twitter feed." Claudia's laugh turned into a snort.

"Marcee, can you hold this on a slant?" Jill asked, ignoring the hecklers beside her and pointing to the vegetable art she'd just created. She used her phone to photograph it from three different angles and then posted it on Snapchat with the caption "One happy vegan girl!"

"Ladies, it's time," Claire said, standing and throwing her bag over her shoulder. "I can't believe I wasted an entire night sitting in the makeup section of a middling department store. Honestly, did that just happen? I could've had a game night with my kids."

"Ugh, I know," Claudia agreed. "Or we could have just met at the Brentwood for drinks. It's not like Gabbi spent any time with us anyway."

"That's actually the only good part about the whole night." Claire laughed. "If I had to hear her talk about the 'miracle powder' that some assembly-line workers in China pounded into a compact, I'd have been off like Risa's weave in an earthquake."

"For $5 and a postage stamp, she could replace it," Claudia added. "So, I'm not really worried about Risa's scalp."

"Well, I'm happy I got to see all of you, no matter the

location," Marcee said, doling out the requisite hugs, kisses and goodbyes.

"Are you always this pleasant?" Claudia questioned, looking at Marcee like she'd just seen a spacecraft land in her yard.

Realizing that Claudia had tasted one too many "Gabbi Green Apple-tinis," Marcee took her by the arm. "Yes, I am always this nice, which is why I'm going to walk you to your car."

"Forget nice," Claire shouted as she left the store with Jamie, Jill and Risa. "You're a fucking saint, Marcee Brookes."

"Claire always goes into bitch mode when she thinks I've had too much to drink," Claudia said as Marcee escorted her to the exit. "She knows every detail of what I've been through with Nick and the divorce — more than my therapist. You'd think she'd be a little sensitive to my situation."

"I'm sure she just wants you to be healthy," Marcee said. Claudia was clearly in a fragile state and had been drinking to dull the pain. They strolled through the outdoor mall, making their way to the garage a few minutes after the others had disappeared in their luxury cars. "Why don't I drive you home," Marcee offered, "and you can Uber back in the morning?"

"Why isn't she more understanding?" Claudia asked, sidestepping Marcee's gesture.

"Maybe it's hard for her to relate to a disintegrating relationship," Marcee suggested. "I mean, she and Rox have been happily married for so long. Perhaps it's tough for her to empathize."

"Are you serious?" Claudia let out a throaty chuckle. "You really think Claire Madison is in a solid marriage?"

"She's never said otherwise," Marcee replied. "And she always talks as though things are great."

"You say 'always' like you've known her more than a

couple of months." Claudia, as inebriated as she was, shook the timeline into perspective.

Firmly holding Claudia's arm to keep her from staggering around the parking structure, Marcee paused. She realized how foolish she'd sounded, talking about Claire's relationship as though she'd shared a years-long history with the woman. *I barely know Claire at all,* Marcee realized. *How stupid of me to offer my two cents about her personal life to her own best friend. Now I look like a wannabe.*

"If you think she's so happy," Claudia mumbled, "go ahead and ask her."

"Ask her what?" Marcee tilted her head, still embarrassed and now confused by what seemed like a riddle.

"Ask her why I call her husband 'Rox Bottom.'"

13

"ROX MADISON TAKES it up the ass? I knew it!" Jordan's voice, with the gleeful joy of a toddler who'd just been given the latest from Fisher-Price, bubbled through Marcee's phone. "I've always known he's a big queen." His giddy arrogance was palpable.

"You say the same thing about every human being with a penis," she replied, playfully shaking her head. "If anyone listened to you, they'd believe that the world is in the middle of a gaypocalypse. *Night of the Walking Homosexuals.*"

"Think whatever you want, but, between me and all of my bromos, we know someone who knows someone who has a friend who actually slept with just about every supposedly hetero celebrity." He sounded proud of his fourth-hand knowledge.

"Well, we can't even be sure of what Claudia was trying to tell me because she passed out in the passenger seat right after she said the words 'Rox Bottom,'" Marcee continued. "Maybe she meant that he has a drug problem and finally hit a low point."

"She's obviously very forthcoming with liquor in her system," Jordan teased. "You should have woken her up and tried to get more information while she was still loaded."

"And why does it matter to you so much?" Marcee asked.

"As a certified versatile-top, I love the idea that I might actually be able to get the world's biggest action star on all fours." His tone was serious.

"Oh, OK, now it's making sense," she goaded, amused by his confidence. "You think you'll wind up meeting Rox, and he won't be able to keep his hands off you. He'll just bend right over." She loved to razz Jordan at any opportunity.

"My reputation as an experienced lover is well-known in Boys' Town," he bragged. "I'm sure Rox would like to know what the fuss is about."

"*Lover?*" Marcee chuckled. "What kind of bodice-ripping romance novel did you just jump out of? And I have no doubt that you're very well established in West Hollywood." Jordan's sexual bravado tickled her.

"You have to find out more, more, more," he instructed. "It's only 8AM, and this has already made my day."

"If Rox actually *is* gay, I'll feel awful for Claire." Marcee was about to arrive at work. "Her life will fall apart."

"I'm sure she'd get a nice divorce settlement and child support," Jordan reasoned. "So, I'm not exactly going to cry for her, Argentina." He was clearly less concerned about the familial fallout than he was about knowing the details of Rox's bedroom proclivities.

"The call might drop because I just pulled into the garage," she said, "but, coincidentally, my lunch today is with Claire and Rox's assistant; maybe she'll mention something. But you know you can't use any of this in your column, right?"

"Come on," he continued, "I'm your EFF; you don't really think I'd compromise that or even consider outing anybody, do you? Never."

"EFF?" Marcee, for the most part, knew the Jordan-to-English dictionary, but this one eluded her.

"*Eternal friend forever.*" He tossed out the term as though it were an often-used, practical acronym. "It's a step beyond BFF."

"If it requires that I be buried next to you, we might have to reclassify our friendship. It's called a final *resting* place for a reason; I don't think I'd have a moment's peace in the afterlife if you're that close by."

"Shut all of your holes," he said, laughing. "Just make sure you have *something* to report later today. There's been a stir in my jeans since the second I pictured Rox, spread-eagle, on my bed."

"I seem to be losing phone service at the perfect moment." She used her voice to briefly mimic cellular static. "Keep your fly zipped, will you?" She pulled into Phyllis's old parking spot, which had been reassigned and repainted, and headed to the elevators.

Addie was waiting at Marcee's door by the time she made it upstairs. "So, how was the Gabbi Green party last night?"

"I don't remember mentioning a Gabbi Green event," Marcee answered with a crooked smile. "Was there some kind of product launch at a department store?" She threw her bag on a guest chair and took a seat behind her desk.

"If you don't want everyone at work to know what's happening in your personal life, you're gonna have to stay out of the press," Addie joked, sitting cross-legged on a nearby sofa. "There's a picture of Brent Wetherley kissing your cheek on the home pages of just about every entertainment website."

"It's so weird," Marcee replied. "I'm used to pitching celeb news to the media, not *being* the news." She logged in to her computer and went right to *Joaquin Richie*. "At least I don't look as bad in these as I did in the pictures from last Saturday. Were you even able to count all my chins in *those* glamour shots?"

"Is that a bid for sympathy?" Addie pretended to file her

nails with an imaginary emery board. "My heart bleeds for the lovely PR executive who's been swept off her feet by a matinee idol."

Marcee began to read the online article aloud. "It looks like Brent Wetherley's budding romance with studio flack Marcee Brookes is continuing to heat up. Here, the couple steps out to support pal Gabbi Green in Santa Monica. Where will the lovebirds pop up next?"

"Where *will* you two pop up next?" Addie wore little makeup. Her smooth, ebony skin didn't require any foundation, and her enviably long lashes framed her large eyes without a hint of liner. "Or should I wait to read about it?"

"Very funny," Marcee shot back. "We're going to the Hollywood Bowl tomorrow night, so don't be surprised to see those photos on Saturday morning."

"You and Brent will have gone out three times this week," Addie pointed out. "Unless I'm missing something, you guys are really into each other."

"Well..." Marcee started. She caught herself before she could mention that the night before wound up being only a red carpet appearance. "I hadn't really thought about it. I guess you're right." Brent's quick departure from Nordstrom had been simmering in the back of her mind, and now, Addie's friendly conversation brought it front and center. *I wouldn't really consider last night a date, but I'm sure tomorrow will make up for it.*

"I'd trade places with you in a heartbeat." Addie sighed with a resigned breath. "I don't think I've had a date with anyone but my mom since my ex and I split. I'll take just a regular guy; he doesn't even have to be a movie star." She must have noticed that Marcee's attention had shifted. "Anyhow, I'm outta here for now. Don't forget that we have to discuss seating for the *Bitter Truth* premiere. It'll be here before you know it."

"Thanks, Addie," Marcee said without looking up from her computer. She had begun to review the readers' comments — which she hadn't thought to do during the craziness of the past week — beneath *Joaquin Richie's* latest posting.

> Who is that free-range porker? That's the best bacon Brent Wetherley could bring home? #oink #trough #dumptheplump

> At least he'll always be the pretty one. Plus, "FAT MEANS YES," so she probably puts out all the time.

As though she'd been struck in the face, she plunged as far backward as her new leather chair would allow. She was accustomed to reading nasty comments about public figures and Luminary movies on various message boards; in fact, she always suggested to filmmakers that they spare their own feelings by not paying attention to the ramblings of online trolls. In an instant, though, she realized she shouldn't have been so quick to give away advice she'd wind up needing back.

> Wow. If losing weight is that hard for her, she should just eat a bullet. #diebitch

> That hag is a sight for closed eyes.

> Having low self-esteem would be good common sense for Fatty McButterpants. What's HE doing with HER? #fail

In one swift motion, she stood from her desk and pushed her monitor upward to maximum tilt. *Why did I even read past the first line?* She locked the door to her office and lay down on one of the couches at the center of the room. Placing an arm pillow beneath her head, she stared at the stark white ceiling. As she closed her eyes, a few tears rolled from all four corners, slowly swelling her lower lids and dampening her face.

Her initial instinct to call either her mother or Jordan was quashed by sudden memories of the elementary school taunts that ate away at her self-worth from the time she was in first grade. To her classmates, she'd been a "Paunchy Pig," a "Goodyear Blimp" and "Bessie Moo," all names that she kept from her parents and the handful of ragtag friends — including Jordan — whom she'd cobbled together. Marcee was deliberate in making certain that the people who loved her didn't know that she was regarded as an outcast by the general population. What if they caught wind of how she was perceived and were suggestible enough to feel similarly? At six, staying silent seemed the best way to maintain a small amount of dignity, and, oddly, it made sense at 42 as well. The big difference? The Internet made public shaming a national pastime, and everyone with a keyboard could see the mud being flung in her face, whether she called it to their attention or not.

Even these strangers can't believe that a guy like Brent could possibly be interested in me, she thought. *I look like a fat dumbass for showing up anywhere with him.* She couldn't chase away the nagging embarrassment that had now taken up residence in her head. The objective audience — those with no dogs in the fight — had declared her unworthy of Brent's affection, never mind that caring people such as her mom, Jordan and Claire rallied behind her. The voices of her family and friends were drowned out by those of malicious web warriors, and it was easier to believe the negativity that had been drilled into her mind from an early age.

With her arms folded across her chest, she remained still, ignoring the passage of time. The sounds of ringing phone lines and e-mail notifications seemed to be happening at a muffled distance. She felt like the only survivor of a tragic accident who was stranded on a raft in the middle of open water; no one knew she was floating alone, and, likewise, she was unable to reach out for help.

Rescue came from a knock on the door. "Marcee?" The rapping on the heavy wood got louder. "Hello? Can I come in?" Lila wasn't giving up.

"I'll be right there," Marcee called out, reaching for the box of tissues that sat on a rectangular glass coffee table in front of her. She patted her eyes and fluffed the pillow that had cushioned her head for an hour.

"Hi, Lila," Marcee said as she opened the door and showed the millennial to a chair in front of her desk. "Everything OK?"

"I should ask you the same thing," Lila replied, looking at Marcee with concern. "Your face is a little flushed."

"My allergies are acting up." Marcee was always good at the quick save. "The pollen has been knocking me out."

"Oh, I totes know what you mean," Lila answered. "I've been sneezing nonstop for about three months. God has blessed me so many times that I needed to start sharing the good fortune."

"If only you could've shared it with someone else," Marcee said in an overly chipper voice. She was trying hard to cover the tremor that the past 60 minutes had left in her throat. "Anyhow, what's going on? Did you need me for something?"

"I have a bunch of invoices for your approval." Lila placed what looked like a ream of paper on the top of Marcee's in-box. "Phyllis used to let them pile up, so we're about two months behind on paying vendors." She stayed in her seat as though she expected Marcee to study them on the spot.

"I'll get to the bills later this afternoon," Marcee answered politely as she repositioned the computer screen and closed out of her web browser. "If there's nothing urgent for the time being, though, I have to finish up a couple of things before my lunch appointment."

"Got it; no problem," Lila said, taking the hint and disappearing into the hallway.

Overwhelmed by the amount of work and management responsibilities that fell into her lap only two days earlier, Marcee began to sort through the heaps of paper that had amassed around her. Stacks of memos, invitations and various reports lined nearly every available surface, which she concluded could help put her out of her misery quickly if a fire were to rip through the building — as well as distract her from the emotional pain that had hijacked the morning.

Before Marcee could lift a single 8.5 by 11 sheet, Addie appeared in front of her. "Knock, knock," she said, having skipped the formality of actually announcing her entrance with the customary action itself.

"Are you alright?" There seemed to be an urgency and officiousness to Addie's cadence.

"Of course, why?" Marcee glanced up, puzzled.

"Lila is telling everyone that you were in tears when she stopped by earlier, so I wanted to make sure you're OK."

"What is it with these kids?" Marcee answered. "I told her that my allergies are wreaking havoc on my eyes and nose."

"If that's all it is," Addie replied, "I'll leave you alone. Lila made it seem like you were having a DEFCON 4 meltdown."

Marcee lightheartedly raised her right arm as though she were addressing her royal subjects. "Please let everyone in the kingdom know that it was nothing more than airborne allergens. But if I don't get through the shit on my desk, you'll be seeing real tears pretty soon."

"Understood," Addie said. "I'm here if you need anything; otherwise, consider me out of the way."

Marcee busied herself by sorting everything into four categories: items that required immediate attention; requests that could wait a week or two; pages to be filed for reference; and useless material left by Phyllis in the wake of her overnight dismissal. She realized that each piece of the bottleneck would likely fall under one of those headings, and putting things into some kind of order created the illusion of control and comfort. By the time the receptionist called at 12:45PM to let her know that her lunch date was waiting in the lobby, Marcee had actually made a small dent in the logjam. She took the brush she'd put in the top drawer of her desk and ran it through her hair before heading downstairs.

In the elevator — paneled with reflective hardware — she was forced to see her entire body. *I really am a fat heifer. All of those comments aren't too far-fetched.* With no one else around, she turned from side to side, examining her waist. She used both hands to scrunch the skin around her stomach, staring at her accentuated midsection disdainfully. *Forget one spare tire; I have a full set of all-terrain tummy rolls.* She thought the pounds she'd dropped by dieting had given her a slightly new shape, but the glass walls *could* talk: she was the same chunk-pot she'd always been.

"It's so nice to see you outside of Malibu," Sarah said as soon as Marcee stepped onto the first floor. Sarah's hair, hanging about three inches below her waist, was held back with two bobby pins. Her pleasantly full face, which had been bare both times Marcee had seen her in person, was highlighted with a shimmery blush and light eye shadow.

It was evident that she'd made an effort for her visit to Luminary Pictures.

"I feel the same way," Marcee replied, giving Sarah a hug. "It'll be great to have time to talk on our own." She tried her best to sound upbeat despite feeling like an unappealing farm animal who should be put out to pasture. "Do you mind if we just grab a bite at the commissary? I can't venture too far from the office because of all the projects we have going at the moment." Ordinarily, she'd have welcomed a change of scenery and restaurant, but her appetite for small talk had disappeared with the morning's online bruising and the harsh criticism of the elevator. She wanted to put the whole day on fast-forward.

"That's perfectly fine." Sarah took a tube of gloss from her Coach bag and moistened her lips. "Anything that's away from my desk is a treat."

"You don't ever run out for a break during a normal work week?" Marcee asked in an attempt to seem engaged. "I would imagine it's good to step away and get a little fresh air." As they walked the 200 yards down the studio lot's main strip and into the cafeteria, she pulled down on the bottom hem of her untucked blouse to make sure it didn't bunch around her unflatteringly.

"There isn't usually time," Sarah said. "It's a three-ring circus at that house if you consider everything happening with Rox, Claire *and* their kids. I barely have a minute to pee, let alone eat."

"I'm surprised there isn't a backup assistant." Most celebrities with whom Marcee had worked had entire support staffs. "You know, someone to help you manage everything."

"You'd think," Sarah remarked, "but they like to keep the number of people inside their home to a minimum. I've been with them awhile, so they trust me, but I imagine that it's hard to feel secure with too many outsiders in your living space." She surveyed the food options and changed the subject. "What are you having for lunch? I was thinking about a grilled cheese and fries. It's the ultimate comfort meal — especially if they have tomato soup to go with it."

"That sounds delicious," Marcee agreed, "but I've been watching what I eat." As the words came out of her mouth, she realized that, while her hips might be best served by low-sodium deli meats, her soul could use something more nurturing.

"I actually noticed that you've lost a few pounds since I first met you," Sarah said. "Have you been on a specific diet? I need to get myself on some kind of health program because I'm at my heaviest. I have only about four outfits that I can fit into at this point."

"Eh, it's an optical illusion. I basically just cut out sodas and drive-thrus," Marcee answered. "I try also to keep healthier snacks around, like baby carrots instead of Peanut M&Ms." *I could actually go for some chocolate today,* she thought.

"Hola, Marcee," Blanca interrupted. The sandwich captain, in a tall paper chef's hat, noticed the two ladies lingering in line. "What are you and your friend having today?"

"She wants the deluxe grilled cheese special, and I'm thinking that I might have exactly the same thing." Marcee was still feeling overwhelmingly fragile and decided that grilled cheddar on buttered white bread would throw a warm blanket over her chilly gloom.

"Please don't cheat on your diet to make me feel better," Sarah insisted. "I don't want to be responsible for standing in the way of your progress."

"Not to worry." Marcee smiled faintly. "It's been a tough day already, and I'm giving myself permission to cheat. I can't deprive myself *all* the time." They stood next to each other with their trays and silverware, waiting for Blanca to plate their meals.

"Why has the day been so crazy?" Sarah asked.

"I don't know if Claire told you, but I was promoted to department head this past Tuesday." Marcee paid for their food and found a two-top table toward the back of the dining room.

"She did, actually," Sarah said. "I meant to congratulate you."

"Thank you, but it has been an adjustment. I'm treading water to keep from drowning, and it's only my second day." Marcee was dodging the truth behind her upset.

"I'm sure it'll all fall into place," Sarah said. "It can take a while to feel like you're starting to settle into a new job. You didn't think it would be totally seamless, did you?" She poured ketchup on top of her steak fries and began to pick at them.

"The transition came out of the blue, so I had no idea what to expect," Marcee continued. "And then, there's the Brent Wetherley thing — which is why today started out so roughly." It slipped out before she could stop herself.

"Really, what happened?" Sarah paused, mid-nibble, and looked at Marcee with heightened interest.

"Gabbi Green sent me a last-minute invitation to her event last night, which I'm fairly certain was her way of getting Brent onto the red carpet," Marcee confided. "I'd met her only that one time at Claire's and then she *happened* to reach out to me right after my first date with Brent hit the papers. That can't be a coincidence, right?" She spoke as though she'd been onto Gabbi's game from the outset.

"You know what it's like in this town," Sarah agreed. "Opportunists are everywhere, even when they're cosmetics magnates in sheep's clothing. Claire will be the first to tell you that Gabbi has no shame *and* no boundaries."

"Well, I asked Brent to go with me because I thought it would give us an extra opportunity to see each other this week." She took a second to savor a French fry, a soothing saltiness that she hadn't tasted in nearly a month.

"I saw the pictures in the press this morning," Sarah commented. "It looked like you guys had a great time." She turned her head to the side while she sipped from her sweetened passion-fruit iced tea.

"It was nice to see Claire and the girls, but Brent wasn't there for long." Marcee took two bites of her grilled cheese. "That aside, when I got into the office this morning, I read the comments that some of Brent's fans wrote on the gossip sites."

"Oh, God," Sarah said. "I can't believe you made *that* mistake. Rox and Claire always make me set up different e-mail accounts so I can go online and offset the negative messages with my own positive posts." Marcee started to tear up. "Shit. Were they *that* vicious?"

"According to @BrentFanNo1 in Santa Fe, I'm too fat to be alive." Marcee tried to hold back — the same way she'd avoided discussing the subject with her mother and Jordan — but her emotional unrest forced her to relent; she figured that Sarah's obvious weight issues would allow her to relate on a different level.

"I'm so sorry." Sarah grabbed both of Marcee's hands from across the table in a consoling gesture. "You have to ignore those losers. They have nothing in their lives but time to make other people feel like garbage."

"I thought I was past the point of being teased about my size," Marcee sobbed, crying into a napkin to avoid making a noisy scene. "I know people judge quietly, but I haven't been outwardly ridiculed since high school."

"Listen," Sarah said, "I'm not naïve enough to think that nobody watches what I put in my mouth when I eat at a restaurant. I'm sure there's someone in *this* room who's thinking to himself, 'That chub could do without the fries.' But I go about my business regardless. The kinds of friends I want in my life don't care if I'm overweight or not."

"I feel the same way most of the time," Marcee answered, "and I try really hard to compartmentalize it. But being flogged in a public square is beyond humiliating." She got herself under control and dried her eyes.

"I can only imagine," Sarah said empathetically. She reached for her bag and began to search through it, not looking up until she found her lip treatment and reapplied it. "I'm trying to think about what it would be like to be in Kathy Bates's shoes."

Marcee looked at her, confused. "Kathy Bates?"

"Every time I do one of those Facebook quizzes," Sarah replied, "I wind up getting Kathy Bates. You know the ones I'm talking about, don't you? 'WHICH FORMER STAGE ACTRESS ARE YOU?' or 'WHICH OSCAR WINNER ARE YOU?'"

"I never take the time to click on those links." Marcee chuckled, genuinely entertained by Sarah's quip.

"Yeah, well, somehow, I never get Jessica Alba," Sarah went on. "Does that make you feel any better? You're having lunch with *Misery* herself. How's that for depressing?"

"Well, if you're Kathy Bates, maybe things aren't *that* bad for me." Marcee all of a sudden felt the fog around her begin to clear.

"Thanks a lot," Sarah jabbed sarcastically. "I'm glad my misfortune has made you feel better. I'll go find a recipe for fried green tomatoes and live out the rest of my life next to a backwoods café in Alabama."

"Don't even think about it," Marcee said. "I have a feeling I'm gonna get used to having you around." The lunch that originally seemed like an obligatory chore wound up lightening Marcee's mood on a difficult day.

"I'm not going anywhere," Sarah confirmed. "I think I'm in for a long tour of duty. I'll probably wind up working for Rox and Claire until it's time to move myself into the Motion Picture and Television Fund Retirement Home."

"Why do you say that?" Marcee inquired. "Are you planning to make a career out of being a personal assistant?"

"Not at all, but my screenplays haven't gone anywhere. I'm kind of stuck at the moment." She told Marcee about all of her writing classes and workshops and relayed the positive feedback she'd received from established industry mentors like Norman Lear and Penny Marshall.

"Can't Rox and Claire put your scripts in front of the right producers or help you get an agent?" Marcee felt like she was belaboring the obvious.

"You'd think so, wouldn't you?" Sarah had clearly been down that road. "They always tell me that I'm talented and that they love my style, but then nothing happens. You could die of enthusiasm in Hollywood."

"If you don't mind letting me take a peek, maybe I can slip your work to our development team," Marcee offered. "There are no guarantees, but it's worth a shot. Us beefier gals gotta stick together."

Sarah's face lit up. "That would be amazing," she said. "You're really kind to do that for me." They'd both finished eating and drank the last drops of tea in their to-go cups. "I should probably let you get back to your office for the time being, though."

Marcee looked at her watch. "If I don't go now, I'll wind up sitting and gabbing with you all day." They stood and took their trays to the "clean up" conveyor belt.

"What do you have on tap for this weekend?" Sarah asked.

"I have a date with Brent tomorrow. We're going to eat

outside at the Hollywood Bowl and then watch the show; it should be a relaxed night. Plus, being under the stars is always romantic. I'll just have to make sure not to read any of the press that runs as a result."

Sarah looked away from Marcee and scanned the room as though she were searching for an exit. She nervously lifted her purse and shuffled through it again, adding yet another coat of balm to the silky lips she's attended to only a few minutes before. "Is everything OK?" Marcee asked. "You seem like you just got spooked."

"Nothing to worry about," Sarah answered. "I realized that I forgot to pick up my prescriptions from CVS. I'll have to swing by there on my way home."

"I'm so glad we finally made this happen," Marcee said as she walked Sarah to her car in the visitors' parking structure. "Let's plan something again soon."

"Definitely, and thanks for lunch," Sarah replied as she swiftly adjusted her seatbelt, started her Kia Sorento and pulled out of the garage. She waved to Marcee through the window, jetting out with the speed of someone whose stomach didn't take well to such a rich lunch. In the past, Marcee had made all kinds of excuses when her own sensitive stomach rejected fried foods and particular dairy items; Sarah's breakneck departure rang all too familiar.

Marcee raced back to her office to find that the mountains of paperwork she'd left behind had waited for her. She vowed to disregard her call sheet and e-mails until she'd powered through at least a quarter of the documents, but when her phone lit up with a personal message from Brent, she dropped everything.

To: Brookes, Marcee <MarceePR@gmail.com>
From: Wetherley, B. <WetherOrNot@wetherleymediagrp.com>

RE: Tomorrow night

Hey, baby.

There's a slight shift in plans for tomorrow night. I have to go to Toronto for a week unexpectedly (I guess Canada can't get enough of me, LOL). I still want to see you, but I'll have to leave at intermission in order to catch the red-eye out of LAX.

Would you mind terribly if I sent a town car to pick you up? This way, you can meet me at the Bowl and then the driver can wait to take you home when the show is over. Naturally, I don't want you to miss Miley and Patrick singing "Shall We Dance?" ☺

I'm sorry this is all changing, but I don't want to cancel. Having an hour or two with you is better than nothing.

XO,

Brent W.

On edge and still nursing her frayed nerves, she dropped her chin to her chest and pulled at her hair from both sides. *Am I being rebuffed? He wants me to graze like a cow on the lawn until he leaves me alone to watch a show? What kind of date is that? I might as well be a loser in private and stay home by myself listening to Yul Brynner on iTunes.* It was time to call for reinforcement; she dialed her mother.

"Mom, where are you? I'm about to lose it."

"Daddy and I are at the Costco in Thousand Oaks, noshing on samples for dinner," Rhonda said. "What's the matter? I thought everything was going well in your world." Her voice had a hint of worry.

"I got an e-mail from Brent about our date tomorrow," Marcee replied, "and I think he's trying to brush me off. Can I read it to you?"

"Let me walk over to the health food aisle," she replied. "There's never anyone there, so it'll be quiet." Marcee waited a beat for Rhonda to situate herself between what she imagined to be the Mayorga chia seeds and the Kirkland Signature whole almonds and then read Brent's note, word for word.

"Honey, what on earth are you upset about?" Rhonda sounded surprised. "He said twice how much he wants to see you. You can't fault someone in his position for having a nutty schedule."

"It just makes me feel like he's squeezing me in," Marcee continued doubtfully.

"Mar, he could've canceled and moved the date altogether, considering that a spur-of-the-moment work trip popped up."

"So you honestly don't believe he's blowing smoke and that he really does want to see me tomorrow?" Marcee felt a wave of relief.

"Why would he go through the trouble if he wasn't sincere?" Rhonda asked. "What good reason could he possibly have to go through the motions?"

"I suppose you're right." Marcee took a loud, deep breath. "I guess I'll go along with it and whistle a happy tune."

14

MARCEE WAS SURPRISED that there were still so many *Hannah Montana* T-shirts in circulation. The Disney Channel series had ended in 2011, but the merchandise seemed alive and well on the front lawn of the Hollywood Bowl. Sure, there were older Miley Cyrus disciples flitting around with pierced body parts and slinky latex garments — not to mention Patrick Stewart allegiants in *Star Trek* gear — but the audience demographics for *The King and I: In Concert* were clearly preteens and gay men.

The chauffeured black Lincoln Town Car that Brent had hired to stay with Marcee for the evening dropped her at the main entrance to the venue at 6:30PM. Traditionally, celebrities valet parked and sneaked into the backstage greenroom through a private artists' entrance, but Brent had insisted that their evening be as "normal" as possible — never mind that he'd likely be inundated by autograph hounds and selfie-seekers. She was warmed by the fact that he was willing to brave the crowds in order to give her a more traditional date.

In a pair of dark denim jeans and a flowing black top, Marcee waded through a sea of theatergoers until she found one empty wooden table. She took a tissue from her bag and wiped crumbs from the bench before sitting and checking her phone.

"Hey, babe, I'm running a few minutes late," Brent had texted. "I got stuck in a meeting with my agent. I should be there by 7:15PM at the latest." Marcee always felt self-conscious sitting alone, and, unfortunately, Brent's "few" minutes really meant "45." She tried to busy herself by scrolling through her Facebook and Twitter accounts, but she ultimately gave up the table to frustrated onlookers who actually had food — and guests — with them.

She walked to the curb at Highland Avenue and watched street hustlers sell bootleg concert swag to passersby. For a moment, she even considered buying a sweatshirt so she'd have a low-cost keepsake from the event. After all, she thought, not much could be funnier — or more collectible — than apparel featuring Miley Cyrus's stint in a classic piece of musical theater. Maybe Danny Glover and Usher on the outward face of a *Fiddler on the Roof* mug.

Marcee was still pacing the pavement at 7:30PM when she glanced down at her watch. She didn't want to bother Brent with a call, but it was getting relatively close to the 8PM showtime. As she looked up, she was relieved to see him walking toward her in a pair of sunglasses and a New York Yankees baseball cap.

"So sorry I'm late," he said, out of breath like he'd run all the way from Beverly Hills. He removed his hat before repositioning his ponytail into a small man-bun. "Will you forgive me?" He batted his eyes dramatically in what looked like an overstated bid for forgiveness. After a fast hug, he handed her a plastic bag from Gelson's Supermarket as though it were a peace offering. "And here's dinner."

Before she could utter much of a greeting, six photographers descended on the sidewalk, snapping pictures. Brent turned Marcee around, his hands on her back, and posed playfully behind and beside her. She smiled and gave them a few cheerful expressions until they disbanded. The flurry of action called attention to Brent's arrival, which generated a small mob of teenage girls — and their mothers — rabid for Instagram photos.

Marcee was jostled to the side by the fans who'd gathered in a circle around Brent; within 15 minutes, both of her feet had been stepped on, her shoulders bumped and her hair pulled at least twice. She backed away to a safe distance and stood on the sidelines until 7:55PM when the group thinned out and headed toward their seats. Having worked with many temperamental stars, Marcee appreciated how gracious Brent had been with his admirers — signing every paper napkin and recording video greetings — yet she couldn't help but feel like a meaningless tagalong.

"It's crazy, isn't it?" Brent said as he made his way over to her. He took her hand and guided her briskly past the ticket takers and the security bag-check lane, showing her to an assigned area in the very first row. "Sometimes, I don't have the energy to go out."

"I can understand that," she said. "Being a public person is a full-time job." She tried to sound sympathetic. He pulled out one of the chairs at a prime table so she could take a seat. "Do you know who's next to us?"

"I bought all of the Section C Garden Box tickets," he replied, "so there's no one else. You can spread out and enjoy yourself." A fleeting twinge of guilt stabbed Marcee in the gut. Five minutes earlier, she worried that Brent had shown up for his fans more than he had to spend time with her. His thoughtful generosity, though, erased any doubts. She unpacked the groceries as he sat opposite her: a small pan of lukewarm lasagna, a bag of Cheetos, a can of Pringles, two Hostess CupCakes and one liter of Coke. Using the paper plates and disposable cutlery at the bottom of the plastic bag, she started to portion out the pasta.

"No, that's all for you," he said, pushing the food closer

to her. "I have to take off for the airport in a few minutes, so I'll eat at LAX."

"Um…oh…" She tripped over her words. "I thought you were staying for the first act and eating with me." Her last couple of words faded into a hush as if the open sky had suddenly closed in with a tight hold on her throat.

"That was my original plan, but then I realized I'd be cutting it too close." He reached across the table and took her hands in his. "Once I found out I had to leave town, I probably should've told you to invite some friends tonight. Selfishly, I wanted you to myself for however long I could be here."

Marcee let go of his grip and turned her head to the side. She felt winded, like she'd been kicked in the chest with blunt force, and didn't want him to see the distress on her face. *He brought all of this for me? Does he really think I eat so much junk? I guess I really do look like a porker.*

"Please don't be upset, baby," he pleaded, moving around to the seat beside her. He put his hands on the back of her neck as she faced the stage. "I don't want to get on a plane knowing that you're unhappy." The orchestra began to play the overture as she turned to face him.

"Go ahead, I'll be fine," she said, forcing a faint smile. "I just didn't realize that I'd see you for only a half hour." He lightly brushed her left cheek with his knuckles.

"Believe me, it's not the way I wanted it either," he assured her, "but I promise that I'll make good the minute I'm back from Toronto." He stood up and blew her a kiss, dashing off before Miley Cyrus came in like a wrecking ball.

It was as if Marcee's clothes — undergarments included — had disappeared like magic. Sitting by herself, front and center, she imagined that she was the focal point of every eye at the Hollywood Bowl. As fast as she could, she put everything but the soda back in its original sack and placed it on the chair next to her. *People must be thinking how pathetic I am, a chubby girl watching a musical alone on a Friday night. "Oh, and look! She brought a convenience store-style picnic big enough for all of the friends who didn't bother to show up. So sad for her."* Her first instinct was to leave immediately until she remembered that Brent had paid for and arranged her transportation; he would likely find out if she wasted the tickets and bolted before the show ended. Instead, she slouched and stared at the stage, trying to immerse herself in the performance. It was of no use.

She opened the Coke and took a few sips, thinking that the sweet syrup and carbonation would settle her stomach. But just as she got her nausea under control, her head began to pound. Trying to avoid making much noise, she reached into her bag carefully and took two Aleve Liquid Gels from a pearlized, round pillbox. She knew they wouldn't kick in for a little while but hoped that the pulsing in her temples would subside sooner rather than later. In the meantime, she couldn't stop her thoughts from barreling through her mind like a fully loaded cargo train on the fast track. *Could Brent have really wanted to see me so much that he came all the way over to Hollywood for 30 minutes?*

As soon as the first act ended, Marcee sprung from her seat and hurried to a rest area so she could call Jordan.

"Girl, you should leave right now and meet me at that churro place near your house," he suggested after she explained what had transpired.

"Do you really think it's OK to take off?" she asked. "Considering that Brent paid for an entire box of seats *and* a car service?"

"If it were me, I would have left during the opening number," he said. "Unless Britney Spears was in it. Then I'd have listened to at least the first 12 songs."

"It's 9:45PM, so, if I call the driver and head home to change into sweats, I can probably be at the restaurant by 10:30PM," she said. "Does that work?"

"Yep," he replied. "I'll jump in the car in 10 minutes. I can grab a table for us if I get there before you do. Oh, and make sure you bring the uneaten food; that'll be my lunch for the weekend."

◇◇◇

MARCEE WALKED INTO the Happy Days Cafe right at 10:30PM. Jordan was already seated at one of two high-top tables against the front windows.

"I'm so happy to see you," Marcee said, giving him a tight hug. "Tonight has been awful."

"Before we get into it, what do you want to eat?" he answered. "I'll go order for us."

"Let me do it, so I can pay," she replied. "You basically gave up your Friday night, and I want to treat."

"Oh, no, no." Jordan winked, motioning with his chin in the direction of the cashier. "I want to take care of this." Behind the register was a tall midtwenties hunk with highlighted blond hair and cheekbones high enough to take flight.

"Now I get it; you didn't come here to soothe *me*," Marcee joked. "You just wanted to ogle..." She squinted to see the man's name tag. "Dallas." She looked closer. "Oh, pardon me: 'Dallas! with an exclamation point." She laughed. "I should've have known there was a reason you were willing to come to my rescue after 10PM in the Valley."

"Please don't let Dallas take the sentiment out of my kind and selfless support," he jabbed. "I may or may not have met a friend here last Friday, and I may or may not have hit it off with a sexy bakery salesman. No big deal."

"Hit it off?" Marcee looked at Jordan suspiciously.

"What does that mean exactly? Was there an exchange of phone numbers?"

"No, but he told me that I'd made a good choice with the Nutella stuffed churros," Jordan answered. "He might as well have proposed."

"Why am I coming to *you* for dating advice?" Marcee shook her head. "You think you're in a relationship with a barely-out-of-diapers pastry seller in Sherman Oaks because he complimented your food selection a week ago? Really? I bet he's not even gay."

"He's gay, trust me," Jordan said as he stood up and took his wallet from the back pocket of his jeans. "And if he doesn't know he is, I'm sure I can help him figure things out." He winked. "What do you want?"

"I'll have the vegan, gluten-free churros and an apple juice," she said. "And ask your future husband if I can get some chocolate syrup on the side for dipping." For some reason, the specialty item made late-night snacking seem less indulgent.

"Gluten-free and vegan? What the fuck is the point?" Jordan scoffed. "Either get something real, or don't bother. This isn't Whole Foods."

"Fine," Marcee said, looking up at the chalkboard menu above the white tiled counter. "I'll have a mint chip churro ice cream sandwich." It didn't take much to change her mind.

She sat sideways on her stool so she could observe the transaction. Nothing besides Jordan's overly wide smile and frequent head tilts seemed out of the ordinary. In fact, poor Dallas looked tired and ready to end his shift. His purposefully distressed T-shirt may have read "Happy Days," but his good time had obviously ended earlier in the evening.

"Did you hear that?" Jordan just about skipped to the

table with an order number, Marcee's juice and a Sprite. "Dallas was practically ready to ask me out. I can probably seal the deal in one more visit."

"Um, Jordan, I hate to break this to you," she replied, "but he was paying more attention to the clock than he was your spastic flirting."

"See, and this just makes it clear why, without my help, you'll be single forever. You don't understand romance." He took a sip of his drink. "Anyway, do you wanna give me any more info about your date so we can analyze?"

"Before I do that, do you mind switching seats? You know I don't like to have my back to a room." Marcee started to stand.

"Nice try, mon amie," Jordan snapped good-naturedly, telling her with his fingers to sit back down. "If you think I'm giving up my view of Dallas, you'd better build a little bridge in your brain and get over that idea."

"Ugh, fine," she said, smirking, "but try to look at me every couple of minutes, OK? So I know that you're half paying attention."

"It's a deal," Jordan replied just as Dallas delivered the desserts to their table.

"I brought you a couple of extra plates and forks," Dallas said, "in case you guys want to share." Jordan gazed at him adoringly.

"Did you hear that?" Jordan asked excitedly once Dallas had turned to clear another table on the other side of the room. "He brought us extra silverware. In case we want to share."

"Yeah, I picked that up." Marcee was entertained by Jordan's enthusiasm for the young waiter. "But what does that have to do with anything?"

"Do you think he does that for everyone who comes in here? Nope. I can't imagine he does."

"I'm fairly sure that's his job." Marcee chuckled. "He is actually *paid* to bring utensils to customers."

"Believe what you want," Jordan continued, "but he is being particularly attentive to me. We've practically fucked with our eyes already."

"Whatever you say," she answered with a theatrical groan. "I can't wait to dance at your wedding. In the meantime, can we discuss Brent Wetherley? At least *I'm* obsessing over someone who actually knows he went on a date."

"Well, from what you said on the phone, it doesn't sound like you were on a date at all." Jordan used the edge of a spoon to cut into one of the caramel churros on his sampler platter.

"It was definitely a date," she explained. "I mean, he brought dinner *and* planned a night out at the theater."

"Yes, but, you ate and watched the show alone. So which part was the date? The 20 minutes he posed for pictures with random people?"

"I think his intentions were good," she went on. "If he didn't want to see me, he could've bailed altogether."

"Listen, you know I've been in favor of giving the guy a chance." Marcee knew that her silence would signal him to continue. "But, after tonight, I'm a little skeptical." He washed another bite down with soda. "This is the third time."

"Third time?" Marcee was bemused. "I see tonight as more of a second. The Gabbi Green party was a last-minute invitation, and he was nice enough to go along with me."

"He didn't really go along with you, though, did he?" Jordan looked her in the eyes. "He showed up, took photos on the red carpet and then hightailed it out of Santa Monica, if I remember correctly."

"But he told me in advance that he needed to leave by

a certain time." Marcee used her fork to pick chocolate chips out of the pale green ice cream smashed between two churro "cookies" and ate them slowly, one by one.

"Just because he managed your expectations ahead of time doesn't make it right. He could have been 20 minutes late to his next appointment — just the way he was tonight — and given you a little more attention. Plus, I personally think he should have kissed you after the first date."

"Well, wait," she said defensively, "that was my neighbor's fault. Sherry ruined the moment with her crazy babble."

"Mar, if a man really wants some kind of action — and his date appears even remotely interested — he'll make a move. Brent could've waited for Sherry to walk down the block with her stupid-ass dog if he had any intention of locking lips."

"What are you getting at?" Marcee put her fork down and began to twist the silver ring on her right hand.

"You're making too many excuses for him. You've explained away the 'no kiss' thing, his 15-minute appearance at the makeup launch and the fact that you were basically stood up tonight."

"I wasn't stood up," she interrupted. "He did come—"

"He stopped by, I know," Jordan answered. "But do you see what I'm saying?"

She fixed her focus on the faux-brick wall behind Jordan's head. He was nothing if not a truth teller, and his astute observations — especially when presented as a cumulative narrative — weren't terribly off the mark. Her disappointment, though, was unmistakable. "You're saying that Brent isn't really into me." She put her elbows on the table and lowered her face into her upturned palms.

"Isn't that really beside the point?" Jordan gently pulled at her right forearm, forcing her to lift her head and look at him. "You need to value yourself enough to realize that *you* shouldn't be into *him*. If he weren't Brent Wetherley the Movie Star, would you even want a fourth date?"

◇◇◇

SATURDAY AND SUNDAY passed glacially. Marcee remained in her Muji pajamas all weekend, tucked away in her bedroom with Italian takeout and a pile of books. She talked with her mother and Jordan multiple times, going over and over her experiences with Brent and the short trajectory of their relationship. Her mood swung back and forth, hitting highs powered by Rhonda's positive thinking and then lows that reflected Jordan's witchy intuition. For the first time that she could remember, the light of Monday morning was a welcome antidote to a draining couple of days.

She was showered, dressed and ready to leave for work just as her cell phone rang at 7:30AM. If it hadn't been Claire, she would have sent the caller directly to voicemail; she liked to have at least one cup of coffee in her system before tackling the day.

"Hi, Claire," she said, walking over to the edge of her bed and taking a seat on the perfectly smoothed-out duvet cover.

"I meant to call you over the weekend, but Rox is away again," Claire whined, "and you know what that means; I had to shift into single-parent mode. One of these days, I'm going to take off for a spa vacation at Canyon Ranch and *he* can try handling all of the parenting responsibilities himself. We'll see which of the three winds up alive at the end of *that*."

"As long as you take me with you," Marcee said in jest. "I could use a little getaway."

"So," Claire said, bulldozing right over Marcee's small talk, "how was your date on Friday?"

"I'm still trying to figure that out." Marcee wanted to respond to Claire honestly without letting on about her own concerns. She wasn't yet sure how she planned to move forward — if at all — and she didn't want Claire to relay anything to Brent prematurely.

"What does that mean?" Claire sounded agitated, like she was put off by having to pull information out of Marcee. "It was either a good time or it wasn't. What's to figure out?"

"Well, we didn't really get to spend too long together," Marcee answered. "He was late because of a business meeting and then had to leave for the airport before the show started. I think we saw each other for about 10 minutes total."

"Welcome to my world," Claire replied. "Your life isn't entirely your own when you're attached to a celebrity, but it's worth it in the end."

"I just worry that he isn't feeling a connection." Marcee was reluctant to open up to Claire completely, but she tossed out a clear fishing line in an attempt to hook even a small amount of reassurance.

"Don't be ridiculous," Claire said firmly. "Brent is really taken with you. He messages me about it all the time. In fact, he texted me on Saturday morning to say how grateful he is that I thought to introduce the two of you."

"Really?" Marcee perked up. "That's so sweet. I didn't hear a peep from him after he left the Hollywood Bowl, so you can imagine the uncertainty that's been swimming around in my head." She relaxed her upper body and leaned back on her arms. *I feel so much less on edge,* she thought. *Brent likes me enough to talk to Claire about it.*

"Don't read into things too much when it comes to how men behave," Claire advised. "Just take what Brent says at face value and enjoy the fact that you've nabbed the town's most sought-after bachelor."

"I suppose you're right." Marcee walked into her living room and took her bag and keys from a basket beneath the tiny kitchen pass-through. "He's a busy guy with huge demands on his time."

"If you're ever feeling doubtful, call me," Claire instructed. "I know the celeb dating game better than anyone — and I lived long enough to write two books about it."

"I absolutely will; you have my word." Marcee stood at her front door, not wanting to lose the signal by heading toward the garage. "By the way, am I going to see you again soon?"

"Oh, yeah...yeah..." She sounded caught off-guard. "We should probably set up a time to get together." The line went dead quiet, as though Claire had activated the mute button for an awkwardly long minute. "Did you not get my e-mail about the TTT dinner a week from today? We're meeting at Cecconi's in WeHo at 7:30PM."

"I didn't see an e-mail, no." Marcee sighed apologetically. "Maybe I somehow missed the note. I'm so glad you thought to mention it."

"You might wind up being *sorry* I said anything." Claire giggled. "I don't think it's going to be the most uplifting evening."

"Why is that? The ladies seemed to be in good spirits at Gabbi's party last week."

"Tons of shit can happen in a few days." Claire must have transferred the call to a Bluetooth device or speakerphone because the audio quality dropped suddenly. "Do you wanna hear the list of everyone's misfortunes?" She didn't wait for Marcee to answer, seemingly anxious — and delighted — to lay down some gossip about her friends. "Claudia is convinced that she has a stalker; Risa got dumped from *Celebrity Ballroom* because the producers found an even less relevant has-been; Jill is panicked that her vegan empire is crumbling because of online rumors that she secretly eats meat; and Jamie found out that her girlfriend likes dick after all." Claire paused. "Did you catch all that?"

"Dear Lord, that's a lot to digest," Marcee answered. "Hopefully, the dinner will help cheer the group up."

"You and I are going to be the only happy people at the table," Claire continued. "Let's just be thankful that our lives aren't as messy as theirs. Anyhow, I have to love you and leave you; my stretching class starts in two minutes."

"Alright, go ahead," Marcee replied. "I'll check in with you during the week."

The impromptu chat with Claire made Marcee feel as though she'd wasted the entire weekend perseverating over Brent's romantic intentions; the seesaw of emotions had been exhausting. Jordan, although smart and practical in his thinking, had no frame of reference for living life next to the rich and famous on a personal level, and her mother's position was wishfully biased. Claire's experiences were better suited to counsel Marcee, and she allowed her new friend's affirmation to put her in a good frame of mind.

As she popped into the Starbucks at the corner of Noble Avenue and Ventura, she eyed the case of breakfast offerings. She knew that a cup of oatmeal without brown sugar was the healthiest and most low-calorie option, but the jollity stirred by her conversation with Claire deserved a thick slice of iced lemon pound cake and a Vanilla Bean Frappuccino. She polished both of them off before settling back into her car.

"Mom?" Marcee wanted to chat with someone during her ride to work and had dialed her mother. "I assumed you'd be awake since it's after 8:15AM. I'm on my way to the office." Her voice had the vivacity of a songbird.

"My eyes just opened, honey," Rhonda replied. "You sound perky today, considering your mind-set this past weekend."

"Yeah, I'm feeling much better," Marcee effused. "Claire called to find out how the date went, and she sort of put things in perspective for me."

"Oh, I see how it is," Rhonda replied. "When your mother tells you how amazing and lovable you are, she has no idea what she's talking about. Yet when the wife of a big movie star offers her two cents, it turns your frown upside down." If Jewish guilt could be bottled and sold, Rhonda Brookes would undoubtedly corner the market.

"You *are* aware that you're completely prejudiced, correct?" Marcee asked. "I'm sure you've wondered why Leonardo DiCaprio hasn't swept me off my feet yet."

"He'd certainly want to if he met you," Rhonda said. "And he'd be a very lucky man."

"Anyway, Claire said that Brent has told her many times how happy he is to have met me." Marcee took a sip of the bottled water that was in the console next to her seat. "So, I feel like Jordan's apprehension might be a little overblown. I know he's being protective, but I think Claire has better insight into this particular circumstance."

"I can't argue with you on that," her mom answered. "Jordan is always looking out for your best interests, but you also have to keep in mind that he might be a little nervous about losing you."

"I actually hadn't thought of that," Marcee agreed. "I hear about 'gay widows' all the time — close friends who wind up hurt when one of the two ends up in a relationship. Maybe he's subconsciously discouraging me from seeing Brent because he's afraid that I won't have as much time for him. Or that I'll treat him differently."

"It's very possible." Rhonda yawned loudly. "Make sure

you give him some extra TLC, and he'll probably lighten up on Brent once he sees that you're not going anywhere."

"I'm on it," she said just as she was about to arrive at Luminary. "I'll call you after work." She parked and made her way to the elevator bank, thinking about how much time she'd misspent worrying over the weekend. If only Rox hadn't been out of town and Claire had had time to call sooner, Marcee wouldn't have agonized about Brent's affections for 48 hours straight.

"Morning, Lila," Marcee said enthusiastically as she stopped by the row of cubicles on the way to her office. "How was your weekend?"

"Nothing to write home about," Lila replied. "I just did my laundry and went to the movies with my roommates. I wasn't at the Hollywood Bowl or anything exciting like that." Lila turned her computer monitor slightly so Marcee could see TMZ's lead story featuring a photo of her and Brent. "How was *The King and I: In Concert*? I bet Patrick Stewart was awesome; he's pretty hot for an old guy."

"He was fantastic, but Deborah Kerr is probably trying to claw her way out of the grave to strangle Miley Cyrus. Let's just say that I don't think NBC will be looking to cast Miley as Eliza Doolittle in *My Fair Lady: Live!* this December."

"Thank God," Lila said. "I'm so sick of those TV musical events anyway; someone needs to make them stop. Did you see the tragedy that was Carrie Underwood in *The Sound of Music*?"

"Ugh, Jesus take the wheel," Marcee answered. "And what about *The Wiz* with Queen Latifah? The networks are ruining everything that's great about theater." Marcee started to walk down the hallway.

"I'm actually surprised you're here today," Lila called out. Marcee stopped and backtracked.

"Why is that?" she asked. "It's a normal Monday, isn't it?"

"Yeah, I guess, but I figured you might have decided to take a long weekend away with Brent."

"That would've been nice, but Toronto is a little far to fly for two days." Marcee was still getting used to the idea that just about anyone could figure out what was happening in her life by tracking Brent in the media.

"Toronto? He's not in Canada." Lila seemed sure of herself.

"He took the red-eye right after our date on Friday night," she said. Marcee didn't want to mention that he hadn't stayed for dinner or the show.

"That's strange; there can't possibly be an overnight flight to Santa Barbara. It's only 90 minutes by car."

"Santa Barbara? Why are you so insistent that he's in California?" Marcee was nonplussed.

"I was on CelebrityBlastoff.com," Lila explained. "You know, that little website that'll post anything to get a click-through? Anyhow, I saw a picture of Brent leaving a Coffee Bean near State Street this morning."

"It must be his doppelganger, because he's working on a project in Hollywood North for the next week."

"Maybe the site got it wrong," Lila said. "They're not exactly the most reputable source. Plus, the person in the photo was wearing sunglasses and a Yankees baseball cap, so maybe he was misidentified."

Marcee's chest started to burn, and her heart skipped a beat. "Can you pull that snapshot up?" She stepped behind Lila's desk and leaned in for a clear view.

15

PANERA BREAD SEEMED like a better place to think. By 9:30AM, the ninth floor of the office would probably have heard from Lila about Marcee's online shocker, and she needed to consider her own state of mind at a place that offered quiet and croissants. A "cake 'n shake" combo from Starbucks had satisfied the happy nerves that flew through her stomach earlier that morning, but only the richness of buttery dough could untie the knots of insecurity.

She left Lila's desk and made her way back to her car in a hurry; she wanted to be off the studio lot before other staffers started to trickle in. As she sped out of the garage onto Riverside Drive, she turned to Stevie Nicks on Apple Music. She always saved "Landslide" for times when she felt crestfallen, the same way that she'd watch *Beaches* during similar mood plunges; it reinforced the notion that someone, somewhere had it worse. If Barbara Hershey could fight to the end, so could Marcee Brookes. And boy trouble, no doubt, promised a better survival rate than viral cardiomyopathy.

The restaurant, only blocks from her apartment, was empty. The early rush had obviously come and gone, taking with it most of the continental breakfast items.

"You're out of *croissants*?" She felt desperate, and a bagel wouldn't be as soothing, with or without cream cheese. "Do you mind double-checking?"

"I'm really sorry," the cashier said, "it's been wild here today. What about a blueberry muffin?"

Marcee thought about the lemon cake she'd eaten only an hour before and then decided that a frosted fudge brownie and an M&M candy cookie — no matter the time of day — were the way to go. The bubbly salesgirl, whose tag identified her as "Mahtob" and included a smattering of rainbow and heart stickers, was clearly instinctive enough to pick up on Marcee's despondent vibe.

"Our brownies are the best." Mahtob smiled. "They make the world a better place." She punched the item codes into her register and then glanced up at Marcee. "You know, you have a free latte on your rewards card. Do you want it today?" She winked as they both pretended that Marcee even *had* an incentive program membership.

"That's really sweet of you, Mahtob," Marcee replied gratefully. "Is it that obvious that my day is off to a bad start?"

"Yeah, a brownie and a cookie at this hour are pretty telling." Mahtob appeared to be empathetic. "But whatever it takes to make it through, right?" She handed Marcee a bakery box. "I'll bring the coffee to you as soon as it's ready."

"By the way, I'm sure I'm not the first person to ask, but..." Marcee looked at the teenager quizzically.

"Yes, you're exactly right...my parents named me after the kid in *Not Without My Daughter*." Mahtob sounded resigned. "I live every day wondering when Sally Field might show up and try to run me across a border." Marcee strained to lift the corners of her mouth. Ordinarily, she would have been more amused by the early-90s movie reference — especially coming from a woman too young to completely understand its pop-culture significance — but at that moment, the allure of baked goods was her only shot at contentment.

Marcee found a booth at the back of the room and plugged her lightning cable charger into the outlet beneath her seat. She logged into the free WiFi network and began to look through her work e-mails. She felt guilty for playing the "suddenly sick" card but needed to make sense of her thoughts before everyone was doing it for her, behind her back.

Luckily, the few messages that had come in weren't urgent, as she was finding it difficult to concentrate on anything other than her unabating concern about the Brent situation. The photo that Lila had spotted on the web placed him only about 80 miles away that morning, and he was wearing exactly the same clothes he'd worn to the Hollywood Bowl. *Why would he have told me he was going to Canada?* It was possible that the snapshot had been taken at another time and erroneously captioned, but he hadn't said a peep to Marcee about having been on any short trips between their dates.

The picture was evidently taken with a fan's phone. Brent looked unaware that he had been snapped, and it wasn't as though established photographers stationed themselves so far from Los Angeles to get celebrity shots. Not to mention, second-tier sites like CelebrityBlastoff.com depended on low-cost images to keep themselves in business. The person who sold the photo probably earned around $50 for his work.

Marcee imagined all sorts of scenarios, mostly those that starred Brent as the handsome man who didn't have the heart to tell a lonely, beefy girl that she didn't turn him on. Perhaps he felt he had to get away in order to build the strength to let her down, but he certainly wouldn't have needed to lie about his location for *that* story. She was perplexed, especially since Claire had just relayed Brent's warm feelings a couple of hours before. Unfortunately, though, she'd been conditioned to assume the worst.

As she stared into the dizzying pattern of the commercial upholstery around her, she recalled the carpeting in the creative-writing classroom of her high school. The low-grade materials were similarly unattractive, and the cold, institutional appointments evoked a familiar unease. If Le Pain Quotidien had better desserts, she'd have camped out a mile down the road, but in exchange for the tastier comfort food, she had to suffer the reminder of being sandwiched between the desks of Meredith Langer and Pamela Goodwin during her sophomore-year homeroom class.

Meredith and Pamela were close friends, skating through their senior years at Harvard Westlake. Of average intelligence and enviable good looks, the attractive duo was rarely spotted apart — they were usually referred to as the Doublemint Twins or Sweet Valley High Schoolers — except during first period. Marcee, who'd been fast-tracked into the advanced placement course, had been assigned the seat between the two young women for the entire semester. She surmised that the teacher was attempting to limit extracurricular chatter by separating the campus besties, but the divide wound up making them more disruptive. They would pass notes frequently throughout the hour, kicking folded pieces of loose-leaf paper back and forth with the tips of their rhinestone-jeweled Keds. Meredith and Pamela had no choice but to befriend Marcee in order to keep their covert communications undetectable, and Marcee accepted the arrangement; it felt good to be acknowledged in the hallways by two of the school's most popular students — even if the day-to-day pleasantries seemed less than genuine.

"You should sit with us at lunch sometime," Meredith

would say every few days, accompanied by an affirmative nod from Pamela. Marcee loved the idea of being spotted among a faster, glittery mix — especially as a lowly 10th grader — and looked for their table every time she walked into the cafeteria at 12:15PM. She knew that being associated with the in crowd would not only elevate her social status inside the walls of the tony private school but would also position her as someone other than a pudgy outsider. Yet, she'd never been able to find them during the meal breaks. As it turned out, that had been by design all along.

Six weeks into the school year, Marcee happened to walk into the restroom while Meredith and Pamela were occupying side-by-side stalls; she could see their signature shoes on the checkered tile. Engrossed in conversation, they obviously hadn't heard anyone walk in.

"You don't really think it's a good idea to have Large Marge sit with us at lunch, do you?" Pamela was chatting away as though she were at a house party and not sitting on a toilet.

"Of course not, numb-nut," Meredith shot back. "I invite her just so she doesn't get us in any trouble for writing messages during class. It has to appear that we actually like her."

"How would she ever find us anyway, considering that we don't go anywhere near the areas where everyone else eats?" Pamela sounded like she was trying to reason out a game of *Clue:* "lunch" in a "secret meeting place" with the "cool kids."

"That's exactly why I continue to bring it up to her," Meredith said. "It makes her think she has a chance with us, but, in reality, it'll never happen. Poor thing will just have to stay on the Island of the Misfit Toys."

"You're so smart, Meri," Pamela answered. "You could totally work in government someday."

Marcee remembered her bottom lip trembling uncontrollably as she ran from the bathroom. She stifled her tears so no one could see her humiliation and never told her mother or Jordan about Meredith and Pamela's shenanigans. She finished the writing class — with an A+, naturally — without even letting the two young women know that she was aware of their mendaciously hurtful slights.

"How's *that* for a latte?" Mahtob said proudly, jolting Marcee out of her daydream. The foam on top of the piping-hot beverage had been manipulated to look like a unicorn floating on a cloud.

"It's almost too beautiful to drink," Marcee said. "Thank you." She took a sip and then wiped the white residue that had created a mustache on her upper lip. As she cut a piece of her brownie with the plastic knife that Mahtob had been kind enough to bring to the table, she saw a push notification from Twitter; apparently, she had a number of new followers.

She opened the social media app on her phone and looked through her feed. Her "nest" was now feathered with more than 12,000 users, which fascinated her considering that she'd been too busy to truly engage with her new virtual friends. She'd sent no more than three tweets with uplifting quotes and was, therefore, plainly drafting from Brent's fan base. The idea made her realize that his activity on Twitter, Facebook, Instagram or Snapchat might reveal something about his weekend whereabouts.

Marcee searched his Twitter account, first noticing that he didn't follow her. *Isn't that contemporary etiquette when you're interested in someone*? she thought. As she read through his posts, she saw behind-the-scenes "throwback" pictures of him on the sets of various movies and general messages wishing his fans "Happy National 'This and That' Day." *Happy National Donut Day. Happy National Music*

Day. Happy National Potato Chip Day. There was nothing pegging him to a specific location at any particular time. The person who managed his online accounts was clearly keeping the process easy and streamlined by using stock film and event photos as well as the exact same public greetings across all of his social media. In the age of "transparency" and "authenticity" — marketing buzzwords that studio executives bounced around like racquet balls — Marcee couldn't believe that no one had exposed Brent for employing a third party to front his online presence.

With the brownie completely eaten, she had no choice but to bite into the candy cookie in an effort to quell her ongoing anxiety. As she nibbled, she refreshed her e-mail accounts to make sure she wasn't missing anything urgent at work. There were only two notes, one of which was from Ben inviting her to hang out at a local dog park on Sunday. *Nothing from the man who* should *be making plans with me? Ugh.* The other message was from Addie.

To: Brookes, Marcee <marcee.brookes@luminarypictures.com>
From: Willis, Addie <addie.willis@luminarypictures.com>
Subject: Checking in…

Hey, Mar. Lila told me what happened this morning. You must have left just before I got to the office.

Are you OK? I'm sure there's some logical explanation, and you'll feel much better once you talk to Brent.

Meanwhile, take care of yourself. Let me know if you need me to do anything for you while you're out, but I think everything is pretty much under control here.

Don't forget that we have a department meeting with Tina Conlin tomorrow at 10AM. She's the Oscar campaign specialist whom Phyllis wanted to hire to promote *Tied to My Heart* during awards season. If you want to reschedule, say the word.

Talk soon,

Addie

The subject of "awards specialists" distracted Marcee for a moment. In her experience, they were overpaid charlatans who postured themselves industry-wide to seem indispensible to studios, filmmakers and actors. They did nothing more than arrange parties, screenings and promotional ads on behalf of their clients, all work that required no unique skill, strategy or savvy. She also marveled at the fact that a number of these freelancers were voting members of the Academy, a boldface conflict of interests. Weren't they likely to pick the nominees that generated their paychecks? It was one of Hollywood's most poorly hidden schemes, and Marcee didn't want to perpetuate it by spending any portion of her already lean budget on Tina Conlin.

On any other day, she would have spent hours stewing in her disdain for yet another group of Tinseltown hustlers, specifically those whose work was rewarded with much higher compensation than hers. In the midst of her confusion about Brent and his intentions, though, she let the infuriating politics of the entertainment business take a back seat. She answered Addie's e-mail with a quick "xo" and decided that, although she was likely to ultimately decline Tina's services, she would be respectful enough to keep the meeting and hear what the "specialty marketing" quack had to say.

Marcee was startled by the earsplitting ring of her phone. She usually kept it at a low volume as not to irritate people around her, but she must have accidentally hit the wrong button at some point. Sarah Lawrence's call came through *very* loud and clear.

"Hi, Sarah," Marcee answered, trying to sound upbeat. "How was your weekend?"

"Too fast," Sarah lamented. "What governing body decides how long the weekend should be? Can we petition someone for a four-day workweek?"

"Get me *that* document to sign, will you?" Marcee faked a chuckle. "I'd even march on Washington with you, if necessary."

"Noted," Sarah replied. "Sorry to bother you on your cell; I tried the office, but the person who answered said you were working remotely today. Claire told me that she talked to you a couple of hours ago about dinner at Cecconi's on Monday?" She delivered the statement with the inflection of a question.

"Yes, at 7:30PM," Marcee confirmed.

"The ladies have decided that they'd rather go to the Palm on Canon in Beverly Hills. Apparently, Cecconi's offers 50 percent off to Soho House members on Monday evenings; Claire doesn't like the 'discount night' clientele."

"The Palm is completely fine with me." Marcee wasn't a big fan of Cecconi's anyway. It had previously been Morton's — home to the exclusive *Vanity Fair* Oscar party — until 2009, and the building conjured so many bad memories. Since she'd started working in the industry, she'd been required to accompany one poorly behaved celebrity or another to the annual bash, chaperoning the talent down the red carpet to make sure he or she wasn't too shit-faced to speak coherently to the press. Once the media got their footage and soundbites, the star celebrated the remainder of the evening inside the lavish soirée while Marcee grabbed fast food on Santa Monica Boulevard and drove home. Walking *to* the front door next to the rich and famous didn't mean walking *through* the door with them, an important distinction that definitively separated those attending as guests and the others who were lowly workers.

In 2007, Marcee escorted Alana Schaeffer, a best supporting actress nominee, through the press line, holding up the train of Alana's dress as the actress stopped and chatted with more than 15 broadcast television crews. Alana was stumbling and mixing up words, obviously high on something; Marcee's job was to keep her from tripping in front of the cameras. Before she entered the party, Alana called out, "Thanks, little dress girl," flapping Marcee away with her hands. When Marcee didn't respond, Alana screamed louder, drawing the attention of every person within earshot. Mortified, Marcee waved back and then hid inside a catering tent until it was time for her to leave. Not exactly the type of work she had in mind when she first dreamed about the glitz and glamour of a Hollywood PR job.

Alana Schaeffer, when compared to Grant Ryder, was a gem. The winner of 2008's best actor award, he scoffed at the idea of being trailed by a studio publicist the minute he stepped out of his chauffeured limo. "I don't want you around," he yelled at Marcee, as though she were a street thug or a downtown bum. Trying to do as instructed by her boss, she stayed nearby the Oscar winner — not too close, but close enough — just in case he wound up needing something and tried to catch her eye. Instead, he walked over to her, unscrewed the top from his bottle of Evian and dumped it over her head. Drenched, cold and disgraced, Marcee was reassigned to another movie star and forced to work for two more hours as though nothing had happened.

Now, Marcee circled back around to her conversation with Sarah. "Are we meeting at the same time?" she asked.

"Yep, just a simple location change," Sarah replied. "I'll let Claire know it's on your calendar." A loud buzzer began to sound in the kitchen, which was just around the corner from Marcee's table. "Are you alright?" Sarah asked. "What's that noise?"

"Oh, some warning alarm on a microwave oven at Panera Bread," Marcee said. "Let me step away." She unplugged her phone, quickly ate the last bite of her cookie and dashed outside to the parking lot at the back of the restaurant. There were some tables and chairs on a small patio that the sandwich shop shared with an adjacent Chipotle.

"You're working from a Panera Bread?" Sarah laughed. "That's where us screenwriters go in LA to steal Internet service."

"I know," Marcee agreed. "In this town, setting up a mobile work space at a coffee or bake shop is such a cliché. But I had to get out of the office for the day; I was feeling overwhelmed." Her voice cracked and then weakened.

"Is everything alright?" Sarah asked. "You don't sound like yourself today."

Marcee was reluctant to unload on Sarah; they had only just become friends. "I'm just really mystified by how everything is unfolding with Brent." She told Sarah some of what had happened at the Hollywood Bowl and then about discovering the web photo that was supposedly taken in Santa Barbara.

"It's a bit odd, I have to admit," Sarah answered in a clipped style. "But dating is a mystery to me in general. I'm probably not the best person to offer any advice." She didn't provide insight into whether or not Claire had mentioned anything about Brent's travels.

"I appreciate you listening," Marcee said, not wanting to push or ask questions that could be perceived as too probing or pointed. Sarah was silent for a couple of beats, making Marcee wonder if the call had been disconnected. "Hello?"

"I'm here," Sarah replied. "I put the phone on mute for a second while I walked into another room. There was too much going on around me."

"I totally understand." Marcee knew too well what it was like to try to have a phone conversation while Phyllis was circling her doorway. "Do you want to chat another time, when things aren't so hectic?"

"Believe it or not, I was going to suggest that we get together this weekend." Sarah was speaking in a hushed voice. "Maybe lunch or manicures — or both — on Saturday? I can tell you more then."

Tell me more? Sarah's tone, coupled with her word choice, gave Marcee pause. "What do you mean, 'tell me more?'" Marcee asked. She began to nervously twist the hair hanging to the left side of her face. *What could Sarah possibly be talking about? More about what? About Sarah's own limited dating experiences? About Brent?*

"Anyhow, thanks so much for making that adjustment to your calendar; Claire looks forward to seeing you a week from today." The officiously swift subject change made clear to Marcee that Sarah was not alone.

"Um…OK…" Marcee stammered, "no problem." She attempted to follow Sarah's lead. "Talk to you soon." She hung up and threw her head back, letting the sun warm her face. *Life was so much easier when I had no social life.* As soon as she looked at her phone again, she saw a text from Sarah.

"I'm so sorry," she typed. "Claire has been home all morning, and I didn't want her to overhear our conversation. I'll try to call this week if there's time, but put me on your schedule for nails and food on Saturday."

"Will do," Marcee replied, slightly relieved that Sarah had explained her erratic behavior but still dying to know what Sarah wanted to say. "Do you want to text me whatever's on your mind?" Marcee asked, making another attempt to alleviate her concern about the words *I can tell you more then.*

"Nothing to worry about," Sarah responded. "It can keep until the weekend."

Marcee drove the few streets to her apartment and powered up her laptop at the living room table. She resolved to get as much work done from Sherman Oaks as humanly possible and struggled to put Brent — and Sarah's cryptic words — out of her mind until she could soak in a hot salt bath later that evening. She noticed that Jordan had tried to reach her a couple of times, but she silenced her iPhone to avoid any further disturbances. It was no wonder, then, that she didn't see Brent's text until nearly 5PM.

"Hi, baby," he wrote. "Hope you're well. It's almost dinnertime in Toronto. I think I'm going to eat early and turn in. I'm exhausted. Talk soon. XO."

I'm on his mind, Marcee thought, her spirits lifting slightly. She considered the fact that he took the time to send a message at all, which, she rationalized, he'd have no motivation to do if he weren't sincere in his interest. His mention of dinner, moreover, added up considering the difference in time zones. *Plus, he has absolutely no reason to lie to me; it's not like we're in a committed relationship yet. He doesn't really owe me anything.* The photo Lila found on CelebrityBlastoff.com was probably a recycled image from their archives, she decided; perhaps it had simply been a slow celebrity news day.

"Hope you had a good meal and that you can get a decent night's rest," she wrote back. "Give me a call when you have a few minutes to catch up. I'm around. xoxo."

◇◇◇

THE REST OF the week was an emotional roller coaster. Marcee initially felt better when Brent texted on Monday afternoon but then climbed up and down a ladder of fluctuating feelings when she didn't hear from him again. Her mother and Jordan did their best to provide phone support — Sara Lee and Häagen-Dazs pitched in, too — but she was living for the weekend. She was hopeful that Sarah planned to reveal something that would set everything straight, or at least provide a small amount of clarity. The constant uncertainty was stealing her sleep and her professional focus at a time when the burden to prove herself weighed heavily on her shoulders.

She slept in on Saturday morning, which meant 8:30AM. At one time, when she was younger, she was able to push the limits of her alarm clock, sometimes staying in bed past noon. The stress and responsibilities of being a grown-up in high-pressure PR jobs, though, ruined her lazy weekend tendencies. She had too much to think about and too many errands; she couldn't afford to waste time on valuable days off.

She met Sarah at 11AM at a nail salon on Montana Avenue in Santa Monica, which was conveniently located near Sweet Lady Jane. Marcee was hell-bent on getting a slice of the cherry pie that had been heralded as one of Oprah's "favorite things," and a to-go container of their famous Oreo tiramisu was likely in the cards as well.

"I'm so glad you picked this restaurant," Sarah said as they stepped inside the shabby chic eatery. "I looked over their menu on my phone while our nails were drying; everything sounds so good."

"It's all delicious," Marcee replied, "but you'll die over the curry chicken salad on challah bread."

"Sold!" Sarah seemed as excited about the meal as Marcee. "Do you want to place the order, and I'll find a spot outside?" The café was busy, and table space was scarce. "I'll give you cash for my food."

"Don't be ridiculous," Marcee answered. "This is on me. Just grab some open seats, and I'll be right there with two iced teas."

Marcee was just as happy that Sarah wouldn't be nearby to see exactly what she was having packed to take home. Once she'd perused the glass case of sweets, she'd added slices of triple berry cake and flourless chocolate decadence to her tab, both of which would keep well in the refrigerator for a few days.

"That's a pretty big shopping bag," Sarah remarked as Marcee set their drinks down on the outdoor wrought iron table. "Is that our lunch?"

"No, they'll bring the food to us," Marcee said slowly so she could spin a viable story in her head. "I picked up some extra things for my parents. They're having a small barbecue at their house tomorrow." It appeared that Sarah fought a battle with high-sugar carbs herself, but Marcee was still compelled to divert any attention from her own.

"If any of this stuff were sitting in my apartment overnight," Sarah said, "it would be gone by the next day."

"I hear you." Marcee could certainly relate but was embarrassed to reveal quite how much. "It won't be easy to keep my hands off these boxes."

"I started going to Overeaters Anonymous meetings recently," Sarah admitted, sweeping a few windblown hairs away from her face. "I haven't told anyone — especially Claire — but then I realized that it's not really 'anonymous' anyway. I mean, it's kind of hard to eat so compulsively and go unnoticed, isn't it?" She delivered the self-deprecating joke as though it were inclusive of Marcee. "Am I wrong?"

Marcee bristled at being labeled an "overeater" — even by someone with similar issues — but she was more preoccupied with what Sarah was trying to say about Claire. "Don't you tell Claire about what's happening in your life?"

Marcee asked. "I used to keep to myself at work, but going out with Brent has kind of pushed me into being open." Marcee always found people to be more forthcoming when she followed a question with a personal anecdote or insight.

"I've learned to be all business at work," Sarah replied, shifting around in her chair. "You know, Claire can be a character." A waitress brought their sandwiches and side salads before Sarah could continue. "Wow, this looks amazing. I'm so glad you introduced me to this place." She stared down at a plate that was large enough to feed two people; her train of thought had obviously been derailed by the portion size.

"What do you mean by 'character?'" Marcee inquired. She cut her sandwich in half and lifted a piece to her mouth. *I feel like she wants to tell me something bigger than the words she's using.*

"Oh, I don't know what I mean." Sarah giggled, seeming noncommittal. She poked her fork into the mounds of chicken salad between thick pieces of challah bread.

"Is there more I should know about Claire? She has been really good to me," Marcee said. She wanted to make clear her own positive feelings about Claire but also give Sarah a safe zone to speak candidly without the threat of being exposed. *It would make sense for Sarah to have a different opinion of her own boss. Sarah works for Claire; I'm friends with Claire. Totally different perspectives and relationships.*

"You just have to be on guard with those ladies." Sarah ate a chunk of white meat. "They can be really judgmental at times."

"Is that what you meant by 'telling me more' when we were on the phone last Monday?" Marcee asked as she stabbed a piece of lettuce and a crouton to create the tastiest bite possible.

Sarah cleared her throat and pushed the food around

her plate. "I guess so," she answered with what sounded like a tentative lilt. "Things get so crazy at the Malibu house that I don't know whether I'm coming or going half the time, let alone what's spilling out of my mouth. I was probably just having a freak-out moment."

It sounded to Marcee like Sarah was covering her tracks, but she didn't want to keep poking. *That can't possibly be all that Sarah was waiting to say; she made it seem like she had some substantial intel.* "I'm used to judgmental people," Marcee said. "Don't forget, I work in Hollywood, too."

"Touché." Sarah smiled. "Claire's a whole different animal, though, so just be a little careful. That's basically what I was getting at."

"I really appreciate you having my back," Marcee said, although still confounded by what came across like a riddle. She finished eating and moved her dishes to the edge of the table as she sat back and watched a group of joggers run by. Her gut told her not to push Sarah any further. "Do you have anything exciting happening the rest of this weekend?"

"If you consider laundry and housework exciting, then yes." Sarah pushed her empty plates next to Marcee's. "Other than that, it's just WebFlicks and Domino's Pizza."

"Ain't nothing wrong with that," Marcee commented as she stood from her seat, "and there's no better reward for being productive than pizza. Well, at least if you add an order of Cinna Stix with a couple of extra packets of icing."

"Oh my God," Sarah shrieked in agreement, "I could live on those. I know it's just dough, butter and sugar, but it tastes *so* good." She walked Marcee to her car, which was parallel parked at a meter a few yards down the sidewalk.

"Have a couple of bites for me, if you don't mind." Marcee hugged Sarah. "I'm going to try to starve myself from now until Monday night." They both laughed. "OK, maybe not. Just until dinner this evening."

"I'll talk to you next week," Sarah said. "Thanks again for lunch."

"It was my pleasure," Marcee replied as she got into her car. "We'll speak after the TTT dinner, for sure." She pulled away from the curb and turned around on a side street. As soon as she was headed in the right direction, she called her mother.

"How are you, honey?" Rhonda asked. "Do you feel like going to a movie with Daddy and me? I think we're going to see that new Meryl Streep film — you know, the one where she plays her own character's mother *and* grandmother."

"I think I will. What time does it start?" Marcee made her way onto the 405 from Sunset Boulevard and headed toward the Valley.

"It runs at 5:20PM at the AMC Promenade and then we can eat back at the house. I'm at the grocery store now, so let me know if there's anything special you want."

"Whatever you're getting for yourselves is fine with me," Marcee answered. "I'll pick you guys up at 4:45PM. Can you talk for a minute now, though?"

"Sure, I'll just have to jump off when they call my number at the deli counter," Rhonda said. "But, as slow as they are at Pavilions, that should give us about an hour."

"So, I just had lunch with Sarah, Claire's assistant, in Santa Monica," Marcee began. "I told you we've become friendly, right? Anyway, she said something today about my needing to be careful around Claire," Marcee relayed.

"Did she explain what she meant?" Rhonda asked.

"No, not really; just that the TTT ladies can be very judgmental. But isn't everyone?"

"I wouldn't give it much thought," Rhonda advised. "Sarah works for the woman, so she probably sees a different side of her. Just the way Phyllis Van Buren likely has friends outside of the industry who think she's a wonderful person."

"That's what I was thinking, too," Marcee said. "Claire has really embraced me; she's brought some great things into my life in such a short period of time."

"Exactly, so filter through what Sarah says, and form your own opinions," Rhonda continued. "Being employed by Claire Madison is not the same thing as being her personal friend."

16

"IT'S WHAT I call win-win-win terrorism." Claire laughed, lifting a glass of iced coffee to her mouth and taking a few quick sips through two thin cocktail straws.

"Sick, but true," Jill replied. "Who would actually want to see Risa Turner opposite Scott Baio in *Love Letters* at some 50-seat theater in North Hollywood? They're probably among the last couple of D-listers to get cast in that god-awful play. I guess Susan Lucci was too busy pretending that *All My Children* is still on the air."

"It's kind of like *The Vagina Monologues,*" Jamie interjected. "I think I'm the only person on the planet who hasn't been in a rotating cast of that snatch-fest."

"And that's only because your lesbian cooch is more like a dick with teeth than a pussy." Claudia downed the last quarter of a martini. "My cleaning lady was even in a production of that vagina bullshit."

Ouch, that's harsh, Marcee thought, stunned by the aggression and hostility at what was supposed to be a girls' night out.

"Anyway, back to what I was saying," Claire continued, grabbing the reigns of the conversation. "The terrorists would feel like they're winning by targeting a historic little theater in Los Angeles; the audience wouldn't have to suffer through Risa's performance; and, more important, it would save future ticket holders from having to watch that dreck. See? Everyone triumphs."

All of the TTTs had arrived at the Palm on time except for Risa, who'd texted the group ahead to say that she was running 20 minutes late because of her rehearsal schedule.

"If the *Celebrity Ballroom* producers hadn't dumped Risa for Jamie Lynn Spears, they would have saved us all a lot of trouble," Jill noted. "Just another reason to hate that tired TV show. Now we'll all have to traipse to the NoHo arts district to watch Risa chew through some of the most banal stage material ever written."

"Enough about Risa for now," Claudia said. "She'll be here soon enough to talk about herself endlessly. Let's just enjoy our private dining space." The triangular James Dean room — which featured an artful caricature painting of the iconic movie star floating at the center of gold, textured wallpaper — could accommodate 12 people, providing a sizable luxury to a dinner party of six.

"It's really nice that the manager gave us this entire section," Marcee commented, looking around from her seat. One side of the room, which was situated just behind the hostess stand, doubled as the front window of the restaurant, and another was a clear glass wall with sliding doors that did a fairly good job of blocking out the noise from the bar and the main dining area. A mesh curtain discouraged peeping patrons but wasn't opaque enough to promise anonymity.

"There's a $1K food and beverage minimum, though," Claudia answered, "so it's worth their while."

"I'm surprised you were willing to shell out so much money considering that you barely have enough to buy a townhouse in Encino," Claire interrupted. "Do you want me to pick up the tab for tonight? I know it's your turn, but I can spot you this one." She threw her head back, pushed some hair behind her ears and took a theatrical swig from her drink, obviously delighting in calling attention to Claudia's financial rut.

"That's not necessary," Claudia snapped, glaring at Claire with widened eyes.

"Did Nick really put you in such a bad place with money?" Jill asked. "How is it legally possible for the Erickson of Erickson Wells to leave his wife of so many years without cash? Can't you at least sell some of that jewelry he gave you?"

"Funny you should mention that," Claire said, suddenly more animated. "It turns out Claudia is entitled to only half the value of each of those pieces." Claire replied before Claudia had a chance to address the question directly.

"Can you explain how something like that happens?" Jamie either had a general interest in divorce law or was looking for information that would help to protect her in her next celebrity romance. Marcee wasn't sure which exactly but figured it was probably the latter based on Jamie's public-relationship history.

"I signed a prenup that entitles me to half of whatever is in only one particular joint marital account," Claudia said. "Everything in his personal account remains his."

"Right, but if he gave you gifts throughout the years, aren't those yours to keep?" Jill sounded confused. "You can do whatever you want with them, can't you? Didn't he buy them for you with his own money?"

"You would think so," Claudia answered, taking a gulp from the fresh cosmo that a waitress had set in front of her, "but I just found out that everything he bought me was purchased with funds from the shared account. So, basically, half of every ring, bracelet and necklace is Nick's. I'd have to pay 50 percent of the appraised value of each piece if I wanted to keep it, or vice versa. At this point, I'd rather *live* on the money than *wear* it."

"He's such a scuzz-bag," Jill said. "Ken and I have an ironclad prenup, but, to be honest, I make more money than he does anyway. Thank God *my* lawyer was smart enough to foresee my earning potential. If our marriage ever combusts, Ken will be worse off than I'll be."

"That's really nice for you, Jill," Claudia snarled. "So, I'm guessing that you're happy with your Beverly Park estate and don't want to go in together on a duplex in the Valley?"

"That's an adorable idea." Jill set her brown, leather-bound menu down on the white tablecloth. "But I'm not in the market for a drunken neighbor, Claudia. If things get really tight, though, I might consider buying a property for you to rent."

"Jill, would you want to be called a 'landlord' or a 'landlady?'" Claire giggled. Clearly, she continued to find humor in Claudia's struggle.

"I'm always a lady," Jill answered. "But, that said, what the fuck am I going to order here? A steakhouse is not the best choice for a vegan."

"'Vegan' is just a nice word for someone who's too stupid to hunt, fish or ride an animal," Claudia said. "You'll have to get the same green salad and steamed vegetable side dish you order everywhere else."

Marcee detected an opening in the chatter and figured she'd insert a harmless pleasantry into the otherwise heated proceedings. "If you do wind up moving to Encino, we'll practically be roommates," Marcee added. "My apartment is only a couple of miles down Ventura."

As though a plate had shattered in a loud, startling crash on the wooden floor, everyone went silent while Claudia's eyes bored into Marcee's face. *Shit, did I say something wrong?* Claudia glanced over at Claire with a look that unmistakably asked, "Did someone just fart? Can you smell it, too?" *It's not as if I were literally asking her to move in with me*. Marcee wanted to crawl under the table until the lingering stench of her embarrassing comment wafted out of the room. Luckily, Risa entered after a 20-second awkward pause, diffusing Marcee's discomfort and setting the biting banter back in motion.

"Rehearsing this play is going to put me in an early grave," Risa announced as she took the one empty seat at the head of the table across from Claire. "Scott Baio is still a lame sitcom actor. Chachi's technique hasn't exactly evolved since *Happy Days* and *Charles in Charge*."

"But *you've* really grown as an actress, huh?" Claire looked at Risa blankly. "I must have missed whichever Broadway play won *you* a Tony award."

"Maybe you were saving money to buy your kids," Risa slammed back, "or were the twins sold as a two-for-one deal? I bet they look just like their real mother."

Marcee didn't remember the last TTT dinner being so contentious, but her second turn at the rodeo gave her a front-row view of the seemingly unburied resentment and crackling competitiveness. Everyone appeared to be carrying daggers with which to impale the weak, making her tentative about adding much to the discourse.

"That's a great top, Risa," Marcee said, admiring the cobalt blue cotton blouse that featured cutouts at the shoulders. "Do you mind if I ask where you found it?"

"I have no idea," Risa huffed with forced hesitation. "I shop all the time, so it's hard to remember where things come from." Marcee looked away, feeling gunned down.

"That's such bullshit, Risa," Claire interrupted. "You once told me that you keep the sales tags from just about everything you buy."

"Maybe I just don't want everyone else wearing the same things," Risa shot back. "If people know where I get my clothes, they'll start to copy me."

"Bitch, please." Claire shook her head. "Nobody wants to duplicate *your* outfits. What alternate universe do you live in? Marcee probably wouldn't even be able to find that shirt if she tried; the stores rarely keep product from two seasons ago."

"Yeah, that definitely isn't current," Claudia chimed in, wagging her finger in Risa's direction. "I'm sure Marcee was just being polite; she could easily get a similar shirt at any Urban Outfitters clearance sale. Plus, that look is so old that she'd be more likely to attract vultures than compliments."

"Speaking of vultures," Jill said, "how are you, Jamie? Did you pick everything off your girlfriend's bones before she decided she'd rather sun herself on Cock Rock than in Poon Pond?"

"Pretty much," Jamie replied, stuffing a piece of bread into her mouth. "She gave me a BMW and about $1 million in cash to 'go away' without talking to the press. I wasn't really that into her anyway, so I made out well, all things considered." She sounded unabashed about her preference for material trappings over her ex's companionship.

"We all know you'll be onto someone else within a couple of weeks, so nothing lost and everything gained, right?" Jill's overly broad smile and light chuckle suggested a disingenuous empathy. "And, Claire, how's the new book coming?"

"Can you even believe I'm actually finishing my *third* book?" Claire responded. "I never imagined that the first two would be so popular."

"Me either," Claudia answered. "Why would anyone think he or she is getting practical, real-life love advice from someone who's been married to a major movie star her entire adult life?"

"Too bad you couldn't benefit from my wisdom." Claire

looked at Claudia and cocked her head. "Maybe I could have helped you tame Nick's roving penis."

"I stopped caring about his little dick before we even got married," Claudia replied. "It was the music publishing royalties that made up for the missing inches."

"Regardless," Claire said, dismissing Claudia with a flick of her hand, "I think this book is going to be a lot of fun; it's a new twist on the memoir genre."

"Wait, you're writing about your life with Rox?" Risa asked. "I thought this was going to be another self-help book."

"It was, until Bartholomew Press gave me a shitload of money to do a compilation of essays describing photos from my Instagram account." Claire took a bite of lobster tail, which had been removed from its shell and served with a side of creamed spinach and mashed potatoes.

"That's impressive," Marcee said. "Bartholomew is like Rizzoli or Taschen. Those hardbound editions are really collectible. I love their stuff, but I've never been able to justify spending $150 for one book."

"I can get you a complimentary copy of mine, Marcee," Claire offered. "Signed and numbered."

"Let me make sure I'm understanding this," Claudia spat in a raspy mumble. "A respected publisher is going to have you caption photos from your social media accounts and then sell them to the public for money? Who would be stupid enough to buy that? They can follow you online for free."

"It's a memoir of my enduring relationship with Rox," Claire explained sharply. "I'm describing it as a love story in pictures *and* words. Essentially, it's a gift to our fans."

"I knew I should have taken a Nexium before I drove over here." Claudia chortled. "Your book is giving me acid reflux, and I haven't even seen a copy of it yet. Excuse me while I run to the ladies' room; maybe my stomach can change the direction of the fluids and send them out the other end." She held on to the edge of the table as she stood and walked toward the bathroom, steadying herself against what was enough alcohol to flatten a baby elephant.

Marcee noticed that the room had quieted briefly in Claudia's absence while the ladies took a moment to enjoy their steaks, seafood and Louis "Gigi" Delmaestro salads. She relaxed and picked at her veal Marsala, grateful that she hadn't gotten too caught up in the conversational crossfire.

"I hope, at the very least, Claudia is *wearing* a Kotex Lightdays," Claire said, laughing, "because she certainly doesn't seem to be *having* any lately."

"Am I the only one who worries about her drinking?" Jamie asked, looking up from her 18-ounce prime New York strip. "She seems to be taking in a lot more liquid since the divorce drama started."

"Are you kidding?" Claire looked to be in disbelief. "Claudia has been on the sauce since I've known her. I'm surprised there's any blood left in her alcohol system."

"I actually like her better drunk," Jill piped up.

"What do you have to compare it to, Jill?" Claire questioned. "When was the last time you saw her without a drink in her hand?"

"Good point," Jill admitted. "Although, I think she passed out on my living room couch once, and her cocktail glass was lying on my rug."

"Do you think we should do an intervention and get her some kind of help?" Risa put her fork down.

"Are you out of your fucking mind?" Claire laughed. "She would love it if we paid for a monthlong vacation at Catalina Mountain Recovery in Arizona, but she needs to start downsizing her life like yesterday. I'm onboard with keeping her in our TTT group for now, though, which I think will definitely help her feel like she's not losing *everything* at once."

"That's a good idea," Risa agreed. "I mean, with no money and no real connection to celebrity, she'll eventually lose touch with our sensibilities, but time will tell. We can always readdress down the line and just phase her out."

"To The Tomb," by its very name, implied to Marcee that inclusion was for an entire life span. Weren't these women true friends beneath their ferocious facades? Or was this just a club of cutthroats that founded its membership on status? The suggestion of a potential excommunication surprised Marcee, especially in the context of a long-standing group confidant such as Claudia Erickson. *What does this mean for me?* Marcee also began to consider why Claire decided to invite her to join in the first place. It sounded as though "fortune" and "fame" were the key words, and Marcee had neither. By a landslide.

"So, Marcee, how are things going with Brent?" Claire changed the subject as soon as Claudia returned to the table.

"Everything's moving along," Marcee replied after swallowing her last bite of veal. "It's just taking time to get traction because he travels so much. He's been in Toronto for the last week." The ladies had been so aggressively pointed with each other all evening, and Marcee didn't want to become the focus of their judgment. She refrained from discussing any details of the previous week or her uncertainty about how the new romance was unfolding.

"Like I said on the phone the other day, when you're attached to a star, things don't follow a traditional timeline," Claire reminded her. "Rox has been in Santa Barbara since last weekend on some retreat with a bunch of studio mucky-mucks, and guess what? I just deal with it. It goes with the territory."

"Frankly, I don't know how you do it, Claire," Jill said,

standing from the table. "I'd be nervous having my husband away all the time. Thankfully, Ken's trips tend to be fast and infrequent." She set her linen napkin on the table, which had just been cleared of dinner plates. "I'm going to run to the powder room."

"Fast and infrequent probably describe Ken's bedroom skills more than his business travel," Claire barked the minute Jill was out of earshot. "I can understand why *she'd* be nervous, though; her husband is notorious for being a beaver-hound. Thankfully, Rox has no interest in anyone else's vagina."

Just as two large pieces of dark chocolate cake and two slices of key lime pie were placed between the women, Claudia reached for a spoon and dug in. "You know I don't like to start rumors, but I heard something interesting from Gabbi Green earlier this week."

"I can't imagine she had anything too groundbreaking to say," Claire answered, "but let's hear it."

"Well, apparently, Jill isn't so diligent in her veganness. Is that how'd you'd say it? Veganness?" Claudia shoveled a second bite of cake into her mouth.

"Meaning what exactly?" Jamie plunged, fork-first, into a slice of pie.

"Meaning that Gabbi and Jill had lunch this past Friday, and apparently, when Gabbi came back from a bathroom break, she noticed that most of the pancetta she'd pushed to the side of her salad plate had been eaten." Claudia took a long slurp from her vodka cranberry and shrugged her shoulders as though she were simply setting out evidence for everyone to evaluate.

"She's such a fraud," Risa said emphatically, like she'd known it all along. "I guess they'll eventually have to reclassify her cookbooks as fiction."

Marcee lifted a cup of decaffeinated coffee to her

mouth, first testing it with her lips to make sure it wouldn't scald her tongue. She stared down into the cup, not wanting to engage in gossip that she knew, firsthand, was true. After all, Jill *was* responsible for Marcee's meteoric professional advancement — regardless of her motivation — and throwing the woman under the farm bus was not how Marcee wanted to repay her.

"You've been quiet this evening, Marcee," Jamie said, almost as though she could see what was happening in Marcee's head. "What's your take on Bacon-gate?"

"Oh, I'm sure it's not what it seems," Marcee answered. "Gabbi didn't actually *see* Jill eat any meat, did she?"

"So, do you think a server ate it off Gabbi's plate while Jill was sitting right there?" Risa questioned. She used the long, lacquered nail on her index finger to pick at her scalp through her woven hair.

"While I was sitting right where?" Jill asked, having re-entered the room unnoticed. She took her seat and looked directly at Risa while the others were quick to busy themselves with their hot beverages and sweets.

"Oh, um," Risa stumbled, "I was just saying, um…"

"Risa was just saying that we didn't need to put any of the desserts in front of where you're sitting because none of them is vegan." Always a fast thinker, Marcee kept the beat going on.

"And I suppose no one thought to ask for a bowl of berries? It's not like I became a vegan overnight. How long have most of you known me?" Jill sighed, reapplied her lipstick and blotted with a tissue from her purse.

"*Overnight Vegan*," Claire said with an exaggerated pause. "That could be a great concept for a new TV show or book. Or maybe *Born Again Vegan*."

Jill put her stained Kleenex on the table and turned her head dramatically to look at Claire. "*Born Again*?"

"You know, like those women on trash TV talk shows who say they're 'born again virgins,'" Claire went on. "They were sexually active hos for years and then opted, after the fact, to 'save themselves' for their future husbands — 30 dicks too late. They delude themselves into thinking they still have their cherries."

"What does that have to do with being vegan?" Jill asked in a suspicious tone, like she knew Claire was ready to strike with a sharpened spear.

"I'm sure there are people who claim to be vegan — or at least who've tried to be — and then secretly smuggle some pork here and there," Claire replied, locking eyes intensely with Jill. "*Born Again Vegan* could expose the chicanery of those irritatingly outspoken animal activists and then get them back on the path to do-gooding."

"That's a fantastic concept," Claudia enthused. "You should produce unscripted television, Claire. Do you have any idea where you might find these undercover carnivores?"

It was obvious to Marcee that Jill — whether or not a true vegan — was being bullied by a gang of adult women. Jumping to Jill's defense could mean throwing herself on the stake but staying silent was more likely to keep Marcee in the club for at least the time being. Fortunately, Jill didn't need any backup.

"I don't think there are too many of those people," Jill said, her neck reddening and pulsing, "and I can't imagine that the audience for a show like that would be terribly large. Probably about the same number of people who would buy a book of your Instagram photos." Her eyes bulged in Claire's direction.

"Maybe you're right." Claire smiled. "I don't know why the idea even popped into my head."

"What does everyone have going on this coming week

and weekend?" Marcee jumped into the ring with an innocuous question in an effort to steer the ship to less volatile waters.

"I'm going with Rox and the twins to Comic Con in San Diego. He has to promote his new superhero movie for Warner Bros., and I think the kids are finally old enough to appreciate the convention," Claire replied. "I, on the other hand, could do without it. I certainly don't need to be rubbing shoulders with 150,000 middle-age pop-culture fans who live in their mothers' basements with PlayStation consoles."

"Ugh; the drive to San Diego on Comic Con weekend is heinous," Marcee added. "I'm so glad I don't have to go there for work this year. Luminary decided to save some money and skip the event this summer."

"Drive? You don't think we'd sit in traffic, do you?" Claire sounded surprised. "The studio is chartering a helicopter to get us in and out in a couple of hours. It costs them only about $16,000, and it saves us so much time. Rox would never agree to go otherwise."

"Can four passengers fit in one chopper?" Claudia asked.

"I think it can accommodate six," Claire answered. "Why, are you fishing for an invitation? You're welcome to come; it might give you a bird's-eye view of the kinds of people you'll be living next to in Encino."

"Are the kids excited about the helicopter ride? I bet it's pretty exciting for 10-year-olds." Risa began to lightly slap both sides of her head repeatedly with her palms, the go-to solution for Itchy-Head-Because-of-Fake-Tight-Hair syndrome.

"I haven't mentioned it to them yet, just in case I decide not to take them," Claire said. "But I'm sure they're gonna love it."

"I don't know how you even tell those adorable twins

apart," Jamie broke in, as if she were trying to join a verbal double-dutch jump-rope game. "I suppose it's easier when you're their mother."

"It's also easy because they're not identical twins," Claire grumbled. "Perhaps you've paid no attention over the years."

"Well, Mary-Kate and Ashley Olsen aren't identical, and I still can't tell which is which." Jamie dipped a tea bag in and out of the hot water in her cup.

"Oh, please," Risa interjected, "the Olsen twins are easy to individually identify. If you watch their direct-to-video movies, Ashley is so obviously the better actress." She howled at her own joke.

"If anybody's interested in what *I'm* doing — and feel free to join — I'm challenging myself to two spin classes per day at Self Search Cycle for the next two weeks," Jill said. "Who wants to do it with me?"

"You've got to be out of your mind," Jamie said, sneering. "Indoor bicycling is a big cult; you might as well become a Scientologist. People who go to those hot and sweaty fitness studios wind up tossing all of their friends in favor of fellow spinners. It's like Jonestown but with Vitaminwater instead of Kool-Aid."

"Whatever, James." Jill smirked. "I'll do it by myself, and you'll wind up drooling over my worked-out thighs and legs."

"Grow your breasts a little more, and the Colonel will sell you in a bucket for $13.99," Jamie retorted.

Marcee looked at her watch; it was already 10:30PM, and it would take her a good half hour to get home. Not only did she have to be up early for work the next morning, but she had been lucky enough to avoid any direct jabs from the TTTs. She decided it was best to quit while she was ahead. In fact, she realized that if she hadn't been sitting among those dipped in Hollywood stardust, she'd probably have taken off by their third nasty barb. She'd never known any so-called friends who spoke to each other so horribly, but the shiny allure of celebrity allowed her to turn a blind eye.

"Ladies, this working girl needs to call it a night," Marcee said. She took her purse from the back of her chair and made her way around the rectangular table to give each woman a hug and kiss goodnight. No one stood to see her out. "I had such a great time, as always. Sorry that I have to be the first one out the door." Marcee always felt more secure when she was able to leave a gathering with at least one other person — safety in numbers — but no one else seemed to be budging from her seat. *I'm sure they'll say something behind my back, but I can't be the last man standing tonight. At the rate they're talking, they'll be here until dawn.*

Marcee walked outside of the James Dean room and said goodnight to the ladies at the maître d' stand as she exited the restaurant. Three valet attendants gathered around her while she stood outdoors on the curb, searching her bag for the claim ticket. After checking every little zipper and pouch for nearly two minutes, she found the card in the side pocket of her skirt. Naturally, it was exactly where she thought to look last.

Then, out of nowhere, she felt a sudden pressure on her bladder, the kind that demanded she use the restroom before buckling in for a 30-minute car ride. "So sorry guys," she said, tucking the ticket away, "but I have to run inside again for a minute."

She swung open the door and pointed to the back of the restaurant, smiling in girl code to let the hostesses know that she'd returned only to use the ladies' room. She stayed to the right of the main dining area, walking alongside the lengthy, fully-stocked bar that was on the far, opposite side of the private room in which she'd just eaten dinner. Even though she was moving quickly, she took a second to notice that the Palm's signature caricature drawings of celebrity patrons had not made the transfer from the walls of their previous Santa Monica Boulevard location to their new digs on Canon. Rather, they'd been replaced with some flamboyant murals of Beverly Hills and a vertical painting of Audrey Hepburn in *Breakfast at Tiffany's.*

The frosted glass door that led to the facilities opened into a small, square lounge. Once inside, the men's room was to the right and the ladies' room straight ahead. As she entered, Marcee heard that the same music that had been playing in the restaurant was being piped into the restroom. She had no problem urinating to Nena's "99 Red Balloons" — floating in the summer sky or anywhere, for that matter — but was surprised by the garish bathroom décor. The Palm's relocation period seemed the perfect time to update, Marcee thought, and yet they'd stuck with someone's idea of what might have been considered upscale in 1970. The patterned, mustard-gold wallpaper clashed with the white and grey squares of tile that were cemented to the floor and stalls, and the black marble vanity countertop was splotched with a brownish-green coloring that recalled mid-flight droppings from a flock of full-bellied birds.

The wooden doors on each of the three cubicles were outfitted with round, brushed nickel locks that displayed the word "vacant" in green when unlatched and "occupied" in red when in use. The first two stalls were noticeably spoken for, so she walked into the largest of the three, a designated handicapped enclosure that also included a changing table. *It's always fun to be reminded that I'm single and childless.*

Marcee had just locked the door and hung her bag on a pewter hook affixed to the back when the song ended. As she started to properly paper the toilet seat, she heard chatter coming from the two cubicles next to her.

"I don't even know how it's gone on this long," one voice said. Marcee moved to the front of the stall and listened closely without making a sound. The others in the bathroom were clearly oblivious to the fact that someone else had walked in. "Remarkable, right?" The inebriated stammer was undeniably Claudia's. Even though the toilet was set too far back for anyone to be able to identify the shoes or calves between the bottom of the door and the ground, Marcee backed up against a side wall and leaned forward. She pressed her ear to the slats above the silver door handle.

"It's fucking unbelievable," the other woman—Claire—replied. "Do you think she'll catch on before Brent's new movie comes out next month?" Whitney Houston couldn't have come back from the grave at a worse time, but, at least "Saving All My Love" was a ballad and not an up-tempo dance tune; Marcee could hear Claudia and Claire above the schmaltzy love song.

"I told him he shouldn't have invited her to the Hollywood Bowl," Claire went on. "To me, that was a dead giveaway. I mean, taking her to a concert performance of an old-school Broadway musical? Really?"

Marcee felt her hands start to sweat, making it hard for her to prop herself against the tile. She stood straight up, letting her feet provide all the support. It was evident that they were talking about her.

"I know," Claudia answered, "I couldn't believe that either. Nothing screams 'gay' like going to see Miley Cyrus in *The King and I*."

Marcee's knees buckled; she took a few steps to the side and quickly grabbed the metal safety rail that had been fastened to the wall. Her insides felt like they had been compressed in a vise.

"I thought for sure she'd be onto the fact that Brent's a

big homo after that, but you know these fat girls." Claire laughed.

"Even if she hasn't figured out that he's gay, I still don't really get why she'd think he'd want *her.* He's hot and famous — what does he need with some wide load from Sherman Oaks? Does she not own a mirror, for the love of God?" Claudia sounded stymied.

"Chubbies want to believe that a guy could possibly be into them. It doesn't matter how smart they are; all logic goes out the window when they think there's a chance that someone cute might want to stick it in them," Claire explained. "He's a fantasy to someone like Marcee."

"Also, I'm sure her friends and family have told her how deserving and worthy of love she is and how lucky *he* is to have her," Claudia continued. "That probably just adds to her delusional thinking. Butterballs are so fucked up."

"The bottom line is, I wouldn't fuck her with *anybody's* dick," Claire said, "but she's definitely serving a purpose."

17

As Marcee looked up at the rearview mirror, she saw that her uncontrollable sobbing had turned her face into a ghastly mess. What little makeup she had put on — some liquid liner and a tiny bit of mascara — was smudged around her puffy eyes and running down her face before she was halfway to work. "*Fat girl.*" "*Delusional.*" The soundtrack in her head was reverberating with distorted laughter and epithets as though she were in a theme park funhouse. She fumbled through her music collection but couldn't find a band or artist capable of stopping her mind from punching her in the abdomen. "*Brent's a big homo.*"

She pulled over and parked against a curb on Riverside Drive. The tears were impeding her vision, and she worried that her control of the car was compromised by despair. "*Butterballs are so fucked up.*" The night before, she was able to drive home from Beverly Hills on the fumes of shock and confusion, but Claire and Claudia's words had sunken in deeply during the torturously sleepless night. Marcee's energy and focus were all but gone. "*He's hot and famous — what does he need with some wide load from Sherman Oaks?*"

She wanted to call Jordan, but she wasn't anywhere near ready to face an "I told you so" moment. He cared for her as though she were family, yet she knew he'd behave like a dog with a bone when it came to a revelation about Brent

Wetherley's sexuality — especially considering that Jordan had already been suspicious of Brent's intentions. And, in the words of her TTT "pals," her mother was likely to offer nothing more than biased support. *"I'm sure her friends and family have told her how deserving and worthy of love she is."* Picking up the phone would simply prove Claudia right, not to mention position Marcee as a pathetic loser to her own mom.

Releasing her seatbelt, she leaned forward, resting her forehead on the car's steering wheel. Had she not recently been promoted and then so quickly taken a personal day off, she'd have turned around and headed home to the security of her bed. *How could I be so fucking stupid?* she thought. *Even if Brent Wetherley were straight, what would make him attracted to me? My thighs? The size of my ass? The winning personality that made Claire and Claudia so hateful?* A chill of loneliness sent a shiver down her back. *I don't even have anyone to call.* She reached into her glove compartment and grabbed a tissue just before her nose dripped all over her purple blouse.

As she patted her eyes with another Kleenex, she looked through the windshield; everyone appeared to be moving in slow motion. Stationed right outside of Sweetsalt, one of her favorite local breakfast haunts, she watched the Valley workforce come and go with coffee cups and bags of morning pastries, the muffins and frosted baked items that would have, under ordinary circumstances, thrown her appetite into high gear. The dyspeptic pains that had persisted since the night before, though, fooled her into feeling full.

Rifling through her bag, she found a packet of MAC facial wipes. She cleaned her face with a disposable cloth and then lowered her window. She restarted the engine and pulled onto the street, letting the wind and fresh air dry her cheeks as she continued toward the studio. Once parked, she lowered her light-up visor and reapplied her eye makeup with a shaky hand. She then did her best to cover her flushed skin with a powder foundation.

Lila was away from her cubicle — likely in the copy room, collating pertinent newspaper and magazine clips into reading packets for Luminary executives — when Marcee walked in. It was still too early for anyone else to be wandering the halls, so Marcee was able to sneak into her office without having to interact with the staff. She turned on the overhead light and closed the door behind her before falling into her chair. Exhausted and depleted from a restless night and an emotional morning, she crossed her arms on her desk and rested her head in the makeshift cradle. As a new flood of tears began to drip onto her fingers, she was startled upright by the ring of her cell phone. *(207) 555-3199?* Marcee didn't answer calls from numbers that were not already programmed into her iPhone. Likewise, she didn't return calls from those who didn't leave voice messages. Whoever was trying to get through was out of luck.

She had just started to go through her e-mails and calendar when she heard three consecutive knocks on the door. "Mar? It's Addie. Do you have a sec?" Marcee stood up and adjusted her top and slacks. She took a plastic headband from her purse and pulled her hair back before opening the door. Addie was standing in the entryway with an armful of color-coded folders.

"Hey, Addie," Marcee said. "Does all of that need my attention?" She pointed to the stack of papers that her coworker was carrying.

"Unfortunately, yes," Addie answered. "I've done as much of it myself as I possibly can, but a lot of it needs your opinion or approval." She followed Marcee into the office and sat in one of the guest chairs facing Marcee's desk.

"Are you doing OK?" Addie asked once Marcee was seated in front of her. "You're a little peaked."

"Actually, I've been feeling kind of sick since last night," Marcee replied, trying to hug the truth as much as possible, "but I know there's so much going on here. I figured I might as well come in and work through it." She gave Addie a half smile.

"Are you sure?" Addie pushed, sounding unconvinced by Marcee's answer. "I don't mean to be disrespectful, but you look kind of rough. If you'd rather work from home, I can mark the pages that most need your input; we can review everything by phone."

"No, no," Marcee answered, "it's important for me to be here. I want to make sure that we do away with Phyllis's antiquated systems and get things streamlined and oiled up as quickly as possible." She was in no frame of mind to be a company cheerleader that day but recognized the importance of morale and team building.

"Works for me," Addie said, smiling. "Speaking of important, there are a bunch of press releases in the pile that need a final sign-off from the legal department."

"I'm actually scheduled to meet with Ben Paull this morning to go over those," Marcee replied. "I should have them back to you today."

"Perfect," Addie answered, "they're at the top of the priority list. We can talk about everything else tomorrow if you want; hopefully you'll be back to yourself." She stood up and turned to leave.

"Addie," Marcee called after her, "would you please ask Lila to let Ben know that I'm going to head over to his office instead of having him come here? I think the walk will do me good."

"Sure thing," Addie yelled back. "The sun is a great cure-all."

Marcee put her mobile phone and the necessary files into her shoulder bag and threw on a pair of aviator sunglasses. The bright outdoors, at the very least, gave her an excuse to hide some of the swollen redness on her face.

She walked slowly around the buildings and soundstages; her meeting wasn't until 10AM, and she'd given herself 30 minutes for what was only a 10-minute stroll. Golf carts whizzed by her, rushing between production offices and various sets. They were busy creating staged Hollywood drama while genuine tragedy was walking among them. Marcee felt as though Claire and Claudia had taped an 8x10 sign with the words "KICK ME" to her back, and now everyone could more easily spot the elephant in the room.

She arrived at the legal building nearly 20 minutes before she was supposed to see Ben and took a seat in the plush lobby. Her eyes still teary, she left her sunglasses resting firmly on the bridge of her nose while she reached for her phone. She had silenced it before she left her office and noticed that she'd missed two calls, one from her mother and another from Jordan. Both messages sounded exactly alike: "Marcee, where are you? I expected you to call on your way home from dinner last night. How'd it go? Hope you had fun and can't wait to hear all about it." She knew she'd have to reply by text later in the day to keep them from worrying, but she planned to put off phone conversations for as long as possible. She couldn't deal with any more embarrassment.

She headed upstairs to Ben's 14th-floor office five minutes early, using the reverse camera on her phone to check her appearance. All she could make out was the undesirable, overweight beast whom Claire "*wouldn't fuck with anybody's dick.*" She lifted her tinted lenses and stared into her own face. "*Does she not own a mirror, for the love of*

God?" Marcee closed her eyes. She could feel four or five weighty teardrops roll beneath her chin and onto the collar of her shirt. As she wiped her right hand across her sniveling nostrils and repositioned her glasses, the doors opened to a floor full of administrative assistants and paralegals.

Everyone must be looking at me, she thought as she walked down the hallway in a pair of shades under the harsh fluorescent lights of the commercial construction. She felt like a supporting cast member from some cable reality show who was conspicuously "disguised" in a sad attempt to be recognized while out in public. *Better that they scratch their heads over the glasses than see the mess of a face that's beneath them.*

"Well, well, well," Ben joked, "look who it is." He stood from his chair and moved over to the doorway the second he saw Marcee. "I was surprised to hear that you'd be coming my way considering how much you usually complain about having to see me in person." She recoiled as he gave her a hug, keeping her arms straight down at her sides. "Is something wrong?"

"Nothing to worry about," she answered, "I just needed to get out of my office and recharge."

"At 10AM? That seems early in the day to be so drained." His brow furrowed as he took a couple of steps back to look at her. "And why are you wearing sunglasses? Is it too bright in here?"

She tentatively pushed them to the top of her head. "I'm fine," she answered, turning her face to the side so Ben couldn't see her head-on.

"It certainly doesn't look that way," he replied, sounding concerned. He pulled two chairs away from the round conference table at the back of his office. "Why don't you sit down." He took two bottles of water from the mini-fridge under his desk and then sat next to her. "What's going on?"

As she removed the paperwork from her purse and laid it out in front of her, she noticed a stack of magazines neatly splayed out at the center of the table. On top, in full view, was the latest issue of *Rolling Stone*. The cover, with a stark white background, featured a seminude glamour shot of Brent Wetherley. She froze, completely immobile, as though she'd come face-to-face with the man himself.

Ben was looking around as if trying to zero in on what had suddenly hijacked Marcee's focus. "Oh, look," he enthused, holding up the magazine, "there's your boyfriend, shirtless, in nothing but a pair of shiny blue briefs, suspenders and a top hat." He looked closer at the photo and then read the headline out loud. "HOW MOVIES AND MUSIC SHAPED HOLLYWOOD'S NEWEST STAR." He thumbed through the pages until he found the article and accompanying pictorial. "He certainly takes care of his body," Ben commented, flipping through what looked like an ad for a Chippendale's show in Las Vegas. "How does it feel to be the girl who gets to stuff dollar bills into those Jockeys?"

"Do you mind if we just quickly go over these press releases?" she asked, wanting to get as far away from the copy of *Rolling Stone* as possible. "I'm in a little bit of a time crunch today."

"Something's rotten in the state of Denmark," Ben commented. "Earlier, you had the time to walk here for a 'recharge'; now you're in a hurry to finish up. And I wasn't going to bring up the fact that I can tell you've been crying."

"I'm just overwhelmed," she said, which wasn't altogether untrue. "Phyllis left the department in shambles, and I feel like I'm running at light speed to pick up the pieces." Also not a lie.

"Marcee, it would take anyone a good few months to feel like he or she had started to make headway in a new job," he answered consolingly. "Just because you've worked in the department for a while doesn't mean there isn't a learning curve to an executive-level position."

"I know," she replied, "I guess I'm just hard on myself." She appreciated Ben's kindness and understanding, but his encouraging words were not the balm for what was really floating through her head. As much as she tried to look away, her eyes kept darting back to the glossy photos. "*Even if she hasn't figured out that he's gay, I still don't really get why she'd think he'd want her.*" She put her hands up to her face to hide the tears that started to flood her lower lids.

"There's something you're not telling me, Marcee," Ben said, trying to pull one of her arms away so he could look at her. "Are things going well with Brent?"

She took a tissue from the travel pack that was at the top of her bag and blew her nose. "Yes, all of that stuff is OK," she fibbed. Ever since she'd first met Ben, he had a soothing style and an unflappable approach to work obstacles; she secretly wanted to tell him everything — about the unsatisfying date at the Hollywood Bowl, the conversation she'd overhead in the bathroom at the Palm and Brent's sexuality. His "big brother" appeal made him an obvious confidant; she imagined that his comforting strength would ease her devastation. Something inside her, though, wouldn't allow any more vulnerability to surface. She wasn't ready to admit that Ben's initial skepticism during their last lunch at the Apex had been warranted.

"I can tell that you want me to shut up," he said, resting his hand on her shoulder, "but please don't hold back if something's bothering you. I'm an excellent listener." He leaned in so his lightly stubbled cheeks were close to hers. "You know I want you to be happy, even if that means dating a *Rolling Stone* cover model instead of a dorky Jewish guy with a dog and no personal life."

On any other day, Marcee would have gotten a laugh

out of Ben's good-natured, "aw shucks" flattery but, she didn't have the energy to dig for any positive feelings. "I appreciate that," she said. "Do you mind if we go through these press releases now?"

"There's really not much to go through," he answered. "I read them over yesterday; there's no language in any of them that raises legal issues."

"So, you were going to walk all the way to my office to say that you have no suggested revisions? You don't think an e-mail or phone call would've been more efficient?" Marcee closed the magazine that had been plaguing her for 20 minutes and turned it facedown.

"More efficient, yes, but more pleasant, no," he replied. "Remember, I didn't ask *you* to walk all the way over here this time around. You're the one who wanted to 'recharge.'" He repeated the word again, this time with a stronger emphasis. It was clear that he wasn't buying her excuse. "I thought it would be nice to see you, regardless of how much — or how little — business there was to discuss. Evidently, you don't share the same sentiment." He closed his eyes and frowned like a mime whose tears were meant to cause laughter.

For the first time, she noticed his beautifully long eyelashes. "You know, those lashes are wasted on a man," she said as she filed the paperwork back into her bag and walked toward the door. She pulled the sunglasses down onto her face. "I have to use four different products to get my eyes to look that good."

"Don't try to make me the pretty one in this relationship," he said, chuckling. She turned the corner into the hall and made her way downstairs. As soon as she was outside, she turned her phone on and saw that the mystery 207 number had tried again. This time, though, the caller left a message: "Hey, Marcee, it's Sarah. I dialed you earlier but didn't leave a voicemail; I was hoping to get you live at some point this morning. I need to give you a heads-up about something, so please buzz me when you can. This is my personal phone, which is why it has a Portland, Maine, area code. Use this line when you call back. Talk to you soon."

Marcee saved the message so she wouldn't forget about Sarah's call, but she had no immediate plan to speak with anyone affiliated with Claire Madison. She'd had less than 24 hours to consider everything that was flung at her the night before, let alone to process the pain and inner turmoil it had caused. And, while Sarah had, in fact, previously offered a general warning to be cautious of Claire's judgmental nature, she'd been cagey and vague in her explanation. Marcee didn't feel emotionally sturdy enough or have the wherewithal to try and decipher any more riddles.

◇◇◇

MARCEE TRUDGED THROUGH Wednesday morning as though she were wading in a tar pit. She hadn't slept a full night since Sunday — her heart raced constantly, even with an increased dose of Xanax — and she continued to dread having to come clean to her mother and Jordan. She didn't want their heartbreak or pity but needed a healthy helping of unconditional love. *I'll call them tonight,* she thought. *Trying to avoid the inevitable will only make things worse; it's time to rip this Band-Aid off.*

Her appetite came and went, but by lunchtime, she craved a cheeseburger with steak fries. She walked to the commissary and had a meal boxed to go so she could eat in the privacy of her office. Even such a short outing felt like a Herculean effort.

"Marcee, I've been trying to call your cell," Lila blurted the second she saw Marcee step off the elevator with her Styro-packed lunch.

"I left it on my desk," Marcee answered without stopping. "I hope it wasn't anything urgent." She'd known she wouldn't be out long and wanted to completely disconnect for a few minutes.

"You have some visitors," Lila said, following just behind Marcee as she continued down the hallway.

"Really? Who'd show up unannounced?" Marcee asked. Before Lila could respond, Marcee had made her way to the door of her office. She looked inside, instantly losing her balance. She grabbed onto a piece of side molding and attempted to appear composed.

"Jill and I don't really *need* to be announced, do we?" Claire questioned from one of the couches at the center of the room.

"My husband *is* the head of the studio, you know," Jill, who was seated next to Claire, reminded her with a laugh. "We don't exactly have to sign in at security. By the way, do I smell meat?"

"It's a burger kind of day," Marcee said, placing her food on the credenza and then taking a seat on the opposite sofa facing the two women. She was caught off guard but tried to keep things business as usual.

"I guess that picture of a slaughterhouse I posted on Instagram this morning didn't touch your cold little heart," Jill replied, shaking her head. Marcee was being meat-shamed by a make-believe vegan who'd downed some pancetta as recently as the week before.

"Jill, none of us cares about your social media posts. In fact, remind me to block you before we leave today." Claire sneered at Jill before turning her attention to Marcee. "Have you seen this?" She pulled a copy of *Rolling Stone* from her Chanel bag and laid it on the coffee table between them. "Look who's on the cover!"

"I saw that yesterday," Marcee replied, sitting back

without reaching for the magazine. She pushed out a phony grin while gritting her teeth, hoping it would pass as authentic.

"It certainly seems like he fills out those underpants nicely," Jill said as she lunged forward to look at the photo. "Has he worn those in person for you, Marcee?"

"I don't think there's been any fooling around yet, am I right?" Claire said. "When's your next date?" She looked straight at Marcee. "Maybe he'll give you a tour under his shorts."

"I can't wait to hear what he's actually packing," Jill added. "Unless the magazine editors enhanced that photo, I would assume that you're in for the hefty log that's been rumored about. Plus, you've heard what they say about thin, trim boys; they're known for their huge cocks. I just hope he's circumcised."

"If you look closely at the pictures with the article, you can kind of make out the head of his dick," Claire said. "I don't think he's driving a covered wagon."

"That's a relief," Jill continued. "There's nothing quite as gross as rolling back that anteater skin and getting a whiff of cheese-and-onion corn chips. I'd rather suck on a sweaty, calloused toe than an uncut penis."

Marcee let the ladies banter between themselves, nodding here and there to feign interest and amusement. "To what do I owe the pleasure of this surprise visit?" Marcee asked, veering the conversation away from Brent's package.

"Jill and I had plans to have lunch with Ken on the lot today," Claire answered, "and we assumed you'd be too busy to join us. But when I saw the new *Rolling Stone* at the studio convenience store, I figured we should at least stop by to enjoy the view with you."

"Yeah, getting out for lunch these days is tough," Marcee

said, indirectly excusing their slight. A week before, she'd have been hurt by not being invited, but now she knew that there was no real friendship between them.

"Anyway, the bottom line is that your boyfriend's face and body are plastered across every bookstore and newsstand," Claire said. "While all the women in the world are drooling, *you* get to be the one on his arm."

"I remember when Ken was that handsome," Jill chimed in. "I wanted to rip his clothes off every time he walked into a room."

"Too bad that was before there were printing presses and paper," Claire jabbed. "Otherwise, he probably would have been a cover boy, too."

"Rox isn't exactly the man he was 10 years ago either," Jill shot back. "We're all getting older."

"Which reminds me, I'm going to continue to age in Paris for the next week." Claire put her handbag on her lap, obviously readying herself to leave Marcee's office. "Rox and I are on a 10PM flight this evening — without the kids, thank Jesus — and then back in eight days."

"Who's watching the twins?" Jill asked, looking down at her light pink manicure. It was apparent that she didn't care.

"They're staying at Halle Berry's house." Claire pulled out her car keys and stood up. "My boys love Maceo and Nahla, so they'll be happy. And, more important, *I'll* be happy to have some adult time, alone." She turned to Jill. "Are you ready? I've gotta get home so I can make sure that Sarah packed everything the way I like it."

"Do you want to take your magazine?" Marcee picked up the copy of *Rolling Stone*. "It might make for some fun airplane reading."

"I've got my Kindle, so I'll be fine." Claire smiled. "You can have Brent all to yourself."

◇◇◇

BY 6PM, MARCEE was in her car and on her way home. Claire and Jill's unannounced "drop in" had thrown her for a loop and exacerbated her feelings of worthlessness; for the remainder of the afternoon, she'd been replaying their conversation in her head to the point of burnout. *Did I sound like there was something wrong? Was I too curt?* She needed some good Chinese food, desserts full of preservatives and her luxurious bed — pronto. She couldn't wait to climb under the covers in a pair of silk pajamas and the cozy sleep socks that she'd bought for $1.99 at T.J. Maxx over the weekend.

Bamboo, her favorite Asian restaurant in the city, was close to her apartment; she decided to pick up her order instead of waiting for delivery once she was already undressed and settled. She fell into the category of people who rarely felt full after a Chinese meal — she always got hungry again 30 minutes after the last bite — so she ordered enough food to see her through the night. Sesame chicken, shrimp in black bean sauce, beef lo mein and Yang Chow fried rice, along with two egg rolls and some scallion pancakes, were all on the menu. And, "No," she answered the telephone attendant firmly, "I don't need silverware for five. One set of chopsticks will be fine." *The person manning the lines obviously can't tell from my voice that I'm a mouth-shoveling fat pig, or whatever Claire and Claudia called me.*

Marcee arrived at the restaurant only about 10 minutes after placing her order, so she pulled behind the building and parked in a spot for dine-in customers. She walked half a block down Ventura Boulevard to the local 7-Eleven and took a two-handled plastic basket. In the candy aisle, she found her favorite Hershey's products. Two king-size milk chocolate bars with almonds were sure-fire home runs, as were the "sharing packs" of Mounds. But where were the prepackaged baked goods? As though psychically on cue, the cashier used a twist and shake of his finger to direct her around the corner to a display of Little Debbie products. He'd clearly seen desperate binge shoppers before.

She reached for a bag of mini powdered donuts and then looked around for any out-of-view surveillance equipment. She felt like a teenage boy sneaking a look at a *Hustler* or *Penthouse* magazine in the back of a Circle K store but refused to be deterred by one swiveling camera and a multidirectional mirror. Tough times called for severe measures, and whoever from 7-Eleven corporate was monitoring her purchases was of less concern than her need for the comfort of Zebra Cake Rolls. She threw some Devil Cremes and three packages of Banana Twins — which were hard to come by — into the mix along with some Strawberry Shortcake Rolls and a handful of P.B. Richies. *Good for "Debbie," being able to stay so "little" while having to taste-test all of her products. Maybe I can take over that job when I eventually get myself out of this Hollywood quicksand.*

"Your total is $50.78," the cashier said after ringing all of her food into the register. "Do you want me to bag everything, or are you going to start eating some of it now?" He wasn't wearing a name tag, which frustrated her.

"It's all to go," Marcee said sheepishly, even though she knew she'd likely take a bite of a Cosmic Cupcake before she even made it back to Bamboo.

Her food was ready and packed by the time she entered the restaurant. She paid the $85 tab — bringing the night's total to $135.78 — and walked through the dining room to the back exit. The smell of soy sauce and cabbage filled her car; she couldn't wait to get home and get comfortable, not to mention dig into her favorite dishes. She wanted to pamper herself and decompress, having been bruised so horribly by her new so-called "friends." She felt entitled to lick her wounds, which were still fresh and deep. *What did I ever do to deserve being treated like this?*

In rush-hour traffic, it took her 20 minutes to drive the two miles to her condo. Tiffany and Debbie Gibson kept her company — a mall singer throwback always helped to temporarily take her mind off her problems — and the bag from the mini-mart, which was sitting on the passenger seat, gave her something to look forward to after dinner.

Between her purse and the plastic sacks from Bamboo and 7-Eleven, Marcee arrived at the front of her apartment building with her hands full. Fortunately, someone hadn't closed the main door completely, so she was able to use her foot to pry her way in. As she fumbled to get her keys into the two locks on her own unit, she noticed a 9x12 manila envelope wedged under the threshold. After she let herself in and set everything down on the kitchen table, she picked up the flat, sealed package and closed the door. "Marcee Brookes" had been typed on a white label and affixed to the golden-yellow pouch. With neither a shipping nor return address, she knew it had been hand delivered and hadn't been processed by the US Post Office or any specialty overnight services.

She opened a stationery drawer beneath her toaster oven and removed a sharp letter opener. Carefully, she ripped through the fold at the top of the envelope and pulled out four thick pieces of card stock clipped together. On top was a handwritten note:

> Hey, there. I'd hoped to reach you earlier by phone but haven't heard back from you yet. I didn't want you to be sideswiped when these photos hit the newspapers this coming Friday. Call me as soon as possible. XO. (207) 555-3199.

18

"IS THAT THE entire length of a dick up Brent's ass? Let me look closer," Jordan squealed, grabbing one of the 8x10s from Marcee. "Oh my God. He's squatting *all* the way down on it." It was as if he'd hit the celebrity porn jackpot. "This blows those nudes of Justin Beiber and Orlando Bloom right out of the water, pun intended," he said. "This is, like, hardcore. I just wish I could see the face of the man Brent's riding." Jordan was examining every detail. "And look at the size of Brent's cock while he's straddling; the tip is resting way above the other man's belly button."

Marcee held three additional photos in her hands, fanned out like playing cards. The images were obviously still shots of a TV screen or computer monitor; the blue tint and slight grain made them less than artful, but they were clear enough for the average eye. As she and Jordan sat at the kitchen table, she stared silently at the pictures, her mouth hanging half open in shock. A few teardrops had gathered at the sides of her nose.

"Do you want to share the others with me?" Jordan nudged. He had come to Marcee's apartment within an hour of getting her SOS phone call and offered to spend the night so she wouldn't be alone. The pictures, however, were obviously making it difficult for him to focus solely on her devastation. He pulled a second print from her hand, this one of Brent giving oral sex to the same similarly well-endowed partner. "Why don't I ever meet men with huge penises?" he lamented. "*Damn.* Look at Brent Hoovering that up."

Marcee turned her head to look at him; her face had the pallor of a white bedsheet. "I don't think I can take this," she said, trying to make her words understood through her congestion.

"Mar, I understand how humiliating it is," he replied. "I really do. I've been the butt of jokes and ridicule my whole life." He put his hand on her arm. "But I never let it mow me down, and I'm not going to allow this Hollywood shit-show to knock you over, either." Before Jordan could swipe another photograph from her, Marcee placed the remaining two images in front of him, fidgeting in her seat as she gazed out the front window. She fixed her eyes on the common courtyard that was visible through the partially open blinds, waiting for him to react.

"Oh. My. Fucking. God." Jordan jumped from a standard sitting position to his knees, poring over the photos as though he were a detective looking for clues. "Brent Wetherley is fucking Rox Madison. I knew it; I knew Rox was gay. I told you the minute you mentioned the drunken comment Claudia Erickson made when you were at that Gabbi Green event in Santa Monica."

"Shhh," Marcee scolded, "the walls are thin." She walked over to the shades and closed them completely and then returned to her chair, facing Jordan. "Sarah's note said these pictures are going to be public on Friday," she cried. "Everyone who's ever seen me in the press with Brent is going to know how stupid I am. I was a lame, fat-ass beard and didn't want to know it."

"Stop," Jordan demanded. "Don't talk about yourself that way. I don't have friends who are losers. You got taken by a bunch of shitty people, that's all. None of it's your fault."

"Really? Not my fault? I'm the one who bought into the fake romance and the fast friendships. Brent and Claire aren't responsible for *my* naïvete." Marcee hung her head, looking down into her lap. "This is one big nightmare; nobody would even believe me if I tried to explain the whole thing."

"What *I* can't believe is that they're both versatile and aren't wearing rubbers," Jordan replied, his attention back on the sexually explicit screen captures. "It looks like they each take a dick equally well." He studied the photos again and began to lay them out in order, like he was piecing together some sort of puzzle made for two-year-olds.

"What are you doing?" she whimpered, using a piece of paper towel to wipe her nose.

"I'm putting these in a timeline, in 'porn order,'" he said.

"What do you mean?" she questioned, confused.

"Have you never seen a gay skin flick?" Jordan gasped, clutching his chest in surprise. "How is that possible?"

"Because I'm not a gay man and don't visit those websites?" she replied as a question, using the same square of Bounty to dry the corners of her eyes.

"OK, well first comes the blow job," he said, placing one image on a corner of the table. "Then, we have the rimming." He added a second shot to the lineup. "Next, we have the intercourse, so Brent getting pounded in the cowboy position. And, in this very special director's cut, there's a fourth segment with Rox getting banged on his back." Jordan had lined up the four photographs as though he were storyboarding a major motion picture. "Voila! If she'd given us a few more snaps, I could have made a flip book."

Marcee moved over to the sofa in her living room and sprawled out, using a throw her mother had crocheted to cover her face and body. "This is all beyond mortifying," she sobbed. "What was I thinking?"

"Listen, you couldn't have possibly known that Brent's a homo," Jordan said, sitting on the arm of the couch and rubbing her shoulders through the blanket. "Why would you think someone — especially a friend who's in the know — would set you up on a date with a gay guy?"

"Yeah, but you realize what people will think, right?" she shot back, muffled by the yarn over her face. "They'll think he took one look at me naked and decided he'd rather fuck a man. I guarantee that half of the online comments will say something like that."

"You can't worry about the comments," Jordan replied. "You have to take care of yourself instead of giving attention to what anyone else thinks. In a year, we'll be laughing about this."

"I highly doubt that," Marcee answered, "but it's not just about the ridiculous dates. Claire and Brent clearly played me like the gullible loser I am. I should have known better. The warning signs were there; you brought them up, my friend Ben brought them up. I just wanted to think that they saw something special in me."

"I don't know one person who wouldn't have been just as drawn in," he said, trying to calm her down. "The fame, money and lifestyle are seductive."

"Yeah, but I've worked in this business long enough to know better, which makes it *more* embarrassing." Marcee uncovered her face and looked up at Jordan.

"I think we need to talk to Sarah," he suggested. "She obviously knows much more about all of this than we do. We're making assumptions at this point. Should we call her now or try to meet with her in person tomorrow morning?"

"I don't know if I can face her," Marcee sniveled, once again masking her face.

"I just made up your mind; we should convince her to come over now," Jordan said, ignoring Marcee's trepidation, "or at least meet us at a restaurant. I think it'll be better for both of you to get everything out in the open as quickly as possible. Otherwise you'll be drowning in even more doubt." Jordan went into the kitchen, took Marcee's cell phone from the counter and delivered it to her on the couch. "Here. Call her now."

"Only if you put those photos back in the envelope," Marcee instructed. "I don't ever need to see them again. Plus, I want your undivided attention, which will never happen if there are dick pics around." He gave the pictures another look and then grudgingly sealed them in their original pouch."

"If I must," he grumbled. "Now, call Sarah." He pulled the afghan away from her face and sat at the end of the sofa next to her feet, massaging them gently. "Now," he commanded as Marcee hesitated to lift her phone.

"Ugh, fine," she said, exasperated and anxious. She went through her voicemail history and found Sarah's message from the day before, taking a deep breath before hitting the dial button.

"Hey, Marcee," Sarah answered. "I've been waiting for you to call. I'm sorry about that special delivery, but I didn't want you to wind up being blindsided on Friday."

"I appreciate that." Marcee took a hard swallow in an effort to hold back the waterworks. "I'm at my apartment with my friend Jordan, and we both have so many questions."

"I thought you might, which is why I tried calling yesterday," Sarah replied.

"We need to talk; could you possibly come over to my place tonight?" Marcee asked, half hoping that Sarah would decline the invitation and put it off a day.

"That works for me," Sarah responded. "I may not get there until 9:30PM. Is that OK? I hope it's not too late; I really want to get everything off my chest."

"I don't think I'll be sleeping much tonight anyway, so whatever time you arrive is fine." Marcee looked at Jordan as he nodded in agreement.

"I'll see you shortly," Sarah confirmed. "And I apologize in advance. I just couldn't let all of this go on any longer."

Marcee and Jordan both showered, changed into sweats and stationed themselves in front of some humorless network sitcom with a bag of powdered mini-donuts. When Sarah rang the buzzer at the front of the complex, it was just about 10PM.

"I guess this is the moment of truth," Marcee said nervously as she remotely released the main gate with a touch of her phone and then headed to the front of her unit. The moment she opened the door, Sarah handed Marcee a plastic container of iced butter cookies from Vons. "I'm a little late, I know, but I figured we'd need these. And, to be honest, I wasn't sure if one package would be enough."

"Not to worry," Marcee reassured her, "I stopped at 7-Eleven on my way home and bought out the entire cake section. I think we're covered." She gave Sarah a tentative hug. "Come on in."

"I wish I could afford more than a studio apartment," Sarah said, taking in Marcee's spacious living room. "But after Friday, it won't matter anyway."

"Sarah, this is my BFF, Jordan," Marcee interrupted.

"It's a pleasure to meet you," Jordan said, reserved but polite. He shook Sarah's hand. "I've heard nice things about you. Can I get some coffee going? How do you take it?"

"That would be great," Sarah answered. "Just black, no sweetener; the best way to wash anything down." Her smile was uneasy.

While Jordan brewed the coffee and arranged the cookies on a serving plate, Marcee guided a quick tour of her apartment and made inconsequential small talk. She didn't want to dive into the drama until all three of them were seated and she had Jordan to lean on — literally and figuratively.

"This is a really nice place," Sarah said. "I'm going to miss having any privacy." She took a seat on the upholstered recliner that faced the sofa.

"Where are you going?" Marcee asked, sitting on the couch with her legs tucked beneath her.

"I'm heading to Maine for awhile, to decompress and then start over," Sarah said. "Who says you can't go home again? I'm moving in with my parents. Can you believe? At my age?" She shook her head as though she couldn't process her own words.

"There's no shame in a time-out," Jordan interjected as he served the snacks and drinks. "Why now, though? What happened that pushed you to send those photos to the papers?" Marcee was relieved that Jordan had jumped headfirst into the conversation; she felt uncomfortable approaching the subject directly.

"Claire has always been a terror, from the moment I started working for her and Rox," Sarah began. "But I needed a job and wanted a screenwriting career — so I put up with being treated like trash, figuring it would pay off at some point."

"Yeah, I get that," Jordan pressed. "But something had to have sent you over the edge." He didn't appear to be backing down. *It must be the journalist in him,* Marcee thought.

"Two things, actually," Sarah said, staring off into a far corner of the ceiling. "Last week, Claire asked me to accompany them to the premiere of *Karate Koala* so I could make sure that the twins were taken care of while she and Rox mingled. Before they walked onto the red carpet, Claire whispered in my ear, 'Try and stay out of any pictures with us. Your look doesn't really represent the public face of our brand.'" Sarah repositioned herself in the chair and locked her lifeless eyes with Marcee's.

"That sounds familiar," Marcee said. "I overheard her saying similar things about me in the restroom of the Palm on Monday night." "*Chubbies want to believe that a guy could possibly be into them.*" Marcee shuddered.

"I've learned to deal with it throughout all the years I've worked for Claire and Rox, so the jabs don't really faze me anymore." Sarah took a sip of coffee. "But even worse was this past Monday morning when she asked me about my latest screenplay and claimed to love the concept. She said she thought it was 'fresh' and 'what audiences are looking for' and then offered to get it to Brian Grazer. I would never have even considered asking her to do that for me." Sarah sat forward as though she were about to deliver the punch line to a joke. "Then I saw the script under some used tampons in a garbage can when I went into one of the guest bathrooms."

"What a fucking bitch," Jordan spat. "How has no one in town put a hit out on this woman?"

"Because she's Rox Madison's wife." Sarah sighed. "You can get away with almost anything when you're connected to a star. And, believe me, I've been sick over the whole Brent Wetherley thing. I was originally trying to stay out of it, but then I got to know Marcee personally, and..." Her voice faded out.

"Is that what you were trying to warn me about when we had lunch at Sweet Lady Jane?" Marcee paused briefly. "You seemed a little evasive."

"That was my first stab at warning you, yes," Sarah admitted. "But I was nervous because I signed so much non-disclosure paperwork when I first started the job."

"Why aren't you worried about any confidentiality documents now?" Jordan cut in. "I mean, going public with such incendiary pictures would be the ultimate breach."

"You know what? I just don't care anymore," Sarah answered. "I have no money and nothing to lose professionally. I'll be writing poetry in New England; they can't get blood from a stone."

"Which outlet is running the pictures on Friday?" Jordan asked. Marcee knew that he was competitive and wanted the name of the newspaper that was going to be on everyone's lips by the weekend

"They'll be on the cover of the *New York Post,* unless some other big world news happens," Sarah replied. "Over the years, Claire had me drop blind gossip items about her friends and enemies — which, in her case, are one and the same, really. So, I developed relationships with the editors. They'll, of course, claim that they have no idea where the pictures came from."

"I wish I could break this kind of story." Jordan wrung his hands. "*Variety* likes to beat the others to the punch but not with anything this salacious."

"It's perfect for the *New York Post,*" Marcee added. "They get a huge exclusive, and Claire gets exposed as a phony bitch." Her eyes were now completely dry and there was a slight tone of strength in her voice. "When are you actually moving? Does Claire know you're quitting?" Marcee adjusted herself, moving her feet to the floor so she was completely upright.

"Well, my plan is to finish packing this weekend and sell whatever I don't need on Craigslist," Sarah answered. "I'll be on the first flight Monday morning." She took a cookie and a napkin from the coffee table. "I assume Claire will figure it out for herself when I stop answering her constant calls — or when she gets back from France and finds that the office has been cleaned out. Or, maybe, her friends will mention that they haven't seen any updates on her Twitter, Facebook and Instagram accounts — since I do all of them."

"You're not wasting any time, are you?" Marcee opined.

"Why bother?" Sarah looked first at Marcee and then Jordan. "I can't seem to come up with a good reason to stick around; I'd just as soon be 3,000 miles away by the time Claire's broom lands at LAX. I want her out of my life as quickly as possible."

"My guess is that I won't hear from her again." Marcee took a mini-donut and ate it in one bite. "But the other TTTs might start asking questions."

"Not all of them," Sarah said. "As long as we're getting real *real,* I might as well fill in the rest of the blanks for you."

◇◇◇

UNTIL THURSDAY MORNING, Marcee's communication with her mother had been limited to a few texts and a two-minute call. She'd hinted to Rhonda that there was trouble with Brent and an upheaval involving Claire but she felt too fragile and too disgraced to engage in a full-blown conversation.

"Honey, Daddy and I have been so worried," Rhonda said with an urgency not typical for 7AM on the average weekday. "I realize you've been upset, but you know I panic when you're not in touch."

"It's been horrible." Marcee turned her car from Dickens Street onto Noble Avenue and then made a right on Ventura Boulevard. "I didn't really know exactly what was going on myself until I talked to Claire's assistant, Sarah, last night."

"She's the girl who told you that Claire can be tricky, right?" Rhonda's selective memory always amazed Marcee. Her mother would recall insignificant details and useless information about the most random situations but then need to be reminded about something as simple as the name of the studio where her daughter worked.

"Yes, you're right," Marcee answered with less enthusiasm than usual. Often, when her mother did, in fact, remember something correctly, Marcee and her father would cheer as though she were a featured contestant on an episode of *The $100,000 Pyramid*. "Anyhow, when I was at the TTT dinner on Monday, the ladies were so nasty to each other; it was really eye-opening."

"You've said before that anyone listening in would think they're enemies."

"Well, the ladies were particularly bitchy, and, by around 10:30PM, I was ready to head home." Marcee hit every red light as she drove down the Boulevard, which, she thought, was just as well considering how much material she had to cover. Even with the traffic signal delays, though, she was at the corner of Ventura and Vantage Avenue before she'd finished telling her mother everything she'd overheard in the bathroom at the Palm. She'd gotten only as far as Claire and Claudia's comments about her body shape.

"If I had those women here, I'd kill them," Rhonda yelled, her voice quivering on the edge of a wail.

"Mom, don't," Marcee said. "I've beaten myself up for two days about believing in those friendships. In hindsight, everything happened too quickly, and I wanted the illusion. You wanted it *for* me because I'm your kid. If we had both been looking at it objectively, we would have seen right through it."

"I think I *am* objective when I say that anyone would be lucky to have you as a friend." Rhonda made Marcee's point. "But if they truly didn't want you around, why did Claire set you up with Brent? That doesn't make any sense."

"You better sit down because the pieces are about to come together." Marcee parked behind her favorite bookstore, which coincidentally shared a back lot with a Starbucks. She plugged her earbuds into her device and switched the call from her Audi's built-in Bluetooth to her iPhone. "Can you hear me?" She began to walk toward the coffee shop.

"Yes, baby, keep going."

"As it turns out, their comments went further than my weight and my 'delusional' sensibility. Apparently, Brent is gay." Marcee stopped in her tracks as she felt a spasm down her right arm; she'd had more than 48 hours to soak it all in, yet the words still brought on a palsy effect.

"Excuse me?" Rhonda sounded as though she hadn't heard it the first time.

"Brent is gay, Mom," Marcee repeated. "A homosexual."

"I speak English, you know," she replied, seemingly frustrated. "If Claire is such good friends with him, how did she not know he's gay?" Standing just behind the Starbucks in an alleyway between Bookstar and Pier 1 Imports, Marcee explained what sounded like a *Days of Our Lives* plotline to her mother. "So, to be clear, Brent Wetherley and Rox Madison are having an affair — which Claire knows all about — and she set you up with Brent just so there'd be evidence of him embracing a woman in public?"

"Essentially, yes." Marcee felt her eyes well up. "All of Rox's earlier indiscretions, according to Sarah, had been isolated trysts with masseuses and gardeners who were paid to keep quiet." Marcee felt like her feet were on fire. She leaned back against the concrete wall, never mind that her light-blue cotton top might pick up some dirt. "When Claire finally realized that Rox's relationship with Brent went deeper than those other quick flings, she basically colluded with the two of them. She promised she'd find an easy mark to be photographed with Brent at industry events — someone who'd be so taken with the fact that a man showed her some romantic interest that she'd ignore all logic. A dumpy dupe who would be standing in the way of any gay rumors, should Rox and Brent's involvement ever strike the media as more than friendly or professional."

"And they thought that person was my daughter." Macee could hear Rhonda blow her nose, obviously trying to disguise the sound of her tears.

"You got it, Fancy Drew." Marcee made a joke in an effort to dilute the fraught emotions that were darting between their phones.

"How do these meshuggahs live like this? Why doesn't Claire just divorce her husband and move on with her life? What's the point of waking up to a lie each day?"

"Two hundred fifty million dollars, three book deals and unprecedented access to anyone or anything on the planet, maybe?" Marcee looked up at the daylight. "Claire is so caught up in appearances and status. If she loses Rox, she becomes the stock Hollywood divorce story with a few million dollars, child support and one property."

"What's to say he couldn't kick her to the curb at any time?" Rhonda asked.

"He could, but *she* knows too much, and *he's* probably well aware that Claire's enough of a cunt to wreak havoc on his career," Marcee said. "Also, she could make it difficult for him to see his kids. From the way she talks about them sometimes, you'd think she adopted them for that purpose alone."

"I don't like the C word," Rhonda advised. "But I'm letting it go in this case. Claire *is* a cunt."

"And, so is Claudia Erickson," Marcee added. "From what Sarah said, Claudia knew what was going on the whole time."

"What about those other women? Your boss's wife and that TV actress — what's her name?"

"Risa Turner," Marcee answered. "As I understand it, Jill, Risa and Jamie Cross were as clueless as I was; Sarah said they still have no idea about Rox and Brent. They must have been wondering why Claire ever brought me into the group — who knows how Claire explained it."

"They might not be wondering any such thing." Rhonda coughed into the phone, presumably to clear her throat. "Maybe they just think you're a nice girl who works in the same industry."

Marcee rolled her eyes, silently dismissing her mother's biased outlook. "Yeah, Mom, you're probably right. But they're all a bunch of frauds anyway, so I'm just going to move on as fast as I can."

"What do you mean when you say 'frauds?'" Rhonda questioned.

"Jill Andrews has built a huge empire on being a healthy vegan, and, meanwhile, she's a bulimic who eats meat. How's that for a start?" Marcee began to walk toward the Starbucks entrance. "And then there's Risa, who's sleeping with the married actor who played her little brother on TV. Oh, and Jamie Cross, the lesbian-about-town? She girl-hops just for money and notoriety."

"And what about Claudia Erickson? I read in *People* that she's leaving her husband."

"Not exactly," Marcee corrected. "Nick dumped her for some Canadian woman. He screwed Claudia over with an ironclad prenup that she was too trusting and inexperienced to understand in her 20s. She's moving to a condo in Encino with what little money she has to her own name."

"I can't say that my heart's bleeding for her," Rhonda replied. "Not that I'm wishing bad on anyone, pu pu pu."

"Well, Claire's life is about to explode — along with Rox and Brent's," Marcee revealed. "Claire pushed Sarah past the point of no return last week, so Sarah sent photos of Rox and Brent, um, in flagrante to the *New York Post*. It's going to be on the cover of the paper tomorrow."

"She has pictures?" Rhonda sounded shocked. "How would she have gotten those photos?"

"Claire's house is wired with cameras in just about every room." Having used the Starbucks app to preorder her breakfast, Marcee was able to walk in, grab her food and caramel macchiato, and walk back to her car without interrupting the conversation. "The twins were at an all-day playdate, and Rox and Brent decided to get naughty in their room. Sarah used her phone to take photos of the security monitors."

"He was having sex in his own kids' room? What is wrong with these Hollywood people?"

"Anyway," Marcee went on, "Sarah decided to bust the whole thing open. It'll definitely impact Rox and Brent's bankability at the box office, but it will also knock Claire down. She won't have much to hold over her husband after Friday, and I doubt that people will take her books about marriage and relationships seriously anymore." Marcee sat in her car and exhaled audibly. "I'm just not sure how *I'm* going to get through tomorrow and the weekend."

"Why? The *New York Post* article doesn't have anything to do with you." Rhonda had never quite gotten a handle on how the media works, even though Marcee tried to explain the mechanics of her job to her mother countless times.

"One of the first things they'll do is dig up photos of me with Brent at Mastro's, the Hollywood Bowl and the Gabbi Green launch. They'll probably do a whole sidebar article about the 'beard.'" Marcee started to hyperventilate.

"Mar, breathe," Rhonda said. "Take a sip of your coffee."

"I just can't deal with the embarrassment. Everyone at work is going to know it was a sham." Marcee figured she'd wind up bawling and had tissues at the ready. "How am I going to face people? They'll be feeling sorry for the dumb fat girl who thought she'd won the lottery. I'm pathetic."

"You're not dumb, you're not fat and you're far from

pathetic," Rhonda insisted. "People can think whatever they want; if they were in your shoes, the same thing would have happened to them."

"You're my mother," Marcee rationalized. "Of course you don't think I'm pathetic."

"Why don't you take tomorrow off? You can sleep over here tonight, in your old bed, and we'll have a girls' day tomorrow." Rhonda tried to soothe Marcee. "By the time Monday rolls around, there'll be fresh news; no one will care about this anymore. I'm sure some pop star will have shaved her head in a public toilet or that actress — whomever she was — will be accused of shoplifting clothes from a high-end department store again."

"I think Winona Ryder is past that phase." Even in her misery, Marcee appreciated the humor in her mother's line of thinking. "But I can't skip work — there's too much going on. Plus, all eyes are on me in this new job. I need to be beyond reproach, especially since I report to Jill's husband."

"That makes sense," Rhonda agreed. "If you'd like, though, I can come over to the studio and meet you for lunch, just for moral support."

"I would love that, but I can't have it look like the head of communications needs her mommy to coddle her." Marcee cleaned up her face and continued on her way to the office.

"I get it," Rhonda replied. "You never wanted me to come visit you at school when you were younger either."

"I love you, Mom." Marcee had just turned onto Riverside Drive when a call beeped in. "Listen, Jordan is trying me on the other line. Do you mind if I call you back a little later? I may want to come for dinner tonight, and I'll probably sleep over this weekend."

"Whatever you'd like, honey. Daddy and I love you very much; just remember that."

Jordan started talking the second Marcee clicked over. "Where are you?"

"I'm just about to get to my office, why?" Marcee could tell something was percolating in Jordan's head.

"Do you think we can get Sarah to meet us for dinner after work? It'll be worth your time and hers — and may just help me out along the way, too." Marcee loved Jordan to death, but he always had an angle.

"I can certainly ask her, but what's left to say? I think she covered everything last night." Marcee was trying to figure out what he was thinking.

"She did say that she handles all of Claire's social media, didn't she?" Jordan asked.

"Yeah, so?"

"Just see if she can meet us at Pace on Laurel Canyon around 7:30PM — or any place that's convenient for all of us. I have a brilliant idea."

19

"ONE OF THE only things I like about this place is the lighting," Jordan groaned as soon as Marcee walked through the front door of the restaurant. He was standing next to the host stand, his backpack still strapped to his shoulders like a grade-schooler.

"Pace was *your* suggestion," Marcee said, giving him a kiss and a long hug. "I assumed it was on your approved dining list."

"I like to bring first dates here, so I'm used to it." He scanned the room. "It's so dark that it makes my skin look perfect. And they have crayons on every table so I can draw on the butcher paper if a guy turns out to be boring."

"Did you check in?" She pointed toward the touch-screen computer at the front desk. "I had Lila make a reservation."

"Yes, but the actress-model-singer won't seat us until our *entire* party is here, even though our table is sitting there empty," he replied flippantly, loudly enough for the hostess to hear. "Maybe she has an audition tomorrow for Annoying Restaurant Employee #3 in some indie film, and she's getting into character early." Jordan had a way of cutting people to the quick when he was subjected to their misguided senses of authority.

"Sarah texted that she'll be here right around 7:30PM, so

we won't have to wait too much longer," Marcee assured him. "How was your day?"

"It was uneventful," he said, "but my editor keeps riding me for a bombshell column item. I think the idea I have for you and Sarah will solve that, though." He shot her a devious-looking grin.

"Tell me now," she pleaded. "You know me well enough to realize that I'm dying to know what this 'brilliant idea' is."

"All in good time, mi amiga, all in good time." He rubbed his chin repeatedly with his right thumb and index fingers, as if he were a cartoon-like villain in an old black-and-white movie. "Let's wait for Sarah so we can discuss everything at one time. Anyway," he changed the subject, "how was *your* day?"

"I could hardly concentrate," she said, "because I know it's the calm before the storm. I can't stop worrying about the *New York Post* story. Everyone will know what a fucking moron I am by the time I wake up in the morning — if I can even sleep in the first place."

"Do you think you're the only woman who's ever been with a guy who turned out to be gay?" Jordan looked upward like he was flipping through a card catalog of celebrity romances in his head. "Liza Minnelli, Carrie Fisher, that girl who dated Ricky Martin for 14 years, Angela Lansbury—"

"Wait, Jessica Fletcher was married to a gay man?" Marcee was usually good with this kind of Hollywood trivia but had missed that tidbit throughout the years. "She could solve a whole murder mystery in under an hour but had no idea that her real-life husband was sleeping with men?"

"The show wasn't called, *Gay, She Discovered,*" Jordan said, laughing. "Plus, they divorced in the mid-1940s, before she'd sharpened her sleuthing skills for *Murder, She Wrote*."

"Regardless, those are mostly old Hollywood stories about women who probably weren't set up by fake friends with ulterior motives." With her arms crossed, Marcee began to massage the cotton fabric covering both of her elbows. "My friendships *and* my dates were bogus."

"True, but the public doesn't know that Claire manipulated the whole thing," Jordan reminded her. "Only the handful of people close to you are aware of the actual details."

"Good point." Marcee squeezed her arms. "So I'll seem like *slightly* less of a loser."

"Unless," Jordan said, "you're willing to put it all out there."

"Why on earth would I want to look like any more of an idiot than I already do?" She shook her head and looked at her phone to see if there was a text from Sarah. "I don't want to talk about any of it publicly — ever. I need to get on with my life and my job like none of this happened."

"So, you're going to let Claire just get away with what she did to you?" Jordan asked.

"She's not really getting away with anything," Marcee answered. "Her big secret is about to be dumped on the world tomorrow."

"Sort of, but she could also wind up getting sympathy from women who believe she was misled by her husband. She may come across looking like the innocent wife and mother who was unknowingly caught up in a lie. The entire Lifetime Television viewing audience could rally behind her."

"What are you suggesting?" Marcee questioned. Before Jordan could go further, Sarah walked down the steps at the entryway.

"Sarah's here," Jordan said, looking straight ahead as she approached. "Let's sit down, and we'll talk everything through."

"Hey, guys," Sarah called out, hurriedly making her way over to where Marcee and Jordan were standing. "I was at the house in Malibu today, grabbing the last of my things. The traffic getting over here was crazy."

"Don't worry about it," Marcee replied, hugging Sarah while Jordan motioned to the hostess. "Thanks for coming to meet us."

"Yes, thank you," Jordan repeated as they made their way to a half booth at the far back of the indoor dining area. He took one of the two chairs facing Marcee and Sarah, his back to the room; the women were seated on a leather bench softened by square, patterned pillows. The brick walls and wooden beams surrounding them were accented by a dim firelight glow and framed black-and-white photos that seemed to have no relevance to the rustic Italian ambiance.

"It's no problem," Sarah answered. "I had to get back over to this part of town anyway. And it's rare that I leave work early enough to have a nice dinner out, so this is a treat. It's too bad I didn't try more of these restaurants before I decided to go back to Maine; I'll be living on lobster rolls and whoopie pies for the foreseeable future."

"That doesn't sound so bad." Marcee looked up from her menu and turned her head toward Sarah. "Maybe I should move with you; do your parents have an extra room?"

"Oh, please," Sarah giggled, "you have a career, a family and friends in LA. What do you want with a bunch of people in Portland telling you that you look 'wicked smaht' in your new L.L.Bean wardrobe?"

Before refocusing on the menu, Marcee thought for a moment about her life in California. Sarah's perception was that Marcee had very good reasons to appreciate her circumstances, and maybe she wasn't wrong in her objectivity. Marcee looked at Jordan, her oldest friend, and then considered her mother and father as well as her studio executive job. Aside from whatever embarrassment might come from being temporarily known as Brent Wetherley's beard — and her weight, which she could manage with a little tenacity and willpower — the sky wasn't exactly falling.

"What's everyone ordering?" Jordan asked. "I was thinking of getting the vegetable salad to start and then the Aphrodite pizza."

"Do you wanna share the pizza, and I'll get my own salad?" Marcee was hungry but didn't want to overeat. At the very least, the effects of too much food would make it even more difficult for her to sleep through the night.

"Works for me." Jordan turned his attention to Sarah. "Anything in particular looking good to you?"

"I think I'm gonna get the cedar wood grilled salmon," Sarah replied, "and maybe a side of roasted potatoes. I usually wind up eating a Snickers bar or some Swedish fish at my desk; forgive me if I go a little crazy."

"Claire doesn't have her chef leave anything for you, especially since she knows you're usually working late?" Jordan sounded surprised.

"You'd think, but no," Sarah answered. "Claire told me when I took the job that I'd have to bring my own meals and that all of the food in the house is for the family, not the help. I basically have to ask if I want to take a bottled water from the fridge."

"She's such an asshole," Jordan said, his tone deepening. "No wonder you've had it with her. I'd imagine the resentment has been eating away at you."

"Pretty much; I've been swimming in it for a while." Sarah stopped to give her order to the server and waited for Marcee and Jordan to place theirs. "That's why I feel totally at peace with the whole *New York Post* situation."

"Speaking of which," Jordan said, handing his menu to the waitress, "I mentioned to Marcee that the public might be sympathetic to Claire depending on how that *New York Post* story is worded."

"I actually thought of that when I decided to go to the paper with the pictures." Sarah took a sip of water. "But there isn't much I can do to control what people think of Claire. I'm sure there are many who will feel sorry for her and then others who will laugh at the irony of her being a self-proclaimed relationship expert who didn't know that her own husband was leading another life right under her nose."

"Well, what if there were a way to let everyone in on the fact that she *was* aware of Rox's sexuality and infidelities and that she was using him — and her friends — to keep her money, her connections and her book deals?" Jordan ate one of the house-roasted almonds on the table and looked directly at Sarah.

"I'm not really sure how that's possible," Sarah said, sounding resigned. "But either way, leaking those photos is as far as I'm willing to go." Sarah noshed on some of the complimentary olives in front of her. "I'm sure Claire will try to come after me, even though she has no proof that I was behind it, and, like I said last night, I don't have too many fucks to give. But I'd rather be in a little hot water than a sea of deep shit."

"Jordan, I don't understand what you're getting at anyway," Marcee said "Is this where your 'brilliant idea' comes in?"

"Hear me out." Jordan took a crayon from the glass jar at the center of the table and began to doodle. "What if, after the *New York Post* runs tomorrow morning, I tip off one of my friends at Joaquin Richie's website; he can post a piece detailing how Claire has known about Rox and Brent's affair for a long time and used you to help keep any curious media away. I can also mention that Claire's known for stabbing her friends in the back and give him some of the dirt that's come up at your TTT dinners."

"I don't like where this is going." Marcee clasped her hands together and set them on the table. "I'll just have to suck it up, deal with the fallout and leave well enough alone. If anything more than those pictures makes its way into the press, Claire will know exactly where it's coming from — and I have no doubt that she'll try to do me in."

"But what if the information isn't technically coming from you?" Jordan persisted.

"Then who's the source? All of those women will assume I'm behind it; they know that my work gives me access to the press." Marcee smoothed the ends of her hair nervously. "I don't want to wind up losing my job on top of my dignity."

"What kind of 'dirt' are you talking about? I hear only bits and pieces of Claire's conversations," Sarah chimed in just as the food was delivered to the table.

Marcee tried to signal to Jordan to stop talking by widening her eyes into near perfect circles. "It doesn't matter," she jumped in. "I'm not getting involved."

"What if Claire admits it all herself?" Jordan replied quickly, as though he were trying to cut Marcee's concerns off at the pass. "What if there is no source, and it all comes right from the horse's mouth?"

"How exactly do you intend to convince Claire Madison to come clean about all of this? Are you going to call her in France and say, 'Hey, you don't know me, but now that your husband has been outed by a rag newspaper and your life is falling apart, why don't you admit publicly to being a total cunt?'" Marcee began to speak in a loud whisper, looking around anxiously to make sure that Pace's largely Hollywood clientele wasn't eavesdropping.

"I don't even have to call her," Jordan answered. "I have a feeling I can get her to own up to everything without so much as lifting a finger. OK, well, maybe a finger." He smiled broadly at Sarah. "Sarah, you mentioned last night that you handle Claire's social media, right?" Jordan wrote the words "TWITTER," "FACEBOOK" and "INSTAGRAM" on the paper tablecloth. "So you have all of her passwords?"

"Yes and yes," Sarah answered. "And I manage Rox's accounts, too. They never do their own posting; in fact, I don't think either of them knows his or her sign-in information. I'm the only one with access."

"So, conceivably, tomorrow morning, you could go onto Claire's social media platforms and begin making public comments about Rox, Brent and her pals as though they're coming from her own fingertips?" Jordan had the half smile of an old-fashioned private eye with a loaded gun. "Am I right?" Sarah, as if in shock, sat silently for an awkwardly long period. "Should I take that pause as a yes or a no?" Jordan asked.

"I'm not sure what to say. I mean, yes, it's feasible, but don't you think that might be poking the tiger a little too hard?" Sarah took one of the pillows from behind her, set it on her lap and hunched forward. "Also, I'm not an Apple genius, but Claire may be able to get someone to trace the IP address of the computer that logs in to her accounts."

"Not if the posts come from a burner phone instead of a computer," Jordan suggested.

"Hmm, yeah. She'll probably assume it's me anyway, because of my access, but at least this way she won't have proof."

"And I'd rather slay this particular tiger than poke it, frankly." Jordan took a bite of the last piece of pizza. "After the heartache that Claire put Marcee — and you — through, I can't believe you have to think twice."

"'Wait, back up,'" Marcee said. "What are you talking about? Aren't burner phones those things that drug dealers and philanderers use for all kinds of shady business?"

"Yes, prepaid, disposable cell phones," Jordan said. "They're called 'burners' because you can just 'burn' or trash them when you're done. They can't be traced back to any individual."

"Look, there's no doubt in my mind that those horrible people deserve whatever's coming to them," Sarah conceded, "which is why I pulled the trigger on the photos in the first place. But this social media 'takeover' sounds risky, like it could wind up biting us in the collective ass."

"Since your job includes posting updates and photos for Claire, it seems to me that this would be all in a day's work," Jordan said. "She doesn't dictate them to you, does she? You do the writing yourself, correct?"

"Yes, I take care of every aspect; she doesn't really know how those platforms work." Sarah turned to look at Marcee. "The night of your first TTT dinner, Claire asked me to make sure she was following you on Twitter. And I'm the one who sent the actual tweet out — the one including all of the ladies. I'm sure Claire never even knew about it, but I thought it was a nice thing to do. Sorry if I'm bursting any bubbles here."

"No worries," Marcee assured her. "I think any illusions I had about Claire being a decent human have been shattered already."

"So, arguably, Sarah, you'd just be doing your job if you sent out a few messages from 'Claire.'" Jordan sounded very matter-of-fact.

Sarah nodded. "And with the burner phone, she wouldn't be able to technically prove her accounts weren't hacked by someone else."

"What kinds of things would you have 'Claire' write?" Marcee asked hesitantly.

"Something like, 'So sad for my bulimic friend @jillandrewsveg. She's started eating meat again & then purging.

Let's get her help @NEDAstaff. #bulimia #vegan.'" Jordan tossed out the 140 characters as though he'd already had them formulated in his mind.

"And you don't think that Jill, if she has even a doubt about where the information is coming from, will have her husband terminate me the same way he did Phyllis?" Marcee took a red crayon and drew a large X on top of Jordan's list of social media outlets. "I have no interest in being fired, thank you very much."

"There's a solution to that," Jordan advised. "We can shorten the posts and tweets and then write, 'MORE TO COME' in all caps at the end of each message. I'm sure those girls have a lot of skeletons they don't want falling out of their closets, and they'll have no idea what else might be revealed publicly if they take any action."

"Give me another example of a possible tweet," Sarah said, suddenly seeming to be giving Jordan's scheme more serious consideration.

"How about, 'Poor @ericksonwellsfrevr; @NickEricksonBand left alcoholic wife w/ no $$$; she's moving to a crap condo in Encino. #EricksonWells #music?'" Jordan was savvy when it came to identifying popular hashtags. "Tweets like that will definitely get all of those shrews to turn their backs on Claire. She'll lose everything — her husband, her friends, her credibility, her following. All gone."

"OK, but how do we reveal that Claire knew about Rox and Brent?" Marcee, still unconvinced, pushed the few remaining bits of chopped salad around in her bowl.

"Just listen to me before you say no, Marcee," Jordan instructed. "We can have 'Claire' post something along the lines of "I'm sorry I set up my fat friend @MarceePRGirl w/ @BrentWetherley; I didn't want people to know that he's fucking @TheRoxMad1. #RoxMadison #oops.'"

"Why do you have to use the word 'fat'?" Marcee gasped. "People will already think I'm a pig when they look at any photos."

"You're not fat, Mar," Jordan said, "but using that insult is important; women don't typically support people who tear other women down. This would put those body-shaming words you overheard in the bathroom directly into Claire's mouth. No one with a conscience will be left standing in her corner."

"How does this plan help you if *Joaquin Richie* is getting all of the gossip that's not in the *New York Post* article?" Marcee asked.

"Before Joaquin Richie's site runs their article, I'll have an industry column all ready to go for *Variety*; in fact, I'll research and write it tonight," Jordan said. "Just after their piece goes live on the web, I'll post mine. It'll dig into the potential fallout for Rox, Claire and Brent — deals that could implode, endorsements that might fall through, and how their secrets and lies might ruin all three careers; you know, the kinds of angles that *Variety* covers. Any associates or brands who weren't already thinking of dropping them from projects will likely reconsider — and I'll have a meaty story under my byline."

"All of the entertainment websites, magazines, newspapers and TV shows — including you — follow just about every celebrity on social media," Marcee noted. "You and your friend at *Joaquin Richie* would have to work ridiculously fast to publish your stories before the rest of the piranhas start feeding." Marcee's PR hat was firmly on top of her head. "The second the blood's in the water, it'll be a free-for-all."

"It's a good thing I'll know what 'Claire' plans to tweet — and at what exact time — before she does, isn't it?" Jordan grinned from ear to ear.

"I don't know, Jordan." Marcee shook her head. "This whole thing is giving me agita. I'm already worked up about the *New York Post,* and the last thing I need is my fingerprints anywhere near Claire."

"I can't say it doesn't worry me, too," Sarah agreed. "Even though I don't have as much to lose as Marcee, a lot of this plan sits on my shoulders."

"But hasn't Claire already been weighing on your shoulders long enough? And imagine the horrible things she's probably done that we don't even know about." Jordan wasn't backing down.

"She really *has* been heinous," Sarah answered, her eyes starting to tear up. "I never told you about the time she took pictures of me eating at my desk, did I? It just popped into my head."

"Do I even want to hear about this?" Marcee put her hand on Sarah's arm. "I feel like I'm going to be disgusted."

"I was having a bad day — OK, who am I kidding, a regular day — and I ran out to get some lunch at McDonald's," Sarah began, looking down at her lap. "When I got back to the house, without my knowing, Claire snapped an unflattering photo of me eating a Big Mac and fries. The next day, she e-mailed it to all of her friends with an invitation to join her yoga class: 'Stretch your muscles, not your waistline. Come work out with me!'"

"Does she have no conscience?" Marcee was outraged. "Claire is a fucking sociopath. How did you find out about it?"

"First, I found the original invitation in her Sent e-mail box, but, then, as everyone began to reply, I had the pleasure of seeing the original note at the bottom of their responses — about 20 times," Sarah went on. "And you know who was the worst? Jill Andrews. She wrote back to Claire with something like, 'Forget a Big Mac; that girl looks like she could eat a Mack truck.' Claire didn't make even the smallest effort to prevent me from seeing it."

Marcee moved her hand to Sarah's back, rubbing it gently. "I'm so sorry that happened. Sadly, I can relate."

"And the two of you still have to decide whether or not we should take this Claire bitch down?" Jordan jerked his head from side to side. "I'd start tonight if I could."

"I really need to think about it," Marcee said, "but I just don't want to have anything to do with Claire anymore. My gut tells me it's best to let sleeping dogs lie."

"First of all, I think Claire is going to have bigger things to worry about than you," Jordan pointed out. "And none of those women will believe her if she tries to throw you under the bus for talking out of school. Why would they think you'd have access to her social media accounts? Not to mention, they'll be too concerned about doing their own damage control. As horrible as this sounds, you probably won't even be an afterthought to them." Jordan continued to make his case.

"On that note, I'm beyond tired." Marcee stood up. "I need to get home, take a bath and brace myself for tomorrow's madness."

"I'll grab the check once you're on your way, but think about everything I said while you're driving. It's time that Claire Madison gets knocked off her throne, and this is a unique opportunity to do it." Jordan gave Marcee a hug. "I'll call you when I'm back at my apartment, in about an hour or so."

"Thanks again for meeting us, Sarah," Marcee said, leaning down to give her a kiss on the cheek. "I'll call you tomorrow." She walked outside and up the metal, spiral staircase to the valet attendants while Jordan and Sarah wrapped up the conversation.

"People like Claire Madison infuriate me," Jordan continued, "and she took a huge dump all over my best friend. I know Marcee is still reeling from the betrayal, and I feel like exposing Claire and her friends as the vile cows that they are will ultimately give Marcee some closure and satisfaction. They're a bunch of elitist mean girls who still behave like they're popular high school cheerleaders instead of evolved adults."

"Listen, I've worked for that bitch for years." Sarah sighed. "No one understands how she and her buddies operate more than I do. But I just don't know if—"

"So, what do you say then?" Jordan interrupted before Sarah could further rehearse her doubt. "Shall we set fire to the rest of Claire's castle tomorrow?"

◇◇◇

AS MARCEE FASTENED her seatbelt and put her car in drive, she plugged her phone into the USB charger and thought about calling her mother. She wanted to discuss Jordan's idea but knew two things for sure: one, Rhonda would discourage Marcee from even considering a revenge plan and, two, she wouldn't understand anything about social media.

Instead, she drove through the winding curves of Laurel Canyon listening to the new Barbra Streisand duets collection. *Is this what Barbra has come to?* she thought as she heard Anne Hathaway attempt to go toe-to-toe with the music legend on a beloved song from *A Chorus Line.* Marcee quickly switched over to the *Guilty* album. *Babs was at her best with Barry Gibb.* She hoped that early-80s, permed Barbra would take her mind off the nightmare that was about to smack her in the face the next day, but no such luck; she turned the music off altogether when the song "What Kind of Fool" came through her speakers.

Just as the traffic light at the corner of Laurel Canyon

and Ventura gave her permission to turn left, her cell phone rang. It was Sarah.

"Hey, there," Marcee answered. "Are you on your way home?"

"Yeah, Jordan and I finished up about five minutes ago. I just got on the road."

"He gets very passionate at times," Marcee said, excusing what she figured Sarah may have perceived as pushy. "But he means well."

"I would kill to have such a loyal friend," Sarah replied. "I can tell that, more than he wants a story for *Variety*, he wants to make sure that Claire and Brent pay for what they did to you. He sees it as though they wronged him, too, by messing with his bestie."

"Crazy as he can be, he's probably the most devoted friend on the planet." Marcee smiled to herself. "He hasn't changed since we were kids."

"Well, it's important to keep those kinds of friends close. They're hard to come by."

"It seemed like you were as nervous about his idea as I was." Marcee shut the air conditioner, which was blowing an uncomfortable chill onto her face. "Believe me, I would love to see everything around Claire crumble — her marriage, her friendships, her writing career — but I'm not sure I have the constitution to dish out revenge. Plus, I'd be so worried about getting caught."

"It would concern me, too," Sarah agreed, "but Jordan does seem to have it all ironed out. His plan makes sense and really *could* work. He definitely put a lot of thought into it."

"It sounds like you're actually considering it," Marcee said. "You do understand that, while I can share some of the TTT secrets with you, you're the one who'd basically have to execute it all."

"That was very clear," Sarah laughed. "But you know what? Jordan's right. My job description includes managing Claire's online voice at *my* discretion. Nowhere does it provide me with any guidelines or restrictions."

"Do you think I'd wind up losing my job, though?" Marcee asked. "Obviously, Jill will know that someone close to her spilled the beans, and Claire might try to convince her that it was me. If Jill mentioned that to her husband, I'm sure he'd can my ass — and possibly try to sue me for defamation."

"First of all, everyone who attends the TTT dinners is aware of Jill's eating issues," Sarah replied, "so that information could be attributed to five different people. And, if I'm correct, there have already been rumors in the press about Jill eating meat. I saw something about it on at least one of the online tabloids."

"Now that you mention it, Claire did tell me early last week that Jill was concerned about some web gossip that could impact her business." Marcee continued to drive through Studio City.

"Right, so it's kind of already out in the universe," Sarah said. "And, if Jordan's right about how this will play out, Claire will be so reviled that none of those women will listen to a thing she says. They'll be scrambling to protect their own images and will probably want to be as far away from the name Madison as possible. Lawsuits would only draw more attention to the gossip, so I doubt any of them would go there."

"That makes sense," Marcee acknowledged, "but I've always been the girl who plays by the rules, even when it works against me."

"I'm not here to change your values." Sarah paused for a few seconds. "But I do think this is a rare chance to give Karma a helping hand."

Marcee stopped in the driveway of her apartment building. "Let me take an hour or so to mull it over. I love the fantasy of dishing out some justice, but I'm just not sure I have it in me."

"That's fair," Sarah replied. "I know that my decision to release those photos affects you, so I'm willing to do my part in Jordan's plan if it will bring you any relief. If you decide to just let it go, that's fine, too. I'll be here to support you either way."

"Thanks, Sarah, I really appreciate your sensitivity." Marcee pushed the button to open the garage gate. "This week has been hell; I just want it to be over with."

"It'll be behind us soon," Sarah said. "Try to get some sleep."

Marcee parked her car, gathered the mail and walked into her apartment. Without stopping to put her bag down, she went into her bedroom and undressed, letting her clothes fall to the floor in a tangled pile. When she first entered the bathroom, the tile was startlingly cold against her bare feet; it warmed up as she stood in place, brushing her teeth and applying lotion.

Capping off her nighttime routine with a .5mg Xanax and a cup of water, she looked at herself in the mirror. *Do I really want to be the bullied teenager anymore?* she thought. *Will I ever win if I'm too scared to color outside the lines?* She picked up her cell phone and looked through her e-mails. There were a few work inquiries that had come in during dinner, but they could wait until morning — or even the following week. She dialed Jordan and waited for him to answer.

"Hi, it's me." Marcee shut the bathroom light.

"Did you get home OK? I was just about to call you," he answered. "About our conversation…"

"Don't say another word," she said. "I'm in."

20

THE ONLINE EDITION of the *New York Post* would hit the web during the night, and Marcee wanted to see the article, photos and layout as early as possible. She knew she wouldn't be able to change anything by being among the first to read the paper, but at least she could get a head start on worrying about what other people might think of the coverage.

She must have dozed off at some point because she opened her eyes suddenly to the disorienting glare of 3:05AM on her nightstand clock. She had a fleeting feeling of relief, as though she'd dreamt that someone close to her had died but then woke up to find the person alive and well. A yawn and a rub of her eyes, though, snapped her back to full consciousness. The past weeks had, in fact, been all too real.

She'd left her laptop in sleep mode on the floor next to her bed. There was no need to turn on a lamp; the bright glow of her computer screen highlighted exactly what she was looking for: the day's top story. Her already racing heart hit the accelerator.

There it was: the photo of Brent with his legs spread across Rox's naked lap. A black bar had been placed across the most explicit portion of the picture with white lettering that read, "MORE INSIDE!" and a headline screaming "HOLLYWOOD'S BIGGEST STAR IN GAY AFFAIR WITH THE

TOWN'S HOTTEST UP-AND-'COMER.'" She scrolled down the page to see the graphic of the actual newspaper cover, which featured the same image and the words "BRENT WETHERLEY ON THE ROX: SHOCKING GAY RELATIONSHIP SET TO SHAKE TINSELTOWN." In the bottom left corner was an inset snapshot of Marcee with the caption "Matronly studio executive became Wetherley's 'beard' to conceal star's tawdry secret."

Dear Lord, no. Marcee put her head in her hands and moved her eyes back and forth across her palms. When she looked up, nothing had changed. *Fuck.* She hit the link to the lead story and began to read. "A steamy sexual relationship between international superstar Rox Madison and screen idol Brent Wetherley is poised to have tongues wagging around the world. In photos exclusive to the *New York Post,* the handsome duo appears to be extremely excited about one another." The three additional pictures — with the requisite censor blurs and pixilation — were interspersed throughout the text.

The article was largely speculative and short on details but did mention Marcee briefly: "Wetherley has been seen out and about recently with Luminary Pictures' plump marketer Marcee Brookes, seemingly a disguise for his same-sex inclinations." *Plump? I guess they want to make sure that readers realize how ridiculous it all is. The only reason someone like Brent Wetherley would want a fat girl around is so he could hide behind her.* She called Jordan from her cell phone.

"I know, I know," he said in a voice that sounded wide-awake. "I'm reading it right now." He didn't even give her an opportunity to say hello. "It's obvious that they kept this feature under wraps and didn't reach out to anyone for comment. Their only real facts are the photos and your name."

"The language makes it read like I was complicit in covering up the affair," she said, "and they throw in the fact that I'm a blimp twice." She felt like she was going to choke on the lump in her throat. Marcee gazed at her screen as though the word "plump" might vanish if she focused on it long enough. She began to sniffle.

"Let's keep our eyes on the prize and not worry about the least interesting adjectives in the entire article," Jordan advised. "The only news people will actually get from this is that Rox and Brent are gay and romantically involved. The real juice will come from the *Joaquin Richie* story."

"Sarah's going to start posting 'Claire's' comments at 9AM Pacific, right?" Marcee asked.

"Yes, she found a wireless store that opens really early, so she'll have the burner phone in hand," he answered, "and we've already formulated all of the status updates, down to the exact number of characters and hashtags."

"I think my stomach just turned inside out." Marcee flipped onto her back. "Are you sure we're doing the right thing?" She heard loud rumblings in her midsection.

"There's not one fiber of doubt in my body," he reassured her. "It's just too bad that it's taken this long for anyone to beat Claire at her own game."

"Are the social media posts going to come out consecutively, one right after the other?" Marcee was trying to get the timeline down in her head.

"Yes, by 10AM, all will be revealed," he said. "And I've already talked to my friend at *Joaquin Richie*. I gave him everything in advance so that he can get his story online the second 'Claire' makes her final statement."

"So, your *Variety* piece is scheduled to go up around 10:30AM?" She closed the computer and cocooned herself beneath her bedcovers.

"Give or take a few minutes, yeah. Why?"

"You don't think it'll seem strange that you'll have such a well-researched and in-depth column within a half hour of the social media rampage?" she questioned. "It would take even the most efficient journalist longer than that to look into all of Rox and Brent's pending studio deals and brand endorsement agreements — let alone write about them coherently."

"Um, well, first, you are talking to *the* most efficient journalist," he replied, "and, second, I can't risk anyone scooping me on this."

"I think you should wait an extra 30 minutes to launch your article." Marcee sat up and pushed the linens off of her face. "Just so it seems more feasible that you'd have been able to gather all of that information, write a story, have it edited and then post it."

"Maybe you're right," he agreed. "Holding a beat might be smart."

"It's going to be around 7PM in France by the time all of this hits," she remarked. "If Claire and Rox are out, they'll have to scurry back to their hotel and camp out inside for the rest of their trip."

"Who cares?" He laughed. "The more awkward and difficult for them, the better. Plus, it's not like they're on a real 'couples vacation' anyway. It's clear that they're just keeping up appearances. She probably goes to spas and shops with his money while he finds French callboys to keep him busy."

"I'm gonna get ready and head to the office." The sun hadn't come up, but she knew she wouldn't be able to go back to sleep. "I'll make sure I'm reachable all day, so call me with any updates." Marcee stood from her bed and stretched. "Love you."

"Love you back, Mar," Jordan answered. "And don't be concerned about what anyone says or thinks. Just get through the day, and remember that you and Sarah are getting the last laughs."

As she disconnected the call, a wave of nausea sent her racing into the bathroom. She barely made it to the toilet before her stomach emptied inside the porcelain bowl, leaving her drained and heaped over the commode. Her whole body began to feel clammy as she threw up a second time. *How did this happen to me?* she thought. *I was minding my own business, not bothering anyone. Living my little existence.* She reached for some toilet paper and patted her forehead and lips. *Now I'm some fat moron on the front page of a gossip rag.* Feeling dizzy, she got up carefully, holding onto the countertop. She splashed some cold water on her face and stayed completely still with her eyes closed for five minutes.

As soon as she regained her equilibrium, Marcee started the shower and waited the 30 seconds it took for the water to turn warm. She stepped in and began to shampoo her hair, feeling her gut clench. She crossed her arms and held her waist tightly, as though such a topical solution might ease the discomfort. She had an urge to scream, to yell at something — even a bottle of conditioner — but all that came out were a few high-pitched heaves and a stream of tears that blended with the spurts raining down on her. *Get it together,* she told herself. *I can either drown in this mess or swim through it.* She rinsed the last remnants of soap off of her scalp and remembered Sarah's comments from the night before. "*You have a career, a family and friends in LA.*"

Within 15 minutes, she'd dried her hair, pulled it back with two plain, silver barrettes and applied a light layer of makeup. Summer Fridays called for casual wear, so Marcee threw on her most comfortable pair of light-blue denim jeans. She decided on a black three-quarter sleeve cotton blouse and some sensible flats along with a pair of small, marcasite earrings. She briefly checked her outfit in the mirror just as the word "matronly" pierced through her brain. *Matronly. I'm a middle-aged, overweight woman. And there's a photo of me on the cover of a newspaper.* Fortunately, the sink was right below her to catch a third round of vomit, which by then was nothing but a tiny bit of stomach acid. *Brush your teeth again, and get it together, Marcee.*

She composed herself and was ready to leave her apartment at 6AM, which, with the light traffic at that hour, would have her at Luminary in 20 minutes. There were no plans to stop for coffee or breakfast — a favor to her insides. She made her way to the garage with her purse and a bottle of cold water, unlocking her Audi and bending across the driver's seat to set her things on the passenger's side.

"Marcee Brookes!" she heard voices scream out, startling her to the point of hitting her head on the inside roof. She looked up to find several grungy-looking men in shorts, positioning small cameras through the bars of the metal garage gate and yelling at her simultaneously. "TMZ viewers want to know how it feels to find out that Brent Wetherley is gay after having just started to date him. Were there any signs at all when you were in bed together? Did he ever mention Rox Madison or call out the wrong name during sex?" The questions were insulting and profoundly offensive.

She knew the paps would be scanning the various websites all night, but she never imagined that they'd care so much about her without Brent by her side; in fact, she never imagined they'd be interested in her at all. *Now they have a shot of my huge 'old lady' ass leaning into the car. Great.* She quickly sat down, slammed the door shut and started her engine, simultaneously pushing the electric door opener. She peeled out of the driveway while the "journalists" scurried to avoid being hit and sped down Dickens Street before they could get to their own cars fast enough to tail her. *Viewers want to know how it feels? It feels like fucking shit,* she thought. She clutched onto the sides of her steering wheel as though she were about to rip it from the dashboard. *Get it together. Get it together. Get it together. There are miles to go before this day is over.*

Marcee stopped at the Sherman Oaks Newsstand, an outdoor, scattered array of magazines and porn, on the corner of Van Nuys Boulevard and Ventura. She parked in front of a red curb, flashing her hazard lights while she grabbed the paper. Angelenos considered the *New York Post* to be a national publication — similar to *USA Today* — so it was readily available and displayed across the city.

"I've never sold so many copies of this particular paper in one day, and it's still early yet," the cashier remarked. "I guess everyone wants to see those movie stars doing nasty things. I don't understand men who like sex with other men."

Marcee handed him a $5 bill with a blank expression. "Keep the change," she called out, getting back into her car and studying the cover. She had no interest in keeping a physical copy for posterity, but she did want to see how it looked in person as opposed to online. She flipped through until she found the two-page spread, read through it again and then folded it in half. She stuffed it underneath her seat and continued on to the studio, even though her hands felt shaky.

Not even Lila had arrived at work when Marcee got to her office, closed the door and sat at her desk. She turned on her butterfly lamp instead of the overhead fluorescents and fired up her computer. *Get it together* she repeated like a mantra in her mind. Knowing that everyone who'd ever saved her number would likely call or text sometime during the day — not to mention the media inquiries that would likely start to come in any second — she switched her phone to "silent mode" and drafted an e-mail to Addie and Lila.

To: Willis, Addie <addie.willis@ luminarypictures.com>, Godfrey, Lila <lila.godfrey@luminarypictures.com>
From: Brookes, Marcee <marcee.brookes@luminarypictures.com>
Subject: Friday

Addie and Lila —

I'm sure, by now, you've seen the *New York Post* and other online coverage of Rox Madison and Brent Wetherley's affair. I'm as shocked as anyone.

I'm in my office if anything urgent pops up, but please try to handle as much as you can without me today. Also, I'm not taking any calls from the press that are related to this situation, so please politely decline all requests. If you need me or have any questions about our current projects, use an internal line or knock on the door.

Thanks for your understanding and support,
Mar

She started to search the popular websites to see how they were reporting the scandal. All of the usual suspects had reposted the four photos with salacious headlines, but Marcee was mentioned — as a footnote — in only a handful of them. *This could've been much worse, I suppose.* By the time she'd scoured every corner of the Internet, it was just about *that* time. She opened the Twitter app on her phone and looked at Claire's account. There had been only a few status updates with photos from France, which

Marcee knew had been organized by Sarah. She stood and paced her office, motorized by anxious energy. *This is what my mother means by "being on shpilkes,"* Marcee thought. She circled every piece of furniture twice and then walked the perimeter of the room as though she were executing an OCD ritual, staring down at her handheld screen until the time changed to 9AM. She refreshed Claire's Twitter feed with her thumb in an instant.

> .@risacloudsTV needs to stop banging her little #TV brother, @RealJeffreyCameron. #Adultery can ruin your life; look at mine. MORE TO COME.

Fuck me. It's happening. Marcee ran back to her desk and waited for the next tweet. A heaviness in her chest pushed out a few coughs.

> .@CrossJamie90 should stop trying to date every #Hollywood lez. We know she wants $$$ and attention. MORE TO COME. #greedy #starfucker

Marcee laid her phone down and leaned back in her chair. She closed her eyes and breathed in and out rhythmically. By the time she looked at her device again, all of the prescribed messages had posted, with the addition of one: "I've seen more of @TheRoxMad1's #dick online today than I've ever seen in real life. @BrentWetherley." Apparently, Sarah threw an extra knife out for good measure.

Marcee navigated to her mobile web browser and went straight to www.joaquinrichie.com. Right on schedule, the article had been posted: "ROX MADISON AND BRENT WETHERLEY SCANDAL CONTINUES TO EXPLODE AS JILTED WIFE GOES ON SOCIAL MEDIA 'KILLING' SPREE."

Marcee couldn't have written the headline better herself;

the plan was unfolding without a hitch, but the potential fallout still had her on edge. She chewed on her left thumbnail as she continued to scroll through the story. "Following a *New York Post* cover bombshell, Rox Madison's wife and bestselling author, Claire, took to Facebook, Twitter and Instagram, lighting fire to her close circle of friends — and her own image. Nick Erickson's soon-to-be ex, Claudia, vegan powerhouse Jill Andrews, professional Hollywood gal pal Jamie Cross and TV has-been Risa Turner all got burned in the line of fire, in addition to Luminary Pictures PR topper Marcee Brookes. And Mrs. Madison promised deeper dish, tagging each of her messages with the ominous phrase 'MORE TO COME.'"

"Claire's" posts were quoted, word for word, next to photos of each of the women who were targeted. Marcee looked away for a few seconds and then continued reading. "Claire Madison, whose personal success, ironically, has come from female-centric self-help relationship books titled *Finding the Man* and *Keeping the Man*, admitted to having set up her friend with Brent Wetherley as a beard for his homosexual interest in her superstar husband. Her online rant not only body shames Marcee Brookes — referring to the innocent bystander as 'fat' — but implies that Rox and Brent were participants in the charade. It looks like she's burned all of the 'bridges to Madison County' in a matter of minutes."

Shit. This is real. Marcee read the whole article again. *There's no going back now.* She glanced at the comments, most of which seemed to disfavor the villains, but she noted a few harsh words directed at the "big girl who was dumb enough to think she was in a real relationship with a movie star." *Get it together, Marcee. Get it together. Carly Simon didn't have time for the pain, and neither do you.*

She could hear that her office phone was ringing off

the hook, and e-mails were flying in fast and furiously. While Addie and Lila fielded the onslaught, Marcee turned her attention to *Variety*'s website. Her whole body tensed up as she waited for the last piece of the puzzle to slide into place — which, indeed, happened at 11AM. "WILL BAD BEHAVIOR AND HOLLYWOOD HOMOPHOBIA RUIN THREE POWER PLAYERS? HOW THE RED CARPET COULD BE PULLED RIGHT OUT FROM UNDER INDUSTRY ROYALTY." Jordan covered every film, television, advertising, product-endorsement and new media deal — domestic and foreign — that Rox, Claire and Brent had in play. His exhaustively comprehensive story painted a potentially bleak picture for the duplicitous notables.

No sooner had she finished reading the entire article than Jordan called. "So, I wrote a damn fucking good column, didn't I?"

"It's very thorough," she replied, her voice quivering slightly.

"Why do you sound so tentative?" he asked. "This whole thing has played out exactly the way we wanted it to. It honestly couldn't have gone better."

"I can't shake the dreadful feeling that this is going to come back and swallow me up," she said. "And I feel trapped in my office. I shouldn't have come in to work today."

"You had to," Jordan replied. "Otherwise, it might've appeared like you knew the ceiling fans were about to turn brown."

"True," she conceded, "but do you think it would seem natural for me to leave now and work from home? I can't really focus on anything here, and I think I want to hole up with my parents for the weekend."

"There's nothing wrong with that," he said. "Just watch your cell in case I need to reach you for some reason."

"Have you heard from Sarah?" she questioned.

"Yep, everything's status quo on her end." His voice became a whisper, as though someone around him in the newsroom might be listening. "She's already smashed the burner phone and tossed it into a Dumpster behind an electronics store on Pico Boulevard."

"OK, good," she answered. "By the way, did you see some of the comments people have been writing online?" She took a tissue from the box on her desk and blew her nose. "Most are supportive, but there are a few that are just horrible."

"I told you on Wednesday night that you can't worry about the comments," he reiterated. "Until the day you can go into Bank of America and get cash in exchange for other people's opinions, put them out of your head." Somehow, that logic made sense to Marcee and calmed her fried nerves.

"You're right." Marcee shot a quick e-mail to Addie and Lila, letting them know she'd be working remotely the rest of the day. "I'm gonna go home now. Talk tonight?"

"Is the Pope's hat tall? Of course we will." He paused. "Nice work today, Brookes."

"Back at you, Jordie." She smiled for the first time in days. Maybe everything was going to be OK, and she simply needed someone who had her back unconditionally to tell her that. She shut her computer down, lifted her bag from the floor and walked quickly to the garage. Fortunately, she didn't see anyone in the halls and was able to get into her car without incident. As she made her way onto the streets of Burbank, she called her mother.

"Are you doing OK, honey?" Rhonda said. "I was surprised I didn't hear from you this morning. Daddy bought the *New York Post* at the deli, and I figured you might want to talk about it."

"I'm on my way to the house," Marcee replied. "I'm

going to set up my computer and work from the kitchen, if that's alright."

"Of course, baby. We'll be home all day."

"OK, see you in about a half hour. I'll fill you in on everything; you won't even believe it." Marcee put on her sunglasses and opened her sunroof. She switched on one of her upbeat 80s playlists and blasted Bananarama with the hope of lifting her mood. It had, in fact, been a very cruel summer.

◇◇◇

EIGHT DAYS LATER, Jordan had chosen the Grill on the Alley on Dayton Way in Beverly Hills for dinner. He often drove to the Valley to meet Marcee, but he had to attend *Variety*'s annual Emmy nominees cocktail party at the Beverly Wilshire hotel and wanted to eat somewhere close by.

"Sorry I'm a few minutes late," he said as he found Marcee in a booth at the side of the busy restaurant. "You know those horrible awards mixers. I got stuck talking to Eva Longoria about some new TV movie she's directing for Lifetime. I wish I'd had one of those lethal kill-pills in my pocket, like the tablets that potential hostage victims carry during wartime. I would have chewed that fucker right in front of her."

"That boring, huh?" Marcee leaned across the table to kiss him.

"'Boring' would be a generous assessment," he quipped. "I mean, I know I'm gay, but not *all* of us love Lifetime. How tone-deaf could she be? Plus, I'm so turned off by the fact the network's newest logo is a red period. You can't convince me that not one executive sat in the creative meeting and said, 'Hm, maybe we shouldn't brand this women's channel with a big red dot." He grabbed a piece of bread, slathered it in butter and began to look at the menu. "I'm starving."

"You didn't have a snack at the event?" she asked. "*Variety* parties are usually pretty lush."

"I didn't have time to even grab a piece of bruschetta," he replied. "All anyone was talking about was the whole Rox and Brent thing, and I wanted to make sure I didn't miss a word."

"You have to tell me everything," Marcee said, taking a second dinner roll from the basket on the table. "It's hard to believe that it's a week ago yesterday since the story went public. I feel like I'm still in the middle of it."

"As Bette Davis would say, 'Fasten your seatbelts, it's going to be a bumpy night.'" He cackled. "But, seriously, I think you'll feel the impact of this for a while. There'll be so many repercussions and related press coverage. You'll know that the uproar is finally dying down when the late-night hosts stop joking about it — and, for the record, Jimmy Fallon's whole monologue was built around Rox and Brent last night. The only possible reprieve for now, and I shudder to say this, would be a natural disaster that steals the media's attention."

"So, what kind of gossip do you have? Anything new?"

"Well, first of all, people loved my article." He pretended to buff his nails on his jacket's lapel. "I got tons of compliments on my reporting and concise-yet-effective writing style."

"That goes without saying," she teased. "But did you find out anything that's *not* common knowledge?" She pushed the crumbs she'd made with the bread crust into a neat little pile.

"I've talked to you so many times over the last eight days that I've forgotten what I've already told you." He looked around the room. "Do you mind if we order now? It's either that, or I'll pass out from hunger while I'm talking." Flagging down a waiter, he requested a glass of pinot noir and a chicken burger with fries.

"I'll have the eight-ounce filet mignon and a side of loaded mac and cheese," she added. "And I'll start with the wedge salad."

"I'm glad to see that this fine Saturday night finds you with a mighty appetite," Jordan observed. "At least you're not on that severe diet anymore."

"I don't know who I was trying to fool." She giggled. "I know I need to get healthy — I'm actually thinking of hiring a trainer — but I'm always going to love food. That's part of who I am."

"Girl, you go with your bad self." Jordan laughed. "Just make sure you're taking care of your body, that's all I ask. Otherwise, no need to go changing to try to please me; I love you just the way you are."

A knowing smile stretched across her face. "Billy Joel couldn't have said it better for you. And you know what? I honestly love you, too. If only we were born in another place and time..."

"I should have known you'd go right for Olivia Newton John," he snapped playfully. "She's such an easy pick."

"Anyway, we're not at a piano bar," Marcee ribbed. "We're in Beverly Hills after a crazy week. Spill what you've heard."

"OK, I told you on Tuesday that I spoke with a representative for Bartholomew Press, right? They've put Claire's photo memoir on indefinite hold. She seemingly no longer represents the kinds of women they're looking to celebrate."

"Yes, we talked about that, but I'm curious to know how the Squibb & Penn folks are going to deal with her first two books."

"Wonder no more," he said. "I actually heard from them yesterday when I was doing follow-up research for a new story I plan to run this coming Wednesday. They're discontinuing the distribution of both titles, as 'obviously, the author is no longer perceived to be a relevant expert on the subjects covered in previous editions of those catalog items.' Oh, and that's a direct quote."

"I can't say I feel sorry for her," Marcee said, "but I *almost* felt a little bad for Claudia Erickson yesterday."

"Why is that?" Jordan seemed bewildered.

"Addie showed me that some longtime Erickson Wells fans started a GoFundMe.com page for Claudia," Marcee relayed. "They're trying to raise money to help her move and maintain some sort of lifestyle. From what I understand, though, there was only about $4,000 worth of donations."

"You felt bad about that? At least she has strangers who care about her," Jordan said. "I don't have the slightest twinge of guilt. She knew that Claire was setting you up all along, and she let it happen."

"Oh, believe me, I'm well aware that she drove the getaway car." Marcee looked down at the food that had been set in front of her. "I personally heard her call me 'delusional' and a 'wide load.' Her conversation with Claire in the bathroom of the Palm is forever burned into me. *Butterballs are so fucked up.*"

"Just take some solace in the fact that a few of Nick Erickson's fans pitched in enough for Claudia to buy a side-by-side washer/dryer set. At least she won't have to clean her clothes in the communal laundry room of her new condo. Let's leave it at that."

"Any further word on what's happening with Rox and Brent?" Marcee finished her salad and started on the steak that had just been delivered. "Luminary shelved *Night Crimes* for the time being, but I know that won't be a huge blow to Rox. He hates that movie."

"I heard that the film he was supposed to start shooting

in Louisiana next month has been recast," Jordan continued. "And so far, his jewelry and credit card endorsement deals have been dropped. We'll have to wait and see what else falls through."

"It's been mentioned in some of the articles that Rox knew why Claire befriended me in the first place. That can't sit well with people, especially women," she commented. "Do you think these companies are backing away because he's gay or because of the questionable way he's handled everything?"

"Well, publicly, they're using coded language like, 'We're taking this campaign in a different direction,' and 'The budget for those ads has run out.' That way, they don't appear to be dumping Rox because he's a raging queen. But we both know that a gay guy can't sell credit cards and watches as well as a hetero action hero." Jordan winked.

"If Rox had just come out on the cover of *People* long ago, like everyone else, these brands would've looked un-PC for severing ties with him," Marcee went on. "Those sex photos were their 'get out of jail free' card." She took a bite of mac and cheese. "Did you find anything out about Brent — other than the fact that the current issue of *Rolling Stone* has now sold out everywhere?"

"His camp has somehow been able to keep things pretty close to the vest," he replied. "You obviously referred him to the best of the PR demons. But don't worry. I'll be poking around next week — as will every other media outlet. It's just a matter of time until it all leaks."

"I got a call from Sarah this morning," Marcee interjected. "She's safe and sound in Maine. Her parents are happy to have her home; they've been doting on her. She sounded pretty relaxed."

"That's good to know," Jordan said. "Did she say if any of those TTT assholes have tried to reach out or go after her?"

"She hasn't heard a peep from them." Marcee finished her steak and took a sip of water. "Speaking of which, neither have I. Don't you think that's weird?"

"Like I said before we even put this plan in motion, they have bigger things to worry about now than some surface friendship with you." He dipped three French fries into a ramekin of ketchup and put them all in his mouth at once. "I don't mean to sound cold, but you, by now, shouldn't expect better from those bitches."

"I just find it odd that not one of them has tried to call," she replied.

"Oh, I'm sure you haven't heard the last from them. Shit floats to the surface eventually."

21

IT WAS NEARLY two months before Marcee started to feel like she fit into her life again. Although Los Angeles had no significant weather changes, summer had passed — Emmy Award voting rolled into pre-Oscar season — and the fall saw her hitting her stride as a bona fide studio executive.

Sitting at her desk, she thumbed through *The New York Times*'s "Arts" section to check out the competitive movie ads. As she moved ahead to the theater pages, she noticed a small photo touting the revival of *Chicago*, "CELEBRATING ITS 22ND YEAR ON BROADWAY." Her eyes were drawn to a red burst of text that read, "NOW STARRING BRENT WETHERLEY AS BILLY FLYNN." The show was notorious for stunt casting a revolving door of celebrities whose stars had lost their shine, and she wasn't disheartened to find that they hadn't broken tradition.

"Sorry to bother you," Addie said, knocking on the doorframe to Marcee's office. "I have a first draft of the PR plan for *A Light in the Clouds*. Do you wanna go over it before your call with the director?"

"I'm sure it's perfect, but I'll read through it once I'm back from my meeting with Ben," Marcee said, smiling as she put down the paper. "I wouldn't have promoted you to senior publicist if I weren't familiar with the quality of your work. And you know how I feel about those ridiculous publicity outlines anyway."

Addie grinned. "This new job means everything to me," she answered. "Not only the pay raise but the designated parking space. Everything."

"Oh, I know the feeling," Marcee replied, walking to the door with her purse. "But the most important stuff is at home, like your daughter and your mom." She followed Addie down the hallway and then made a turn for the stairs. "I'll be back in about an hour; hold down the fort."

As she made her way outside and onto the main lot, she noticed that the waistband of her size-14 steel-grey skirt was cutting into her sides — never mind that the silver Dior pumps put a classy glide in her movement. She loved the outfit but not how tightly it clung to her body. *No more excuses; I'm buying a gym membership this week.* The studio had a complimentary, private training facility for high-level employees, but she didn't like the idea of working out in activewear next to a bunch of colleagues. She knew she'd feel more comfortable at 24 Hour Fitness in the Sherman Oaks Galleria where she could sweat, unnoticed, on an elliptical. A couple of visits per week would keep her clothes fitting nicely.

Because she'd left herself just enough time to walk to Ben's office, she didn't take a scenic studio tour. Instead, she passed the commissary and the animation department and took a sharp right at the Luminary Lighthouse building, home to the company's top brass. Had she not looked up from her phone while turning the corner, she never would have made eye contact with Jill. *Shit.* Marcee felt her whole body tense up and noticed that Jill's posture appeared to stiffen as well. It was like *Alien vs. Predator* at first, only more awkward and prettier.

"It was going to happen eventually, wasn't it?" Jill

approached Marcee in a pair of black capri jogging pants and a purple hoodie. "My husband *does* run the place; our paths were bound to cross."

"Here we are," Marcee said, the corners of her mouth turning upward into a faint smile.

"We *are* here, aren't we?" Jill shrugged her shoulders with a laugh that sounded as phony as her vegan platform. She looked past Marcee for a moment, as though something in the distance had grabbed her attention.

"How've you been, Jill? I've wanted to reach out, but it's such a busy time of year work-wise." Marcee struggled to seem pleasant.

"Who are we kidding, Marcee?" Jill asked. "I think both of us has dreaded the possibility of running into each other, am I right?" She put her hands in the front pockets of her sweatshirt.

"I wouldn't say that, no," Marcee lied. "I figured we'd see each other when we were meant to." Marcee wasn't a fatalist by any stretch, but Jill wouldn't know better.

"Well, it hasn't been the easiest time for me," Jill remarked. "I would've lost my whole business if Ken hadn't had such strong relationships with every network, publisher and website. Claire's accusations came *this close* to ruining me."

"Yeah, well, she didn't exactly do me any favors either." Marcee shifted her weight from one foot to the other. The heels looked fantastic and were the perfect accessories for an intricate political tango, but they weren't terribly practical.

"Just so you know, I had no idea that Claire was setting you up," Jill said. "It *did* seem weird that she brought someone new into our group out of the blue, but I didn't give it much thought at the time."

"Have you heard from the other ladies?" Marcee questioned. "Nobody has touched base with *me*."

"I was in contact with Risa for a little while after everything went down," Jill answered. "She got pregnant by her boyfriend, and, apparently, *his* wife wasn't really happy about it. Go figure. She couldn't decide if she should keep the baby, especially at her age and under the circumstances. But guess what? She's due in February."

"Wow. Lucky for Risa, Claire didn't know about *that* situation before she went mental on Twitter, Facebook and Instagram," Marcee said, not breaking eye contact with Jill. "It would have been even more fodder for the press."

"Risa said exactly the same thing." Jill loosened her arms and then ran her hands through her hair. "Claire must have been building up so much anger and resentment over the years, clawing at glass to keep an illusion. But trying to take us all down with her? Unforgivable."

"Did Claire contact you?"

"She tried," Jill said sharply. "I didn't respond, so she left a ton of messages. Can you believe that she had the audacity to try to gin up some sympathy?"

"Sympathy?" Marcee acted surprised. "After having burned the whole group to the ground? I thought the circle was called 'TTT' because it was supposed to be a safe place to talk openly. Your confidences were supposed to go *to the tomb* with you, no?"

"Well, in her voicemails, she claimed to have been devastated by the revelations about Rox, as if the *New York Post* story was news to her." Jill rolled her eyes. "And she insinuated that her social media accounts had been hacked by her assistant—or one of *us*—just to pour salt on her open wound."

"I don't buy that," Marcee answered. "Which one of us

would have been willing to say such horrible things about ourselves in front of the whole world?"

"Exactly!" Jill exclaimed. "We all know she's a fucking liar. The woman tried to claim that I eat meat and am bulimic, for Chrissake. Really? The 'valiant vegan?'" She cocked her head to one side and looked at Marcee through slightly narrowed eyes.

"I feel your pain, trust me." Marcee met Jill's gaze. "She knowingly set me up with a gay man whom I actually started to like and then called me fat online. I think you and I both got carved up."

The twisted dance went on for another 15 minutes. It was evident to Marcee that the disingenuous discourse was representative of whatever semblance of a relationship she'd have with Jill going forward, which would likely consist of similarly infrequent encounters on the studio lot and at industry events. Marcee wanted to protect her job and Jill her professional empire, so the truth would serve only to put each of their positions at stake.

It was an ice-cold war between them, predicated on secrets that both preferred to keep hidden. Jill's tone and body language suggested that she knew Marcee was aware of her dietary transgressions, and Marcee was unsure if Jill actually believed that Claire was the only whistleblower among them. *For all I know, she suspects that I had some hand in this.* Liking each other and needing each other were two different things — and Marcee was well aware of which side they were on.

"All I can say is that I hope Claire is resting in peace," Jill said.

Marcee was stunned that Jill had taken the conversation to such a dark corner. "What? Resting in peace?"

"She said in one of her messages that Rox had filed for divorce, and she was heading to some recovery resort in Montana for a couple of months. She wanted to 'reset her mind.'" Jill made air quotes with her fingers. "I would imagine that it's very restful and peaceful there."

"I see," Marcee said, nodding her head and forcing a smile.

Jill took a pair of shaded, reflective sunglasses from her purse and covered her eyes. "You didn't think I was wishing Claire dead, did you? God forbid."

They shared a frigid hug and then started to walk in opposite directions, both taking a fast look back at each other before continuing on. Marcee raced to the legal building, now 30 minutes late for her meeting with Ben. She hurried into an open elevator and headed straight upstairs.

◇◇◇

MARCEE HAD NEVER taken time to appreciate the view from so high up. She stood quietly, looking over what appeared to be miniature model homes and surrounding greenery.

"You got so quiet all of a sudden. What's on your mind?" Ben walked over and stood next to her.

"I just don't remember it being so breathtaking." She hadn't been to Runyon Canyon in years, probably since a high school field trip as a teenager.

"You mean all of that?" he asked, pointing out toward the great expanse in front of them.

"Yes, the skyline, the trees, all of the lives happening below us." She wished she could stop her eyelids from blinking for just a few minutes so she could take it all in, completely uninterrupted.

"It's really stunning, isn't it?" He paused and stared down over Los Angeles with her. "And your footwear is pretty stunning, too."

Marcee started to laugh. "Are you making fun of me?" She knelt down.

"Me? Make fun of blindingly bright, hot pink running shoes? Nah."

As Marcee self-consciously tightened her laces, she removed a small rock that had become wedged under her right foot. "I don't want to hear a word about fashion from Mr. Brooks Brothers himself," she teased. "I rarely wear sneakers, and these were on sale at the Designer Shoe Warehouse."

"They definitely make a statement." He tugged on the black nylon leash that was giving Jackson a little too much freedom. "See, even the dog is spooked by the brightness of your feet." They had obviously been in one spot for too long; the regal-looking Weimaraner was ready to move on.

"Calm down, Jackson," Marcee cooed, bending over to rub his chin and ears. "Don't worry, we're going. I don't get here twice a week like you two, so forgive a girl for lingering." Jackson licked her hands.

"You've been asked many times," Ben reminded her. "This is the first you've actually agreed to hike with us."

She'd always treated Ben's invitations like they were coming from a little brother who was offering to spend time with his sister out of obligation. But when he insisted on a weekend hike and lunch during their last work meeting, the idea of an altogether different dynamic crossed her mind for the first time. She still found it hard to believe that any man could think of her as a romantic possibility, but she felt a tiny flutter of hopeful excitement that finally pushed her into taking him up on his offer.

"Yeah, well," Marcee admitted, "I've decided to start caring for myself a little more. Plus, I really need to spend time outdoors. I signed up for a gym membership last week, but I like being in the sun sometimes." She didn't let on that anything more than exercise was running through her head. *Smart + Handome + Funny + Jewish.* She wasn't sure what it would ultimately add up to but was now interested in solving the equation.

"That works for us, doesn't it, Jackson?" He patted his dog on the head and continued walking along the trail. "We love to have company." The wind blew through his wavy hair, brushing some strands onto his forehead. "You seemed pretty busy there for awhile, with those fancy work friends and that jerk of a celebrity suitor who shall remain nameless. I wasn't sure if we'd ever really get a chance to hang out."

"My schedule has lightened up in the last two months," she said, "but you'd have no way of knowing that, would you?" She smiled and purposely bumped her left shoulder against his right. "It's not like it was all over the papers and Internet or anything."

"I hate that you went through that, but, if I'm being honest, I'm not too upset that you have some time on your hands these days." She loved that he approached the subject delicately and without a hint of *I told you so* or *You should've listened to me.*

"So, you find my empty dance card appealing?" she joked. Ben lifted his white, sleeveless T-shirt to wipe some sweat from his forehead. A light dusting of hair covered his adorably flat stomach and trailed past his belly button into the elastic band of his blue running shorts. *He's really kind of sexy,* she thought. She loved that he seemed to put minimal effort into his appearance and was appealing regardless. He was cute but didn't have the attitude of someone who knew it.

"Only if I'm allowed to book time in some of those empty slots," he said. He lightly grazed Marcee's back with his fingertips. His touch felt good, but she tried to avoid reading too much into the gesture; leaping ahead and projecting hadn't served her well recently.

"I'm sure I could fit you in here and there." She'd known Ben for 10 years and yet was suddenly a little nervous with him.

"Well, if I'm taking you hiking again next Saturday," he smiled, flashing his perfect teeth, "you're going to have to get different shoes. That shade of pink belongs on a paper cocktail umbrella, not on a dirt path." His hazel eyes glimmered in the sun.

"I'll see what I can do about picking up a new pair this week," she answered, stopping in her tracks as he and Jackson walked on.

"Are you coming?" he called out, looking behind him and stretching his arm as though he were reaching for her. She breathed in the fresh air and took another glimpse of the view from the canyon's highest point. Then she turned back to Ben and walked forward, slowly.

Acknowledgements

ENEMIES CLOSER WOULD not be possible without my dear friend and brilliant editor, Benée Knauer. I'm forever indebted to this insightful and extremely patient force of nature who walked into my life five years ago without realizing she'd never be allowed to leave. Thanks to Silvio Gonzalez and Renny Gonzalez for sharing her with me.

Victoria Sanders, Bernadette Baker-Baughman and Jessica Spivey comprise the best agenting team in publishing; I'm incredibly lucky to have them.

My work has reached a larger audience because of my close friend Lita Weissman, who has been my personal and professional champion since the day we met. Now she's stuck with me — whether she likes it or not.

A huge thank-you to Jill Abatemarco, Edward Ash-Milby, Josh Coffey, Andy Drummond, Evonne Drummond, Maya Gittelman, Gwen Jones, Jeanne Kingston, Oscar Moreno de La Rosa, Frank Parra, Crystal Perkins, Lennie Rohrbacher, Ariane Sherrod, Yuka Shikami, Frank Varela, Amanda Youngman and all of my bookseller friends. They've fostered my work since I started on this writing journey; I'm honored to know them.

I'm grateful to Thelma Adams, Jessica Anya Blau, Wendy Broudy, Amanda Cagan, Claudia Cagan, Emily Cagan, Marilyn Cheek, Lauren Fox, Nancy Grace, Gigi Levangie

Grazer, Terry Greenberg, Amy Hatvany, Jessica Horwitch, David Mack, Sarah Pekkanen, Barbara Pflughaupt, Tammy Rubel, Michelle Sobrino-Stearns, Trish Suhr, Kate sZatmari and Susan Wenger for lending their eyes, ears, counsel and kind words to this novel.

Nic Flower offered an endless amount of love and care during the writing of this book. His constant cheerleading got me through many long days and nights.

My sister and brother-in-law, Nancy Sabarra and Jason Karlinsky, and my nieces, Bethany and Ella, provided much-needed support throughout the process, and my amazing parents, Howard and Deborah Sabarra, are the gold standard. I love them always.

About the Author

BESTSELLING AUTHOR JOSH Sabarra is a veteran marketing executive and television producer who has held positions at the Walt Disney Company, Warner Bros. Studios, Miramax Films, New Line Cinema and Lifetime Networks. He resides in Los Angeles, California, where he is the president and CEO of his own public relations firm, Breaking News PR®. His first book, *Porn Again: A Memoir,* is available worldwide.